"The action scenes were absolutely packed with great descriptions that played like they were straight out of a movie. I could picture every intense moment. Murray does a great job of balancing the crime, romance, and emotional moments. Overall, The Gangster's Game is a fun, gripping read with just the right mix of action, romance, and heart. I highly recommend it if you love fast-paced thrillers with a bit of romance."

K.C. Finn for Readers' Favorite

The Gangster series is best enjoyed in order:

The Gangster's Daughter
The Gangster's Mistake
The Gangster's Game

The Gangster's Game

The Gangster's Game

Jodie Leigh Murray

Jodie Leigh Murray Books

For my feisty little "angel" Brooke.
May you always have that fire in you
to keep fighting for everything you believe in.

Chapter One

The waves of the Atlantic Ocean crashed against the sandy beach almost violently, before retreating with a gentle pull. It captured my attention as I stood with my bare feet buried in the wet sand, the water brushing against my shins each time it surged. Even living on the upper west coast, I rarely went to the beach. Maybe I would if the weather compared to this.

As soon as Naomi, Hannah, and I got off the plane in Myrtle Beach, I knew Cape Haven had significance. More so when the ferry let us off on the island.

The balmy September day on the secluded island, off the coast of South Carolina, was unmatched by any weather I had experienced even while growing up in southern California. If I knew what heaven felt like, this had to be it.

I was glad I'd worn a pair of cutoffs, though I was in no immediate danger of getting wet. The weather here was perfect. An ideal opportunity to wear a bikini, I mused. I had thrown a loose-fitting knit top over it, but it barely concealed anything. I hadn't been able to wear this type of clothing since my last visit with my dad two years ago, which filled me with a touch of sadness. Too long.

The beach had grown increasingly crowded during the few minutes I had been standing there.

When I called Riley to tell her we'd landed in Myrtle Beach and were catching the ferry, she shrieked in my ear with excitement. For the island to be crowded with visitors after Labor Day was rare, especially nearly two weeks after the holiday. With the weather being unseasonably warm, people were eager to squeeze in last-minute vacations. Looking around, I saw lots of children playing in the waves and others building sandcastles. People lined the beach, sunbathing in chairs or on colorful beach towels. Others played games like frisbee and volleyball, and I couldn't blame them. I breathed deeply, the smell of sunscreen and suntan lotion mixed with briny sea air and it tickled my nose.

The only difference was me.

I could have stood there staring out at the ocean all day, but I had flown across the country for a reason. My best friend had found the love of her life and would marry him tomorrow. Of all the people I knew, she deserved this the most. I sucked in happy tears just as my phone vibrated in my back pocket.

It took less than a minute for me to read through the text from Evan. I would have laughed at the absurdity of him calling it quits after only seven months of casual dating if it hadn't been delivered via text. Fury surged through me. Half a year wasted on a man who couldn't even be bothered to break up with me in person or, at the very least, pick up the phone to call me. I wished I could be upset about the fact that he'd dumped me, but the manner in which he did it infuriated me.

Retreating a step, I drew back my arm as though I would throw my phone as far out into the water as I could. No. He wasn't worth it. I growled and pulled back, before shoving it into the back pocket of my cutoffs with enough silent curses to make myself feel better. As I did, I caught sight of a trio of men walking by, the one closest to me immediately capturing my attention.

Trapped by the intensity of his eyes, my breath hitched and held. I couldn't tell if it was the electric blue or the way they pierced through me, but I had never seen such a vivid color before. His gaze met mine as he neared, almost as if he slowed down while passing. He had dark brown hair with a slight curl, hanging nearly to his shoulders. The dark slashes of his eyebrows were raised.

Exactly the type of man I would have pounced on in my younger years. While his eyes lingered on me, the upward curve of his lips screamed danger. If I wasn't mistaken, my heartbeat had quickened. It had been a long time since a man had made my pulse race like this. True, he wore only a pair of athletic shorts, exposing his sculpted chest to my roaming eyes, but there were plenty of men on this beach dressed the same way. I caught a brief glimpse of the dark swirling tattoos covering part of his chest and arm before I heard Hannah yelling and waving from halfway to the beach house.

As soon as I broke my gaze away from him, I felt a sense of loss. What the heck is wrong with me? I got dumped less than a minute ago. I shouldn't be ogling other men. But as soon as the thought slipped into my head, my eyes glided back to him while I walked toward the row of houses along the beach. He seemed to have the same idea, turning his head to watch me as he continued down the beach. Now, all three of them were looking at me.

I've never been the type of woman to blush and shy away from attentive men, but having all of them looking at me suddenly made me self-conscious, especially since there were so many other women on this beach, most of them dressed in less clothing than I was. I needed to focus on where I was walking before I accidentally stomped on someone sunbathing, smiling to myself as I turned back to Hannah.

She wore her light brown hair in a careless bun atop her head, much like mine. Riley always teased us for having the same sense of fashion. I couldn't help that, even though *they* were sisters, they were exact opposites. I only hoped Ty would rub off on Riley with her messy, distracted ways. I'd tried for years to get her to eat healthy and take better care of herself, but with no luck.

She'd been working as a junior private investigator when she met Ty while investigating the kidnapping of a famous pop singer's little dog. Naturally, Riley took it further than she should have, since it involved a dog. Ty, a detective working undercover to bust a gang, caught her sneaking around. All hell broke loose after that, despite Riley and Ty's efforts to prevent it. Ty's partner saved them both. If Jack hadn't been cunning enough to know there was more to the case than either of them realized, Ty and Riley would be dead. Riley escaped with a gunshot wound to her arm, while Ty took a pretty severe beating. And tomorrow, they would be married, with a baby arriving in just seven short months.

I met Hannah halfway to Regan's beach house. Other than Riley, I'd never met a stronger woman in my life than Regan. Smart and resilient, she didn't stand for any nonsense from anyone. Only her husband, Cameron, could get away with it, and that was only sometimes.

The way they looked at each other struck me with a longing I still didn't understand. They lived about a mile up the beach but kept her beach house, Regan proclaiming she couldn't part with it. I couldn't blame her. The house was gorgeous and in the center of all the beach activity.

Riley and Ty would stay in Regan's beach house for a few days after the wedding, while Naomi, Hannah, and I would be there just for the weekend. Hannah needed to get back to school on Monday. Since it was her senior year, she couldn't miss more than a couple of days, even though her grades were superb.

"Aren't you going to check out the house?" Hannah asked, breathless from her jaunt to meet me.

Her eyes sparkled with excitement. Oh, to be seventeen again.

"I did when we got here," I replied with a calm smile.

Naomi had known my dad since he became best friends with her son, Ricky, over twenty-five years ago. After my mom died, Naomi brought Hannah and Riley to live with me, since my dad had been on tour. As a drummer in a rock band, Lex Edwards simply couldn't leave. I know it hit my dad hard when she died, but I remember talking to him on the phone after her funeral.

Even at a young age, I understood. He needed to stay on tour to keep his mind off her passing. Now that I'm a therapist, I realize he needed that time to heal.

Hannah was only seven, and Riley was fifteen. Ten years ago, I mused. They were my sisters, despite not being blood related. Riley and I bonded over her troubled past, which led me into a career in therapeutic services. I enjoyed helping people. At least, I thought I did. I'd gone to school for it, but lately, it seemed monotonous. Still, it kept money coming, which helped even though I didn't have to pay a mortgage while I lived at my dad's house.

"I might have died and gone to heaven," she said, linking her arm with mine and pulling me toward the gated house.

From the beach, the house appeared to be one level, but it had a partial second level that Gavriel De Luca had remodeled into a dance studio when Regan was young.

Vibrant bushes and tropical flowers flanked the house, creating the illusion of a tropical oasis, even though winters here could be chilly. The black iron gate, at least a foot taller than us, loomed as we approached. It wasn't locked, allowing Hannah to open it easily. Three steps led us to the deck, where a large sparkling pool awaited. I'd crossed the deck when we arrived, but the private oasis still stunned me.

An inviting hot tub nestled between the pool and the house, surrounded by lush greenery, looked serene even without the jets on. A few lounge chairs flanked the pool, and a patio table sat near a second set of French doors that led to the master bedroom suite.

"Isn't this just like paradise?" Hannah squeaked, tugging my arm as she pulled me around the pool. "God, I could live here forever."

"You'd have to take that up with Regan and Cameron. You could probably pull off online schooling. But I don't think it's like this year-round, Hannah."

I allowed her to pull me into the house, which was equally

impressive. The open concept living room, kitchen, and dining room shared a spacious interior, separated by a breakfast bar.

We passed a glass dining room table on our way to the kitchen, which was divided from the massive living room by the breakfast bar. I couldn't say a single word before Riley screeched and launched herself at me.

"Easy," I said, my mouth quickly smothered by her thin shoulder. Her petite figure had always evoked a little envy in me, as I had to work to stay slim. "Riles, you're squishing me."

Lord, she was strong, despite being a couple months pregnant. She laughed, waiting a full minute before pulling away and wiping her eyes. "I'm so happy you came. I couldn't do this without you."

I shrugged. "I needed a vacation."

"Naomi is lying down. She's tired after the flight."

Holding her by her arms, admiration flooded me as I thought of how far she'd come in just the last six months. My thumb swept over the black semicolon inked on the inside of her wrist, and I smiled when I met her gaze.

"Seems this symbol is right on target," I murmured. "Your story is far from over. About to get married to the man of your dreams, a baby on the way, and two wound-up dogs who are likely to drive me nuts when I get home in a few days."

As if on cue, Ty strolled out of the bathroom, absently scratching behind his ear while eyeing me warily. That was the detective in him. Always suspicious. When his arm slid comfortably around Riley's waist, I smiled despite my jealousy. I loved Riley as though she were my true sister.

Masking my envy, I looked around. "This place is magnificent."

Riley scoffed. "You've lived in big houses your whole life, Cass."

"True, but that doesn't mean I can't admire them." I walked the perimeter of the living room, glancing into the master bedroom. "Plus, I've lived in Seattle for a long time. Been a while since I've been anywhere remotely warm."

"Seattle gets warm." Even as Riley said it, she laughed. "Warm-ish."

I turned toward them. "I'm going to get settled into my room. Assuming I have one?"

"You do!" she said. "There are three bedrooms behind the kitchen, and another two upstairs, but they aren't finished. Not even close, Regan said."

"My parents and brothers are at the hotel." Ty reluctantly released Riley and headed into the kitchen for a bottle of water, then grabbed two. "Cassie, Hannah, water?"

Hannah reached out for one, but I shook my head. It seemed like there was more he wanted to say. I walked across the room toward him with a raised eyebrow. "I can understand why it would be crowded here, but . . . "

He took a chug from his water before lowering it slowly, eyeballing me. I got the feeling he was putting his detective skills to work on me. I should be suspicious, so I glanced over at Riley. I hadn't seen much of her in the last few months. They'd been tucked away in Ty's house in the woods during that time, and I couldn't blame them after their ordeal.

"Ty's friend Jack is staying here," she blurted. "I hope that's okay."

"Why wouldn't that be okay?"

"Well, you know," she said. "He insisted on staying on the couch."

I shrugged, knowing exactly where she was going with this. She'd told me about him and his reputation for never settling down with anyone. I assumed he and Ty were around the same age, nearing thirty, since they'd grown up together. Riley mentioned that he'd even hit on her the night she spent with Ty, even though she was only pretending to be Ty's girlfriend.

"I'm an adult, Riles. If I can't handle myself, you have permission to slap me. If Ty's friend wants to stay on the couch instead of in a hotel room, he can." I gave her a reassuring smile.

"In fact, I don't blame him. I hate staying in hotels."

I didn't miss the low chuckle from Ty, but I ignored it. Whatever the reason Jack had for staying here, I was certain he would mind his manners with Hannah since she was underage. Plus, I was sure that if Ty didn't warn him away from her, Riley would. No one messed with her little sister. Naomi wouldn't allow anyone to get close to Hannah, either. Both Naomi and Riley knew I could handle myself, always keeping everyone at a distance.

Curiously, my bedroom faced the beach. I had a feeling Naomi told Riley she didn't care and that I could have the room with the better view. I'd grown up spoiled with two famous parents, but I didn't need to be. I would have taken any room.

Everyone knew me as Cassidy Nichols, daughter of rockstar Lex Edwards and actress Jenna Nichols. Jenna Nichols had been at the height of her fame when she'd overdosed, leaving behind her only daughter. During her life, she gained massive popularity on the big screen, but she had a problem. And it killed her. No one knew that I'd been the one to push her over the edge. I would take that secret to my grave.

Lex Edwards had equal fame with his rock band, followed by his marriage to Jenna Nichols. Their divorce only propelled them further into the spotlight. Following the divorce, the drugs pulled my mom in deeper. And when she confessed that she'd been lying to me all my life, that my dad wasn't my real dad, it blew my entire world apart. I never asked him. I didn't want it to be true. I would always consider him my dad.

Most people recognized me as Jenna's daughter because I looked so much like her and I shared her last name since they weren't married when I was born. My dad had been in the picture, but they hadn't decided on marriage until the following year, and with my mom's acting career, the timing hadn't been right.

I lived in my dad's house in Seattle because he never used it. Not even when they were in town on the tour. Why not live there since it was empty all the time? I told myself that once I established my career, I'd buy a house of my own. But I'd grown so accustomed to living with Naomi and Hannah that I never did. My dad would help anyone in need. The apple hadn't fallen far from the tree. I turned out the same way, to a fault. He would never consider selling the Seattle house and putting any of us out. He wouldn't do it. Little did he know, we would survive if he sold the house and we had to move.

I glided through the bedroom, boasting a decent-sized window with a slight view of the beach through the greenery, but it didn't match the massive size of the master bedroom. The master suite occupied the entire opposite side of the house and included a private bathroom. This room featured a simple queen-sized bed, a side table, and a tall dresser. There was no walk-in closet, but it had one of those barn-door closets.

I wouldn't be here long enough to unpack my small bag, I thought sadly. Riley and Ty would take part of next week for their honeymoon before heading off to Las Vegas for some quality time with Riley's dad, Reno. They needed this solitude after the stress of the last few months. I would never intrude on that. Besides, I had clients to see next week, and someone would need to pick up Riley's two-year-old Labrador retrievers, Gus and Gatsby, from the doggie hotel.

Just as I was about to flop down on the bed, I heard another male voice in the house. My eyebrows raised, wondering if that was Jack. Curiosity would eventually get the better of me, although I knew better than to get involved with someone who would undoubtedly walk away. It was getting old, being dumped. But at least I'd had relationships. From what I'd heard, Jack didn't waste his precious time on relationships.

I couldn't think of a single one-night stand I'd had, or even a friends-with-benefits situation. I had plenty of short-lived relationships, especially when I discovered they were only with me because of ties to fame. That had happened more times than I cared to admit. The rest left because I struggled to let anyone into my life, trusting them with knowing the real me. Cold, that's how Evan had described me in his breakup text.

Sighing, I decided I shouldn't dwell on those memories, so I left my bag untouched and went back into the kitchen. I hoped that Regan and Cameron would be around. When they had stayed at my house several months ago, I had the best time. Another pair who were most definitely suited for each other.

As I rounded the corner, I slowed my steps at the sight of the man standing next to Ty between the living room and the breakfast bar. The same intense blue eyes from the beach turned my way, followed by that devious smile. My heart wavered in my chest.

"Cassie." Riley wound her way around Ty to meet me in the middle. "This is—"

"Jack," I blurted.

She shot me a sideways glare. "Jack, *this* is Cassie."

From the way she said that, I could only assume she had told him about me. Trying to keep my deep breath inconspicuous, I stepped closer and reached out to shake his hand. His warm, surprisingly powerful hand slid into mine and held it longer than necessary while he dipped his head ever so slightly.

"Meeting you has been long overdue."

God, the way he purposely drew out his words had to be against the law. No wonder women fell at his feet. With his sinfully deep tone and his unrushed way of speaking, it felt like just the two of us were in the room. His eyes were locked on mine, my hand in his. A rush of warmth flooded me from head to toe.

He wouldn't release my hand. It felt rude to tug, but I couldn't understand why he still held it. My eyes widened when he pulled my knuckles up to meet his lips, and my mouth popped open. Oh, for the love of God, what did he think he was doing? His warm lips against my skin made me tingle, lingering longer than necessary. I didn't dare look at Riley because I knew her mouth was probably hanging open.

Finally, he released me, and I caught my breath. I could have blurted out that I had a boyfriend, but I had to remind myself that I didn't anymore. Of all the guys I'd met over the last few years, none compared to how dangerous this man could be to my well-built wall. The gleam in his eyes convinced me it would be a colossal mistake to let him close.

"I hope my staying here won't bother you," he said.

With a voice that was low and sultry, sliding over me like the finest silk, I wondered if it came naturally to him or if he needed to work at it. Damn, I cursed silently. This would be trouble.

"Unless you sleep naked, it's no bother. I'm an early riser, so I'll try not to wake you."

I could swear I heard a quiet gasp from Riley, but her rolled eyes told me I'd surprised her yet again.

"Don't sleep naked," Riley warned him. "But she is an early riser. She'll go for a run, maybe do her yoga, have her tea, and look perfect before anyone even thinks of rolling out of bed."

I gave her a gentle shove. "Not perfect, just taking care of myself."

I couldn't help but notice the sparkle remaining in Jack's eyes, but I turned away before he could do something even more disgustingly noticeable, like sweep them over my body. Even as a therapist, I had my own issues to work through. Yoga and tea helped me with that, but running really helped. No one needed to know, though.

Chapter Two

Judging by the muffled laughter coming from behind my closed door, guests were arriving for tonight's pre-wedding gathering. Everyone who had come to the island for the wedding was heading to Regan's beach house tonight for dinner and to visit with each other, along with Riley and Ty, since we were all here for such a short time.

One last time, I checked my appearance in the full-length mirror on the wall. I didn't know why I was nervous. Who was I kidding? I knew exactly why nerves had crept in. It had been years since I'd attended any type of social gathering outside of Reno, Cameron, and Regan visiting my house earlier this year. I sometimes went out to the bar with my co-worker Tish after work, but I had a feeling tonight would be far different. This setting couldn't be more intimate. Ty's family was here, and Riley's family was here, including some of her extended family.

Before I could take another minute to ensure this was the outfit I wanted to wear, the door burst open, and Hannah breezed in wearing a yellow sundress that complemented her dark blonde hair, which she'd left loose for the occasion. She would break hearts when she grew up, I thought. I hoped she was smarter than I was, and wouldn't get duped by men like I seemed to do.

"You look amazing, Cass!" she said. "I never get to see you wear anything other than your business attire, workout clothes, and regular colorless outfits. This has at least a bit of color."

I smiled. "Gee, thanks."

It was a simple blue dress with tiny straps over each shoulder and strings resembling the ties of a bikini on the bottom of each side of the skirt, which reached just about to my knees. I twirled to show Hannah the back of the dress, where matching straps crisscrossed to my lower back, leaving it mostly exposed.

Her mouth dropped open. "I'm not sure I've ever seen you look like this," she whispered. "Come on, before you change your mind."

I laughed as she linked her arm with mine, dragging me out of the bedroom and into the hallway. "Pretty sure Riley would barge into my room like you just did to drag me out."

We were still laughing when we joined the others in the living room. My laughter died when I caught Jack's eyes across the room and noticed the unmistakable darkening of them as he took in my attire. I could say the same about him dressed in a pair of tan dress pants and a blue dress shirt rolled up to his elbows. The shade of his shirt made his eyes seem even lighter. I tore my gaze away and looked at Regan, who had Nicco tucked in her arms.

"Ooooh," I whispered, looking down at the sleeping baby. "Regan. Cameron. He's beautiful."

Cameron grinned beside her. "If you want to hold him, now is the best time. When he wakes up, he's going to scream this house down to be fed."

I let out a breathy laugh as Regan handed the tiny one-week-old bundle to me, cradling him in my arms and running the pad of my finger over his rosy cheek. "He's absolutely perfect."

"Not when he's screaming in the middle of the night, he's not," Cameron said, slipping his arm around Regan's waist.

When she looked up at him with a smile, that pang of jealousy hit me like it always did. Quickly, I looked back down at Nicco with his tuft of dark hair and puckered mouth. I was sure I would never become a mother myself, so I would enjoy Nicco while I could.

"The rest of your siblings couldn't make it?" I asked Cameron.

"Not all of them have come to terms with having a half-sister yet, but they'll come around. Zoey would have, but she has school. She and Hannah got along so great when she visited last summer, they exchanged numbers. Peter and Emma, and my handful of a nephew, are staying with her to make sure she stays out of trouble while my parents are here."

I laughed softly. "Isn't she a senior in high school like Hannah? How much trouble can she possibly get into?"

Cameron's dark brows raised. "You'd be surprised at how much my little sister can get into when no one is around. I like to think she's calming down, but I don't think that will happen until she's college-bound next year."

"Georgetown, right?" I asked, recalling Hannah mention it. "Isn't that where she decided to go to college?"

"I'm impressed that you remembered that." Cameron grinned just as Nicco's eyes fluttered open.

"That's my cue," Regan laughed, scooping him back out of my arms as he yawned, before he could let out a wail for food.

I watched her whisk him away for privacy and looked back at Cameron, shaking my head. They had to be the most perfect family. "I am so happy for you," I said.

Cameron reached out to touch my arm. "Thanks. We can't thank you enough for your hospitality earlier this year and for everything you've done for Riley. Anytime you need anything, even if it's coming here for a getaway, just say the word."

How did he know I needed a longer vacation than this? He must see the weariness on my face, even though I'd tried my hardest to hide the dark circles beneath my eyes. Regan called him and he excused himself, moving away from me. A scrumptious-looking array of food and drinks in coolers sat on the table and deck, so I wandered out to grab a drink.

"Are you Cassie?"

Just as I was reaching into the cooler for a bottle of water, I heard a voice behind me. Straightening, I saw the two guys Jack had been walking on the beach with when I'd first seen him. They had to be Ty's brothers. They shared his blond hair and blue eyes though they were clearly younger than him, but not by much.

"I am. And you are?"

The taller of the two reached out. "Marc." He jerked his thumb at the other one. "This is August."

"Auggie," he growled, shoving his brother. "I can talk to her, too, you know."

"It's nice to meet Ty's brothers," I said, laughing at the playful shoving and thinking how nice it must be to have siblings.

"We love your dad's band," Auggie said.

"Thanks." My stomach sank. I couldn't go anywhere without someone mentioning my dad or my mom. But they were close enough to family. I liked Ty, suspicion and all. I needed to suck it up. "Have you been listening to his music for long?"

They both lit up. "Ever since we could get away with it. They just got back from tour, didn't they?"

I thought about it for a minute. "Last week, I think."

"Do you get to see the band a lot?"

When I moved toward the edge of the deck, away from the coolers to give others access to the drinks, they followed me. "I haven't seen them for a few years, but I suppose I used to see them a lot. I used to go with them during summer tours."

Auggie's mouth dropped open. "Shut up!"

Maybe talking about this with them wasn't so bad. They seemed to have such a good time discussing it, and I didn't mind the memories. It had been a few years since I visited my dad, though I talked to him often. As often as I could.

I nodded. "When I was a kid until just before my senior year. Then I went to college and stopped going." I didn't add that I'd had a fling with their roadie that year, and it kind of ruined it for me to go back after my senior year.

My relationship that summer with Watts Campbell ended in heartbreak, although I'd seen him many times since that tour, the shock of seeing him locking lips with another girl devastated me.

As the band manager's son, he knew my family's entire history, and while it seemed our relationship had been encouraged, he still did it.

"That is so bad ass!" Auggie exclaimed, eyes still bright. "Does he ever come up to Seattle?"

"Not unless they play a show there, but they stay on the tour bus or in a hotel. Next time they're in town, I'll hook you up to meet them. How about that?"

They exchanged high-fives like teenagers, even though I swore Ty had told me his brothers were in their early twenties. It was that easy to please them. My dad and the rest of the band would give me backstage passes for anyone. All I had to do was ask. That might be the issue I had with people trying to get close to me, I thought.

"Marc! Auggie! Leave the poor woman alone!"

My gaze snapped to a woman in the doorway, dressed in a sundress like Hannah's, except in a light pink color. Blonde hair, like theirs, was swept up stylishly. She made a pretty picture. I had to assume this was Suzie Cavanaugh, Ty's mom. She stepped onto the deck and marched over to them. I almost expected her to take them by the ears.

"What did Ty tell you about cornering her?"

"Sorry, Mom," Marc said, hanging his head.

"Sorry, Mom," Auggie grinned at me, showing no remorse whatsoever.

"Don't say sorry to me. Say sorry to Cassie."

They looked at me, both smiling as if they had a secret. "We're sorry," they said in unison.

"Will you still hook us up?" Auggie asked.

"I promise."

Suzie shooed them away, leaving me alone for a minute. I shuffled to the edge of the deck, leaning over to peek through the shrubs at the ocean as the sun began to set. It was probably the worst idea ever, but I pulled out my phone and called Evan.

When more people from inside came out, I moved down to the beach while the phone continued to ring. I should have known he wouldn't answer, the coward.

As soon as his voicemail picked up, I smiled bitterly. "The least you could do is pick up your phone and talk to me, you coward. Breaking it off with someone by text is the worst thing you can do, especially after seven months. I deserved to at least be told to my face when I came back, Evan. But I would hate for you to have to endure my coldness any longer, so have a nice life. Prick."

I hung up, blowing out a breath and taking a quick glance behind me to see if anyone at the house might have heard that. Sure enough, Jack leaned against the deck next to Ty's brothers, his eyes on me. Then he smiled. Damn. Reaching down, I slipped off my heels and walked toward the water, hoping he wouldn't follow me. I needed a moment, and sitting by the water was my favorite place to think.

A while later, Riley came and plopped down next to me. She slung her arm over my shoulder and pulled me slightly toward her. I rested my head on her shoulder.

"I'm so glad you came," she whispered. "I can't get married without you here."

"Of course you can't. I'm your witness."

Laughter erupted from her. "That's not it, but okay. All the same, you have been my rock when I needed someone the most, Cass. Naomi saved me and Hannah, but you . . . you saved *me*."

I heard a sniffle. "Are you crying?"

"I'm so emotional these days. It's because I'm pregnant. I can't help it."

I threw my arms around her. "You'll be alright, Riles. You have Ty now. He's probably the one who really saved you, if you think about it. Now you'll be like Regan and Cameron. When I look at you, I see such profound happiness that I get jealous."

She sat up, wiping away the wetness from her cheek. "You're jealous? Of me?"

I nodded.

"But you've got it all together. I'm a mess and you are always orderly, fit, and so dang healthy." She shook her head. "Perfect."

"Stop saying that. I'm not perfect. Maybe I look that way on the outside, but I'm a mess on the inside."

Bringing up the fact that Evan broke up with me earlier wasn't an option, otherwise she would make everything about me, and I didn't want that. This entire weekend was about her, and I'd make sure it stayed that way. She deserved this.

"Reno thinks so much of you, Cassie."

That shocked me. So much so that I pulled away from her, my mouth hanging open. Riley had only known of her dad for a few months. Reno was a powerful person, much like Regan's dad. He and I had shared many deep discussions while he stayed with us after Riley's ordeal. Still, he hadn't scratched the surface of the real Cassidy Nichols.

"He talks highly of you anytime you're mentioned. I think you made a big impression on him when you let him stay at your house last summer."

My eyebrows drew together. "I'd have done that for anyone. You know that."

She shook her head. "No. You don't let just anyone in, and you let him in a smidge. He admires you."

I couldn't understand why, but I didn't need to. We'd all be going our separate ways on Sunday, and I didn't know when I would see him again. "The feeling is mutual. I like your dad. He's a great person to talk to. Very intelligent."

"Sneaking off without me?" Regan shouted from behind us, plopping down on the other side of me. "Abandoning me in there, brats."

"Cameron never leaves your side," Riley said, but she smiled as she said it.

Regan sighed. "I know. He's overprotective. Especially now with Nicco."

"You're so lucky," I said, shocking myself for having said it. "Married, in love, cute little baby. Lucky."

"You'll get your turn someday, Cassie," Regan said, pushing her shoulder into mine.

"I'm not counting on it. I don't think I'm wife material."

Tossing her head back, Regan laughed. "I didn't think I was, either. And look where that got me! Good luck with that. I bet within a year, you'll be married."

She extended her hand, and I stared at it.

"A thousand bucks."

I don't gamble. I limit how much alcohol I drink, and I rarely curse, but I grabbed her hand, determined not to lose this bet. "You're on," I said. "And you're going to lose, Regan Moretti."

"Not on your life."

Chapter Three

"I can't believe you're getting married tomorrow."

I stretched my legs out and leaned back as Ty glanced at me. We sat on the sandy beach in front of Regan's beach house, watching the waves roll in while we could. Everyone else had long since left or gone to bed, leaving the house quiet and dark. Tomorrow would be busy with the wedding, and I didn't know when I'd see my best friend again. It might be a long time with what I had to deal with back home.

"I can't believe you're wearing shirts on a normal basis," Ty teased. "Especially since you're ditching Seattle and heading to LA. You can't tell me you won't go down to the pier and maybe do some surfing."

"Guess it's time for a change."

"Bullshit," Ty coughed into his fist.

I grinned. "I'll be working while I'm there. Maybe not all the time, but I am looking forward to doing a little surfing while I'm there. The perks of having a brother who works in a surf shop."

"Are you sure you want to do this? I mean, Working for that bastard . . . "

Ty shook his head when I glanced over at him. I knew he meant well, that he was concerned I was putting my life in danger, just like when we were undercover—maybe worse. There was no doubt in my mind about the decision I'd made. I had packed up my apartment in Seattle, sold my car, and shipped everything down to a house I rented in Santa Monica for my brother, Ezra, and me to share. I would take care of him. I always did.

"If one of your brothers was in trouble, would you ignore it?" I asked, trying not to sound defensive. He knew Ezra's troubled history.

"Absolutely not. That's not how either of us operates. I'd do what I needed to do for Auggie or Marc. But you've been rescuing Ezra for so many years, Jace, and he keeps at it. When is enough gonna be enough?"

I sighed, looking up at the dark sky, littered with twinkling stars. Ty was right. I'd been Ezra's shield for his entire life, and nothing had ever changed. I had to be his shield. It was partially my fault. The youngest child, "the dumb one" as our old man called him, he didn't fit the mold Fred Taylor wanted for his boys. We were expected to serve in the military. I wouldn't do it, although becoming a cop was close enough. Ezra was nothing but trouble, and it only got worse as we grew up.

"They would have killed him if I hadn't taken this deal," I murmured.

Ty stared me down. "For a long time, I always wondered why you had rules when it comes to women. Now, I understand why."

"You don't know shit. And why'd you tell Riley that I'd do anything to get a woman into bed? I told her enough lies while we were undercover. Did you really have to go and tell her that?"

He laughed. "It wouldn't have mattered. She was mine from the start, and you knew it. She isn't your type anyway." Seriousness returned to his pale blue eyes. "But seriously, you're going to be very lonely when you get older if you don't ease up on your rules and let someone into your life, buddy."

"What's Cassie's story?" I asked slowly, wondering if he was going to jump to conclusions as soon as her name came out of my mouth. "Is she shy or what?"

I'd tried my hardest not to make it obvious every time I looked at her earlier that night. The blue dress molded perfectly to her figure. Even Auggie and Marc had something to say about it. They wouldn't stop talking about her. But those two boneheads would drool over just about any woman. The fact that her dad was a drummer in one of their favorite bands only made them pant after her more.

I had to remind myself she was just a woman. But something in her eyes when I first saw her on the beach, standing in the water as if she were about to vault her phone into the surf, caught me off guard. The gentle slope of her neck, with wisps of windblown blonde hair framing her face when she turned and met my gaze. Pouty lips and big blue eyes—it heated my blood just remembering the vision.

Every time I headed in her direction, she'd catch me and traipse off to talk with someone else, like it wasn't obvious she was doing her best to avoid me. I couldn't recall a time when a woman had point blank avoided me like that. Cassie Nichols wouldn't be easily caught.

"You're kidding me," Ty said, yanking me out of my thoughts. "She would never let you close enough. Both of her parents are famous. Her mother was Jenna Nichols."

I frowned. "Should I know who that is?"

"Think back about ten to fifteen years ago and all those action movies we watched that starred Stirling Montgomery as the hero—she was the hot blonde in them. Hot to two young punks like us, anyway."

My mouth dropped open. "That was her mother? Holy shit."

Ty grinned. "Yup. And her dad is the drummer for a heavy metal band that both of my brothers listen to, which is why they got yelled at for cornering her tonight. Now you understand why she keeps her distance. People only want to get close to her for the fame."

"Damn, her mom doesn't hold a candle to her."

Ty shrugged. "She doesn't, not that I'm looking."

"She should have gone into acting like her mom."

"Cassie doesn't like that attention. There's a reason she's up in

Seattle and not living in LA."

I pushed him over. "So, she hides herself up there in Seattle, away from the spotlights of LA. What a damn shame. She's gorgeous."

"Damn, dude. I don't think I ever remember you getting wound up over a woman before. Remember your rules!"

Exactly why I had rules. No woman would fit into my life as it was. It was too risky, and that was assuming any of them would stick around—not to mention I'd never met a woman worth having stick around. In a way, I was like Cassie, holding everyone at a distance.

"Doesn't matter anyway. She'll be going back to Seattle, and I'm heading to LA."

"She visits her dad from time to time and has friends down there. Don't rule that out, Jace. Plus, Cassie and Riley are best friends. There might come a day after this weekend when you see her again."

Staring out at the ocean waves washing onto the shore, I thought about Cassie. She had gone to bed hours ago, and the house felt empty as soon as she did. But with Ty's words, a thrill of anticipation shot through me of laying eyes on her again in the morning.

Chapter Four

I could count on one hand how many weddings I'd attended, and I hadn't cried at any of them.

Yet, as Riley walked out of the house on the arm of Reno, my eyes instantly welled up. The dress, the flimsiest thing I'd ever seen her wear, made her look classically beautiful. It was her bare feet that nearly did me in. This was my friend, one of my *best* friends, and the look in her eyes, her gaze solely on Ty, was the unmistakable stare of someone utterly, deeply in love.

When my eyes darted to Ty, the breath caught in my throat. The look in his eyes matched hers, unwavering in his feelings. Happiness swelled in my heart for them, so much that it ached to witness. Envy aside, I couldn't be happier for them.

My thoughts drifted to my most recent disaster of a relationship, and I wondered if I would ever walk down the aisle. When I said I wasn't wife material, I meant it. When I'd made that bet with Regan last night, I knew I wouldn't lose, and in a year, I'd be a thousand bucks richer. My lack of love for Evan, and my indifference over the breakup confirmed my belief that I wouldn't get married. I couldn't let anyone in enough for them to want to marry me. The breakup stung, but I was far from crushed.

The wedding ceremony itself didn't last long. It was simple and sweet, just as Riley wanted. She'd never been one to prolong anything. When she told me the news of her upcoming nuptials and invited me to the island under complete secrecy, I was surprised that she didn't elope.

I looked around at the crowd gathered on the beach in front of Regan and Cameron's house, their sailboat bobbing up and down with the waves at the end of the long dock behind the makeshift altar. The people here were all important to Riley and Ty, and we all loved the two of them.

When Ty pulled Riley into his arms as her husband, I tried not to sigh at the hunger in their kiss. I couldn't imagine what it would be like to have someone love me or to love someone like that.

People moved around as Riley and Ty chatted with those rushing up to them to offer congratulations. I had a feeling it would be some time before I could get to them, but I knew I would. I would need to sign the marriage certificate as a witness. Regan and Cameron quickly commandeered their time, followed by Riley's mom, Simone, and Ty's two brothers. As much as I wanted to stand at the water's edge with my thoughts, it would be rude, so I joined the small throng of people.

Unlike Regan's beach house, massive trees surrounded this two-story house on all sides except the beachside. The windows on that side of the house reflected the beach from top to bottom. What a view, I thought.

I spotted Jack standing off to the side, talking with Naomi. By the dreamy look in her sixty-seven-year-old eyes as she stared at him, I knew without a doubt that his charm had reeled her in. I had avoided him last night, but I hadn't escaped his gaze. Every once in a while, I'd feel his eyes on me, and sure enough, he had been watching.

Instead, I strolled toward the low, multi-tiered deck at the back of the house, where I spotted Reno near Ty's parents, William and Suzie. He was listening to them, but he wasn't talking. I stepped up next to him.

"Riley told me last night that you've taken a particular liking to me," I said.

It couldn't have been my sparkling personality. No one except a few close friends knew me well enough to feel that way. To be honest, I didn't understand why Reno had told her that.

Reno turned away from the group, smiling down at me with his warm brown eyes from his imposing height. He was handsome, even with dark hair tinged with gray at his temples. "Did she now?"

Taking me lightly by the elbow, he led me toward a table with refreshments and handed me a glass of lemonade. Because Ty and Simone had issues with alcohol in their past, they chose not to serve it at their wedding. That mattered very little to me, as I wasn't a big drinker myself. I accepted the glass and took a tentative sip.

"You know I would open my home to anyone Riley cares about. Especially her dad."

His brown eyes sparkled. "That's not it, sweetheart."

He moved closer, as if about to share a dark secret that no one else should overhear. Startled, I wasn't sure if I should step away. There were reasons I didn't let people get close to me, both physically and emotionally, and Reno would be no exception.

"You want everyone to think you're all sweet and innocent. But we both know deep down that isn't true. Don't we?"

That stunned me. After a pause, I barked out a laugh so loud that it caught the attention of several people around us. Did he just insult me? It only made me more curious about what had led him to think I could be anything but innocent.

"You may fool many people, but I see a woman with a lust for life. And if you ask me, you're ruining it by hiding up there in Washington."

He had guts. I'd give him that. It made it easier to understand what had shaped him into the man he was today. Reno Moretti didn't take shit from anyone, and anyone could tell that just by looking at him. The apple didn't fall far from the tree with Cameron, and I was sure it was the same with his two other sons, Stefan and Peter. Even Riley, despite not being raised by him. It must be in their blood, I mused. Cameron got lucky when he found a wife like Regan.

"Am I?"

"Without a doubt. If you ever feel like cutting loose, Las Vegas is the perfect town for it. Give me a call. I know people who can make your stay there an experience you won't soon forget. They don't call it Sin City for nothing." He flipped me his business card, edged in expensive gold. I studied it, wondering if it was made of actual gold, running my finger along the edge. "And please don't take this as a man twice your age hitting on you, sweetheart. This is me trying to help you."

With a nod, I turned to walk away, tucking his card into my clutch.

"Cassie?" he called softly after me.

I turned halfway around and met his eyes.

"I'm here if you ever need my help."

Wondering what on earth I would ever need his help for, I could only stare at him. I'd put in too much work constructing my own defenses. Ever the gentleman, he touched my arm lightly and excused himself, brushing past Jack as he went. Dressed in a loose-fitting pair of pants and a thin, almost translucent shirt, Jack's hair blew in the breeze as he eyed me.

"Cassie," he said, reaching around me to grab a glass of lemonade. "There wasn't much opportunity for us to talk last night."

I sipped slowly. "Lots of people around."

He purposely looked around, and I knew why. The same people who were there last night were here now. He thought he could one-up me by casually pointing out my bullshit excuse. "Are you avoiding me?"

"Should I be?"

"I can't think of a single reason why."

"Not a one?" I feigned shock.

God, I was a brat. And that was the problem. People thought I was some perfect girl, dressing flawlessly in the blandest colors, with not a hair out of place and a picture-perfect life. They couldn't be more wrong, and I would never let them know that. I did it on purpose so I wouldn't stand out any more than I should. His smile, slowly touching the corners of his lips, made my heart skip a beat. Or two. Holy smokes, he had a sexy smile.

Mentally shaking myself, I doubled my efforts to keep this man at arm's length. I'd dated men like him in the past, and I'd had enough of those.

"You don't like me very much, do you?" he asked.

"To be fair, I don't know you. I only know that you hit on Riley when you first met her." His dark eyebrows raised. "Do you deny it?"

"No."

That was the quickest I'd ever heard him speak. I shook my head. It didn't count since it was only a one-word response. "Rather ballsy of you to do that when you knew she was with Ty, don't you think?"

"Rather shallow of you to judge me."

"I have reason to," I shot back.

His laugh, low and sultry, washed over me as he stepped closer. "So, you've made up your mind about me?"

I stared into his eyes. Hard. How could I explain that I didn't want to take a chance on getting hurt without sounding shallow like he said?

"Are you in a relationship right now?" I blurted.

"No. You?"

Trained in psychology, I surprised myself with the slip, but his admission wasn't shocking in the least. His reputation spoke for itself.

"Yes." The lie came easily.

"That's not what I overheard last night. Are you sure?"

Oh, he would be the death of me if I stayed around him any longer. I knew he'd overheard! I calmed myself before responding with a simple, "Yes."

He tilted his head to the side. "I saw you running earlier." "I run every morning. It helps me."

"With?"

I sighed. He was going to pull everything out of me, or at least try, wasn't he? As a detective, I imagined he was just as used to peppering people with questions as I was as a therapist. I smiled at the uncanny commonality between us, shaking my head.

"Something funny?"

"It helps me cope. I have a lot of demons," I admitted, looking into his eyes.

As soon as our eyes met, I realized my mistake. I could drown in those eyes. As beguiling as they were, no wonder women fell at his feet—with his eyes, his voice, and his physique. I tore my gaze away.

"I'm sorry to hear that. If it helps, I have a lot of demons, too."

"Anything you want to share with me? I am licensed, which means it would be a violation if I were to share what you tell me with anyone else unless you give your approval."

The corner of his mouth lifted. "I'll book an appointment with you when I'm ready to talk about my demons. It would take a long while to unleash them all."

"I'm not taking new clients right now. Maybe you should try running. Pumping out all that sweat seems to help me, followed by calming yoga and a cup of herbal tea. It does wonders."

"I prefer lifting weights, although I'm not as dedicated to it as you are with your morning ritual. I appreciated the sight last night, though."

My face warmed at his reference to my dress. Was this his offhanded way of complementing me? I knew I'd captured his interest, as much as I'd tried to avoid him during the get together, but to point it out so blatantly made my heart thump uncontrollably.

I wasn't sure what to say to him after that remark, like I'd been robbed of forming coherent words. Flustered, I did the only thing

I could think of: I walked away. Walking away from him in the middle of a conversation had a distinct feeling to it. It felt like a statement.

Reno had been right. I had success, a decent house, and while I couldn't deny my high maintenance, it didn't have to be a relationship-breaker. I truly didn't know why men never stuck around. But Jack Taylor could be a disaster for me if I let him.

Chapter Five

The lull of the waves washing against the beach of this paradise put me in a daze as I waited for my tea to steep. Leaning my hip against the granite countertop, I tried to peek through the slats of the window coverings for a glimpse of those waves. No luck. Afraid to wake Jack, I hesitated to get up and make myself a cup of tea at this ungodly hour. I had already skipped my run this morning, and now I would have to skip my yoga routine as well.

The sun had barely risen, and the screaming of seagulls searching for a morning bite was just beginning, but I couldn't sleep. Restlessness plagued me, as it always did. I could hear Naomi, still snoring in the room next to mine, in my subconscious: "Cassie, you need to meditate. Clear your mind. Then you won't be so dang restless."

Bobbing the tea bag up and down in a steaming cup filled with water in a touristy *I Love Island Life* coffee mug, my lips quirked up. Naomi Monroe had easily filled the role of mother when my mom died. Ricky Monroe and my dad had been friends since their teenage years after my dad came here from England. Who better to step in and take care of me than Ricky's mom, who already had her two granddaughters in her care?

After my mom died, Naomi moved Riley and Hannah twice in less than a year to escape Simone's dangerous living conditions, which involved drugs and alcohol. On top of that, she had to contend with teenage me who had just lost my mother and felt responsible for it. She had to be a saint to survive those years.

Screw it. No one would be up for a while. I couldn't think of a reason not to take my restlessness outside and enjoy the sound of the waves from the deck. There was less chance of waking anyone up. I darted a glance at Jack on the wide couch, lying on his stomach with the thin blanket shoved down to his waist. His muscular back created a striking image, the dark swirls of ink covering his shoulders and impressive upper back. Holy smokes, I thought. Good thing I was leaving today. The man's physique was magnificent.

Taking my tea, I padded lightly across the floor, nearly making it to the French doors leading to the patio when my cell phone rang.

"Shoot," I muttered, nearly spilling my tea as I scrambled to open the door quickly, hoping not to wake him.

The door clicked shut behind me before I finally answered the call, setting my cup down on the table until I could bring the phone up to my ear.

"Dad," I said in a frantic whisper, even though I was outside where no one could hear me. "What on earth are you doing up this early?"

"Hey, baby girl."

The low, scratchy voice of Lex Edwards came through. His British accent still made me smile, and I would never tire of hearing it. It had been too long since we'd last talked, and I didn't care if it was barely four in the morning in California or what he was doing awake right now.

His call, though early, shouldn't have surprised me. He'd always been a night owl. I supposed that rockstars usually were night owls, playing gigs well into the night and then partying afterward.

"Dad? What are you doing up this early?" I asked again. "Or are you still up?"

"Can't a dad be concerned about his daughter? My *only* daughter?"

Was I? I thought silently to myself, squeezing my eyes closed and pinching the bridge of my nose for a moment to collect myself. I loved him more than anything in this world, real dad or not. As far as I was concerned, he *was* my dad. Even though he'd been on tour when my mom died, he was there for me afterward. And I went on every tour with him after that instead of just once in a while, even if it was only part of a tour.

"I worry about you, I do," he said, interrupting my memories. "We haven't talked in ages. What have you been up to?"

I let out a small laugh, taking my tea with me toward the edge of the deck to overlook the vacant beach. "I'm up to the same things as usual. What are *you* up to? You can't be thinking about me this early in the morning."

"Ricky's girlfriend is about your age." I could hear him take a deep drag from a cigarette, grimacing at the habit I always hoped he would kick.

His voice had a scratchy sound to it for a reason, and smoking only contributed to that. Backing vocals for his band made up part of it, too. He'd been the drummer for many years, giving his heart and soul to this band.

"Ugh, he's too old for her then. And why would I give you a reason to worry? I have a boring career, not much of a social life, and I just got dumped by text, so my dating life is pretty dull, too."

"Dating? My little girl? Who's the stupid fuck that would break up with my little girl by text? Should I kick his ass?"

"I don't want to talk about him. What are you doing up so early, Dad? Is everything okay?"

He paused for a moment. "Don't avoid the question, Cassidy. Who's the guy?"

"He's a lawyer. Not the fancy criminal defense lawyer like you'd think, though. He's a corporate lawyer. Don't worry, I left him a nasty voicemail on Friday night."

"Ack, he's crackers. Better off without him. Dim, he is."

I couldn't agree more and laughed. My dad might think Evan crazy to break it off with me—maybe not smart—but in truth, he'd probably done us both a favor, though my life was bound to be seriously dull now. Until I found someone else to date for a while, who would end up dumping me because I couldn't open up. Seriously. What kind of therapist can't trust people?

"How was the tour?"

"Smashing. Just got back a little over a week ago. Been in the studio this past week working on new stuff." He paused again, taking another drag from his cigarette. There was an edge to his voice that I hadn't noticed before. "When are you coming for a visit? I've got a lead on a superb piece of art for sale at a gallery opening next weekend."

Nostalgia swept through me, hearing the excitement in his voice. If music was his love, art was a close second to it. "Soon. I was just thinking about that."

"See that you do, baby girl. I'll let you get back."

"Bye, Dad. I love you."

"Ah, my love to you, baby girl. Ba-bye."

I pulled the phone away with a frown. A strange feeling washed over me. Like he wanted to say something else, but he didn't. Staying up late into the night was normal for him, but he rarely called me this early. I sighed, wishing I could talk to him more. As usual, it had been too long since I'd had a decent conversation with him. He'd been on tour for the last several months, and now that they were back, it was about time I went to see him. My high school friends, Mac and Kya, were due for a visit. It was surprising they weren't blowing up my phone since it had been a few years.

I glanced up, amazed when I shouldn't have been, to see Jack walking toward me with his sinfully muscular chest bare and a pair of thin sweatpants riding low on his hips. A man should not look this good this early in the morning, especially a man like Jack, who was off-limits to me.

"Everything all right?" came his slow, deep drawl, still laced with sleep.

My mouth instantly dried, leaving me no choice but to hastily grab my tea for a quick sip. The warmth of the tea offered me a much-needed reprieve, but I couldn't find my voice. I could only shake my head, barely managing that.

"No?"

He stepped over to me, leaning his smoothly sloped arms over the edge of the deck to look out at the waves lazily coming in. Other than the swirls and swaths of black tattoos, there were no blemishes on his olive-toned skin. His hair, tousled from sleep, nearly touched the top of his broad shoulders. I tried my hardest not to stare at him or at the way the tattoos banded around his arm, curling down in black swirls. Holy smokes, he had smooth skin. The kind that made you want to run your palm over it just to feel the texture.

I shook my head again. "Everything's fine."

He chuckled. "You shaking your head tells me something different. You sure it's all fine?"

With his eyes fixed on me, those vivid blue irises rimmed with green, I lost my words. Not only were his eyes captivating, but the way he spoke felt almost lazy. I was certain I'd never heard anyone speak that way. It was like he took his time. I wondered if he took his time in everything.

Giving myself a hard mental shake, I whipped my gaze back to the shimmering water before I did something seriously stupid.

When I looked at him again, he still stared at me as though he hadn't stopped. He knew his game; I'd give him that. This wasn't like me. I wasn't some dumb kid stumbling around, talking to a boy for the first time. I remembered all too well being that dumb kid, and it hadn't ended well for me.

"Everything is fine, Jack."

"Jace."

I held his gaze, even though it made me feel things I had no business feeling. "Excuse me?"

"My name is Jace. Jacek, actually, but people call me Jace. I only went by Jack when I was undercover with Ty."

"And you're just saying something now?"

When he smiled, the tiniest dimple appeared, making him look even more charming. But talking to him was dangerous for me. Bad boys had always drawn me in like moths to a flame. If I wasn't careful, he'd have me hooked. Getting involved with someone like him was something I'd put deep into my past. I dated men like Evan now—safe. Evan had cared about being successful, and that suited me well. Until two days ago.

He shrugged. "You can never be too sure."

"Around Ty's friends? Are we dangerous?"

I watched the light in his eyes grow sultry. "You might be a danger to me, Cass."

The way he elongated my name caressed me like a finger dragging lightly down the center of my back. Slow, calculated.

"Cassie," I bit out. "My name is Cassie. The only danger I might be to you, *Jace*, is walking away." "Again?"

"I'm not interested in being another night in your collection."

When he took a step back, slapping a hand against his bare chest, I winced. He hadn't said anything direct about being interested in me. I had only stupidly assumed. I noticed more black swirls of tattoos on the other side, along his ribs, curling around his shoulder.

"Is there a reason you loathe me?"

"I don't loathe you. I already told you yesterday what I learned from Riley, and you didn't deny it."

Interested in his response, I tilted my head and waited for him to deny it again. He hadn't given me much yesterday other than an agreement.

"I was undercover. Playing a part."

"That's BS, and you know it. She said it was just the two of you in the kitchen then. No one else was around."

When he stepped closer, my heart sped beyond my comfort zone as I felt the heat radiating from his body. How could he be so hot? The chill from the ocean breeze had little effect on me. I didn't have time to consider the possibilities of what could happen between us. His eyes locked onto mine, capturing my gaze and demanding my undivided attention.

"I was still playing a part," he whispered, so close that his breath stirred the hair at the curve of my ear. "I've known Ty for a long time. Undercover or not, he would have told me if he had a woman in his life. Playing my part was essential at the time because I knew Ty, and there was something not quite right about why Riley was suddenly there."

I breathed deeply when he pulled away, not realizing I'd been holding my breath.

"Turns out, I was right."

And he had been. Riley had gotten caught sneaking around the house where they had been working undercover, and Ty had saved her. When he came to her rescue, it forced her to spend the night. A small shudder slid through me as I wondered what it would have been like to be in that situation—having to sleep in the same room with a man I hardly knew. And now they were married. I couldn't wrap my head around it.

"And now they're married," I whispered aloud.

"Better him than me."

I ignored his comment, wondering if he was right. Having a bet with Regan, I would have to agree with him, even if I didn't voice it. I couldn't let him think I would agree with him on anything.

"I'm not sure I want to leave the warmth of this paradise." Turning back toward the beach, I could see the sun make its hazy presence in the sky known. "This is something I could get used to. Are you on the same flight as we are?"

"I'm not going back to Seattle."

My hands curled around the mug as I sipped my tea, savoring the herbal warmth. "No? Don't you have another undercover assignment or something?"

"I quit."

"Why? You saved Riley and Ty. Isn't that what you do? Get the bad guys and save the day? That's your job. Why would you leave that?"

I couldn't believe it. What he'd done had been heroic, no matter his feelings about relationships. As a detective, he'd been damn good at his job when it mattered the most.

"I have some things to take care of back home. Guess I need a break from being someone I'm not."

Trying to keep my frown hidden, I continued to watch the gentle roll of the waves as they caressed the flawless sand. What I didn't want Jace to know was that I could relate all too well to that. Being the daughter of two famous people—one whose death from an overdose at the height of her career thrust me even further into the spotlight—I had to pretend to be someone else more than I ever wanted.

Having famous parents gave me a popularity I never wanted and drew people to me who wanted to get in with the famous crowd. I'd kept an extremely private life, ducking away from paparazzi like my mom had taught me. At one point, I considered changing my name like Riley had. Instead, I remained private and moved far from Hollywood.

Only Mac, Kya and a few other select friends, including Riley, knew the real Cassidy Nichols. None of them would betray me by talking to the paparazzi or the press.

Chapter Six

Three days later, I still hadn't gotten used to the Seattle drizzle, even though I'd settled into my usual routine. Naomi, Hannah, and I returned to a fine rain that cleared soon after we arrived home. I could only be thankful for that after picking up Gus and Gatsby for Riley. Riley and Ty stayed in Cape Haven for a few more days with Cameron and Regan before heading to Las Vegas to spend some time with Reno. That left her wound-up two-year-old Labrador retrievers for Naomi to handle while Hannah had to get back to school and I went back to work.

The carpet in the office lobby muted the heels of my stylish ankle boots when I walked in on Wednesday morning, ready to get the midweek done and over with. My conversation with Jace had stuck in my head most of the way home. Though I'd sworn him off, he had done nothing to come onto me.

Almost a pity, I thought for the briefest moment. No, it was better that he stayed away and didn't tempt me. My life was content even without Evan.

My schedule was full with clients today, but I planned to text Evan later to see if we could meet for a drink and maybe talk through whatever issue we had. I would never crawl back to him, but I deserved a proper explanation for being dumped. It was the least he could do. There'd been no response to my voicemail, although I had to admit it had been vicious enough to warrant being ignored. Who was I kidding? I needed to see Evan to get Jace out of my head, though getting back together with him wasn't an option. Jace shouldn't be in my thoughts, anyway. He was hundreds of miles south, somewhere in LA.

After a quick greeting to the receptionist sitting at the front desk, tapping the keys of her computer, I slipped into my office and closed the door. I was one of the lucky therapists to have a window that overlooked the bay, though I had to trade the view for a smaller office. Despite the size, I'd created a cozy atmosphere for my clients with a chocolate-brown suede couch big enough to sit two people comfortably, flanked by two side tables and muted lamps that provided warmth. The only decoration was a lightly colored watercolor painting of the Seattle skyline by a local artist.

I set my bag down next to my chair and eased into it, opening my laptop to review my appointments for the day. I knew the day would be full, but I always reviewed who my clients would be to refresh my memory on what we'd discussed during our last sessions. My last session would be with a new client.

Oh, goody, I thought sarcastically. I needed to ensure I wouldn't accept new clients after this. The reputation I'd built for myself made me sought after, and my workload had increased even after only a year in the field.

The day breezed by uneventfully but was incredibly busy. I barely had time to grab a bland salad for lunch before the onslaught of afternoon clients began. With a sigh of relief, I walked to the waiting area to fetch my last client.

"Bethany?" I scanned the two women waiting and smiled warmly as a thin woman with light brown hair stood.

"That's me!" she said, extending her hand.

"It's nice to meet you, Bethany." I shook her hand politely. "I'm-"

"Cassidy Nichols."

She matched my stride back to my office. "I prefer Cassie. Cassidy is too formal, and no one calls me that."

"Oh, absolutely! It's so nice to meet you finally. I've heard good things about you as a therapist, and I've had to wait a while for an appointment to open up."

I ushered her into my office and closed the door, waiting for her to sit on the couch before taking my seat in the matching chair. She chewed on her lower lip while I reached over to grab my notebook and pen.

"I've wanted to meet you for years. What was it like growing up with your dad? I have all of your dad's bands' CDs. He is such an amazing drummer!"

The bottom of my stomach dropped, but I managed a small, quiet laugh to ease any tension. "Bethany, we're not here to discuss me. I leave my personal life outside of this office. I'm here to help you."

"Oh, I'm so sorry!" She leaned back against the couch. "I didn't have a good upbringing. My parents were pricks. Partying and leaving me with my little sisters and brothers. You had no brothers or sisters?"

I gave her a stern look.

"Right. Anyways, I feel like I grew up before I should have, ya know? All of my relationships have failed because I keep picking these losers to date, and I end up alone. I've been fired from six jobs now."

"How many brothers and sisters do you have, and how old are they?"

"I have two sisters and three brothers." She laughed softly. "I don't even know how old they are. I think my sister Janice is two years younger than me."

"Are you using drugs or drinking alcohol?"

She looked up at me slowly. "I haven't for a while."

"What do you consider a while?"

"A month maybe." She sighed. "What are you writing in your notebook?"

"I need to make notes for your file so I can remember what we talk about for our next session. Do you feel you have a problem?"

"Your mom died of an overdose, didn't she? Did you live with your dad after that?" She gasped. "Did you get to go on tour with him? And hang out with the band? I bet you get to hang out with rockstars and famous people all the time."

My stomach tensed. "Bethany, I'm going to tell you one more time not to ask questions about my personal life. This is about you, not me."

"I'm sorry. It's just been so long since I've wanted to meet you! And now you're here, and I'm just in awe. You're so pretty. You look kind of like your dad but really more like your mom."

I sighed. "Bethany, did you seek me out as a therapist just because of who my parents are? Because of my dad?"

After she visibly swallowed, she nodded. "I mean, I need therapy. I need help. But I really wanted to meet you. I'm sorry."

I tried my best not to swear. I really did. At least not out loud. But I felt the urge rising. Calmly, I set my notepad and pen down on the coffee table between us.

"No. I'm the one who's sorry. Bethany, I'll have your session rescheduled with another therapist."

When I stood up, she jumped to her feet. "But why? I'll stop asking personal questions, I swear."

"I'll make sure you get the help you need. Thank you for coming in today. The receptionist will help you schedule another appointment."

She balked when I opened my office door, but after a long pause, she walked out in complete dejection. We walked in silence to the lobby, where I left her with the receptionist before returning to my office and closing the door, trying to keep my frustration at bay.

"Damn!" I uttered.

No one else could hear me. Thankfully. I didn't want to shatter my impeccable reputation, though I was far from perfect.

Dropping my hands, I sat at my desk to text Evan. I needed that glass of wine I foolishly thought I'd be having with Evan, even though I hesitated several times before finally sending it.

After a minute, he texted back to say he couldn't get away tonight. The case he was working on would consume a lot of his time this week, but maybe this weekend he could carve out some time. I dropped my phone onto my desk just as a couple of knocks sounded on my door.

Tish poked her head in. "Tough day?"

I groaned, burying my face in my hands. "The worst. Can't I just go back to the beach for a few more days?"

She laughed, closing the door behind her as she walked into my office without an invitation. Tish knew me well enough to know when she could tread on my turf. Dressed in a colorful red suit, it only darkened her complexion and hair. With her lithe figure, she was a beautiful woman. And now that her divorce was final, she was single again. Her ex-husband had moved on with a petite young woman ten years her junior.

"Only if you take me to the beach with you. What happened?"

"Apparently, my new client in my last session sought me out for my famous background. She admitted it after bombarding me with questions about my dad and my life."

Tish threw her head back in laughter. "Are you serious?"

"When did a therapy session become 'ask the therapist questions'?" Shaking my head, I scoffed. "I need a glass of wine. I tried to get Evan to talk to me, at least to explain the text dumping, but he's too busy."

"Well, if you ask me . . ."

My eyes snapped up to meet hers. I knew her opinion about Evan, and it wasn't good. Tish disliked Evan immensely, and she had since we'd started dating in March. She thought dating him was a waste of my time. Apparently, it had been.

If I was being honest with myself, I didn't want to see him. True, I wanted Jace Taylor out of my mind, but I really just wanted to move on from Evan. I'd convinced myself I needed closure, but did I? Maybe I wasn't as upset by it as I thought. Maybe I just needed a bubble bath instead.

"Let's go have a drink, then," she said, rising and pressing out invisible wrinkles in her suit jacket. "Come on. You deserve it. God knows I deserve it."

"One drink, Tish," I warned. "No more than that."

I laughed, touching my hair to make sure it had stayed in place. Satisfactory, I determined. Why the hell not? It had been a while since I'd been out for a drink. Maybe I'd have the guts to let some hot guy take me home for one night.

"Let's do it. It's been a while since we've had happy hour."

Chapter Seven

Cassie

An hour later, Tish and I bellied up to the bar with drinks in our hands, ogling a bartender in a black t-shirt stretched over one helluva an enormous chest. If he wasn't a bodybuilder by day and a bartender by night, I wasn't the product of two famous parents. Flashing us his perfectly straight, white teeth, he left us to our drinks and wandered down to the other end of the bar to wait on other patrons.

"Cheers to all the single ladies," Tish said, lifting her rum and coke.

"Cheers."

Our glasses clinked together, and I sipped my red wine. The tart flavor lingered for a moment before sliding down my throat, and I resisted the urge to take another sip right away. Usually, if I indulged in alcohol, it was white or red wine; rarely any more than one glass. Riley made fun of me for it, being the opposite of me in almost every way. Both my parents were prone to addiction, and I refused to follow in their footsteps with drugs or alcohol, allowing myself only a glass of wine on occasion. I exercised, going for a morning run followed by yoga, and I only ate healthy foods. Caffeine, other than what's in tea, was off-limits, and I usually took my time to look my best. I did so as blandly as possible, opting for neutral colors to melt into the background where no one would notice me.

"Why didn't you stay at the beach longer? You can't tell me you don't have enough vacation time. You never take time off."

True. I had built up an enormous amount of vacation time, only because there hadn't been reason to take any. Tish couldn't be more right. I should have stayed longer or traded one beach for another; Miami wasn't far from Myrtle Beach.

"What can I say?" I cupped my hands around my glass. "Responsibility is a bitch. I didn't want to leave Naomi to handle the dogs alone."

"She isn't *that* old."

My thoughts drifted to my dad. I hadn't seen him for a while and hadn't been to LA to see my friends in years. If anyone was overdue for a vacation, it was me. To be honest, I'd been neglecting myself without realizing it.

"I hate it when you're right, Tish," I grumbled, taking another sip. "I'm due for a trip down to LA."

Tish grinned. "Who've you got if you don't have me here to remind you?"

I laughed. "Naomi reminds me all the time but I never listen. But you? You'll badger me until I give in."

We dissolved into laughter, earning a curious look from our cute bartender, who caught Tish's slight wave and fixed her another cocktail. I shook my head at a second glass of wine, but Tish insisted. I knew I would have a raging headache in the morning. Although it was rare for me to let loose, it wouldn't be the worst thing in the world to cancel my appointments in the morning. I'd feel awful about it, but it didn't happen often.

"Uh-oh."

Staring deep into my glass and thinking about the blue eyes of Jace Taylor, I barely heard Tish. She nudged me with her elbow until I turned her way, just in time to see Evan step through the door.

"Guess he changed his mind," I said, straightening on my bar stool.

I mentally prepared my already alcohol-riddled brain as he pulled a slim brunette toward him, snaking his arm around her waist and guiding her across the bar to an empty table in the corner. Confusion swept through me. I followed their movements with my eyes, waiting until they sat across from each other before looking back at Tish. She raised her eyebrows.

"Must be a business meeting," I said, turning back to my drink and taking another sip. I knew better than to believe that flimsy excuse.

"Um . . ."

I didn't need to hear anything else from her before I whipped around to see the two of them nestled close to each other. Business meetings rarely, if ever, involved two people sitting so close together, and they certainly didn't involve the man having his hands entwined with the woman's. Sliding off my bar stool, my boots hit the floor with a thud.

Before I could take a step, Tish grabbed my arm, nearly making me topple back into her. "Let me go."

"Cass, don't do it. It's not worth it. *He's* not worth it."

There were enough people around that Evan couldn't see the disturbance Tish and I created at the bar. Gracious, she was strong for her five feet, six inches. Her arm around mine wouldn't budge.

"I'm just going to tell him he was right to break it off with me before moving on. If that's what he did."

She spun me around, the small amount of alcohol I'd consumed nearly knocking me sideways into the bar. Her eyes narrowed. "You go over there, and your true colors are going to show. People will notice."

"God, I hope so." I wrenched my arm out of her grip and spun back around, determination urging me on. I had kept my true colors on a leash for too long.

Tish called after me, her voice distant to my ringing ears as my feet moved of their own volition toward the small table in the corner. The club had filled with customers since Tish and I had arrived, the voices all sounding as distant as Tish. When I stopped at the table, I had the pleasure of seeing Evan glance up for a moment before looking down. Then his eyes snapped right back up.

"Busy at work, huh?" I asked. "I completely understand."

"Cassie." He put a small distance between his body and that of the woman, but not nearly enough. And it was entirely too late. "We were working late, and—"

I leaned forward, bracing my hands on the table and giving both him and his date a full view down the front of my shirt. He opened his mouth. "Save it. While I have no doubt you broke up with me to move on, I do have serious doubts you waited to. And by the way, while you were here cozying up to another woman—apparently this one—I was in Cape Haven fucking someone else. I'm about done with you and your boring-ass job, anyway. Don't call me."

I walked away with a purposeful sway of my hips. God, how easily the lie had slipped from my lips. Maybe I should have slept with Jace in Cape Haven if the opportunity had presented itself. Tish hadn't been completely right about my true colors. I had been calm enough not to cause a scene, but I gave Evan a glimpse of anything but the frigid woman he had just broken up with. I didn't like to cause scenes because they created unwanted attention.

Tish's eyes widened when I rejoined her, growing wider as I turned to see Evan still staring after me in disbelief. I whirled around, gave him the finger, and had her rolling with laughter.

"True colors," she muttered.

Very few people had seen them. And had I allowed Jace anywhere near me, others would have known a much more diverse side of Cassie Nichols. He'd gotten enough of what I didn't normally let out when we'd spoke after the wedding. I couldn't allow that to happen. I was calm, just as cold as Evan had told me in his text. But after he'd sent that message, something had snapped, and I'd let a tiny hint of the real me out last weekend. I was not an indifferent person, even if I still didn't like scenes.

"That felt good," I said, tossing back the rest of my wine and motioning for the bartender to pour me another just as someone changed the channel on the television screen over the bar to one of those notorious paparazzi news channels.

An uneasy feeling swept over me at the sight of an airplane crash being reported on the news. If Tish spoke, I wouldn't hear her. The closed captioning at the bottom of the screen reported that a private plane flying over rural California toward Nevada had crashed with no survivors. The report mentioned the airplane may have carried members of the rock band Skeletons of Disciples. My stomach pitched, and for a moment, I thought my drinks would come up all over the bar top.

My vision swam, and my heart thundered.

"What in the hell?" I murmured. "This isn't something a person learns about on the news, Tish."

I reached for what was left of my wine, but a violent trembling in my hand made me pull back. No. This couldn't be happening. They'd just returned from the tour. What could they be doing on an airplane headed toward Nevada? Playing a last-minute gig in Las Vegas? Why hadn't he mentioned that when I talked to him on Sunday?

If my hand hadn't been resting on my clutch, I might not have noticed my phone vibrating. I fumbled to dig it out in a panic until I finally brought it to my ear.

"Hello?"

"Is this Cassidy Nichols?"

My breathing slowed as I leaned against the bar stool, slapping my clutch back onto the bar. "This is Cassie Nichols." "My name is Officer Davison from the LA Police Department. I'm sorry to bother you, especially on the phone, but I wanted to reach out to you. We believe your father, Lex Edwards, was aboard an airplane that crashed."

If my lips were trying to form words, none were coming out. I cleared my throat. "What makes you think he was on that plane? Was the whole band on board?"

"We can't comment on any other occupants at this time. He was listed as a passenger. Unfortunately, it might take some time to investigate the scene. It would be a good idea for you to come to the station and prepare for the worst. If his remains are found, we'll need you as his next of kin to identify them."

My eyes closed as anguish swept through me. I felt Tish's hand on my arm; little did she know that if her hand weren't there, I might have toppled to the floor. They had to be wrong.

"Of course," I whispered. "I'll come as soon as I can."

Once he gave me his phone number and instructions to contact him when I got into town, I pulled my phone away but kept it gripped tightly in my hand.

"Talk to me, Cass."

I shook my head. "They're wrong, Tish. He wouldn't be on a plane." My eyes turned to hers, filling with tears. "Would he?"

The bartender placed another glass of wine in front of me, and I grabbed it with shaky fingers, taking a quick sip. My last phone conversation with him had been only days ago, while I'd been in Cape Haven. My mind scrambled to remember our brief conversation.

When my watery eyes lifted to hers, I sensed she was about to pull me into her arms, and I shook my head. Not after having had a messy episode with Evan. No way did I want him to think this had anything to do with him.

"He should be working with the band, not on a plane somewhere."

I covered my mouth as tears spilled down my cheeks. Her hand remained on my arm, but she made no further attempts to hug me. "Honey, I'm so sorry."

"I can't lose another . . . I can't lose him, Tish. I just can't."

She shook her head, pulling me against her despite my feeble attempts to resist comfort. "Cassie, you know that I love you," she whispered. "If they're already reporting this, you need to get out of here. It's only a matter of time before people recognize you for who you are. Let me get you home."

That seemed like the best idea she'd had all day. I quickly finished my wine, something I knew I would end up regretting, while Tish paid our bar tab. She whisked me out of the bar as quickly as she could, tucking us into an Uber.

Cm

As soon as I stumbled to the front door, I realized I wouldn't be drinking this much again, possibly ever. Riley would be incredibly disappointed if she could see me. She would be shocked out of her mind if she ever saw me this way. Dear God, how many glasses of wine did I have? Punching in the key code couldn't be this hard. I wouldn't dare ring the doorbell and wake Naomi and Hannah. Not when they'd both have to be up early in the morning.

Tish insisted on staying, but I wouldn't hear of it and told her that I needed to sleep off the wine before I processed this. Drinking wouldn't bring my dad back, but I needed time alone. From what I could recall, the news reported that it had been a private charter.

I blew out a breath, pressing my face up to the door, determined to press the right numbers. Sleeping outside on the doorstep wouldn't be ideal in this chilly weather, but I'd do it if I had to. Finally, with intense concentration, I hit the right numbers, and the door swung open.

Thanks to Riley's issues with her adopted brother at a young age, always trying to find her, we had the best security system. I enabled the system again before kicking off my boots, nearly falling headfirst into the wall.

As tempted as I was to brew a pot of coffee, I was fairly certain I wouldn't be able to work the coffee maker. I couldn't remember the last time I'd had a cup. Instead, I crawled my way upstairs to my bedroom and closed the door behind me just as my phone rang.

Evan, I thought, as I struggled to get my phone out of my purse. If he thought my near-mental breakdown at the bar had anything to do with him, he was about to get another tongue-lashing. Apparently, my voicemail wasn't enough. Finally extracting my phone, I looked at the screen. What the . . . I looked again. Were my eyes deceiving me? It was my dad's number.

I shrugged off my jacket and let it fall to the floor before I took the call. "Dad?" I said, the panic rising in my voice. "Is this a dream? What's happening?"

"I'm in some bloody deep rubbish. I was *supposed* to be on that plane, but someone tipped me off."

I considered pinching my arm. This couldn't be real. I had to be dreaming this conversation. After falling back onto my bed, I pressed the heel of my hand into my forehead.

"I don't . . . I don't understand. I saw the news. I talked to the police. How are you talking to me?" I took a deep breath, my head suddenly clearing as though I hadn't just downed a few glasses of wine. "What do you mean 'you're in trouble'?"

It sounded like he was walking, out of breath. "It wasn't my fault the nicking went wrong. He saw me and Ricky. If he can't find me, we're all safe."

"Nicking? What the hell is that? Where are you? Who is coming after you? Why?"

"I was trying to help. Yeah, I know it was dim. Don't lecture, baby girl. Vissar Loukas is pissed. Far as anyone knows, I'm dead. Gone. Don't tell anyone I'm alive. Anyone, baby girl."

I sat up, the room spinning around me. "Are you kidding me? Dad, the cops already called me. They aren't going to find you in the wreckage. They'll know you're alive. Tell me where you are."

"Can't do that. You be careful, too, baby girl. Don't do anything stupid. Stay the hell out of it. And I need to tell you about Skyler. She-"

"Dad!" I shouted into the phone, holding it away from my ear for a moment. "Dad!"

When the line went dead, I jumped to my feet and nearly threw my phone across the room in frustration. He would do anything for anybody, especially Ricky, but what the hell? Assuming he did something to someone named Vissar Loukas, who apparently blew up a plane he was supposed to be on? I immediately tried to dial him again, but it went right to voicemail. He must have shut it off.

Naomi burst into my room a second later, her white nightgown flowing around her and her eyes wide with horror. Drunk or not, guilt instantly gnawed at me for waking her with my shouting. I hoped I hadn't woken Hannah, too.

"What's going on?" She took a step toward me, her eyes widening when I swayed unsteadily on my feet. "Oh, honey. Let's get you into bed."

When she reached out, I swatted her away. "Naomi, I'm fine. My dad is . . . " Even in my sobering state, I couldn't tell her. "Sorry to wake you."

I didn't bother disguising the bitterness in my voice, even after seeing the flash of hurt in her eyes. Damn it, what was wrong with me lately? I'd pushed people away my whole life, but I hadn't been so blatantly rude about it for a long time. Nothing I could say would excuse me when Naomi backed out of the room, closing my door softly behind her. Now, I really wanted to swear.

Despite how much wine I'd had, the bottom dropped out of my stomach. What an emotional rollercoaster today had been. I'd just talked to him a few days ago. He hadn't let on that anything could be wrong. Then, I thought, for the last several hours, he was dead. Now he was alive, but in danger? I needed to sleep before I could think. Squeezing my eyes shut, I took a few gulps of air.

Before I could feel bad about it, I hung up and tossed my phone aside. What was he going to tell me about Skyler? She'd been cleaning my dad's house for the last few years and must still be doing it. Although I'd met her once, she was about six years older than me. She was the one person I knew of with access to his house who might know something. What had she done? Was she involved?

Lex Edwards could never turn down helping someone. He'd offered her a job as his housekeeper after her abusive boyfriend kicked her to the curb. That boyfriend was a friend of his in another band, now a former friend. In saving her, he had caused an irreparable rift between them that had never mended. I knew there was more to their relationship than just cleaning his house, but I never said anything to him about it. That was his business, not mine.

I flopped onto my bed and stared at the ceiling for a moment before closing my eyes and letting the darkness take over. My last thoughts hoped my dad was telling me some fabricated story and not something he'd actually gotten involved in. But the feeling in my gut was anything but reassuring. What a nightmare.

Chapter Eight

Cassie

Sunlight streamed through the windows as I peeled my eyelids open the next morning, jolted awake by the blare of my alarm. The aroma of coffee greeted me, a smell my stomach didn't appreciate after a night of too many glasses of wine with Tish. I rubbed my hands over my face, hoping to ease the aching in my head as the memories of yesterday came flooding back.

Had I imagined the entire thing or been having a nightmare? With one hand, I patted around on my bedside table for my phone, not caring what I knocked over in the process until I found it and brought it in front of my face without moving my head. Sure enough, there was an incoming call from my dad around eleven last night.

With the greatest care not to move my head too much, I sat up and barrel-rolled off the bed to start my routine, even though every part of me screamed in protest. While I went through my bathroom routine, I texted the office to inform them I needed bereavement time and that my appointments would need to be rescheduled. Not five minutes later, my cell phone rang. That would be Tish, calling to check up on me. Therapists, I thought with a dramatic eye roll that pierced my head. I picked up the call.

"I'm fine, Tish. And I never take a day off, so save it," I said, although my tone was far from snippy.

"Good," Riley shot back. "You deserve it. Did Naomi put you up to it?"

The reflection in the bathroom mirror looked more like a zombie than me. What had I been thinking last night? Mascara smudged beneath my eyes, a trail of dried drool at the corner of my mouth, and hair still swept up but going every which way made me look like a Barbie doll that had gotten stuck in a vacuum cleaner. I scoffed. I had to pretend that my dad had died yesterday and not tell anyone the truth. How was I going to pull that off?

"Cass?" Riley prompted. "You okay?"

"They think my dad died in a plane crash yesterday, Riles. He was listed as a passenger," I whispered, putting on my top acting skills. "I'm doing my best."

After I heard her sharp intake of breath, I knew her emotions had overflowed. She couldn't muffle her sobs for long. Calmly, I waited for her tears to subside.

"Ty! Pack our stuff, we're going to LA!"

"Riley, no. Just . . ." I put my hand on my forehead.

She sniffled loudly in my ear. "What's going on, Cassie? You love your dad more than anyone. If you're bottling this up-"

"Don't even try giving me therapy. Yes, I'm compartmen-talizing. I was a mess last night, but Tish was with me."

"Were you drinking?"

"Yes, but it was before I heard about the crash. Tish is a bad influence."

I could hear Ty in the background, trying to find out what was going on but Riley ignored him. She probably waved at him to quiet down, hoping to try getting me to buckle and accept help.

"Where's Tish now? Where is Naomi? You shouldn't be alone right now."

"Riles, I appreciate your concern. I love you for it. I really do, but you know me." I swallowed the lump of guilt in my throat. "I need time alone to process this. I promise you I won't have a meltdown or do anything stupid."

"Okay, but you know that I'm here if you need me. We're here. Ty and me."

"Absolutely not. You're on your honeymoon. I'll go down there, have a funeral, deal with his accounts, the house . . . " As I ticked things off in my head, I overwhelmed myself with how I would manage it all, knowing it was all a lie. I felt like throwing up. "Something tells me this plane crash was on purpose."

I didn't want to spill anything I shouldn't. Although I'd had more to drink than I should have, I remembered his warning. But I refused to allow him to disappear forever if I had friends who could help me figure it out for him. Not if I could help it. Riley and Ty were investigators. They knew what to do, and I itched to tell her the truth. But I'd wait until I got to my dad's and poked around before I spilled my guts and swore her to secrecy. I couldn't help but think of Jace, who was somewhere in LA, uninvited excitement rippling through me.

"What makes you say that?" Riley asked slowly, her tone gaining an edge.

"I don't know. I'm just wondering why he would be on a plane when they just got back from tour." I stared at myself, struggling to believe my dad could be involved in something so serious. I had to assume he meant stealing when he said "nicking". He'd mentioned being seen, so he had to have been caught doing something. I mean, stealing? Really? I couldn't remember a time he'd ever been in trouble.

"Let me get down there. They still have to investigate."

By her heavy sigh, I could tell she didn't like having to sit and wait this out. If the police found anything indicating my dad had been on that plane, I'd need to contact everyone I knew for a funeral. Only I knew they wouldn't, but I had a feeling I wasn't the only one who knew that.

I scrubbed my mascara off before picking up a brush to untangle my bramble-like hair. "I ran into Evan last night. Showed up with some brunette, like he hadn't been screwing her all along. I might have told him off."

Riley breathed out, wanting to laugh but too somber to do it in light of the news I'd broken to her. "It couldn't have been because you were drinking or anything."

The teasing didn't help my mood, but I kept my mouth shut.

"It was only going to be one glass. You know me. One glass, then water."

"I know," she whispered.

If Ty and Riley were anything, they weren't judgmental of people who liked to drink or party. They were just two people who didn't partake. Riley had never touched a drop of alcohol after living with a mother who struggled with drinking and drugs. Ty had his issues during and after college, went to treatment at Jace's insistence, and hadn't touched the stuff since. Hannah was much like Riley, with avoiding drugs and alcohol, underage or not. But where Hannah was as sweet as an angel, Riley got into trouble in other ways.

"It's not like I want to go down there to deal with this," I said, changing the subject away from my terrible decisions last night. I may have stumbled in very late, but I clearly remembered every single word I said to Evan.

Riley sighed. "You're an adult, Cass. Just be careful. If your dad got mixed up in something, it could be dangerous. You just never know."

"Stay out of trouble," Ty called out from the background and it took extreme effort to hold back my laughter. She really found a good guy. "Seriously, Cassie. And Jace is there."

"Ty!" Riley exclaimed, and I couldn't help but smile at her scolding tone. As if I would go looking for Jace. "Please be careful. And call us if you need us. Regan and Cameron are headed to Cali at the end of the month. Call them if you need to."

Riley and Ty were two people I would undoubtedly call if I ever needed help, with Cameron and Regan being a close second.

My mind wandered to Jace again after Ty mentioned him. Why would he have bought him up? I wondered. Riley told me Jace was starting his own independent private investigating firm when he went back to LA. I didn't know where he would be, but as soon as the thrill shot through me at the thought of him for the second time, I quickly banished it.

"You'll be the first one to hear from me," I promised. "I've got to finish getting ready and see what arrangements I can make on short notice."

"Let us know when you get there."

"Got it."

After hanging up with Riley, I finished getting ready, albeit slowly. I took a long, hot shower and reapplied my makeup before dressing in a baggy off-the-shoulder sweater and a pair of stretchy capri leggings. Barefoot, I went downstairs to find Naomi dancing around the kitchen. If you could call it dancing, it seemed more like drifting. Probably some kind of hippie thing, I thought.

"There's hot water in the kettle for you," she said without turning toward me, "and a bottle of ibuprofen next to your mug."

I groaned, setting my laptop on the breakfast bar before reaching for my lucky cup and herbal tea. Naomi was a saint, and I didn't deserve any of her sympathy. She had known my dad for many years, and I hated to break the news to her this way.

"Did you watch the news last night?"

She wrinkled her nose. "No good comes from watching it. Why?"

I swallowed the lump in my throat. "There was a plane crash in California last night." This was even harder than I had expected. "It's suspected that my dad was on it. They aren't releasing any other names, but he was on the passenger list."

When I looked up, Naomi had stopped dancing. She stared at me for a moment before rushing to my side and pulling me against her. I wrapped my arms around her, letting her cry it out. I knew this would hit her hard.

I hated lying to her like this. When my dad moved here, he left his family behind in England and rarely saw them again. At eighteen, he couldn't wait to leave London for America and travel the country of dreams, doing what he loved most: music. He was an amazing drummer and songwriter. Ricky was his first good friend, and Naomi filled the role of his mom just as she had filled that role for me. That was her nature, and I shrugged it off. I would find out what happened and bring him home, even if I wasn't a detective.

When she pulled away, she wiped the tears from her face but they still glistened in her eyes. This would be a long road to travel, and Naomi wouldn't be the only one shedding tears. My eyes filled again, but I blinked them back.

"I need to go to LA to close out his estate and plan the funeral, although he always told me he didn't want a big thing. It'll be small."

"I'll go pack right now. Yolanda will cover for me while we're gone, and Hannah will be fine with missing more school. She's at the top of her class."

I shook my head. "I need to do this myself. I'll call you with the details after I get there and figure everything out. I still need to go to the police station, and then I'll need to identify . . . " I blinked, tears forming again. "I know he didn't want anything big, but I will let you know when services will be held. It won't be for a while yet, I think."

It had to be the weirdest thing for a rockstar in the spotlight, I thought. When he and my mom got married, it had been a small ceremony. I supposed that sometimes people in the media's attention just needed to escape from it sometimes.

Once I had my tea bag steeping in the steaming water, I opened my computer and started a web search for any recent Lex Edwards sightings. As much as following the paparazzi grated on my nerves, I knew this might be a way to get some answers.

If he escaped the plane crash, he must have been thorough in disguising himself to avoid detection. I wish he'd told me exactly what happened, or at least where he intended to hide. Where would he go that he could be completely out of the public eye?

"Naomi, I owe you an apology."

She didn't resume her dancing and appeared somber now. "You don't owe me anything, dear. It's obvious you had a troublesome night, and now I understand why."

"That's no excuse. I'm sorry I snapped at you." "I wish you'd told me last night."

"I should have." I sighed. "I ran into Evan at the bar last night, snuggling up to his new woman."

"He never deserved you anyway," she said without missing a beat.

I snorted and returned to my web search. It seemed I didn't lose too much when he'd broken up with me. No one seemed to like him much.

"He did me a favor by breaking up with me last weekend. Should have done it a long time ago, to be honest."

Even as I said it, I couldn't help but feel that deep ache inside. Though I could never picture settling down with someone like Evan, I wanted someone to share my life with. I deserved that. Didn't I? Talking to Riley and Ty and hearing how happy they were in their marital bliss gave me that stab of jealousy again. No matter what relationship I had, good or bad, they all seemed destined to fail. I supposed it had to do with my parents' marriage being cut short when they divorced. I was eight and it still hurt.

I remembered going on tour with my dad the following summer and spending summers with him after that. It was never quite the same with my parents separated. The paparazzi had a field day with that for a long time. My dad dated but never settled down with anyone. I never asked him why, but I often wondered if it was because of how badly his marriage ended with my mom.

My mom, I scoffed. I loved her, but she hurt my dad badly. When she died, it was almost as though he lost her all over again.

Naomi moved around the kitchen like it was a natural place for her, her colorful gauze shirt settling around her after she stopped. "So many people loved your dad," she murmured, sadness sweeping in again. "Anyone who ever traveled with the bands he'd been in, that woman who used to cut his hair. He hated how she cut it, but then he started dating her."

I noticed a ghost of a smile touch the corner of her mouth. "Gina," I said. "He thought if he started screwing her that she wouldn't cut his hair anymore. How wrong he was."

"Or Faith. Wasn't she a groupie who thought she'd snagged your dad, then skipped off with the lead singer of another band?"

"He couldn't hold on to anyone, even the good ones," I said.

"Apparently, neither can I."

"I know you want a permanent relationship, Cass."

My head snapped up, my gaze meeting hers. Knowing me for as many years as she had, Naomi knew exactly how to get my attention. She'd mastered it.

"I see how you look when you're around Riley and Ty," she murmured, turning to pour herself more coffee instead of resuming her dance. My eyes widened, even though she faced away from me. "And Regan and Cameron. Anyone in a happy relationship."

When she finally turned with her coffee, she met my irritated gaze. Her golden eyebrows raised while she sipped, daring me to argue with her about it. Dang it, I couldn't. Naomi, wise beyond her sixty-seven years, was right every time, and I would never admit it to her. I eased back on my irritation with a tight smile.

"What do you want me to say? I would love to have a relationship like Riley's or Regan's," I said, popping some ibuprofen, followed by my cooling tea. "I would. But not with someone like Evan. I don't think it would have ever been with him, if I'm being honest."

She shook her head. "You're going to sabotage yourself every time, Cass. Not every relationship is going to end like your mom and dad's. Maybe the fame got to be too much for your mom."

I scoffed. "Yeah, so much that she had to involve herself with drugs and men. No, she knew exactly what she got herself into. She killed their marriage and hurt my dad in the process."

But I'd loved her and missed her despite what happened between them, and I hated that she got into drugs. I should have helped her. Naomi knew how I got when we talked about my past and brushed it off.

She headed for the stairway between the kitchen and the garage. "I'll stay home from work today and help you plan everything out. Please tell me you aren't going into the office."

No amount of discouragement would stop her from insisting on helping me, but at least she wasn't insisting on coming with me. I shook my head slowly, not wanting to move it more than necessary. "Not only did I make poor choices last night, but they'll understand that I won't be going back for a while. I don't know how long it will take to deal with everything."

Before Naomi disappeared upstairs, she halted mid-step and turned back. "I'll go up and get ready. We'll book your flight and make a list of things you'll need to take care of when you get there."

She considered my dad a second son. I wondered what in the world Ricky had gotten him into or what both of them had become involved in. Whatever happened didn't sound good.

Naomi disappeared upstairs, and I returned to searching websites. One report mentioned him catching an Uber from his house yesterday. Beyond that, there was a list of sightings from the first week of September, when their summer tour ended in Saratoga Springs. They'd been back since just after Labor Day.

I waited until I heard the shower running before I called the one person who could answer all my questions in a single conversation. Naomi didn't need to know anything about it, unless he wanted to fess up to her himself.

"Ricky, it's Cassie," I said as soon as I heard his gruff hello on the other end of the line, as though I'd woken him up from a deep sleep in the middle of the afternoon.

"Cass, what're you doin'?" he mumbled.

"Making arrangements to get to LA to talk to the police about the plane crash my dad was reported to have been in. Then, I suppose I'll be planning his funeral, which we both know is not true. So talk."

Silence greeted me in response.

"Ricky, talk to me. What the fuck happened? Do you know where my dad is?"

"Stay out of it, Cassie. You aren't going to find anything down here 'cept trouble."

"Dammit, Ricky. You know something. He said you were seen. And now someone is after him."

I could hear his heavy breathing on the other end, then what sounded like him running his hand over his face, as if he'd just woken up.

"You'll be in danger if you come down here. Stay where you are and stay out of it."

Click. I pulled the phone away from my ear, staring at it. Oh, hell no, he did not just hang up on me. Fuming, I sent a text to my dad. I stared at the word beneath my message, waiting for it to change from "delivered" to "read." Please, I murmured silently. Please, Dad. Part of me knew it would go unread after what he'd told me. If he really was in trouble with this Vissar person after him, he'd have ditched his phone to be safe.

Regardless of where my dad was, I could still visit my hometown, and I didn't give a crap what Ricky said. I'd prefer to take a vacation visiting my dad and friends instead of digging into my dad's things and personal business.

Abandoning my web search, I pulled up my schedule and reviewed my appointments for the next week before calling Tish. She sounded somber and quickly pressed me about my feelings, but I assured her I would be fine. I handled things in my own way, and suppression wasn't an option. She agreed to take the lead in rescheduling my appointments. After I booked my flight, there was nothing else to do but pack.

Chapter Nine

Cassie

The weather in California didn't hold a candle to that of Seattle. After contacting Officer Davison for an update on the investigation, he informed me that the information he had could wait until I arrived. I waited until the next day to fly out, making sure I'd packed everything and giving myself sufficient time to talk with Naomi and Hannah, all the while trying to contact my dad. Still nothing.

The two-and-a-half-hour flight I'd planned for catching up on reading ended up being consumed by worry. My dad always answered me when I texted or called. If not immediately, then soon after—unless he was playing a show. It was strange not hearing from him. It didn't matter if he was in the middle of a tour, working on new material, on vacation, or even out of the country; he would have gotten back to me by now.

By the time I landed, picked up my bags, and headed to catch a ride to my dad's house, I was tired. There was no need to call ahead and bother anyone to pick me up.

Still irritated that Ricky had hung up on me yesterday without bothering to at least explain what happened, I adjusted my heavy bags on my bare shoulder while toting my rolling bag. Not knowing how long I'd be here, I packed enough clothes for warm days and cool nights. I anticipated shopping for evening wear, as my friends would undoubtedly drag me out to parties and clubs during my visit in an effort to cheer me up. I would go, but in due time. I didn't have much fashionable clothing with me. It was early enough to fit in a trip to Santa Monica Place today if I needed to.

As soon as I landed, I contacted Officer Davison to let him know that I'd arrived and would be at the police station as soon as I dropped off my things at my dad's house and picked up his car.

I looked up to see a skinny woman with a smattering of freckles on the bridge of her nose running directly toward me. Mac! Pushing past anyone in my way, I rushed to her despite my heavy bags, and we crashed together in a hug.

She clung to me, sniffling against my neck.

"You talked to Naomi, didn't you?" I asked. "That's how you knew to pick me up."

When she pulled away, tears rolled down her face. "I know it's been a couple of days, but how are you not more broken up about this? Cassie! I can't believe you look so refreshed, walking through the airport like you own it."

I managed a small smile, reaching up to brush the tears away from her freckled cheek. "Believe me, I've processed it, and I'm broken up about it. It's only going to get worse as I go through his things. I'm glad you're here."

"I just can't believe this," she murmured, slipping her arm around my waist and leaning her head against me as we continued to walk through the airport. "It hurts. Like losing one of my parents, you know?"

"I know, Mac. And it's going to be okay. I'll be okay."

"Kya and I were about to drag you down here for a visit, but now I wish we hadn't talked about it. I feel guilty, like we shouldn't have even been thinking it."

I snorted. There was no doubt in my mind they would have done that.

"What's going on?"

"I'll tell you in the car. And I'll need to do some shopping while I'm here," I said as we walked out into the bright sunshine. "I brought nothing appropriate to wear with me. I might be here for a while, handling all of his accounts."

Her long brown hair blew in the breeze as we crossed the street to the parking garage, and I smiled. Like me, she had two parents who were big-screen actors. Mac hadn't followed in their footsteps into acting; instead, she worked behind the scenes as a set designer. Mac was a busybody and knew a lot about a lot of people. It seemed like she knew everyone, and everyone knew her. Though her parents had split years ago, they remained close to Mac and her two brothers.

After we put my bags in the trunk, I waited until we were safely pulling out and on our way to my dad's house before I revealed that my dad was alive. He swore me to secrecy, but someone had to know what I was up to in case something happened to me. Her tears had long since dried, replaced by relief, then livid anger.

Two hours later, Mac finally pulled into the driveway of my dad's multilevel house across the street from the beach near the Santa Monica Pier. I groaned at the sight of people lingering outside on the sidewalk with cameras, trying to look inconspicuous. Nice try.

As I slid out of the car, nostalgia swept over me. I had spent little time at his house over the years. The times I had been here were when I was much younger, usually across the street at the beach.

"Ms. Nichols, can you tell us what happened to your dad? Where was he going? When was the last time you talked to him?"

I glanced at them as Mac opened the trunk before jumping out to help me. I ignored the two men trying to get me to say something while Mac assisted me with my bags, including the shopping bags we had.

We'd only shopped for an hour, which was longer than necessary, but she insisted on picking out the most revealing dresses in addition to a modest black dress for the funeral, though it wouldn't be necessary. I had little opportunity to wear dresses like the ones I bought, hoping it would be worth it.

"Please, Ms. Nichols. Give us something. Anything."

Not bothering to turn toward them, I slammed the door, earning a disapproving look from Mac. "I have nothing to tell you. I don't know what happened."

Liar, liar. With that, I followed Mac up the steps to the front door and punched in the code to let us in. Once inside, I let out a deep sigh of relief. They'd better not camp outside for as long as I was here. I couldn't tell them anything I didn't know, and I didn't know the complete truth. Sharing anything would only risk blowing my dad's cover, wherever he might be, and it could throw me right into danger, just like Ricky said.

"Not so many of them," Mac remarked about the reporters.

"Thankfully."

I left my luggage by the front doors, setting my other bags next to them while Mac dropped the shopping bags. Most of the house featured modern décor in warm beige, white, and light browns. The kitchen boasted all the latest appliances and a tall island with two stools, while the dining room table for eight sat across from it, and the living room occupied the far side of the space. The ambiance was inviting with a sectional couch in front of a decent-sized fireplace and a TV mounted above it, reminiscent of the house in Seattle.

I wandered into the kitchen, Mac following behind me as my stomach growled. It hadn't occurred to me to stop at the farmer's market to pick up some food.

While Mac scoured the pantry, I opened the fridge. She found crackers, and I discovered fruit that still looked fresh. Quickly, we grabbed some plates and laid everything out on the island. It felt good to be off my feet for a minute as I slid onto a stool while she leaned against the white farmhouse sink.

On the kitchen island was a pile of mail, and on top was an invitation to an art gallery opening. I lifted it up, my curiosity piqued as I recalled the conversation with my dad from last weekend. He'd mentioned a piece of art for sale at an art gallery opening. I couldn't possibly know which one, but it didn't diminish my attention.

My eyes lifted to Mac as I held it up. "It's an invitation to an art gallery opening tonight."

"You look interested."

"Invitation by Vissarion Loukas." My mouth curved into a smile. "If I'm not mistaken, this person has a piece of art for sale that my dad wanted to buy. It might tie into whatever he was doing at his house that led him to flee."

"You're seriously thinking about going out tonight? Won't people wonder why you're not in mourning?" she asked. "I mean, I know they haven't officially announced that he was on the plane, but they did leak that it might have had members of the band, and they've all been accounted for except for your dad."

"My dad was a huge connoisseur of art. He wouldn't have wanted me to miss this gallery opening." I waved the invitation. "Not if there was a piece he wanted to buy. I'll be going in his honor."

"I've got to work tonight, but I can-"

"No, I'm going alone."

"Maybe Kya-"

"No. I'll be in a room full of lots of other people. I'll be in no danger."

As much as I didn't want to attend something like this alone, I knew it would be my chance to find out who Vissar Loukas really was. I wanted to see if he knew who I was, and if he did, how he would react to hearing my dad's name. As far as he knew, he'd already gotten rid of my dad. He wouldn't be expecting Lex Edwards' daughter.

She popped a grape into her mouth, her soft brown eyes filled with concern. "Be careful. Which dress are you gonna wear?"

I ignored her question. "Despite what's going on with my dad,

I'm not here looking for a relationship, Mac. I know you and Kya, but people think he's gone and I have to play it that way."

"Thought you were dating some hot-shot lawyer, anyway."

"He dumped me last weekend. All the more reason to stay away from any men while I'm here. Or did you know that, too?" I eyed her suspiciously, eating a grape.

Laughing, she shook her head. "He must not have been worth it, but no, I didn't know. Someday, you are going to meet that one guy you won't be able to resist."

"You know as well as I do that I can't open up to anyone, and it drives them away faster than I can explain. Guys don't want that. They want to know at least something about the person they're spending time with, and I can't do the just sex thing." I sighed, my mind drifting automatically to Jace Taylor. "I wish I could."

"I can't yell at you for it. I'm still single, too."

With a groan, I pressed my forehead into my hands. "You don't push people away like I do. I can't help it. It's just so hard to trust anyone." I dropped my hands and looked back up at her. She leaned over the island, propping her chin on her hand. "Just don't get any ideas about setting me up while I'm here. Please?"

"Deal."

The front doorbell rang, interrupting us. We exchanged glances, knowing the press wouldn't be bold enough to come right up to the door.

"Do you want me to haul your stuff up to the guest bedroom while you get the door?"

I smiled. "You're the best."

We left our fruit and crackers where they were and headed back into the entryway, splitting ways. Mac grabbed the bags and headed up the stairs while I opened the door to a younger-looking guy with short light brown hair dressed in blue jeans and a t-shirt. He smiled.

"Officer Davison," he said, flashing his badge. "Cassidy

Nichols?"

I opened the door wider. "People call me Cassie. I could have come to the station, Officer."

"You can call me Adam."

"Fine." I closed the door. "What can you tell me, Officer Adam?"

He chuckled as he followed me into the kitchen. I waved him toward a stool while I cleaned up the mess Mac and I had made. Anything to keep my hands busy, I focused on rinsing the dishes, afraid of what he might tell me and terrified of what he might not.

"Do you know where your dad might be, Cassie?"

I froze, bent halfway over to put the dishes in the dishwasher. He didn't need to say anything else for me to know that they hadn't found anything in the wreckage to indicate my dad was on that airplane, which meant it would soon be out that he was not dead but simply missing.

Mac called my name in a hushed voice from the top of the stairs, but I waved my arm at her to be quiet without looking at her. I would have told Officer Adam to hold on for a minute, thinking she'd found something, but I needed to know what else he would tell me.

My heart thumped as I wondered what Ricky and my dad had gotten caught up in. He wouldn't steal anything, but to help someone out? Maybe he would. Maybe he and Ricky had been wronged or set up, or someone had made a mistake. Based on my conversation with my dad, it hadn't been a mistake.

"I'm sorry?" I asked, straightening and closing the dishwasher before turning around.

"I think you heard my question. Can you tell me where your dad might be? Because he wasn't in that airplane crash. They picked through the wreckage and have identified the remains, none of which were Lex Edwards."

I heard Mac urgently whispering my name again.

"How would I know where he is?" I replied.

"You're his only relative, at least in this country. If he's hiding, it stands to reason he'd contact you." He stared at me, making me uncomfortable. "Do you know of anyone who might have wanted that airplane to crash? Did your dad have any enemies?"

I swallowed the lump in my throat and shook my head. "I think you may have wasted a trip coming here, Officer Adam. I don't have anything to tell you. I don't know where my dad might be."

He stood. "Are you telling me the truth?"

"What reason would I have to lie?"

He sighed. "This wasn't a wasted trip, Cassie. There are other people I need to see. I figured I would save you a trip down to the station and help you avoid the press until you get settled in here. They'll be releasing who *was* on that aircraft soon."

I walked around to face him. "I appreciate you coming here. If I find anything out, I'll certainly let you know."

The glint in his eyes told me he didn't believe me, but it didn't matter. He could badger me all he wanted. I couldn't tell him what I didn't know.

As we walked back toward the front door, I looked up to see what Mac so urgently needed. She didn't have a chance to speak before the front door opened, and a boy of about eleven or twelve walked in with a backpack slung over one shoulder and a skateboard tucked under one arm. From the top of the stairs, Mac's eyes widened, and she slowly walked down a couple of steps.

The kid looked at the guy, who gave him a nod and slipped out the open door before shutting it behind him. What a bizarre day, I thought.

The backpack slipped off his shoulder, landing on the floor with a thump, but he held on firmly to his skateboard as he looked between Mac and me. With blond hair that brushed the tops of his shoulders and brown eyes, he looked like he belonged among some beach-bum natives, dressed in cut-off jean shorts and a t-shirt.

"Who are you?" he finally asked, setting his skateboard carefully down next to his backpack before cautiously moving toward me.

I stood up. "I'm Cassie. This is my dad's house. You might want to tell me who you are and what you're doing here."

His blond eyebrows shot up. "Lex is your dad?"

Chapter Ten

Lex had another kid? I had a brother? Confusion pushed into my already stressed mind as I backed up until my ass hit the chair with a plop. Mac came down the rest of the stairs and moved over to me, leaning over the island.

"Who's your mom?" I asked.

"Skyler. She cleans for Lex."

"And your dad? Who is he?"

He shrugged. "Mom said Lex is my dad."

Torn between bombarding him with more questions and dialing Skyler to demand answers, I could only stare at the little guy. What in the hell was happening here? Was this kid really my dad's son, or was Skyler just trying to be a gold digger? She'd only been cleaning his house for the last three years. I knew she'd been doing more than just cleaning his house, given my dad's reputation for his charm, but this kid was clearly older than three years old, so someone was lying. Why would this kid be here if my dad was supposed to be dead? He had to be as confused and surprised as I was. Except he looked calm, even tilting his head to the side as he took me in.

"Do you live here?"

"Sometimes we stay here."

"That's what I was trying to tell you while you were talking to the officer!" Mac whispered. "There's a boy's bedroom upstairs."

I swallowed, not wanting to freak him out with questions. "You have a bedroom here?"

"Yes."

"Before I pepper you with more questions, do you have any for me?" I asked slowly.

He stared at me, but I could tell his brain was working overtime as he tried to come up with a good question. Instead, he shook his head. I figured he must be as freaked out as I was.

I blew out a heavy breath. I didn't need a kid underfoot while I was here trying to figure things out. "How about I fix you a snack, and you start with telling me your name and how old you are? You know . . . all that fun get-to-know-you stuff."

His eyebrows shot up. "You're . . . going to fix me a snack?"

I moved around the breakfast bar and started opening cupboards, Mac staying quiet while she helped me. "Got a problem with that?"

When I turned partway around, he had taken my spot on the stool and was watching me in the kitchen with unmasked fascination. He shook his head.

I found another box of crackers, opened it, and took a nibble to make sure they weren't stale. Opening the refrigerator, I found some carrots that looked to be in fairly good condition. Thankfully, the bottle of ranch dressing hadn't expired yet. I collected everything on a plate and set it in front of him, waiting while he looked at it for a minute.

"Good?"

He shrugged. "No one makes me a snack when I get home from school."

Mac pointed upstairs. "I'm just gonna . . . start putting your stuff away while you guys talk."

Ignoring the urge to roll my eyes, I put the food away while starting in on my questions. Poor kid had the same life I had growing up. I had to fend for myself, even before my mom died. "So. What's your name, shortie?"

Snorting, he replied, "Quinn. And I'm eleven. I'll be twelve in December." He chewed on a carrot and continued, "Can I ask you questions, too?"

"Absolutely." I leaned against the counter near the sink. "You don't think I'm going to get all my answers and leave you hanging, do you?" He shrugged again. "I don't work that way."

I couldn't help but notice the corner of his mouth quiver as if he might smile.

"I come here every day after school. Then, when Mom gets done working, we go home. Or sometimes we stay here. Where have you been? Why am I only meeting you now?"

The last time I visited, I stayed with Mac. Now that she had another roommate, I didn't want to be crowded or uncomfortable. The last time I'd visited, Skyler had been his housekeeper, but I was fairly certain she didn't stay here then. I didn't understand why he never mentioned that Skyler and her kid occasionally stayed here.

"I live in Seattle. Where's your mom?" I asked.

Another shrug. "Sometimes she's not here when I get home."

That struck a chord. Wasn't she supposed to be his housekeeper? I pushed away from the counter, leaned over the breakfast bar, and rested my face in my hands as I looked at him. Maybe I was imagining it, but he resembled Lex a little. Lots of kids had long blond hair in this town. That would be impossible. This kid said he was eleven.

Quinn stared back at me, a cracker held in his fingers while I studied him. Inwardly, I groaned. I couldn't leave him, even if he didn't technically live here all the time. I needed to go tonight. Guilt I hadn't known existed gnawed at me.

"What do you mean, sometimes she's not here? Like, a lot?"

He munched on crackers, speaking with his mouth full. "Sometimes. Sometimes, I spend the night at my friend Ray's house. Like on weekends."

"Are you going there tonight?"

"I wasn't going to. Why?"

"I have plans to go out tonight." He looked at me with big brown eyes hanging on my words. "When she isn't here when you get home from school, she does come here eventually, right?"

Another shrug, which aggravated me further. "Sometimes." "I'll be home tonight, just probably late."

With pride, he puffed out his chest. "I can take care of myself."

I wanted to ruffle his hair. "I know you can, shortie. You just shouldn't have to, and I'd like to get to know you if that's okay. It's lonely being an only child. I had friends, but it just wasn't the same. Get me?"

That gave him something to think about for a minute. I'd met his mom before, but no one had ever mentioned she had a kid. A kid who was supposedly my half-brother. I was glad she wasn't here, as I wouldn't have anything nice to say right now, especially considering how mouthy I'd been lately. He seemed healthy and happy enough. I'd been that way, too, at that age. But I'd been on my own for as long as I could remember.

"What do you like to do, Quinn?" I slid a glance at his skateboard. "Skateboard?"

"Uh-huh. Hang out with my friends."

"Do you surf?"

"Sometimes, but we skateboard more." He eyed me. "Do you?"

I let out a short laugh. "It's been a few years, but I used to surf all the time when I lived down here. Maybe we can catch some waves while I'm here before all the good ones are gone. And maybe you'll let me come watch you and your buddies at the skate park?"

Briefly, his eyes lit up, followed by a shrug.

"I'm here to take care of some things, and I'm probably not going to leave until I do. So you might as well get used to me hanging around. Is that okay?"

"Sure," he mumbled. "Where is he? Where's my dad?"

"I'm not sure."

Holy smokes, I thought as I straightened. This was going to be an interesting trip. When he finished his snack, I took care of the plate before following him upstairs. Mac was happily putting away all my clothes in the guest room to the left, which had the same color scheme as the main room, with whites, beiges, and light browns. The queen-sized bed had a fluffy white comforter and a short wood headboard that looked solid. A private bathroom further into the room contained a deep tub and a stand-alone shower.

I followed Quinn into his room on the right, fully understanding what Mac had been whispering so frantically about. If we'd gone upstairs first, it wouldn't have been such a surprise when he came through the door.

"How'd you get past the reporters?" I asked as he opened the door.

"I slipped in through the bushes. Same as I did yesterday."

Following him into his room, I could only shake my head. The kid seemed like a master at evading paparazzi. I'd have to find out how he did that and learn to do it myself.

Quinn's room had some personality, with colorful skateboarding pictures on the walls, clothing strewn everywhere, and skateboarding equipment like various decks, wheels, trucks, bearings, and grip tape. All the skateboard terms I'd learned by asking him questions. Once I'd asked, I couldn't get him to stop talking. Eventually, Mac came in to tell me I needed to get ready because she had to go.

A half hour later, after a long shower, I stared at myself in the full-length mirror in my room. The pattern of the short pink dress made it look as though it shimmered. The skirt barely hitting mid-thigh with a little flounce at the edge. I turned halfway, looking at the open back, crisscrossed by tiny straps similar to the blue one I'd worn at the beach party last weekend.

"I can't wear this!"

Mac brought over the heels I'd bought to go with the outfit. "You're going to," she retorted. "You're the one who bought it."

"It didn't look like this in the store! My boobs are hanging out the sides, Mac!" I exclaimed, covering the sides with my hands.

"They are not." She swatted my hands away. "Here, put the shoes on. You'll be an inch taller."

I laughed. "I don't need height. I need more cover."

As I reached down to put on the sling-back heels, she pulled the pins out of my hair until the heavy mass swept down. I gasped, my hands flying up as I straightened.

She wagged her finger. "Not tonight. You're leaving it down. From now on, you leave it down. No more therapist looks, Casanova. You aren't yourself while you're here. Fit back in. It's only a matter of time, if it hasn't been reported already, that your dad wasn't on that airplane after all."

Ugh, she was right. Maybe I had grown into a cold, undesirable woman hiding out in Seattle. I glanced at my reflection again. If I was the only woman dressed like this at the art gallery opening, I was going to die of embarrassment. I turned halfway to look at the open back, my hair cascading down in waves. It had been so long since I had left my hair down that I didn't realize it needed a cut, almost hanging to mid-back.

"Plan for a night out tomorrow," she said. "Your dad may be technically missing, but at least we know he's not dead. I've gotta go. You're wearing the silver dress tomorrow night, and I don't want to hear another word about these dresses. You look amazing. When I pick you up, if you're wearing something different, I'm dragging you up to change."

I shot her a dirty look.

"Have fun tonight. And be safe!"

Mac darted out of my room, leaving me to finish getting ready. I touched up my makeup and made sure I had everything in my clutch, including my courage. It took everything in me to go to this alone, not knowing who would be at this event.

Quinn had a movie playing in the living room when I stepped downstairs, not bothering to turn around as my heels clicked across the floor. It seemed he had gotten used to Skyler not being there after school, as she was supposed to be. I wondered where she could be and how often she left him alone.

"I'm locking the door and setting the security system," I told Quinn while checking my clutch once more to make sure I had my cell phone.

Quinn finally turned his head, his eyes widening. "Wow!"

I laughed. "Too much?"

His golden hair swung as he adamantly shook his head. "You look like you're ready to party."

I snorted. "What do you know about partying? You're eleven!"

"Almost twelve!"

"Yeah, well, twelve is still too young to know what it looks like to be ready to party," I grumbled. "I don't know how long I'll be out, but I left you my number."

Suddenly self-conscious, I looked down. Nope, I'm not changing. I had never been to an art gallery opening, but this was LA. An event like this, especially one by invitation only, would have to be a dressy affair. I had to look as strikingly beautiful as I could.

"Call me if you need me. I can always come home early. I'm taking the convertible."

"Have fun," he called, already turned back to his movie.

Tweens, I smirked to myself as I hurried out. I knew he wouldn't leave his movie, which was probably for the best since Skyler still hadn't made an appearance. I entered into the garage and smiled at my dad's MX-5 Miata convertible. He'd never let me drive it before, and this would be fun.

Chapter Eleven

Cassie

As I entered the modern building, bright lighting from multiple ceiling fixtures illuminated the high-priced art displayed against the white walls. From what I could see, the reception area seemed to be where most of the guests had gathered, while individual rooms beyond with the same white walls contained vibrant art. Soft music played through the audio system, and I stepped carefully into the swell of the crowd.

Women dressed similarly to me allowed me to slip right in after showing my invitation at the door. People in high-quality attire clustered in the main room, chatting and sipping from champagne flutes. I noticed several guards in all black, standing straight against the walls, their eyes scanning the room. My heart raced as I moved deeper into the crowd, nervous about being solo for the evening.

"Cassie!" A breathy voice tore me from my thoughts, and I turned to see my mom's best friend, someone I'd known since birth, hurrying toward me. "Why didn't you tell me you were going to be here? When did you get into town?"

The brunette squeezed her way toward me with a glass of champagne in her slender hand. I hadn't seen her since my last visit. Like Mac, Darlene Brannon was well-connected and usually had the scoop on all the gossip and happenings, with an uncanny ability to recognize anyone. She snatched another glass of champagne from a passing server and handed it to me.

"Just today, actually!" I said, leaning in to give her a hug. "How are you, Dar?"

Throughout my childhood, Darlene and my mom were always together when they weren't on location working. Even after all these years, she still looked amazing, with her long hair and lithe figure. As a big-screen actress, she had to.

Dar gave me a slow examination. "You look amazing, Cassie! God, girl, you need to get into the acting business with that body. My bet is you'd outdo your mother—no doubts."

I smiled and accepted the glass of champagne from her as I followed her deeper into the massive crowd, thanking my lucky stars I knew someone here. She slipped her arm around my waist with familiarity.

"God, if your mom could see you now. You look just like her, you know. But with just a touch of your dad."

I took that as a high compliment. My mom had been beautiful. "You heard my dad was involved in a plane crash?"

"I did, girl. I'm sorry. How are you holding up?"

"I can't talk about it," I admitted, tilting my head to the side as we stopped near a tall table draped in white cloth. "I saw your last movie. It was fantastic."

"Wait until you see this one coming out. Oh! Tell me you'll come to the movie premiere next weekend. You just have to come, Cassie. Please."

I shook my head vehemently. Of all the things I did to stay out of the public eye, going to a movie premiere was at the very bottom of my list. "No, I would rather not jump in front of the cameras."

"Please?" she begged. "Your dad loved being in front of the camera, especially with your mom. What better way to honor his memory, Cassie! Say you will. Do it for your dad."

Ugh. She had to mention that my dad would have loved to go. Just as I was here tonight, alone, playing with possible fire.

"Only because you're right, I'll go. My dad would have loved to go, and if he was here, he would undoubtedly come with me."

"He would have been here tonight, right?" she asked softly. "He loved art."

"Loved" didn't describe it. He was passionate, curious, mesmerized by art. He absorbed it with his eyes like his ears did with music. His house was filled with many expensive pieces he'd collected over the years.

"Ah, here's Stirling."

A man who had at least six inches on me strolled over, the delicate stem of a champagne flute resting lightly between his long fingers. I looked up at the man who had been my mom's on-screen leading man in most of her movies. His dark hair had no hint of gray, his deep chocolate brown eyes held the same sparkle, and he sported a smoothly shaven, rigid jaw I curved my hand against when he bent down to kiss my cheek.

"Cassie, what a wonderful surprise to see you," he said, his deep, gravelly voice the cause of many women swooning.

When he straightened and moved to stand next to Dar, she beamed and took a sip of her champagne. I knew they'd been together for more years than I could remember. These days, it surprised me that they'd lasted through the spotlight.

Dar looked up at him. "Cassie is going to join us at the movie premiere next weekend." She turned to me. "It's a little bit of a ritzy affair."

I would quake like a fool, and I needed to find something appropriate to wear, which I didn't have. Not necessarily Oscar-worthy, but something camera-crowd appropriate. I'd need to grab Mac again for another shopping trip, except this one would be much more expensive. Thankfully, I had enough money to live on for a long while.

"That's wonderful to hear." Stirling stared at me. It had been a number of years since he'd seen me. "Forgive my staring, my dear. You look just like your mom."

"Which is why I stay out of LA, for the most part."

Dar grabbed my hand, sipping her champagne with the other.

"You will have a blast next weekend, I promise. Your parents loved you so much, Cassie. You know that before your mom died, they were trying to make it work, right?"

No. I couldn't have heard that right. My dad and mom were trying to repair their marriage before she died? "Excuse me?"

"You heard me. They were trying, but there were a lot of things that kept getting in the way. Still, I think they were in love the entire time, even when apart. She regretted hurting your dad the way she did." She touched my arm. "I didn't mean to make you sad."

I smiled. "I never knew."

"All water under the bridge." She smacked her lips. "We'll have lunch while you're here, since I'm on a slight break. Stirling and I should get back to our friends. It was good to see you, honey. I'll message you the details about the premiere. Bring a date."

A date? Where would I get a date? I hoped she wouldn't be upset when I showed up alone, as nervous as I'd be. Attending a movie premiere with as many reporters as would be there, especially after the news about my dad broke, was bound to be chaotic.

"You're leaving me?"

"Vissar Loukas is coming this way with his eye on you."

Without another word, she swept up her champagne and walked away with Stirling by the arm, blowing a kiss to me as she went. The man coming my way indeed had his eye on me, wearing a high-end suit with light brown hair edged with a tinge of grey at his temples, like Reno. Green eyes boldly drew me in.

He extended his hand, an expensive watch dangling loosely on his wrist. "I don't believe we've had the pleasure of meeting yet. Vissarion Loukas, but please call me Vissar."

I shook his hand and smiled, wondering about his accent. I couldn't place where it might be from. Here goes nothing, I thought. "Cassie Nichols."

"Cassie Nichols." He paused, my name not registering on his face. "Who is the lucky man to have you on his arm this evening?" Crap, I thought. I didn't want him to think I was available, but I also didn't want him to think I had scammed my way in. "I found the invitation in the mail. I'm so sorry if I assumed it was for me."

He smiled, revealing straight white teeth. "In that case, I'm happy to have you. If I may, may I show you around since you're without a date?" He offered his arm, and I hid my deep breath as I slid my arm within his. "Who was the invitation addressed to, if you don't mind my asking?"

I laughed nervously as he guided me through the crowd. Now would be the true test of his reaction. "My dad. Lex Edwards." "My apologies. I heard about his unfortunate accident, although I'm surprised to see that you would be out after such a loss." His hand covered mine as he glanced down at me. "And if I remember correctly, you lost your mother several years ago as well. To have lost both of your parents now—that's truly sad for you."

"Don't feel too sad. I've been on my own for a long time. Longer than you think." I stared at him, boldly. "I'm sure you know my dad was a huge art connoisseur. I believe he was interested in a particular piece tonight, which is how I ended up with this invitation."

"Such a shame that he couldn't be here himself," he murmured.

Without a doubt, I knew my dad's disappearance had something to do with this man. The way he said that set off all kinds of alarms in my head. Whatever my dad had done, it had angered this man enough to take down an airplane and everyone else on it.

"I agree." I glanced around. "He always loved a good party, too."

"I'm glad you accepted the invitation, anyway. I'd never turn away an exquisite woman, especially if it makes me the envy of every man here."

My gaze snapped to his, but I bit my tongue. "There are many women here, far more beautiful than me. Such an extravagant event. And the art—it just takes my breath away."

"Allow me to show it to you."

The crowd was thinning as people moved into other rooms throughout the building, viewing the breathtaking art. When I first arrived, I didn't realize it would be more crowded than I had thought. I spotted more bodyguards in each room, and I realized how big this event was. Guarded to the hilt against any issues, my heart faltered when one caught my eye.

He stood rigidly against one of the walls. His black shirt stretched across a muscular chest that I imagined had black swirling tattoos beneath, paired with black pants secured by a black belt and black boots. Wires draped down behind him from a radio secured to his shoulder and attached to the belt. He looked strikingly like Jace Taylor. My eyes narrowed as I studied him. He had sinfully dark hair, cut short, olive-toned skin, and electric blue eyes, even though he was facing forward instead of looking at me. My breath hitched.

What was Jace Taylor doing here? Was he working as one of Vissar's bodyguards? I thought Riley told me he was starting his own investigation business. It didn't seem like he noticed me, and I didn't want to cause a scene. Or maybe he was purposely ignoring me because of last weekend. While his reputation as being a ladies' man preceded him, I had snubbed him, and now he seemed to be doing the same to me.

As Vissar guided me through the room toward the adjoining areas, I tried to catch Jace's eye, but with no luck. He refused to meet my gaze, keeping his eyes fixed straight ahead and stood rigidly. If I wasn't mistaken, I could see his jaw tense as we passed by.

"Why are there so many bodyguards here tonight?" I asked, trying to pose it as casual conversation rather than prying.

"A man with as much money as I have can never be too sure, Cassie." He tugged me closer to the first piece of art splashed with vibrant reds and oranges. "I won't brag, but these pieces here are worth millions. I will sell them to the highest bidder, only adding to my worth," he said, followed by a chuckle.

If only I could believe that he made his money honestly. I wasn't that naïve. It appeared Vissar had as many bodyguards as the president had Secret Service agents.

"What do you think?" he asked.

"I don't think you're bragging."

Rocking back, he barked out a laugh that caused several people to glance our way. He placed his free hand on my arm. "About the painting, my dear, although I am pleased to hear you say that. I wouldn't want to come off as arrogant."

I smiled. Oh yes, I could pull off this acting bit. "The art is exquisite. You say you've imported these pieces? Are they from different countries or the same?"

"These pieces are from Greece, from high-end artists I've commissioned there. There will be more art coming in, but only these for now. I wanted to test the waters to see how they sold before bringing in more. It may be that I add more art galleries into the fold. I'll be attending many events in the coming months."

I continued to sip my champagne, pretending to be interested in his art dealings. I wish I knew which piece my dad had an taken an interest in. I also wondered what type of illegal activities Vissar was involved in. I knew he was. There was no way he had this many bodyguards just because of some pieces of art.

As we wandered into each individual room, my anxiety grew. He'd said nothing further about my dad and made no mention of any conflicts he might be involved in. Not that he would to a woman he'd just met. It didn't stop all the questions from racing through my mind. I could hardly pay attention to the art.

Despite my worries, Vissar behaved like a gentleman the entire evening as we walked from piece to piece. When the crowds thinned, we moved toward the reception area, and I noticed Jace had moved as well. Once again, I tried to catch his eye. No luck. What was wrong with him?

"I must say goodnight to you, my dear," Vissar said, releasing my arm. "It has truly been a pleasure in your company tonight. Thank you for coming."

Oh no, I thought as he leaned closer. Jace stood only a few feet away, and Vissar was about to kiss me with him right there. I felt mortified. We had just met, and the fact that he thought he knew me well enough to kiss me made my blood boil with irritation.

Instead, he leaned in and kissed my cheek. "I'm having a small party at my house tomorrow night. I understand that you've just lost your father, but I'd be delighted if you would come."

I raised my eyebrows. "A party?"

"An exclusive party. I'll put your name on the list."

With one last kiss to the back of my hand, Vissar relinquished me to one of his other bodyguards. As I was guided toward the door, I glanced back at Vissar, who was walking toward Jace. Our eyes met and held, and the same jolt of electricity I had felt the first time I saw him flooded through me, heat rising within me. I allowed the bodyguard to take my arm, leading me out.

Chapter Twelve

"Jace, a word?" Vissar asked, stepping toward me.

Inwardly, I swore. It wasn't bad enough that I had to watch him all night with a woman I hadn't been able to get out of my mind since I met her last weekend; now I had to talk to him. It was harder than I thought not to meet her eyes all night, knowing she was watching me. She knew it was me, even though I'd cut my hair. All I wanted to know was why she was here and why the hell she was with Vissar. I intended to find out.

But now, I had to deal with Vissar. He was one of the toughest people I'd ever had to do business with, and being in this position as one of his bodyguards was degrading. This wasn't what I signed up for when I agreed to work for him while getting my own business off the ground. I had agreed to do surveillance, although I could think of a dozen worse things he could have me do, such as illegal things.

"Did you see the beauty on my arm this evening?" he asked.

I stood ramrod straight, my spine feeling like it would snap if it were any straighter. "Yes," I bit out, unwilling to admit that I knew that beauty-and beauty didn't fully describe her.

"I want you to watch her."

My eyes clashed with his. "Watch her?"

"Watch her. I want to know what she's doing, who she's with, and where she's going. Everything. I want pictures."

Fuck. "Is there a reason?"

"I don't give reasons. You'll do it. No questions," he said, smoothing out his suit jacket before raising his cold eyes to mine. "I shouldn't need to remind you that I've taken care of your brother's issue."

"We both know that money was a drop in the bucket for you, Vissar."

"It's still *my* money, Jace. I could have refused and let them kill him."

I kept my mouth closed, knowing better than to argue with him. It wouldn't do any good. Saying no, or arguing with Vissar, never ended well for anyone. And he had a point. Ezra put himself in this position, and I had to bail him out. Again.

"You'll continue to work for me until I deem his debt is paid. Is that understood?"

I jerked my head in agreement. "As long as you agree, I won't be doing anything illegal for you."

The corner of his mouth lifted. "You'll do anything I ask of you, Jace."

Vissar had been trying to get me for years because of my connections to the police department, but I would never stoop so low as to be a dirty cop. He didn't need to know that I was already working with the police department as a contracted investigator, working behind the scenes to take him down for the illegal activities he was involved in. Now, however, I had to tail Cassie, and that wasn't ideal. But it was better for me to do it than any of his other thugs.

"Illegal wasn't part of the deal. You know what that could do to my reputation in this town? I can't have that on me."

"That's right, along with your reputation as a ladies' man." He stepped closer. "I bailed your brother out of a deep mess with his drug problem. I did it at your request. Never forget that I didn't have to help him."

Oh, I would never be able to forget it, I thought.

"I asked you to do surveillance for me, and you will. But you will work for me as an extra bodyguard whenever I need you. And that might be for a while, since I'm now enemy number one for Gavriel De Luca. If I need you for something else, I expect you to do it without argument. Watch Cassie Nichols. Get close to her. Into her good graces. Find out if she knows her father's whereabouts."

I took a deep breath.

"Do you understand me, Jace?"

My fists clenched at my sides as I nodded.

"Say the words."

"I understand."

As I watched Vissar stride away, motioning to his other bodyguards, I remained where I was to regain control of my anger. I could have beaten him bloody, but then all the other bodyguards would have returned the favor. Ezra. I shook my head. I loved my little brother, but this had to be the most painful job I'd ever done in the name of family. For him. Humiliating, I thought, pushing away from the wall and hurrying out of the gallery.

I unlocked my car and climbed in, striking the steering wheel several times and shouting at the top of my lungs. My blood boiled, even after letting off steam. How dare he order me to watch Cassie and get into her good graces? If this got back to Ty, it could ruin our friendship. Who the hell did he think he was? I started the car and headed for home.

The house I rented with Ezra and his friend Milo usually took twenty minutes to reach on a good day, but on a Friday night in this town, the traffic was a nightmare. It was well into the early hours of the morning when I finally parked in front of the driveway, surprised to find a spot available.

"You've got to be kidding me," I muttered.

Cars lined the street, and I didn't need to get out of the car to hear the pounding music coming from our tiny house. All I wanted to do was retreat into my room after such a long day, maybe grab a beer and lie in bed to relax for a minute. It didn't look like that would happen anytime soon. Not until I got all these people out, if I could.

As I walked in through the front door instead of the garage, the smell of pot assaulted me. I waved a hand in front of my face as I entered a haze of marijuana mixed with vape fog. If anyone was in my bedroom, I was going to come unglued. My room was the first one on the right, the master bedroom suite, if you could call it that, since I paid the larger portion of the rent.

I opened my door and quickly scanned the small bathroom to the right before stepping into the main bedroom, breathing a sigh of relief. No one had turned my room into a party space. Slamming out of my bedroom, I entered the sea of drunk people in search of Ezra. In the kitchen, a girl sat on the counter with her legs wrapped around some guy, waving her arms in sync with the music. The living room beyond the kitchen was packed with people dancing.

Pushing my way past the kitchen to the two other bedrooms, I scanned the crowd but couldn't see Ezra anywhere. I ducked my head into his bedroom. No luck there. I strolled to the next bedroom and spotted his tennis shoe in the bathroom doorway between the two rooms.

I crouched down to make sure he was still breathing.

"Ez," I said, earning a groan in response. "Yep, you're alive. Come on, bro. Let's get you up and into bed."

"Jace?" he asked, his voice groggy as he struggled to sit up.

I pulled him to his feet. Lucky for me, he was a skinny little shit, and I wrapped my arm around his waist to guide him to his bedroom. If he hadn't been somewhat walking, I would have had to throw him over my shoulder. I shook my head. Four years younger than me, at almost twenty-five, he should have outgrown this. But he hadn't.

"What'd you take tonight, Ez?"

"Mmmmdoooknnnooow." His head lolled to the side.

"I need to know what you took. Come on, Ez. I'll bring you in if

I have to."

I kicked the partially open door to his bedroom, causing it to swing wide and bang against the wall. His room smelled nearly as bad as he did. I would need to call Mom to see if she could swing by and help me clean up. God, this house was going to be a wreck tomorrow. Having a brother mixed up in drugs sucked. I'd tried for years to get him clean, but it only kept getting worse.

"Speed," he whispered.

"Drinking too?"

"Yup." At the solid pop of the word, I shook my head and eased him onto his bed.

At least he was lying on his stomach, I thought as I knocked some junk off his bed and onto the floor before pulling a blanket over him. He'd need to sleep in his jeans.

I'd done a lot of things as a cop and then as an undercover detective. Taking care of Ezra was a big job and the main reason I moved back here. He'd gotten himself mixed up with owing a lot of money to people who weren't happy about not being paid. I didn't have any choice but to go to Vissar and ask him to bail Ezra out.

Ezra knew what I did, swearing he would get clean. I shook my head and headed back to my room, taking a detour through the kitchen and ignoring the girl on the counter who was waving her arms at me. She was one of Ezra's beach-bum friends, someone I recognized from the last time I'd been down here.

Growling at the oversized baggie of marijuana on the counter, I snatched it up despite the loud protests of the two other guys in the kitchen. When I swung my glare around to them, they appeared ready to pounce.

"Milo!" I bellowed.

He and Ezra knew what would happen if the cops were called. My neck would be on the line just as much as theirs, and I wasn't going down for this in my own house. Clutching the baggie, I headed toward the bathroom shared by Ezra and Milo.

While I'd been helping the police department with investigations, I didn't have the authority to carry a firearm or Taser. Probably a good thing, I thought, as one of the guys grabbed my arm.

"That's mine."

"Not in my house, it's not," I growled, throwing him off. "You want this amount of drugs, do it in your own house. Since it's in mine, it's going down the toilet."

"Dude!" Milo cut through the crowd, his blond, nearly white hair standing out in the dim light even amid the sea of bodies. "Don't do it, Jace!"

My jaw clenched. "Milo, this is not happening in my house. You know I can't allow this. Not now, of all times."

His bloodshot eyes blinked. "Please. Don't flush it. I'll get these people out of here. Just . . . don't."

It went against everything I stood for as a cop to not flush the entire thing down the toilet, but I thrust it back to the guy. "Stuff this down the front of your fucking pants and get the hell out of my house." He stared at me but reached out for it and did as I ordered. "Now!"

Milo's eyes widened at my authoritative voice, likely not having heard me so pissed off. Tonight was not the night to push my buttons. I swung around, scanning the small kitchen and living room, surprised the neighbors hadn't called the cops yet. Once the guy stuffed the baggie down his jeans, he made a fast retreat out the front door with his buddy close on his heels.

"Everyone out!" I yelled, grabbing at people as I headed toward the partially enclosed kitchen. "Out! Out!"

Milo had the good sense to help me herd people out, although his voice was much calmer than mine.

"Jace!"

A brunette with hair piled on her head, reeking of pot and sweat, launched herself at me. Her arms wound around my neck, her body pressed provocatively against me. Ah, Jesus, I swore, trying to push her away without touching what I didn't want to touch.

"I've been waiting for you."

"Not interested, Luci," I said, continuing to walk despite her arms still wrapped around my neck as I tried to dislodge them. "You need to leave just like everyone else is."

"Jace," she growled. "Come on, don't be like that."

"Come on, Luci." Milo pried her away from me. "Sorry, Jace."

I nodded at Milo as the music abruptly cut off. People shot me a mixture of glares and disbelief while moving like a mass crowd leaving a concert. How the hell they'd all fit in this miniature house, I had no idea.

Once I had a cold bottle of beer in my hand, I needed to get out of this swarm of people and into the quiet of my bedroom.

"Make sure these people are out and lock the damn door behind them, would you? Ezra's out, and I've had a long day."

"Will do, bro." Milo gave me a salute and turned with Luci, even though she shot me a pouty look and a glare. Two seconds later, she was laughing at something someone else said while they exited.

Not even close to being interested, I thought as I continued to push my way through to my bedroom. Finally, I closed the door behind me and locked it. Leaning against the door, I closed my eyes, thinking about how good it was to see Cassie tonight.

Damn, she looked gorgeous in that dress—almost as daring as the one she'd worn last weekend, which had showcased her slender back. This one was a tad shorter and the top was narrower. I groaned, pushing myself away from the door and taking a deep pull from my beer as I walked further into the room. The drone of voices grew fainter until silence settled in the house, granting me a sigh of relief.

During our time in Cape Haven, she'd always had her hair up. Tonight, it flowed down her back, golden and thick. I'd only seen her wear it up before.

Seeing her with Vissar shocked the hell out of me. Of all the people to be with, why him? And now I had to tail her. Get close to her. Why? I intended to understand it; there was no doubt about it.

I clicked on the lamp beside my bed and set my beer down. The dark gray bedding wasn't nearly as messy as Ezra's, but I hadn't taken the time to make it up decently that morning before leaving. I eased out of my black boots, kicking them out of the way. The black t-shirt, belt, and pants required of Vissar's bodyguards landed in a heap on the floor. I crawled into bed with a groan, visions of a blonde vixen in a shimmering pink dress plaguing me.

Chapter Thirteen

Cassie

By the time I arrived home that night, Quinn was already asleep, and I slipped into my room with heavy eyes. The day had been exhausting, and I had learned next to nothing. As I crawled between the whisper-soft sheets, I sighed, thoughts only of Jace filling my mind and how good he looked, even in black. He looked even better with short hair. I couldn't shake the image of him looking straight at me as I left.

Quinn had left the next morning before I woke up, leaving a note that he'd gone to a friend's house. I went for a run, did my yoga, and had my tea. After getting the kitchen stocked, I made calls regarding my dad's finances to ensure everything was in order. After an unanswered call to Ricky, I checked in with Naomi to share the news that my dad hadn't been found in the plane crash wreckage, but I wasn't a tattletale and didn't mention any of this mess Ricky and my dad were apparently involved in. At least I didn't need to make any funeral arrangements. By the end of the day, I felt an edge that needed to be aired out.

There had been no sign of Skyler, but Quinn came home shortly before I was ready to leave for a night out with the girls. I made him a quick dinner, watching him eat despite his irritation at being stared at.

"You know the drill: lock the door after I leave," I told him.

I hated to leave him again, especially since I hadn't seen Skyler at all. How could she stay away from her kid for so long? Thinking about it only made me angrier. I didn't want to start anything with her, but this was not okay.

I carefully made my way down to Mac's convertible. With the top down, I withdrew a hair tie from my clutch and quickly tied my hair back. She had to be crazy to have the top down. While the temperature hadn't dropped too low, it soon would with the sun setting.

"Girl!" Mac called from behind the wheel. "You look amaaaazing!" she sang.

I walked around the car to Kya, who slid out from the passenger side in her white sheath dress and pulled me into a tight hug. "I missed you, babe," she said, releasing me so I could climb into the backseat.

Dani, a distant friend I hadn't seen in a long time, sat in the backseat. Like me, she had long blonde hair. We could almost pass for sisters from a distance. She gave me a warm smile and extended her hand. "Long time no see."

"Right? What have you been up to, Dani?"

"Working with Mac on sets."

Mac never wanted to be in the spotlight like her parents, settling for the background. That was my choice, too, but I had chosen a profession further into the shadows, as far from the movie scene as I could get. Far from letting people in to get to know the real Cassidy Nichols.

"Are you sure you want to go to this party?" I laughed as Mac reversed faster than she should have out of the driveway and headed down Ocean Avenue.

I wasn't sure I would have been able to go to this party alone, and I knew that it would have been too risky to. That the girls had agreed to go out, despite the heightened stress with my dad in trouble and missing, I needed to find out who might be in Vissar's trusted circle. By going to his house, maybe I could find out what it was that my dad supposedly took.

"We aren't wasting this invitation!" she shouted over the whir of the wind.

I noticed the corner of Kya's mouth tilt up a fraction. "She's right. You don't turn down an invitation from up there."

Kya was beautiful and had a knack for stealth. The matchmaker of our childhood, she would sneak up on you without warning, and before you knew it, you'd be on a blind date. I needed to be careful while I was here, or she'd have me hooking up with someone regardless of reasons why I was here in the first place.

"Just so you know, this isn't a party we'd usually go to," I responded, watching Kya's eyes widen. "Vissar has buttloads of money."

"They all do!" Mac sang. "So? How was last night?"

"It was an event, but uneventful. But I got an invitation to tonight, didn't I?" I shrugged. "Oh, and I need to go shopping again. I'm going to a movie premiere next weekend."

"Shut up!" Mac exclaimed. "You?"

I chuckled. "I ran into Dar. She pointed out how much my dad would have loved to go, and the sentimental sucker in me agreed to go."

The car swerved when Mac took her eyes off the road for a second to look back at me, shocked. "Casanova! Do you know how many cameras are going to be there?"

She didn't need to remind me of that. Attending it was so far out of my comfort zone. Last night's art gallery opening wasn't anything compared to what this would involve. Plus, Dar expected me to find a date. I wasn't sure I could pull that off.

"I'm aware," was all I could say.

Mac's laughter filled the backseat, wrapping me in a sense of nostalgia at being back with my friends. God, I'd missed them. The only person missing was Riley and her spunk.

Dani tapped my hand. "How long has it been since you've been back?"

"Oh, probably two or three years? Three years, Mac?"

"Sounds about right."

"What's been going on around here while I've been away? Tell me you've got significant others, at least." My question hung in the air. Kya and Mac exchanged glances again. "Seriously? What are you doing? Playing the field?"

"Something like that." Mac met my eyes in the rearview mirror. "Dani met someone, haven't you? His name is Connor. He's some kind of investment broker, working in the stock market and helping people with their finances."

Good for her! Dani, even though we'd all been friends since high school, was the most rigid among us. I knew her well enough to understand that she could kick back and have a good time, but she definitely had a serious side. Kya likely set her up with this guy. Maybe she was working on Mac. And hopefully, she wouldn't be working on me while I was in town. I was fairly certain I'd gotten over Evan, but I still didn't want to be sucked into a relationship so quickly.

As if reading my mind, Kya swiveled in her seat. Her hair blowing around wildly in the vicious wind amused me. If she didn't realize it would be a tangled mess by the time we reached the party, she soon would. And she wouldn't care. "And you? Last we knew, you were dating a lawyer."

"Not anymore. But it's okay. I'm okay." I glanced over at Dani, who was listening to our exchange intently. "He did me a favor."

"I heard Watts may be interested in picking up where you left off," Mac announced.

I gasped louder than I ever had before. "We're friends. Nothing more."

"Everyone expected the two of you to end up together. Even we thought you would, especially since you were underage when you were dating him," Kya pointed out.

"Forget it," I interrupted.

Mac's laughter echoed in the back of the car. "He never got over you."

"I'm not interested."

"Oh, is that your ex-boyfriend?" Dani asked. "The one you lost your virginity to?"

"Yes," I groaned. "And I am not getting back together with him."

The cars lining the streets leading up to the estate on top of a slight hill made the three of us balk at the walk when Mac pulled into an available spot. The driveway itself had to be a quarter mile long with a high wrought-iron gate surrounding the villa.

"Now, *this* is a party," Mac said, ushering us along.

I could hear the thrum of the music from where we were. It had to be an amazing party if we could hear it from a mile away. Our high heels clicked on the pavement as we hiked our way up the incline toward the house. As we neared, the sheer size of the house had me gaping. It had to be two, if not three, of my houses combined. And clearly, it was some type of Italian villa.

Cars lined the driveway past the iron gates, which were open with at least five security guards standing around. The lights on either side of the pale brick pillars did little to illuminate the area, and all the guards wore black boots, pants, and shirts just as they had at the art gallery opening. Each of them had a gun strapped to their waist. I didn't remember seeing any guns last night, but that didn't mean they didn't have them. It made me wonder if Jace had one on him.

One guard stepped closer as we approached, while the other guards hung back and continued their conversation. "Name." His clipped, no-nonsense tone matched the straight line of his lips.

Mac and Kya exchanged looks before turning to me. Just as I opened my mouth to give him my name, Dani stepped forward.

"Don't you know who I am?" she snapped. "I'm Cassidy Nichols."

Too flabbergasted to correct her, I just stared. What did she think she was doing? The guard stepped back, looked at his phone, then returned and shook his head.

"You're not on the guest list tonight, Ms. Nichols."

"Well, check again," came her bitter retort.

This time, he cracked a stiff smile that didn't reach his eyes. He stepped away, pressing the button on the radio strapped to his shoulder. I caught my name somewhere in the mix, frowning. Dani could snap at him all she wanted. Vissar may have verbally invited me last night, but maybe I'd been too hopeful that he would actually add me to his guest list.

The security guard stepped back to us, returning to his stone-cold, passive demeanor. "Welcome to the party, Ms. Nichols and friends."

Dani tossed her hair over her shoulder, and we followed her inside, though I still couldn't find the words to process what had just happened. How in the hell . . . what just happened? I struggled to gather my thoughts when a golf cart zoomed toward us, turning around in front of us. A kid who looked like he hadn't hit puberty yet grinned at us.

"Hop in, ladies."

Better than walking, we piled in while chatting about who might be on the guest list for this party. I tried to ask Dani what she was thinking, but we arrived at the door quicker than I'd expected. Mac wouldn't stop talking about the size of the house.

As exclusive as it was, the cars lining the street and filling the driveway were some of the most expensive vehicles I'd ever seen. When the golf cart stopped in front of the house, I stood up and took in the sight of the illuminated structure.

An Italian villa, indeed. The tall, narrow windows and massive arches made the house look as if someone had plucked it from the Italian countryside and placed it in California. The front of the house was a shade of brown, slightly darker than sand, almost hidden by the ivy that covered its surface. Once we stepped inside, the interior matched the exterior, with warm browns and dark wood accentuating the columned arches and high-beamed ceilings.

People were everywhere, the music pounding from an audio system, and I felt like this was the place to be tonight. Mac slipped her arm through mine, pulling me through the giant entryway with two staircases leading upstairs. Bypassing the intimidating stairs, we walked into a living room with couches whiter than white, a grand piano, and a fireplace twice the size of mine.

I tried to pay attention to those who looked at us as we walked through, curious about where Vissar could be in this massive crowd. He'd be the only one here I would know, though I had run into Dar and Stirling last night. Kya and Dani trailed behind us until we found a makeshift bar close to the kitchen. I couldn't help but peek into the kitchen, where staff bustled around preparing food and drinks. Dazzled by the sheer size, I could only think of Naomi in a kitchen like this, with every type of convenience imaginable and an island twice the normal size covered in black and gray swirled granite.

"Hey, isn't that Petra Gordon over there?" Kya elbowed me.

My eyes scanned the room, landing on the black-haired beauty from our school days who had the gall to use me for my parents' fame. One of many who'd gotten close enough to almost succeed. Petra had been the new girl and used her charm to befriend me, pretending to actually like me when all she wanted was to make a name for herself by associating with people who had connections. Mac had been included in Petra's deception, but wasn't nearly as hurt as I was by it.

"Guess she's making her way up in the ranks," Mac said dryly. "Bitch."

I laughed. "That was so long ago."

"She got close enough. We're going to mingle," Mac said before she and Dani wandered away into the swell of the crowd, steering well clear of Petra.

Kya waved at the bartender, who poured us each a glass of wine.

"Can you imagine living in a place like this?" she asked. "I'm not sure I'd leave."

I shook my head. "I'm not sure I'd want to live in a house this size. It's intimidating, don't you think?"

Looking around, I sipped the dry red wine and let the taste linger on my tongue for a moment before swallowing. I couldn't determine how expensive the wine might be, but it had to be pricey in a house like this. Just one glass, I reminded myself. That was my rule. I wished I'd asked Dani what she had been thinking by giving my name at the gate like that before she walked away.

"Ladies."

I perked up at the deep voice, the accent hard to forget. When I turned, Vissar walked toward us, exuding charisma. Kya's eyes widened when she saw him.

He stepped between Kya and me, and I felt a sense of danger I hadn't felt at the art gallery. Of course, we were in his domain. Not once did his gaze leave mine. A two-finger salute to the bartender produced an amber-colored drink in less than a minute, his hand curling around the exquisitely cut crystal glass.

"Welcome to my home," he murmured before taking a sip. "I'm glad you accepted my invitation."

I tried to calm my growing anxiety, meeting Kya's saucer-like eyes. It seemed I wasn't the only one aware of his significance. In this grand house, Vissar Loukas was an important man. Those around us were merely puppets in his game. A game I had no business being in.

With unspoken permission, he reached down, taking my hand and boldly caressing my knuckles with his thumb. I would have expected him to kiss my hand, but he continued to smooth the pad of his thumb over them. He never once stopped looking at me.

"I'm pleased you accepted my invitation. Tell me, my pet, what do you think of my house?"

His dark eyebrows raised, and he still held my hand with no promise of letting it go. I tilted my head to the side. "I'll tell you under one condition."

Deep, rumbling laughter bubbled out of him as he tossed his head back. "What . . . a bargain?"

Kya looked uncomfortable. I gave her a jerky nod and watched her step away from us out of the corner of my eye. I hoped she wouldn't go too far, keeping my gaze fixed on Vissar, my hand still a prisoner of his.

"What is this . . . condition?"

Tearing my eyes from his, I drew in a deep breath to bolster my courage before looking back at him. Before me stood a man who could be far more dangerous than Reno Moretti. Courage, don't fail me now.

I stepped closer to him, which required him to release my hand. When I tipped my head up to maintain eye contact, his lips parted and his eyes brightened. Gracious, but I was playing with flames that wouldn't just burn me; they would obliterate me. If not now, then in the future.

"That you never call me your pet again."

Instead of laughing, his lips curled. "And what would you have me call you?"

I was playing with fire, a fire I didn't know how to extinguish in a hurry. "I do not give my time, precious as it is, to married men. Just so we have that straight, Vissar."

"I won't call you my pet. Answer my question."

"It's beautiful," I whispered.

"I might say the same about you. I don't give a damn whether you don't give your time to married men. You've come to my home at my invitation; there must be some merit in wanting to see me."

"You realize I wasn't on your guest list?"

"How did you get in?"

"Maybe I snuck in."

His eyes darkened. "My security team would never allow that to happen."

"Are you so important, then?" He stiffened. "Relax. A house as beautiful as this can only belong to an important man. I'm in town burying my dad. I'm not here looking for someone to jump into bed with, especially not with a married man."

"My wife does not mind my pets."

My stare strengthened my courage. "I'm not your pet. I'll never be that."

He lifted his drink and took a long gulp. "My dear . . ." He raised an eyebrow, and I nodded in consent, "my wife does not delve into my activities, nor do I into hers. One could say we have a marriage in name only. It is nothing for me to take a mistress, and I would treat her far better than my wife."

Ah, medieval crap, I thought, my lips tightly closed. "I am terribly sorry to disappoint you, but I don't sleep with married men. I never will."

"What can I say to convince you?"

I shrugged, finally sneaking a sip of my wine and realizing I might need something much stronger after this conversation. "You won't." I looked around the room, as pointless as that was. "What is your wife's name?"

"Veronica is not here this evening. She's gone overseas."

Damn it. With a wife out of the way and a man likely possessing more money than I could dream of in a house like this, this wasn't a fire; it was an inferno. It could be charm, but this man had a persuasive nature, and I suspected he didn't like to be told no. I couldn't let him win.

I sighed, shaking my head. "I'm not sure what it is you're after, Vissar, but I'm not available for you."

His eyes narrowed at my firm refusal. If I had known he'd invited me to his home to try to get me into his bed, I would have thought twice about coming here. "I have other guests to attend to. Do enjoy yourself while you're here."

My heart thumped wildly in my chest as I watched him leave. Just like that. I couldn't believe I'd escaped the encounter unscathed. How could he be so confident that I would be interested in a man like him? It made my skin crawl to think about it. Vissar may be handsome to some women, but not for me. Not at all.

I craned my neck, watching him leave and noting whom he might stop to speak with. I spotted Dani talking to a couple of bodyguards before following them out of the room. She'd get one of them in trouble with her flirting, I determined. By then, Vissar had vanished, which didn't surprise me. Mac was talking to a group of people. She couldn't go anywhere without knowing someone or someone knowing her.

"Oh my sinful God," Kya sputtered as she returned to my side, sliding her hand down my bare arm to my wrist. "I'm normally a selfish person, and everyone knows I'm a matchmaker at heart. There is a sinfully gorgeous man walking this way, and he has his gorgeous eyes locked on you, babe."

No matter how many times I explained to her that I wasn't interested in being set up with anyone, she was forever trying. With a heavy sigh, I turned to see what I'd be dealing with in a few moments, unsure if I wanted to after that interlude with Vissar.

My eyes widened. Sinful be damned, Jace Taylor looked downright wicked in his black pants and dark slate-gray button-up shirt rolled up to his elbows. The collar was open just enough for me to see part of the dark swirl of a tattoo. That was him last night, all right. He'd cut his hair, making him look even more dangerous. But when my eyes met his, they caught me off guard. That deep electric blue drew me in like a drug.

Chapter Fourteen

Looking entirely too beautiful for her own good in that wisp of a dress, Cassie's eyes locked onto mine as I stalked toward her. They were so intense that I had to take a sip of my drink to moisten my mouth. Women rarely, if ever, had this much of an effect on me. I had yet to figure out what it was about this woman that affected me so deeply, but I was determined to find out. I should have known she would be at this party after seeing her with Vissar last night.

The same thing happened when I met her a week ago, standing on the beach in her loose-fitting shirt over a very skimpy tank top and tiny pair of shorts. When she'd walked away from me at the wedding, my blood heated like it never had before. Damn it. I needed to cool it, or I'd be in trouble with this woman.

 I couldn't get her out of my thoughts last night, even after finishing a beer. If anything, it got worse.

"Cass," I said coolly.

Her friend's mouth dropped open at my familiarity. Damn right I knew her, and I intended to find out why she was at the art gallery opening on the arm of Vissar Loukas and now here in his house. Find out why he needed to know if she knew where her dad was. This was definitely not the place for her. These people were not the type of people she should be associating with.

"Jace," she returned, putting her back to the makeshift bar. "Funny running into you here."

"I could say the same. How did you get in?"

Her friend laughed, and Cassie shot her a look. "It's an interesting story," she murmured in her breathy voice. "What are you doing here?"

Cassie had a reputation for being morally uptight. If I told her what I was doing here, she would never let me within a hundred feet of her again. I didn't trust Vissar, and she shouldn't either. I knew it was only a matter of time before he pulled me into his illegal business. For now, I'd stayed clear, working on surveillance to some of those in his employ he didn't trust, an extra bodyguard, and now spying on Cassie.

"I have business here," I finally answered, only a partial lie. "Same."

"Do you want to get out of here?" I moved closer to her, but she remained where she was and stood her ground.

I did not intimidate this woman one bit. It felt as if she saw right through all my bullshit. I assumed her time spent with Riley Cavanaugh and Regan Moretti was the culprit, and damn if it didn't make her more attractive. This was not a woman who threw herself at men. No, she would never do that.

"I just got here," she said, a slight pout to her mouth.

"You shouldn't be here."

I chose my words carefully, but apparently not carefully enough, because those gorgeous blue eyes flashed with defiance. Heat coursed through me. I'd handled enough women. If that was all it took to rattle me, I needed to calm down. But this woman was unlike anyone I'd ever met.

"The security guards let us in, Jace. It's not like we broke in. I doubt we would have been able to." She tapped a slender finger against the rim of her wineglass. "Kya and I were having some wine and enjoying the ambiance."

Trying to distract me wouldn't work. God, she looked like a vixen in that dress—curves in all the right places and lightly toned elsewhere. She worked out just enough to maintain it. Staying in a house with her for a few days in Cape Haven, I came to appreciate her healthy outlook on life: running on the beach early in the morning, followed by yoga and a cup of herbal tea.

She was the yin to my yang, as I was about as unhealthy as you could get. Living with Ezra and his best friend Milo, who both worked at a surf shop, our refrigerator was stocked with beer and leftover pizza. Only when Mom stopped by did we have a full stock of real groceries and a clean house. I tried to keep things fairly tidy, but she was far more organized than we were. In my line of work, I had to stay in shape, but I wasn't as conscious about food—not like Cassie.

"You're staring," she retorted.

"Hard not to, with that dress."

At the brightness in her eyes, my lips curved into a smile.

"Your moves don't work on me, Jace. Remember?"

I tipped my head back to laugh, just loud enough to let her know I didn't believe her. Little did she know about my moves. Rule number one: I never made the first move. Ever. But I could hardly recall a woman ever walking away from me like she had.

"That's right. Immune to my charms. Why is that? I'm still confused about what you dislike about me so much."

"It's not dislike. I just don't play that game."

"Ah. More of the 'take me on some dates first' kind of woman." Her eyes glazed over with a wounded look, instantly making me regret saying it. If she just said the word, I would gladly take her home and right to her bed.

"Right now, I'm not looking for anything." She took a sip of her wine.

"Jace?"

I felt a slender hand on my forearm as Natalia's auburn hair brushed against me. Great, I thought. This is just what I needed.

"Who's your friend?" she asked, her voice innocent.

Natalia was anything but innocent. From the look in Cassie's eyes, she recognized it immediately. Good. I should warn her about Vissar's daughter. Natalia could be just as cunning as her old man. Maybe even be more so.

"Cassie, this is Natalia Loukas. Vissar's daughter."

Cassie extended her hand. "Nice to meet you."

It didn't take a rocket scientist to hear what Cassie wanted to know, as distasteful as I thought it would be. Was I sleeping with Natalia? Absolutely not. I needed to get her away from Natalia, and fast. The two of them together would be a disaster.

"Natalia, don't you have guests to see to?"

"Actually, I'd like to speak with our friend Cassie a bit more."

"Maybe another time," I said, grabbing Cassie by the elbow and almost making her spill her wine. Setting my drink down, I guided her away from Natalia. I didn't want to hear another word out of Natalia's mouth. "Can we take a walk, maybe in private?"

She exchanged a look with her friend, who shrugged in response. "Kya, I'll be right back."

"It was nice to meet you," Natalia called sweetly after us.

Kya gave us a little wave. Cassie abandoned her wine on a high table, allowing me to take her by the elbow and lead her away from the bar and toward the back of the house.

"You seem to know your way around this house. How long have you been working for Vissar?" she asked as we walked down a dim hallway beneath high arches.

"Long enough," I answered quietly, keeping my hand on her.

For whatever reason, I felt the need to maintain my grip on her, as if I would lose her if I let go. I would never forgive myself if I lost her to Vissar. The man didn't even try to hide the fact that he was a bastard, and I would not let him sink his claws into Cassie. It might already be too late.

She didn't seem to mind my touch, which made me feel better. Maybe she didn't see me as the womanizer everyone else did. I had a reputation for a reason, and I would always carry that weight with me. It was better that way. I led a complicated life— one that a woman didn't fit in. That was why I had rules.

The corridor led through another sitting area and past Vissar's study before reaching the back of the house. She stopped, mouth gaping as she stared ahead.

"Is that a pool?" she asked, looking down the steps just past the curving stairway leading to the second level.

"Yes."

Pressing her to the left, I opened the double French doors onto a covered patio that spanned half the length of the house. I lost my grip on her when we stepped outside. The backyard sloped down to two paths: one led to the outdoor pool and guest house, while the other led to the tennis courts.

"Nice to see he has a putting green," she drawled as we strolled down the path.

I sighed. "Vissar has more money than he knows what to do with."

Silence enveloped us as I glanced up at the second level to ensure Vissar wasn't on his balcony. He had guards posted everywhere, hidden from view except for those stationed at the front of the house. I'd be lying if I said this wasn't the most dangerous job I'd ever been on.

Casting a glance at the beauty beside me, I realized how much more dangerous this situation with Cassie had become. I couldn't understand how she had ended up here, of all places, instead of being safe in Seattle.

"Why are you here, Cassie?" I asked softly, watching the hand swinging by her side, tempting me to grab it just to keep her close. To claim her. I wondered if she'd allow me to touch her again. She knew my reputation, not me.

"Mac wouldn't take no for an answer about going out tonight—"

"Why are you in LA?"

Her eyes darted to mine, fear shining through. Unmistakable fear. I'd seen it a thousand times before. She couldn't hide it. Not from me.

"My dad was reportedly in a plane crash on Wednesday. They can't locate his remains, though."

"I'm sorry," I whispered.

"He shouldn't have been on that plane in the first place. He was running from someone. For something he didn't do." She released a breathy sigh. "He's always helping someone. I think he might have gotten caught in the middle of something."

I blew out an unsteady breath. "Need my help?"

She shook her head. "I've got it handled."

I doubted that. "Do you know what kind of trouble he was in?" She glanced away. "I can help you, you know. I was an undercover detective before I moved back here, and I'm working on getting my license as an independent private investigator. I have connections. But you can't stay in this house. You should stay away from Vissar. Natalia, too. There are dangerous people here."

"I'll keep that in mind, but I'll be fine."

We stopped in the middle of the path. As much as I wanted to lead her further away from the party, I also needed to get her back inside and right out the front door. I kept my eye on the second story. Vissar had told me to get into her good graces, and he would be watching any chance he could to make sure of it.

"Would you consider taking down my phone number? Just in case?"

A smile touched her mouth in just the right spot, hitting me in the center of my chest like a punch. This was no ordinary woman. I couldn't quite figure out what it was about her, though.

"That's not necessary. I'll probably be heading home in a week."

"I'm not asking for yours, Cassie. Just take mine. Please."

With a slight huff, which she tried to mask, she took her phone out of her clutch and entered my number into her cell phone. That made me feel better.

"Vissar is dangerous," I told her again, hoping to get her to trust me and stop thinking of me as a total prick. "Extremely dangerous. The people who associate with Vissar are dangerous. Your being here puts *you* in danger."

When she met my eyes, I prayed she recognized the seriousness I was trying to convey. I couldn't detect even the slightest hint of humor from her. With a nod, I offered her my arm, but she turned and walked without my help. I tried not to take it personally. Those who knew me were aware of why I was how I was.

"Who does Vissar associate with? Anyone who would purposely take down an airplane to be rid of someone? Anyone I would know?" she asked.

"Cassie," I growled. "Don't get involved with him. He doesn't associate with anyone you would. Trust me."

"You tell me to trust you, but I don't know you."

A valid point. "Do you honestly think Ty would ever forgive me if I let his wife's best friend get hurt? It's in my best interest to earn your trust."

With the house still packed full of people, I followed Cassie back to the bar, where we found her friend Kya talking to a group. My eyes swept the area for Vissar, as they had the entire way back inside and through the house. His eyes met mine from across the room, eyebrows raised. The sinking feeling in the pit of my stomach would remain until I was rid of this assignment. Hurting Cassie was the last thing I wanted to do, despite her indifference toward me.

"I see you made it back in one piece," another woman next to her friend Kya said, her warm brown eyes sparkling with mischief. "Who's your friend?"

Cassie sighed. "Jace, this is Mac and Kya. Two of my oldest friends."

They exchanged glances, and my lips quirked up at their charming display. They were trying to be inconspicuous in finding a love interest for their friend. Little did they know that Cassie didn't want anything to do with me.

"This is Jace."

"And you just ran into him here? Of all places." Mac's eyes widened. "How did I miss that?"

Cassie merely shook her head, and I noticed her looking across the room at someone. I was about to ask whom she was staring at when another woman joined us, shoving right into me from behind, knocking me right into Cassie. This woman appeared flustered. My arms shot out to catch Cassie, and I couldn't help but smooth my palms around her small waist, earning myself a glare until she straightened. The glare was worth it.

"We have to leave," the woman sputtered. "Now."

"What the hell, Dani? You look pale," Mac pointed out.

"Yes," Dani snapped. "I want to get the hell out of here right now. Apparently, it was stupid to give them your name at the gate." She looked pointedly at Cassie. "They mistook me for you, and it wasn't to make friends. I'll be waiting in the car."

When she whirled around and let the crowd swallow her up, I realized she resembled Cassie with her blonde hair, but that was about it. Cassie had an undeniable glow. The two other women appeared confused and upset, huddled together and discussing what Dani had said.

As they walked away, I caught Cassie's wrist. "You'll call me?"

"I won't need to, but thanks for your number anyway."

All I could do was watch her walk away, admiring her grace. She had fire and ice in her veins. I didn't know why, but I itched to find out. I just didn't know how yet.

"Hey," her friend Kya said, and my eyes darted to her. "She likes to go to the beach at sunrise."

"Does she?"

I looked back at Cassie and her other friends, but she'd disappeared into the crowd with them. I remembered her sitting on the beach, watching the water whenever she could last weekend, especially at sunrise.

"It's her favorite place to be," Kya continued. "And right now, I have a feeling she's going to want to be there."

"Why are you telling me this?"

Kya stepped in front of me, as if to prevent me from going after Cassie. "I've known Cassie for a lot of years. She needs someone she can trust. If I'm not mistaken, I saw the way she looked at you . . . Let's just say she doesn't look at just anyone that way."

I tried not to scoff at that. "With disgust?"

"Cassie isn't who she pretends to be." She leaned closer. "She'll try her hardest to mask it, but no one can maintain a pretense one hundred percent of the time. But I think she can trust you, Jace. Tell me I'm wrong."

I shook my head. She could trust me. Despite what I was doing for Vissar, she could trust me. I had good intentions behind all my actions. If anything, I was doing it to protect her. He could have asked one of his other minions to tail her, but he'd asked me. At least I could control what I'd fed back to him.

Kya smiled before leaving me standing there, wondering what the hell had just happened. I needed another stiff drink—just one to keep my wits about me if I was to survive this.

Burning questions swirled in my mind. Had I heard correctly that her friend had mentioned Cassie's name at the gate? If so, why in the hell had she done that? And why did Vissar's men pull her aside as though she were Cassie? I intended to find out all of this. And it wouldn't be by asking Vissar. I had to find another way.

Chapter Fifteen

Digging my toes into the sand, I listened to the waves swishing against the shore. Like the island of Cape Haven, this was exactly what I needed to calm my frayed nerves. The sun was barely up, and no sane person should be awake. Just when I thought it couldn't be more perfect, I spotted Jace Taylor strolling toward me.

Kya, I muttered silently. She must have told him last night where I liked to go to think. I should have known she was up to something when she lagged behind us when we left the party. I needed this morning to think, so I kept my eyes on the ocean, focusing on the sound of the waves. He didn't say a word when he sat next to me.

After we'd left the party, Dani told us that two men had pulled her into a room and questioned her relentlessly about her life, her dad's life, and what he was doing before he died—and if she was sure he'd died. Hearing that irritated the hell out of me. It didn't matter that I knew he wasn't dead. It hadn't been confirmed he was or wasn't dead, and no one had the right to question someone so aggressively right after they learned they may have lost a loved one.

When she couldn't provide the answers they were looking for, they became forceful. She told them she wasn't who they thought she was, but by that time, they didn't believe her. I couldn't understand it since Vissar knew me now. They had to know that

Dani wasn't me unless his guards stupidly mistook her for me while I'd been speaking to him.

Stupid. Even as a joke, she shouldn't have given them my name. Dani admitted she thought of it at the last minute just to be funny, and now she regretted it. Whatever happened had clearly spooked her.

I needed to figure out why Vissar's guards were questioning her and not me. Was that the reason Vissar had invited me? And if so, why was he flirting with me when he intended for his men to question me forcefully?

I looked over at Jace. He watched me, his piercing eyes devouring me. Had anyone ever looked at me so intently before? He seemed entirely too comfortable sitting next to me and saying nothing. It was as if he knew something.

I had to break the ice. "What is it that Vissar really does for money?"

"Tell me what you know."

"Do you know anything about my family?"

"Your mom was a big-time actress. Died when you were fifteen from a drug overdose. Your dad is a drummer who was on tour when she died, so you lived with his best friend's mom, and you have ever since. You hate being in the spotlight like your parents were, so you live in Seattle."

"God," I muttered. "Did Riley tell you all that? Or did you use your investigative skills to look into my past?"

"Most is public knowledge. But, no. I asked Ty."

"I told you last night I think my dad got mixed up in something." I sighed. "I went to the art gallery opening to see if Vissar would have a response to me showing up there."

"And you didn't find it strange that an invitation was waiting for you when you arrived?"

"It wasn't for me. It was for my dad. Vissar wanted him there." I could only guess.

I swallowed, waiting for him to ask questions, but Jace stayed quiet, listening. I told him what Dani shared with us last night after we left: that they had questioned her about me and my dad, even threatening her.

"Dani thought it would be funny to give them my name at the gate. Before I realized what she was doing, they let us in. I mean, Vissar did invite me."

"Sounds like you need my help."

"This isn't funny, Jace. Vissar knows who I am. Why would his guards hassle Dani?"

His face showed not even a glimpse of humor. "I'm not trying to be funny. There's a reason he had his men question her and not you. I'm not sure why. Vissar is about as ruthless as they come. Not only does he pick up young women, regardless of what his wife thinks, but he's also known for a slew of illegal activities, including selling young girls."

My mouth dropped open. I knew about human trafficking, but I didn't know anyone involved, and I hadn't treated any young girls who had experienced such horrors. The thought of it made me feel nauseous, especially if what Jace said was true.

"No one can pin anything on him, of course."

I scoffed. "That doesn't sound like anyone my dad would hang out with. But would Vissar have something to do with my dad disappearing?"

"Disappearing?" he asked slowly. "Or dying?"

Damn it. "Dying."

"Cassie, if you think I enjoy working for Vissar, you're wrong. I don't trust him. He'll use anyone to his advantage. That's why I wanted you out of there so fast last night. But I had nothing to do with your friend being questioned. I would never repeat what you say to me."

I blew out a breath. "My dad didn't get on that plane," I whispered. "He must have known and didn't get on it. He called me that night. Told me he'd gotten into trouble and had to run."

Jace stayed quiet for another minute, digesting what I had admitted. I prayed I could trust him with this. We were both playing a dangerous game if I couldn't.

"I'll tell you what I think happened. When the guards at the gate called in to check if I was on the list, they gave the guards in the house her description. Vissar was talking to me and didn't know his guards had pulled the wrong person. And he wouldn't do the dirty work himself, would he? But the question is why he wanted answers from me in the first place? I don't know a thing about this."

He shrugged, drawing a circle in the sand with his finger. "He's cunning. That's why you need me. I'll find out."

"How do *you* know him?"

The muscles in his jaw clenched for a moment. "There are certain things I need to get my PI license in this state, so it's going to take a little while. In the meantime, I took a job offer from him."

That didn't help me. "Why? Why him?"

"I had to."

I felt a sinking feeling in my stomach. "Please tell me you aren't helping him sell young girls."

He looked hurt that I would ask such a thing. "Of course not. I'm working for him because I need the money. I only hope that when the job is over, he doesn't keep me for another one. Vissar doesn't take no for an answer. He's dangerous, even by my standards. I don't want you anywhere near him."

"I have to find out where my dad went and what happened."

"You think your dad stole something from him?"

"My dad doesn't steal or get into trouble. Unless he was helping someone or got caught in the middle of something. Vissar knows my dad is on the run, and my dad isn't safe until I figure out why."

The way his jaw clenched told me I had said something he didn't want to hear. But he had no say over what I did with my life. Jace barely knew me.

"I wish you wouldn't," he finally said, then gave me a wry smile. "I can't change your mind?"

Saying nothing, I felt a strange comfort in his presence. "I'm just taking it one day at a time, but just know—" He looked away, and I reached out to touch his shoulder so he'd look at me. "I don't want to be in his company. He scares the living daylights out of me. But I won't lose another parent, Jace."

"Does that mean you'd rather be in my company?"

I laughed. "It means that if I have to be in his, I won't like it. So, what now?"

He looked back out at the ocean. "Let's go surfing. The sun's almost up, and the waves look perfect."

Glancing down at my sweatpants and baggy sweater, I realized in horror how terrible I must look. "Pretty sure I'd get arrested if I tried surfing naked. And it isn't exactly warm enough outside for that. Plus, I didn't bring my board."

The wicked smile that curved his mouth made me realize why women fell at his feet. That grin made his eyes flash.

I had barely slept last night, crawling into bed late and unable to shake the events of the evening from my mind. My thoughts refused to quiet. What had I gotten myself into by coming down here?

"Can I take you for a cup of coffee or tea?"

"Is that what they call it now?" I teased.

When he tilted his head and the ocean breeze ruffled his short dark hair, it took my breath away. If I thought he looked good with longer hair, he looked even better with it short. "That's not what I meant. But I suppose if you wanted to . . . "

"I'm not the type of girl who does one-night stands."

"Who said it would be one night?"

"Jace, stop it."

"Stop what?"

"Stop trying to get me into bed."

He laughed, his voice deep and full of soul. "Maybe it's more than that."

That gave me pause as my thoughts shuffled around. He couldn't be serious. Jace Taylor didn't settle for relationships. Riley told me he had a reputation for it, and everyone knew it. He didn't keep a girlfriend and rarely called any woman back. Deep down, I understood that. Didn't I? I hardly knew the man sitting next to me. With a deep groan, I dropped my head back. I didn't have time for this.

"I'm not here for relationships, sex, or anything else."

Staring into his eyes, I tried to force him to be serious.

"Let me help you, Cass."

God, the way he said it—slow and sensual—warmed me inside and out. He had a way with words, no doubt about that. I'd given up on trying to get him to stop calling me that. Everyone called me that, except for the few who called me Casanova. But my name on his lips felt like a caress. With my jaw set, my decision to accept his help remained unchanged.

"I'll let you know if I need it."

I should have known Jace wouldn't accept no for an answer. He wouldn't have the reputation he did if he gave up so easily. When we parted ways on the beach, I hadn't made a firm commitment to accept his help, but I hadn't outright declined either. I was somewhere in between, I mused as I crossed the street toward the darkened house.

Skyler hadn't come here last night; I'd checked when I got in, and my dad's room remained empty. I would have woken up if she had come in after me, having left my door open a crack. Even though Quinn was asleep by the time I got home, I figured he wouldn't be up this early. I cast a quick glance back at the vacant beach before going inside, seeing no sign of Jace. I would be lying to myself if I didn't admit that part of me wished he'd been watching which house I went to. He'd watched me walk away, but only so far; I knew that much.

For a while, I stood in the kitchen, debating whether to catch a bit more sleep or brew a cup of tea. In the end, I went back to bed. The house, still a little dark and silent, wouldn't provide much of a companion this early in the morning. No one would be up for hours yet, and I figured a few more hours of sleep would clear my mind.

Chapter Sixteen

"You're here," I said, noting Skyler's outfit as I glided into the kitchen.

With her dark brown hair flowing down her back in perfect waves, her outfit was impeccable and of high quality, which I found interesting for a housekeeper. She wore a black tank top and matching leggings, with a hot pink kimono that nearly reached the floor. Dramatically, I rolled my eyes, but she didn't catch it as she poured herself a cup of coffee.

The week had passed quickly with the calls I made to clients. Quinn had come here every day after school, but Skyler hadn't come in when she picked him up. I had a feeling she didn't want to talk to me. She probably didn't want to know what would happen now that my dad was gone, and I didn't blame her for that. I hadn't heard anything more from Vissar or Jace, but I went shopping with Mac to find a dress for the movie premiere tonight. I still hadn't found a date.

"Good morning to you, too." She turned, leaning her lithe figure against the counter by the sink as she brought her mug to her lips.

Foregoing tea for the moment, I slid into a chair at the breakfast bar. "It would have been nice if you'd been here last weekend when I got in."

She raised her dark eyes to regard me, keeping the mug at her lips. If her intent was to make me feel inferior to her, it wouldn't work. Brushing it aside, I managed a half-smile.

"And yet," she eyed me, "here you are. What do you need me here for?"

I didn't want to fight. I barely knew her, and ignoring her snide comments seemed like the only plausible option. "Is there anything you want to tell me?"

"What could I possibly tell you?"

I could rattle off several things she could clue me in on, but it wouldn't do any good, given how closed off as she already was. Did she even care that my dad was gone? Finally, she set her coffee down and folded her arms in front of herself.

"It would have been nice if someone told me about the living arrangements around here. And Quinn. That was quite a surprise. He told me Lex is his dad."

She shrugged. "That would have been up to your dad to tell you. It's not my fault he never did."

Was she always this snarky? I wondered, feeling the need to count to ten and back to calm myself. It might take more than that to get through one simple conversation with her. A few deep breaths, and I'd be ready to resume the discussion. She was right that my dad should have told me. But she was the only one here to handle it, and she should have been present.

"What was my dad doing before he disappeared? Can you remember your last conversation with him?"

She blew out a frustrated breath. "Not really. We weren't always together, you know."

"You're his housekeeper, and obviously more than that since you're living here, Skyler!"

Her crossed arms told me everything I needed to know. Argh, she aggravated me. "We only live here part of the time. And he wasn't always here, *Cassidy*."

I didn't want to be at odds with her, but now that he was supposedly gone, she didn't need to be here. I would have to decide what to do with this house and whether to keep her as the housekeeper. If I never found him, I would have to get rid of one house. Which one would I sell? It made my stomach churn to think about that decision.

"I suppose you'll sell this house now, and I'll be out of a job," she said, as if she'd been reading my mind.

"For now, no. I haven't decided what I'm going to do."

I watched her pick up her coffee cup and take a tentative sip.

"Were you and my dad having problems?"

Her eyes snapped to mine, bold with irritation. I could have laughed at how easily I could rattle her, but she maintained her smooth tone. "That's none of your business."

"You're right." I slipped from the chair and moved around her to grab a coffee cup and heat water for tea. "But my dad is gone, and that might be a piece of the puzzle. So, I suggest you tell me what you know."

We stared at each other, dislike simmering in her eyes. I didn't care.

"No, we weren't having any problems."

When she broke eye contact, I knew she was hiding something. I'd have to keep digging if I wanted any answers. They wouldn't be coming from Skyler. And here I thought it would be so easy.

"Mom?"

"Quinn."

She shoved away from the counter as Quinn stumbled into the kitchen with tousled hair, wearing SpongeBob pajama pants and a white t-shirt.

"Morning, shortie," I quipped, setting my mug of water in the microwave to heat.

He grumbled something while Skyler glared at me, taking her coffee and leaving the kitchen. Wow! She didn't fix him something to eat or ask how his day at school was yesterday. There were several epithets I wanted to hurl at her back, even if only in silent frustration. But I would never do that in front of her son.

"What do you want for breakfast?" I asked him, rummaging through the refrigerator and making a mental note to stop at the grocery store for some food.

He yawned and plopped down in a chair. "You're making me breakfast?"

"Depends on what you want. I'm fairly simple with cooking, so if you want anything crazy, you're going to have to get a job and hire a personal chef." That got a smile from him, albeit a sleepy one. "Eggs? Fruit?" I opened a drawer and found some bread that looked decent. "Toast?"

"Alright."

I retrieved my hot water to steep the tea before making him a quick breakfast, chatting about the movies he liked to watch. His favorite movies were those dumb comedies, horror films, or action flicks.

"How long are you staying?" he asked, his mouth full of scrambled eggs while holding a piece of toast in his other hand.

The urge to ruffle his already messy hair made me chuckle. Instead, I settled against the counter where Skyler had been and considered the question. When I booked my flight, it was only a one-way ticket. I didn't know if it would be a quick visit or an extended one.

"Looks like it might be a while unless my dad magically walks in the door." When he dropped his eyes, his face crestfallen, I added, "But I'll be talking to some people today to see if I can find out more."

Quinn looked up at me, opened his mouth as if he were going to say something, then thought better of it and stuffed the toast in instead. I wished I could tell him something different. My heart ached for him. This kid didn't have his mom around to share what was going on in his life, and now the man he thought was his dad was gone. No one around to ask him how school was going, or what he liked and disliked.

At that moment, Skyler breezed back in wearing the same outfit but with a different wrap over and a large bag slung over her shoulder. She waved her hand, clutching a pair of dark sunglasses.

"I'm leaving."

She leaned down and kissed the top of Quinn's head, despite his grimace.

"When should we expect you back?" I asked, a smile tugging at the corners of my lips.

"Don't. I'll be back when I get back. Quinn knows the routine." When my eyes met his, it felt like something snapped into place, and we both understood. Our lives were so similar it was scary. We were on our own. While I preferred my life that way, I didn't want this for Quinn or any kid. I had been managing this for so long; it felt automatic.

I sighed. "I grew up the same way."

The way his eyebrows drew together made me realize just how young he truly was. I knew he wouldn't turn twelve for another couple of months, but he looked so young—too young to bear the weight on his shoulders. And to think I was only three years older when my mom died.

"My dad was always gone on tour, and my mom was an actress. No one was ever home for me. I fixed my own breakfast, snacks . . . usually dinner." I pursed my lips. "No one to talk to about how my day at school was or what the mean girls were doing."

Slowly, he lowered his toast and left it on his plate before raising his eyes to meet mine. "You . . . didn't have anyone around, either?"

I shook my head. "My mom died when I was fifteen. I still went on tours with my dad, or sometimes only part of them. I grew closer to him after she died, but he was still gone a lot."

His eyes brightened. "You went on tours?"

"Sometimes."

Picking up his toast, he resumed eating. "That's so awesome."

Damn her, I thought with a cringe. I had my hands full getting my dad home, and now I had an additional worry about this little dude. Skyler would never listen to a word of advice from me, especially since I didn't have any kids. I didn't even have any prospects of marriage, though I didn't need to be married to have kids. I scoffed. I wasn't even in a current relationship, and none of my serious ones had lasted.

"Don't you have school today, shortie?"

He scrunched up his face. "Are you always going to call me that?"

"Technically, this is my house now. It's my right to tease you every chance I get." His dramatic eye roll only charmed me more. "So? School, Quinn?"

"No school today. Teacher workshop. Might go to the skate park with Ray and Leo."

"Want to hang out with me for a little first?" He shot me a look of doubt. "I have some calls to make, but after that, I need to run out. Would you want to come with me? We can stop by the skate park if you want."

"You'll drive me to the skate park?"

The disbelief in his question made me assume that Skyler had never once taken him to the one place that apparently brought him the most joy. To be fair, she didn't seem like the type to hang out at a skate park. My heart ached again.

"Sure. Give me an hour to get ready and make those calls, and I'll let you know what the plan is."

Kids were not my area of expertise, but when he pushed his plate away and bolted from the kitchen, I couldn't help but feel that he might be excited. That only made my mission seem more worthwhile. After rinsing his dishes and putting them in the dishwasher, I hurried to make myself presentable for the day.

A half hour later, I clicked on the lights in my dad's soundproof studio in the basement and wandered around the spacious room, waves of nostalgia rushing over me. Blinking away tears, I sat behind his drum set and picked up the sticks from the snare. The smooth wood beneath my fingertips brought back such an onslaught of memories that I knew I would either need to put them down or beat on the drums.

The vibration of my phone, scaring the living daylights out of me, saved me from making that decision. I snatched it out of my back pocket. It wasn't my dad. Disappointment weighed heavily on me.

"Riles," I said with a smile.

I set the sticks back down.

"Cass. We haven't heard from you."

I sighed. I never would have thought Riley would turn into a 'we.' The jealousy would eat me alive if I didn't get over it. "I know, but I haven't found anything."

"Not a single lead?"

I huffed out a laugh. "I'm not the PI here. You and Ty are. And Jace."

"Jace?" She latched onto that quickly. "You've seen Jace?"

"Mm-hmm. Ran into each other at a party. Some hotshot guy he's doing a job for." I purposely let out a slew of things I'd been up to since I arrived.

"Be careful, Cass."

Riley had been through a lot in her life. I knew she could get scared easily, and there were times when she had every right to be spooked. But warning me about Jace? I only needed to be careful of him charming his way into my bed.

"Reno already told me to call him if I needed help." I had never told her what he'd said on the island. It was odd that he'd mentioned it, almost as if he sensed I would need his help.

"Cass, what's going on?"

"I'm just trying to find out why my dad left in the first place. I need you to stop worrying about me so much. Can you do that?"

I could sense her hesitation through the phone. "Tell me you're being careful."

"Riley! I'm not a fucking baby."

"No need to swear at me," she shot back.

"I'm sorry for swearing at you."

"That's unusual for you." She sighed heavily. "I understand, though. Your dad is gone, and I . . . I know he meant a lot to you. I'm sorry for being so overbearing. It's the baby. I'm just all emotional."

"We all are. At least you have Ty now," I breathed. "Shoot, someone else is calling. I promise I'll be careful. Love you, Riles."

"Call soon."

I didn't answer her before I ended the call and bit my lip. How easily I had slipped. I had never been a liar. Well, I might have told a few lies in my teenage years to stay out later or avoid getting caught skipping school. But my ways had changed so much since then. No one was calling. I just couldn't do this with Riley right now. And be careful of Jace? Really?

I sat on the stool, looking around my dad's domain. This room was his pride and joy. He loved music. God, I missed him. More than I usually did.

Dialing another number, I perked up at the voice on the other end. "Shawn," I said, keeping my excitement at his answer in check. "Is the band getting together today?"

"Yes. We're at the studio, trying to accomplish something without one of our main songwriters." His response contained a hint of irritation. "You stopping by?"

"Was thinking about it. Will I be in the way?"

I knew Watts would be there. Even though he was a roadie for the band and had nothing to do with songwriting, his dad was the band manager, and he hung around the band more often than not. The band, like Shawn's, was Watts' life. No wonder they expected us to end up together. There had been a promise to, but that hadn't panned out. Not that I was shocked it didn't. I should have known not to trust Watts.

"Absolutely not. The guys would love to see you. Been way too long. We'll be here through lunch, until late afternoon at the very least."

I glanced down at my watch, more for looks than telling time. Perfect. "I'll be by then. And I'll bring lunch too."

A playful growl came through. "You really should move back here. If nothing else, to bring us lunch."

That didn't surprise me. "See you soon."

After I slid my phone back into my pocket, I picked up the drumsticks again and twirled them between my fingers like my dad had taught me. It had been so long since I'd seen the guys in the band that I couldn't help but start banging out a song on the drums.

However long it had been since I'd played, I didn't know, but it was something not easily forgotten. It wasn't until I finished that one and started another that Quinn wandered in with wide eyes.

I grinned at him, continuing to beat out a song despite the perspiration that threatened to ruin my recent shower. At least I had dressed in a pair of wide-legged pants and a light shirt. I had planned to grab a light cardigan to throw on if the weather turned out cooler than I expected. Now, I'd have to change my shirt entirely.

Once I stopped, I set the sticks on the snare where I'd found them and wiped my sweaty palms on my pants before standing up. Quinn leaned against the doorframe, still staring at me with wide eyes.

"I didn't know you could play."

"Do you play?" He shook his head, and I laughed. "It's the one thing my dad taught me. Do you want me to teach you?"

He brightened again. "You'd do that?"

"Well, I'm not nearly as good as my dad but I can teach you some basics."

"I think you're good."

This time, I laughed louder and ruffled his hair as we left the studio. I'd come back later to rummage through the desk. Papers littered the surface and could contain important information. For now, I'd talk to the band.

"I appreciate you saying so, but you don't have to lie."

"You *are* good."

We walked up the staircase to the main level. He followed me into the kitchen, watching as I opened the cupboard to retrieve the keys to the convertible. "If you want to meet up with your buddies, we can do it now or after we meet with the band."

His eyes widened again. "We'rc . . . going to see the band?"

Jesus, how sheltered was this kid?

"I need to talk to them about my dad if I'm going to find out what happened to him. Do you still want to come with?" He nodded vigorously. "Your choice is whether to meet up with your buddies now or later. We can still go to the skate park. I told Shawn I'd pick up some lunch, but we can always order and have it delivered if we go to the studio instead."

He nodded again. "Leo's at Ray's house already. I'll find out when they want to go. The park is right by Ray's house."

"We just have to stop and pick up some groceries on the way back. Find out from your buddies and grab your board. Let's go." I was just about to open the door to the garage when a shadow appeared at the front door, the doorbell ringing a second later. Quinn looked just as confused as I was about who it might be, but he quickly retreated to his room for his board while I opened the door to a delivery guy holding a massive bouquet of red roses.

"Cassie Nichols?" he asked.

I blinked. "Yes."

Without another word, he thrust the roses into my arms and dashed back down the steps as if he were behind in his deliveries.

Quinn stared at me, the board tucked under his arm and his eyes wide. There had to be at least two dozen roses in the bunch.

"Who are those from?" he asked.

Plucking the card from amidst the fragrant red mess, I carried it into the kitchen and set it on the breakfast bar. No need to search for a vase; the bouquet already included one with water and everything.

Vissar Loukas. I should have known as soon as I opened the door. Silently, I read the card, my stomach plummeting to the floor: "Meet me for dinner Sunday evening at seven. If you don't, I would hate for there to be an accident on the set of that movie your friend MacKenzie is working on. I look forward to seeing you again."

My mouth fell open as I read the address of the restaurant below. He had to be behind the attack on Dani, and he knew she wasn't me. He was fully aware of who my friends were. I looked up at Quinn, who was still staring at me, holding his board and waiting for us to get going. Something told me I was about to venture into dangerous territory.

"A guy I met at the art gallery opening last weekend," I mumbled. "Let's go!"

Chapter Seventeen

Cassie

Trying to put the chilling note and the impending dinner out of my mind, Quinn and I left the house. It was fun to drive around in my dad's convertible, especially with a kid beside me who seemed to enjoy it just as much. With the top down, we zipped through the streets of Santa Monica, taking a detour so he could show me the skate park, his school, and his friends' houses. The band's studio was located south of Santa Monica, toward Venice, and Quinn and I enjoyed the sunshine and beautiful weather as we drove.

I imagined Quinn didn't get around much if Skyler left him to himself most of the time, but I bet my dad took him out when he was home. My dad loved kids.

It seemed like Quinn divided his time between their two houses, not finding it odd when no one was home. Skyler's behavior was a mystery. Who knew what she did with all her time? Still, I had to admit the house looked fairly clean.

Gavin opened the door when we arrived, pulling me into a hug before I could even say hello. With shaggy dark brown hair and deep chocolate brown eyes, he always looked boyish. Gavin was the band's bass guitarist and youngest member, even though he didn't look a day past forty.

"You don't age, do you, Gavin?" I teased.

Quinn tentatively stayed behind me. When Gavin pulled away, he kept his hands on my shoulders and simply stared at me. I had grown up considerably since he last saw me.

"You've got to come around more often. We miss you." My brow arched. "I miss you," he amended with the same accent as my dad. "I'm positive I'm not the only one."

Throwing my arm around Quinn, I pulled him into the dimly lit studio beside me. I didn't know how they could work with hardly any light. "This is Quinn."

Gavin looked at him, scratching his head. "Hey, Quinn. Geez, been a while since I've seen you, too. Your mom sure hides you away."

All I could do was shake my head as I closed the door behind us, giving the other bandmates a nod. Apparently, they knew Quinn. We were off to a good start, and I was right that my dad took Quinn out when he was home. I tried to push it out of my mind as we walked into the control room, attempting not to bristle at Watts sitting on the couch against the far wall with his eyes on me. Old boyfriend or not, I had to admit he looked good. Older than me by only three years, I still saw him like the nineteen-year-old I fell in love with instead of someone inching toward thirty.

The recording studio was split into two rooms: the control room and the live room. The control room housed the computers, controls, and mixers, along with a sitting and kitchen area where the band took breaks and did their songwriting. The magic happened in the live room when the band recorded the music.

"I ordered pizzas," I said, dumping my purse on an empty chair. "Figured I couldn't go wrong with pizza."

All I heard were deep voices of agreement before the rest of the guys rose to come and greet me with hugs. I pushed them away, all of them having at least a foot of height on me. Poor Quinn, I thought. He'd had the good sense to stay back, at least.

"Hey, dude." Wes leaned down to him, his hands resting on his knees.

Of all the band members, Wes had always been the quietest, with short dirty blond hair and piercing hazel eyes. He sported a scruffy chin but no hair above his lip. From what I could see, he also had the most piercings in the band: ears, nose, eyebrow, and tongue.

"Hi," Quinn replied, his voice sounding small.

"Why don't you come on over and sit with me? Ever played guitar before?"

Quinn shook his head and followed Wes over to the couch, soaking up every word Wes said. Dave, with his dark dreadlocks, threw his arm around my shoulders and pulled me in closer, his lips pressing against my temple.

"Baby, you're looking good."

I pressed my hand into his lean ribs, covered with colorful tattoos beneath his shirt. "If my dad were here, you wouldn't be standing so close to me."

My growl only made him laugh and tug me closer.

"Were I ten years younger, Casanova."

This time, I pushed him away until he stumbled back. Jesus, these guys really needed to stop hanging around so many groupies and start having actual relationships. Maybe they could have a life like my dad used to.

After a quick glance toward Quinn, I turned to Shawn. Watts had the good sense to stay on the couch and not approach me with the rest of them.

"After you got back from the tour, what happened?"

I followed Shawn to the controls, and he pulled out a rolling chair for me. Once we sat down, he leaned back until I thought his chair might fall over.

"We took the rest of the week off to recoup, like we usually do. Worked all the next week, and then that Wednesday, we saw on that news show that he might be on a plane that crashed."

That damn trashy station, I thought. Breaking that false news without knowing the truth. I still wasn't certain if it helped or hurt my dad's need to get out of sight. It seemed, from the threat I'd received from Vissar, that it helped. He obviously couldn't find my dad, either.

"He didn't say anything before that? No signs that something else was going on?"

Out of the corner of my eye, I could see Watts staring at me. I wanted to groan. I had enough to deal with already.

"He took a call on Wednesday the week after we got back from tour. Seemed a little agitated afterward, but we don't know who it was." Shawn moved closer to me, blocking my view of Watts, and I knew he did it on purpose. His voice lowered. "He never got over you, you know."

I grunted. "He got over me while he was still with me, Shawn. He's your son, and I know you want to defend him. I know you wanted us to be together." I met his gaze. "God, I was sixteen!"

His hand found my arm, fingers curling around my biceps. "He's different now. More mature."

I looked him in the eyes. "Oh, Jesus Christ. Will anyone give it a rest? I am not here for a relationship. I'm here to find out what happened to my dad."

Getting up and walking away seemed like the best thing I could do. I made my way to the table where Gavin sat with Dave, poring over the pages of what they'd written so far. I slid into a chair beside them, picking up some pages to read what they had.

"Well?" Dave asked, leaning back and locking his hands behind his head.

I often wondered what he would look like without the dreads. Like Wes, he had scruff on his chin but no other facial hair. Dave's hair was so dark it was almost black. The only piercing he sported was in his earlobe, a common feature among the band members, except for Gavin. I thought Gavin might be the most well-behaved of the group.

"You need a shave," I teased Dave.

He stuck out his tongue.

"I missed you too." I set the papers down and flattened my hands on the table. "Can either of you think of anything odd about my dad before he left that day? Other than the call he took that upset him? I mean, don't you want to know why he was suddenly getting on a plane when he was supposed to be here working?"

Dave sat up, suddenly serious. "I've wracked my brain trying to think of why he would do this. There is no plausible reason, Cass. It's just not like him. We were working hard on new shit, and he was on it." He snapped his fingers. "More so than usual. Pumping it out like he had some kind of epiphany. And then, gone."

I looked at Gavin. Even younger than my dad, he was closest to him because they were both from the UK and had a lot in common. Even Shawn wasn't as close to my dad as Gavin was. It surprised me that Gavin knew nothing at all. He *had* to.

By the time the pizzas arrived, Quinn had withdrawn from whatever shell he'd displayed when we first arrived. He sat at the table, trading playful jabs with the rest of the guys as if he had known them all his life. My heart swelled with happiness that he'd clicked with the guys so well.

This only fueled my determination to get my dad back, wherever he might be. I thought about the last time I'd spoken with him, trying to recall anything in the background. He'd been out of breath, but I couldn't remember anything else. I needed to talk to Ricky and make him talk to me somehow. Ricky was his best friend, and he knew what happened; otherwise he wouldn't have hung up on me.

"You're thinking too hard." Watts stood in the doorway to the live room with his hands stuffed in his pockets.

My eyes lifted. Clad in light blue jeans ripped at the left pocket and a loose-fitting white t-shirt, Shawn's son and roadie for the Skeletons of Disciples band looked nervous. "I have to find out what happened, Watts."

Almost ten years had passed since our summer fling. That summer, Watts made me feel special. The nostalgia that plagued me now made my heart thump. My young heart didn't think I'd ever get enough of him. I still didn't understand how my dad, or even Shawn, had allowed us to continue our relationship. Even though I was sixteen and Watts was nineteen, I felt so cool for having an older boyfriend.

It had ended with him cheating on me, or at least kissing another girl, leaving me with a broken heart that still hurt when I thought about it. I realized how young and naïve I had been, but out of everyone I'd known, Watts knew cheating would crush me. I knew nothing about what I wanted for the future, and I still had a lot to live and learn. Still, I hadn't turned a blind eye to it, just like my dad.

I stayed where I was and stared at him. How many women would he have cheated on me with if I hadn't walked in on him kissing that girl in Chicago? I dragged my gaze away.

As he settled in next to me, I inhaled and exhaled deeply, as if it would change something. I'd take anything at this point. "Don't beat yourself up about it."

"I'm not."

Watts made a slow perusal of me, his light hazel eyes sweeping from my high ankle boots to my wide-legged pants and light shirt, if you could call it that. It covered my black tank top but had a see-through look to it and a wide neck that bared my shoulder. I had no choice but to change my shirt after my drumming workout. As usual, I had my hair swept up into a messy bun, with chunky wisps escaping.

"Damn," he said, his throat bobbing. "You look . . . amazing."

I kept smiling. "You look the same, Watts."

Same shaggy brown hair that looked like it direly needed a trim and that lanky build. I fought the urge to close my eyes against the onslaught of memories. No. I wouldn't be revisiting that relationship again.

My brows drew together again. "It won't be the same without him."

Concern deepened in his eyes. Charming, I mused, not about to be taken in by it. "He was the same old Lex around us."

Roars of laughter from Quinn swiveled my head around to look at them, laughing around the table and having fun. My heart lurched again. I wanted this for him. I wanted Quinn to continue to spend time with the band. He deserved this. That thought brought a smile to my face as I remembered the good times I'd had with my dad on the road.

The second a tear hit the corner of my eye, I swiped it away. "Why didn't anyone tell me that Skyler and Quinn were staying at my dad's sometimes?"

If that surprised him, he didn't show it. "What . . . you think Quinn is his?"

"Quinn said Skyler told him he is. But that's absurd." I snorted. "She's only been around for the last few years. Quinn's almost twelve."

He shrugged. "She lied to him? Why would she do that?" "Beats the hell out of me, but I've never liked her much. Seems like she's in it for the money. Not such a strange thing from my angle."

"Never was." The corner of his mouth lifted. "What've you been up to?"

"Same thing I've been doing since graduating from college."

"Do you like it? Being a therapist?"

I swung my chair back and forth, using my foot as leverage, while he reclined like his dad did earlier. "It pays the bills, I suppose."

"You always did like helping people. I've missed you, Cass."

"Don't start, Watts. I'm here to take care of my dad's stuff and try to find out what happened to him. I just got out of a relationship, and I'm not looking to get into another one."

"Come on, Cass. You can't hold this over my head forever. I made a mistake ten years ago. Can we please move past it? We're adults now."

"You were an adult then." I hung my head. "I want to stay friends. Can we at least do that?"

His hazel eyes stayed on mine, challenging. He could do that all he wanted. Watts might be a good-looking guy, but I would never shake the vision of him kissing that woman while we were in Chicago out of my mind. He nodded.

"I got over it a long time ago. It happened. We wouldn't have lasted anyway."

"We were meant to. I promised you."

I bit my lip. He had promised me, and my immature heart had clung to that promise. The one thing that probably stung the most. "We've been through this already. I didn't break that promise. You did."

When he glanced up, clearly losing patience with me, I felt guilty. "You never let me explain. What you saw wasn't what you thought. We could be married by now, Cassie."

"If we were, would you be putting your lips on other women?"

"That's not fair." His jaw clenched. "Look at you. What man in his right mind would ever do that? You forget, I might have technically been an adult then, but I was young, too. Groupies were throwing themselves at me, trying to get close to the guys. You just happened to see one catch me off guard."

I stared at him, not having heard him explain it so forcefully in all the times we'd been in each other's company since. Mentally shaking myself, I snapped out of it. The subject needed to change quickly.

"If you know anything about what my dad might have been up to, now would be a good time to tell me."

He knew my tactic, allowing me to change the subject. The air in the room had grown too thick with our drama. "I wish I could, but I don't. None of us do."

I sighed, tired of coming up empty. I might have to call Jace after all, or I'd need to stay here much longer than I'd expected. Calling him would be wise after receiving that threatening bouquet of flowers from Vissar, I thought.

Watts gave me an impish smile and stood, rejoining the party around the table a second later. He seemed to have accepted the impasse in our age-old relationship argument. I stayed where I was, watching Quinn enjoy his time with the band.

We lingered a while longer before the band had to get serious about working. Quinn and I had monopolized enough of their time, even after bribing them with lunch. Gavin walked us to the door, leaving me with parting words that lingered long after we left.

"There's a party tonight," he said. "You should come."

"I can't. I'm going to a movie premiere. Technically, I'm not here for partying, and I keep getting roped into them. I'll try to make it, but I can't make any promises."

"Ah, jumping right into the fire, huh?" His eyes stayed on mine as he quietly added, "You're going to want to be at this one, Cass."

❦

I sat on the bench, watching Quinn make moves with his skateboard, while his friends seemed more interested in me than in skateboarding. Tweener boys, I mumbled to myself. They were right at that age where they began noticing girls, but I was much too old for that. Ew. I hoped they were paying attention to girls their own age.

Kids packed the skate park. I was lucky to find a spot on the bench to watch them; otherwise I'd be leaning against the fence like the other onlookers were doing.

What did Gavin mean? Why would I want to be at this party? Would someone be there who knew something? If that were true, Gavin *knew* something. Ugh. When I slammed my back against the bench, I winced. I didn't know the first thing about detective work.

Just as my thoughts drifted to Jace, my phone vibrated with an incoming call. I quickly checked it, not wanting Quinn to think I'd brought him here just to keep him occupied. It meant a lot to me that he knew I was interested in his life-interested in him as a person.

Unknown number. Nope, I didn't do unknown numbers. Even if it didn't say "potential spam," there were too many crazed fans out there trying to get to my dad. I shook my head. Me included. Except my excuse was far more important, and I hadn't gotten any further than I had a few days ago. I'd contacted Officer Davison, but there was nothing new to report. The entire wreckage had been cleared, with absolutely zero indication that my dad had been involved, which meant everyone who had perished in the crash had now been accounted for, and it was common knowledge that my dad was alive. No one knew where he was, though. I'd managed to avoid the paparazzi and press, at least.

The last thing I wanted to admit was that I needed Jace, but his offer remained open. He'd been up at dawn, seeking me out at the beach because Kya told him where I'd be. Why? Although I'd heard certain things about Jace Taylor, he didn't strike me as the type who chased after women—only the kind who strung them along. Riley had mentioned that Ty said Jace would do anything to get a woman into bed. I had no clue what his motives could be when it came to me as aloof as I'd been around him, but if he was after getting me into his bed . . . the thought heated my body mysteriously.

I picked up my phone.

"Cassie! Are you watching?"

I looked up to see Quinn yelling and waving at me from the top of a halfpipe. I ignored my phone and watched him ride his skateboard down and back up another one. I didn't know what it was called, but he had his feet and board in the air, one hand holding the board and the other on the edge of the halfpipe. Impressed, I jumped to my feet and clapped as hard as I could, whistling through my teeth.

People stared at me, and it embarrassed him, I was sure. I laughed and sat back down. As soon as I did, his friends started calling me to watch them, too. Resigned, I watched the boys do their crazy moves for a while until my phone rang.

The name that popped up was the same one I'd programmed into my phone last weekend: Jace Taylor. That was funny. I distinctly remembered not giving him my number.

"How'd you get my number?" I answered.

"Hello to you, too," came his sultry murmur, making my heart skip several beats.

"Jace?"

"The one and only." His smooth voice sent a pleasant warmth through my skin. "Nice of you to take my call."

"How *did* you get my number?"

"How do you think?"

Of course. A cop for how many years, an undercover detective, and now he was working on becoming an independent private investigator. God only knew what other tricks he had up his sleeve. He would find my number another way. That was why he gave me his. I could have saved him the hassle and just given it to him, but where was the fun in that?

I warmed again, and it had nothing to do with the sun. Had he known I was thinking about texting him? Weird.

"Why are you calling?"

"Been thinking about you."

I snorted. "Classic pickup line. Try again."

"I've been doing a little digging."

"And?"

"Can you meet me?"

What was with these men wanting to go somewhere with me? As much as I wanted the deep love that Riley and Regan had, I couldn't handle a relationship—maybe ever. Not to mention, I had a bet to win with Regan. But unless he was bluffing, I needed whatever information he had.

"I'll make you a deal," I said, taking a deep breath for what I was about to ask. God save me from the road I was about to go down.

His sultry chuckle sent shivers along my skin. He could have been sitting right next to me, given how much his voice affected me. "What kind of deal are you offering me, Cass?"

"Do you have a suit?"

"A suit? I can get one. Why?"

"I need a date tonight. At least a fake date. It's a lot to ask of you, but . . . "

"Spit it out, Cassie."

"To a movie premiere, but there's a party afterward, I think someone has some information for m-"

Out of the corner of my eye, I saw Quinn fall, tumbling a few times before landing on his back. I swore and jumped up, ready to sprint toward him. "Quinn!"

"Quinn?" Jace asked. "Who is Quinn?"

I watched Quinn with wide eyes as he got up, shaking himself off and running back to his friends. Thank God for helmets and pads, I thought. No skinned knees or broken bones. But my heart thumped wildly still.

"Uh." Damn, how would I explain him? "He's the housekeeper's kid. I'm watching him at the skate park."

He laughed. "Why are you doing that?"

I ignored his question. "Do you want to go with me tonight or not?"

I couldn't admit how terrified I was of going to this movie premiere, even with Dar and Stirling with me. Being in front of cameras had never been comfortable for me, and I'd be doing it willingly this time. For my dad, I reminded myself. This wouldn't just be a few cameras; it would be an entire lineup and likely some questions. I wondered what Jace would think. He might not want to do this.

When he said nothing, I thought I'd scared him away. Maybe he was busy tonight. Oh God, maybe he had a date already. Then, "I'll pick you up at five. Dinner, then we'll go to this premiere. And a party after that."

Presumptuous, I thought. "That sounds like—"

"See you then."

He hung up before I could say anything else. All I could do was laugh. As a detective, he'd have my address, but why did he hang up so quickly? Did he think I would change my mind? I wanted to so badly, but I couldn't do that to Dar. She'd already called to make sure I was coming. I didn't confess to not having a date yet. And then it hit me. I'd be spending my entire night with Jace.

Chapter Eighteen

From my car, I looked through my binoculars at the skate park, focusing on the gorgeous blonde sitting on a bench, watching the kids skateboarding. When I saw her jump up, her lithe body taut with concern, I felt an uncomfortable rush of blood to my groin, as if I were no older than the boys she was watching skateboard. Damn, it didn't matter if she wore the tiniest dress or the pair of pants she had on today; she looked stunning. Well put together. Perfect, Riley had said once.

Yet the more I was around Cassie Nichols, the more she grew on me. I knew she wasn't perfect, but she looked it, and I could appreciate that.

I'd been following her all day, wondering about the kid she had with her and amused when they ended up at the skate park. To my knowledge, Cassie didn't have any kids. Her explanation about the housekeeper's kid suited me fine. I hadn't taken a single picture of her and the kid, and I wouldn't.

Vissar could badger me for information on her all he wanted, but I'd only be giving him what I chose and when I chose to. It didn't seem like there was much information to glean from her based on what she'd told me. Cassie was doing the same thing as Vissar was. They were both looking for her dad. I had to find out Vissar's reason.

Walking a fine line between Vissar and the police department, now involving Cassie in this, put me at a huge risk. I lowered the binoculars. This wasn't anything I hadn't gotten used to during my years on the police force or while working undercover. Danger always lurked somewhere. Only Ty knew that was the sole reason I didn't have a woman in my life. It wouldn't be fair to bring someone into a life that might eventually tear us apart, nor could I focus on my job knowing a woman could be used against me. Not that I'd met a woman worth it.

Almost tempted to pick up the binoculars and watch Cassie more, my cell phone rang, interrupting thoughts. I groaned at the name on the screen. Being a busy man, I would have thought he'd have better things to do than bother me, but he seemed to do it often enough.

If I wasn't spying on Cassie for him, I was spying on one of his lower thugs to ensure they weren't deceiving him. I rolled my eyes, answering the call.

"Vissar," I answered. "What can I do for you?"

"Jace," came his clipped voice. "I haven't heard anything from you about our friend Ms. Nichols. With so much on the line, I would have thought you would provide me with something by now."

I ground my teeth together. "I already gave you information about her friends. You know as well as I do that they are innocent of anything she's doing. Her friend didn't deserve to be roughed up by Tito and Xion."

He had the gall to chuckle. "Minor. They could have done much worse. I told you to get in good with her. What have you found out?"

"Not a damn thing," I snapped. "She doesn't know where her dad is. Why is this so important? If she doesn't know, she doesn't know."

"Careful, Jace. You forget that you have as much to lose if I get irritated. Never mind the fact that your little brother has a drug problem; I would hate for your mother to have an unfortunate accident."

I bristled. "I am doing what I can to get you what you need.

There is no need for threats against my family. If there isn't anything to report, you can't fault me for that."

"Right you are. But if I find out otherwise, you'll learn the hard way. That's all for now. You'll hear from me soon enough unless you find something out. Until then."

Click. I would have punched my steering wheel if I thought it wouldn't draw attention. Instead, I stuffed my knuckles between my teeth. The man knew how to irritate the hell out of me. My attention was drawn back to Cassie, who was now standing up and cheering on a boy she watched with keen interest. Lucky kid, I thought, sitting up straighter in the driver's seat.

And I had a date with her tonight. A date, I mused. How in the hell had she gotten me to agree to such a thing? No time to think about that now. I started the car and abandoned my watch on her. I had a suit to get, and I needed to stop by the police station to talk to my buddies.

An hour later, with a fresh new suit in my trunk that had set me back more money than I cared to admit, I parked my car in the police station lot and hurried inside. I'd sold my car in Seattle and used that money plus some from savings to buy a new one. It might have been frivolous to buy a BMW, but it was worth it. I'd saved up a fair amount of money working since graduating from the academy, living as frugally as possible.

I spent most of my time in my car, having to spy on people. It was one small comfort I wanted, considering the house we rented was a borderline dump. For three of us, it was cramped, and the rent was extraordinarily high. Luckily, I received a decent contractor wage from the work I was doing for the police department.

"Jace!"

Adam Davison sat behind his desk, standard-issue boots propped up next to a pile of paperwork I knew he'd been putting off. I strolled in with a tight grin. I'd known Adam since my days on the force when Ty and I had worked it before moving up to

Seattle a couple of years ago. I would never admit that I much preferred it down here to dreary Seattle, but Ty had issues back then that I wouldn't abandon him for.

"What brings you in today, buddy?"

"I got that wiretap installed for you without detection," I said, half-sitting against his desk. "If I get found out, he'll kill me for it. Just so you know."

He grinned, as though I hadn't just told him I would lose my life for putting a wire device in Vissar's head bodyguard's car. Who knew what would come of it, but I knew Vissar dealt with trafficking, and damn if I would let it continue. Even if I could do a small part to stop it, I would. Adam knew to keep it quiet should Vissar have someone inside the force working for him.

"Man, you've got guts." He sat up. "Anywhere else you can put one? His office would certainly help."

"Vissar knows I was a cop. He won't allow me in his office. Vissar's trust only extends so far, and it doesn't extend to me. In fact, he won't bother killing me; he'll take out those I care about instead, just to watch me suffer."

"The benefits of the job," Adam murmured.

"Any leads on the location of Lex Edwards?"

His eyebrow lifted. "And why would you be interested in that case?"

"You do know Ty's wife is best friends with his daughter, don't you?"

When Adam's head kicked back in laughter, I wondered if I should have even brought this up. If I could get information and get Cassie home, out of danger, I would in an instant. As much as I liked seeing her, she didn't realize the amount of risk she was in while she was here.

"I did not know that. Interesting, though. I saw her last week when she just got into town, broke the news that her dad wasn't on that plane." He planted his elbows on his desk, serious. "She doesn't know where he might be. That sucks when there's a missing person, a missing famous person, and the family has no idea where they are. The odd thing is, she didn't seem all that worried."

"Meaning?"

"She knows where he is."

I laughed. Cassie didn't strike me as a liar, but her mom had been a big-time actress. Had she been playing me and really did know where her dad was? Not that I would share that information with Vissar, but it would mean she really didn't trust me if she'd just lied to me.

"I don't think so," I breathed.

"You've talked to her?"

Damn it. "Yeah, I know her. She doesn't know where he is, Adam. If she did, I doubt she'd be down here. Cassie doesn't like being in the spotlight like her parents did."

"Huh," was all he said before leaning back in his chair and locking his hands behind his head. "She's a beautiful woman, isn't she?"

If he was trying to get me going, that was certainly one way to do it. I wasn't sure why, but I instantly went into protection mode.

My eyes narrowed, and he held up his hands in surrender. "Pretty sure you have better things to do than chase tail, Adam."

He barked out a laugh. "Coming from you! Jesus, Jace. What the hell has gotten into you? Seattle changed you, my man. Do me a favor, and if you find out anything different about Lex Edwards, let me know. I'll do the same if we hear anything incriminating through that wire."

When I stood up, Adam remained where he was, but his eyes followed me. "Please do. As soon as we get Vissar for anything, I want to be the first to know."

Chapter Nineteen

Cassie

Something I hadn't considered when I thought of this plan was that I'd actually be going on a date. With Jace. Did Jace even date? While I had a strong attraction to him when we first met, it had grown considerably each time I saw him. I thought about him constantly, and once again, I'd be leaving Quinn alone as Skyler had made herself scarce again.

"Caaaassiiiiiie!" I heard Quinn yell as I stepped out of my private bathroom.

I came downstairs to find Quinn closing the door behind Jace, and I nearly stumbled back at the sight of him. Dressed in a black suit that fit him perfectly, all the blood suddenly rushed to my head. Jace could easily fit in with any other celebrity. His eyes sparkled as they swept over me from head to toe.

I had left my hair down again and chose a slim red dress that hugged me from the bodice to just past my thighs, flaring slightly before ending at the floor. My shoulders were bare, and thin straps barely graced them while the neckline took a daring plunge, complemented by a simple diamond necklace that dripped low. Quinn rolled his eyes and walked away from us.

"You didn't have to come in," I said, carefully stepping down to him.

Jace reached his hand out to me, but I was already down the stairs and wouldn't stumble. Before I could question what he was doing, his palm smoothed up my arm, and with a quick jerk, he pulled me against him. His face was so close to mine that I thought he might kiss me. Instead, he pressed his nose against my cheek and inhaled deeply.

"You look stunning," he whispered, his voice unusually slow and deep.

Holy smokes. I could feel the strength of his arm around my waist and the hardness of his torso molded against me. The subtle smell of his cologne attacked my senses, instantly turning my insides to liquid. I felt his lips brush my cheek where his nose had just been, and my eyes fluttered closed as I welcomed the sensation churning within me.

When he pulled away, my eyes shot open. He stared into my eyes, keeping his arm firmly around my waist, his blue eyes shining. Up close, I could see rings of green around the blue, mesmerized by the color. If I thought I was in trouble with him before, I knew it without a doubt now.

Slowly, he released me as though reluctantly. My mouth wanted to form words, but it couldn't. Instead, my gaze shot to Quinn, who stared at us with wide eyes.

"Should we go?" Jace's throaty voice pulled me out of my daze.

All I could do was nod.

It took me a minute as Jace pulled me toward the door to clear my voice enough to say, "You know the drill, shortie. I'll see you in the morning."

Quinn flopped down on the couch with his movie and called over to me to have a good time, the little butthead. I couldn't help but smile as Jace led me out the door. I was growing on Quinn as much as he was on me, even though it had only been a week.

As Jace guided me outside into the cool night air toward his dark gray BMW, I briefly reflected on the events of the last few days. He kept his hand lightly on my lower back the entire way to his car. Smoothly, he opened the door for me. It didn't escape my notice that he maintained contact for as long as possible, just as he'd done when I had run into him at Vissar's house. He might have thought I hadn't noticed, but I did. He withdrew his hand, only to hold it out for me to get in. As soon as I did, he slowly slid his hand up my arm until I was settled in, then leaned down to ensure my dress was tucked into the car. Flames ignited my entire body at the contact, slight as it was.

Before he closed the door, I caught his eyes, which held an innocence I knew better than to believe. Was I really that boring? I couldn't play games with him, not the kind he likely wanted to play. But the burning feeling, mostly on my arm where he'd touched me, lingered.

"Tell me what you know," I said as soon as he got in and closed the door.

Firing up the engine, he tipped his head and laughed but didn't answer as we pulled onto the street. He was toying with me, I told myself wryly. If he thought to draw this out as long as possible, I could become a huge bitch. I instinctively put my hand over my mouth as if I had spoken the word aloud.

"Your dad might have been seeing someone."

My brows shot up to my hairline. "No way. He's been sleeping with Skyler. He definitely wouldn't be sleeping around."

"Skyler?"

"Shortie's, I mean Quinn's, mom. His housekeeper for the last few years. Obviously, they've been sleeping together." I shuddered at the thought of my dad's sex life. "He wouldn't be seeing someone else."

Jace kept his eyes on the road, but I could tell he was glancing at me from the corner of his eye. "When you talked to him last, did he sound different?"

"Yes, like something was bothering him. And the night the plane went down, he sounded out of breath, like he was walking." I frowned. "Look, when he and my mom split up, it hurt him. My mom wasn't faithful to him, not the other way around."

When he looked at me, I couldn't meet his gaze. I didn't know what Riley might have told him about my relationship issues. Regardless, I wouldn't tolerate being cheated on. Period. Maybe that was why I didn't want to give Jace a chance. It had burned me bad enough in the past with Watts and then Evan. I couldn't be with someone involved with other people, regardless of whether a relationship existed. I would invest too much in that person.

"When she died . . . " I paused, looking out the window and watching the houses pass by as I carefully chose my words. I didn't like to talk about it. Normally, I didn't. What was it about Jace that made me open up to him? It was as if he pulled these things out of me. "When she died, it tore him up. He went on a bender, and that was the last time he ever did any drugs."

"I'm sorry."

"That's how I know this has nothing to do with drugs. He'd never cheat on Skyler if they were together. And since she still sleeps there occasionally, I have to believe they are."

He looked so relaxed driving as I studied his profile. While he fit the classic mold of a man who guarded his heart, each time I talked to him, I sensed there was more to Jace Taylor than met the eye. He had a reputation for never getting into a relationship, but did anyone really know why?

Riley told me that Ty had said he'd do anything to get a woman into bed, and she was married to his best friend. Ty would know. But did Riley really know Jace? He *had* saved them both from being killed. I knew it had nothing to do with his personal life or any women he may have had. That was his job. Was he helping me now because of his instinct for saving people?

"Why are you watching me so closely?" he murmured.

When his tone was that low, it sent shivers up my spine. No wonder women threw themselves at him. If he spoke like that and we were, say, in my bedroom, I'd likely fall right into his arms. I shuddered.

"Thinking."

"About?"

"Why do you close yourself off from relationships?"

His jaw set. "Why do you?"

Riley, I muttered silently. I didn't know if I wanted to go down this road. Part of me knew why. "It's been said that I'm cold."

Rather recently, I thought.

"It doesn't seem to me like you are."

That was because I'd been slipping into my old ways for no apparent reason. That had to be the only reason he thought differently from everyone else. If I hadn't found Watts kissing another girl when I was sixteen, would we be married now? His promise had been forever, but it hadn't been a proposal of any kind. He'd promised me we'd be together forever. To my sixteen-year-old brain, that meant forever. Even I had to admit I was more fun back then. Gradually, I'd become stiff, closed off completely, cold.

I sighed. "I don't like being used."

How he'd pried that out of me, I didn't understand. I didn't talk to people about my private life; that was mine to hold on to.

"My parents split when I was younger, too," he said. "No one cheated on anyone, but my dad is a real big asshole. They did nothing but fight, and that's on them both. I guess my first actual relationship didn't end well. I was kind of a dick back then, too. She ran off with another guy."

So he'd had a relationship and been cheated on like me. That was brutal honesty. After that, nothing I could say seemed to measure up, although I itched to ask how long ago that had been. He'd been honest with me. I knew it had to be the truth because what would be the reason for lying about something like that? Now, I felt bad for giving him such a hard time.

"Don't you ever get tired? Of having woman after woman?"

He laughed. "Who told you that?"

I would never admit that.

"You have to know that you have a reputation," I said, and he looked at me with the corner of his mouth tilted up. "That's why I told you I'm not the one-night-stand type of girl."

His eyes swept over me and back up, heating my blood. "A man can't describe you as a 'girl' in a dress like that, Cass. Or any of the dresses I've seen you in."

I smiled at the compliment. "Are you trying to tell me you don't have a reputation following you around?"

"I'm not saying that. God knows I'm not innocent in that regard. But I may not have as many women in the picture you're painting." He grinned. "I don't sleep with just anyone, Cassie. I have standards."

Though I hated agreeing with him, I had to. I had standards too, some of which weren't worth the time I'd given them. Most recently, Evan. Prick, I muttered beneath my breath.

"Did you just call me a prick?"

I laughed. "No. The guy who broke up with me while we were in Cape Haven. He was a prick."

"I knew it," was all he said, albeit slyly.

It didn't take us long to reach the quaint restaurant tucked into the outskirts of Santa Monica. Jace came around to help me out of the car before I could get out myself. Thankfully, because I was worried that if I moved the wrong way, the dress would rip. That would be embarrassing. He kept his arm slung casually around my waist, just enough to ward off any wandering eyes. I had to admit, it gave me a titillating thrill when he caught the gaze of several men, who glanced away. Anyone who looked our way would see we were overdressed. When we arrived at our table, he dropped his arm and pulled out my chair. At least he acted like a gentleman, I thought.

"Tell me about this guy who broke up with you. Is that why you're not interested in another relationship?"

I eyed him with caution as the server approached for our drink order. The restaurant had an intimate atmosphere, with dim lighting and candlelit tables. I could see the glimmer in Jace's eyes. He truly made me curious about him. That was something.

I told him about what happened when we first saw each other on the beach and the text I'd just received from Evan. Then, I shared the details about going to the bar with Tish and what had transpired, ending with me nearly sleeping on my doorstep. He listened attentively without interruption, even when the server returned to pour two glasses of red wine.

"Sounds like a prick."

"I don't drink much." He raised his eyebrows. "One glass limit. Except that night, I might have had more than one. Pretty sure he didn't think I'd be there with Tish."

When he took my hand and drew his thumb over the back of it, surprise coursed through me. His touch felt like the barest brushstroke of a paintbrush. "I promise not to let you sleep on your doorstep tonight."

"Thanks, but I don't think I'll be drinking that much for a while."

"That's a relief."

"What? Why?"

"You would hate me in the morning." He had the decency to look guilty and pulled his hand away from mine to emphasize his point. "I find it hard to keep my hands off you. I have a rule never to make the first move with women, and I'd hate to break that rule with you."

That shocked me. He had rules? "I'm not sure what to think about you, Jace."

My blatant honesty slipped out so easily. At least it wasn't a lie. His eyes lit up, making him more enigmatic. I hadn't completely closed down the idea of us. Together.

"You asked me to go surfing last weekend. Didn't you grow up in Seattle?"

He nodded, sipping his wine. "Until my parents split. I spent the summers here and the school year in Seattle. I came down here for college and the police academy."

"And your brother?"

"Ezra. He packed it up and moved down here right after graduation. He works in a surf shop down the road. Our old man wanted us to go into the army like he did. Pissed him off that I didn't become a military man. But becoming a cop was close enough, I suppose."

"And he's still in Seattle?"

As he nodded, the server returned to take our order. We were so engrossed in our conversation that we hadn't looked at the menu. I enjoyed talking to Jace. It came so easily. How interesting it was, splitting his time between here and there—a little like me going on tours with my dad.

Jace pointed out a few things we could order and share, knowing that I liked to eat healthy. It seemed like he knew me pretty well based on what Riley had told him, which made me curious about what else she might have said.

"What did Riley tell you about me?"

He frowned, leaning back. "What do you mean?"

"She must have told you something."

"I don't talk to Riley as much as you think I do. What I know about you is that you take care of yourself. I only know that because we shared a living space for three days." He shrugged his broad shoulders. "But who was counting?"

A smile lifted the corners of my mouth. He paid enough attention to me in Cape Haven to be cautious of what I put into my body. What he didn't know was that while he did that, I had been doing the same. I knew he worked out by his physique, but he didn't do it routinely like I did. We'd both been lazy about it while in Cape Haven.

"I *try* to be healthy," I corrected.

"Then you won't beat me up for having pizza and beer in my fridge?"

A laugh burst from my throat.

"I take that as a no."

A wisp of hair slid down my shoulder when I shook my head. His eyes darkened. "If I judged others for their lifestyle, wouldn't that give them the right to judge mine? Unless their lifestyle hurts me, I can't do that." I turned serious. "The last thing I want is to be hurt. That's probably why I'm keeping everyone at arm's length."

"I understand. But what's it going to take to bend your arm?"

I stared at him, thinking about how he had pulled me to him so suddenly earlier. I couldn't recall a single time when a man had been so spontaneous with me. Respectful, yet giving me all the signs that there might be a spark of something more. My eyes closed. I had done this to myself by choosing only safe men to date. I also chose men who eventually walked away.

"Hey," he said, the soft drawl of his voice reaching me before he took my hand, and my eyes popped open. "You okay?"

I shook my head. "I'm fine."

"You're telling me something different again."

His eyes held mine, filled with concern, while his tone carried a hint of teasing. I let out a soft laugh. "I'm okay. Just lots of years . . . closing myself off."

"Cassie," he murmured, his slow drawl captivating my attention and making me hang onto his every word. "Nothing I say is going to convince you that I'm not out to hurt or use you. But I don't set out to use people or hurt them. That's just not me."

We kept the conversation casual, even after our dinner arrived and we picked at the food. Jace hardly touched his wine, but I needed to keep drinking mine to occupy my hands. I kept to my rule of only having the one glass. When we finally left the restaurant for the premiere, my head swam with emotions.

The feel of his hand resting low on my back as we approached the car heated my skin through the thin fabric of my dress. His fingers, strong and sure, grasped mine to help me into the car, causing my heart to thump erratically in my chest. There was no doubt in my mind that, where Jace was concerned, I was in deep.

Chapter Twenty

I gave Jace directions to Dar's house, and we arrived just in time to join her and Stirling in a limousine taking us to the arena.

The four of us chatted while we drove, my nerves growing all the while. Jace kept his hand on mine, as though he sensed what I was feeling. I had to admit; he didn't appear to be star-struck. He behaved perfectly normal. Like me.

When we pulled up to the line, slowly inching toward the red carpet, Jace squeezed my hand. "Are you ready for this?" I leaned over and asked him.

"Are you?"

I smiled. "Have you ever done anything like this before?"

"Absolutely not, but it doesn't bother me like it does you. I'll be right by your side, Cassie." He lifted our joined hands and kissed the back of my hand. "I won't let you go."

"There'll be cameras. Lots of them," I warned.

"I've watched TV."

I laughed. Watching entertainment programs and reading about them in magazines was far different from actually attending them, I thought. He'd find that out as soon as the limousine stopped at the red carpet.

Dar and Stirling got out first and started down the line. Jace got out next, straightening his suit before turning to offer me his hand. Like a gentleman, he waited until I made sure my dress was properly straightened.

Groups of celebrities dotted the red carpet in clusters, talking with reporters and posing for pictures. The décor for the movie premiere was jungle-themed, reflecting the action-packed setting of the film. I stared down the aisle with wide eyes, my heart beating uncontrollably.

Jace tucked a wayward strand of my hair back. "You should wear your hair down all the time. I love it."

My eyes widened even more when the usher directed us to walk. After a deep breath, Jace grabbed my hand and held it tightly as we began our descent in front of the rows of flashing cameras. I could see Dar and Stirling further down, chatting with the host and wondered how they'd gotten through so quickly.

Glancing up at Jace, he looked cool and collected. I wished I could be like that. He'd been honest when he said he wouldn't let me go, holding my hand as we walked and periodically stopping for photos. The bright flashing lights were making me disoriented and dizzy after drinking wine at dinner. Every so often, we stopped to talk to reporters asking questions about Dar and my relationship with her. Most were polite and didn't ask probing, uncomfortable questions. We were almost through.

Then a reporter yelled out to me, "Ms. Nichols, can you comment on your dad not being in that airplane crash as originally reported?"

The air in my lungs seized, and I felt Jace's hand tighten around mine. He took a step toward the reporter while I maintained my composure, holding his hand back. Don't do it, Jace, I silently pleaded. They love scenes.

"Ms. Nichols has no comment at this time," he said smoothly, pulling me away from him—not in a hurry—but fast enough to create some distance between us.

I released my breath when we reached the host, glancing up at him with wide eyes. He brushed his knuckle against my cheek and leaned down to kiss the spot he had just touched.

We bypassed the host, not needing to do an interview since we had no part in the movie. I wasn't sure I could have stopped for an interview after that. The reporters we'd spoken with had been respectful. This one had blurted that out like I would confess everything I knew about the situation. True, he hadn't been on that airplane but everyone knew he hadn't been seen, either.

As we entered the building, I accepted a champagne glass, and we drifted in to join Dar while she chatted with some other A-list actors. I knew them, of course, introducing Jace to anyone I could to make him feel more comfortable, even if I didn't feel the same way. He seemed so at ease, like this was nothing to him. The reception went by quickly before we were ushered into the theater to take our seats.

"Maybe I should have talked to that reporter and asked him what he knew."

He shook his head. "Wouldn't that just invite more rumors?" He was right. "Keep it under wraps for now. Enjoy the evening. You made it through the lion's den like a champ."

I smiled. I made it through.

After the movie played, the crowds moved through the reception area and prepared to leave for the after-parties. Dar hugged me tightly, as if she wouldn't let go, while Jace talked to Stirling.

"You should come to the after-party. It'll be so much fun, and it's been such a great night already," she said. "Please, Cassie. I beg you. Your dad-"

"Dar," I replied, knowing she would make me give in to her begging. "I already promised someone I'd stop at another party. Truly, I can't thank you enough for inviting us tonight, though." I glanced over to Jace, who caught my eye with a wicked grin. "It wasn't nearly as bad as I thought."

"See? Maybe you want to go into the business like your mom?"

I stared at her in horror. "Absolutely not."

She laughed. "But it's so fun! Your mom loved it, and she was an amazing actress. We truly lost some talent when she died."

My stomach pitched every time I thought about that night ten years ago. I could have been the one to prevent it—damn me. What a horrible person I was. Shaking it off, I smiled at Dar, engaging my best acting skills.

"We did," I agreed.

"We'll do lunch before you leave for Seattle?"

"If you can fit me into your busy schedule. When is your next movie scheduled to shoot?"

I dreaded the thought of going back to dreary Seattle already, even though I'd been here for a week. I loved my home there, along with Naomi and Hannah, but being here brought back something I didn't realize I'd been missing. The last time I had been here I hadn't felt the same nostalgia as what I was experiencing now.

"I leave for New Zealand in a week. We'll see if we can fit it in. If anything, maybe you can come over for a visit."

Jace and Stirling rejoined us, with Jace sliding his arm around my waist protectively. "I'll see what I can do," I said as she leaned over to kiss my cheek.

We said our goodbyes and walked back to the waiting limousines. I said nothing, lost in thought about going home. The absence of a rigorous schedule felt different. Surprisingly, I didn't miss it as much as I thought I would. This freedom was something new. Not that I didn't want to work—I did. I just wasn't sure if being a therapist was still my calling.

"You okay?" Jace murmured.

I shook my head. "Mm-hm."

"Cassie," he growled, "you're giving me mixed signals again."

We reached the limousine, and the driver opened the door for us. Jace extended his hand, but as soon as I slid my hand into his I realized he wouldn't release me until I gave him a straight answer. I smiled.

"I'm fine."

Once I was inside, he climbed in and sat next to me. "Are you telling me the truth? You had a very distant look on your face for a while. Want to tell me about it?"

"No."

I closed my eyes. This was exactly how I pushed everyone away. Jace would interpret my silence as coldness, and he would run the hell away from me. I had let him into my life more than I intended, more than I had with anyone else. When I opened my eyes and glanced at him, he was looking at me with a raised brow.

"I never wear red," I blurted.

He laughed softly. "I don't think that's what you were thinking so hard about."

God, how could he see through me so clearly? I let my head fall back against the seat with a small laugh. "But it's true."

Pulling my hand into his, he rubbed his thumb over the sensitive skin of my knuckles. "I would never use you as a ticket to fame. That is not something I would ever do, despite what others in your past may have done."

"I'm sure you knew about me before the wedding, and you didn't come chasing after me, so I think that's safe enough to assume." I sighed, meeting his gaze. "Not everyone has used me for that, though. I've just learned to be very private over the years. I've told you more about myself in this last week than I've told anyone in an entire seven-month relationship."

He grinned. "I'm honored."

"You probably should be."

C∿

By the time we arrived at the party, I felt comfortable with Jace in a way I hadn't thought possible after our conversations in Cape Haven. I might have misjudged him. That didn't mean I would fall into his arms by the end of the night, although I allowed him to touch me again as he helped me out of the car. It was almost as if I couldn't get enough of him. The fact that he told me he never made the first move, yet admitted he had a hard time keeping his hands off me, made my heart race.

Possessive without being overbearing, he didn't put his arm around my waist as we entered the house party. Instead, he slipped his hand into mine and intertwined our fingers. When he looked at me as we went in, silently asking for permission, I smiled.

"We are severely overdressed for this party," I told him as he opened the front door and the loud music blasted us.

He chuckled. "Just makes for more interesting conversation."

The house had windows all around the main level and was one of the more unique places I'd ever seen, with a large office immediately to the left of the entryway and a massive open stairway with floating steps leading up to the second level. People were everywhere, and the music blared so loudly from the sound system that it was a surprise the windows were still intact.

All I heard were whistles as we walked in, my face betraying my embarrassment at being the center of attention once again. It would never end, I thought, as Jace pulled me further into the house.

"Cassie!" I heard from the kitchen in the far right corner of the entryway.

Over the heads of the crowd, I spotted Dave holding up a beer can. Jace tugged my hand and pulled me through the throng, nearly having to push people out of the way. It had been a while since I'd been at a party packed with this many bodies.

Dave and Wes were in the kitchen in front of a blender, happily mixing drinks for the crowd. I couldn't hear anything they were saying until Jace and I were standing right next to them.

"Ooh, girl!" Dave's eyes lit up at my attire, waggling his eyebrows at Jace with a grin before chugging his beer.

Wes leaned down, pushing his shoulder into mine. I felt Jace's hand tighten around mine and glanced at him, noticing his jaw was taut. When I looked back at Wes, his eyes hadn't moved past the neckline of my dress. I gave him a shove back, earning myself a devilish grin before he returned to his spot next to Dave.

"Almost twice my age," I murmured to Jace, who eased his grip on my hand but didn't let go. "My dad would kill him if he touched me."

Dave raised his eyebrows after hearing my comment to Jace.

"You too, asshat," I growled.

"Casanova!" Dave admonished, pushing the button on the blender and taking another chug from his beer. He looked at Jace. "You let her kiss you with that mouth?"

"Not yet," I murmured, trying to keep my voice low.

The smile that lifted Jace's mouth was anything but innocent. I knew that if it kept up, I wouldn't be able to resist him. Not after such a lovely dinner and for keeping me grounded at the premiere.

Jace leaned down, his lips nearly touching the curve of my ear. "Casanova?" came his delectable whisper.

"You guys want a beer? Margarita? Wine, Cassie?" Dave asked, and I nodded.

One glass at dinner, which was hours ago. And the small bit of champagne at the movie premiere reception, a glass of wine now was safe enough. So long as it was only one and didn't lead to two. My resolve had always been a lot stronger, at least when not around Tish.

"None for me," Jace replied.

Ignoring him, I yelled at Dave, "Where's Gavin?"

He shrugged. "Around here somewhere."

I turned toward the crowd, wondering how soon I'd be able to find him in this mob. Jace grabbed the glass of wine from Dave and handed it to me. For a heavy metal band, the music playing surprised me: hard rock, but not heavy enough to get the blood pumping. I didn't need any help in that area with Jace next to me and his hand wrapped around mine.

As I took a sip, I eyed him. "My last glass was hours ago. I'm safe enough having this one."

He leaned down, his breath tickling the hair around my ear as he whispered, "I trust you."

The room suddenly grew very warm. I sipped my wine, hoping the heat didn't bring a flush to my face. I've never been someone who blushed easily. He might trust me, but did I trust myself?

As we pushed our way through the crowd, Jace kept at least one hand on me until we finally found Gavin. He leaned over to kiss my cheek but refrained from staring at my chest, as Wes so blatantly did.

"Gavin, this is Jace. Jace, Gavin is one of my dad's bandmates. He plays bass guitar," I said, smiling at him with pride. "One of the best."

"Any friend of Cassie's is a friend of mine," Gavin said, shaking Jace's hand.

Gavin jerked his head toward the back of the house, leading us to a deck with far fewer people.

I welcomed the clear, cool air. The end of September brought slightly cooler evening temperatures off the coast and tonight had a slight breeze to top it off. I needed the cool air.

"Thanks for coming by the studio today, Cass," Gavin said.

The twinkling lights of LA surrounded us, making the view from where we stood spectacular. I watched Gavin's shaggy hair blow in the breeze. He couldn't be more right. I was glad I'd gone to the studio and taken Quinn with me. It felt good to be back, although I wished I'd visited sooner and more often. I missed it here in some small way.

We moved toward the side of the deck, away from the door where people were coming and going. Jace stood close to me, blocking the breeze. Ever the gentleman, I thought with a smile.

"You don't mind me spilling secrets in front of him, Cass?" Gavin asked.

"No, please do."

"There are things I didn't want to say in the studio." Gavin scratched his head. "To be honest, I'm not sure this is the place to say them, either. But since you're here, you're going to see it soon enough."

"See what, Gavin?"

I was freaking out a little, finally getting something that might lead me toward answers. My hand fell to my side, reaching back until I felt Jace's hand slide solidly around mine. How, after knowing this man for such a short time, had he become my rock so quickly? Easy. With my dad gone, I had no one else.

Gavin looked around before moving closer. Jace tightened his grip on my hand. I held my breath and waited.

"Skyler and Shawn are having an affair."

Chapter Twenty One

Disgust built in the center of my chest, threatening to crawl up into my throat. Quinn . . . I closed my eyes and shook my head. If this was true, she didn't deserve a single ounce of my dad or his time.

"How long?" I whispered. "Are they truly together, Gavin? I mean, is it serious enough with my dad that if she's carrying on with Shawn, it's cheating?"

He nodded. "They've been serious enough, but you haven't been around to see it. Not something you tell your daughter over the phone. I've only known about this thing with Shawn and Skyler for about a month. Who knows how long it's been going on?"

"Does . . ." I cleared my throat. "Did my dad know?"

Gavin shrugged. "If he did, he never told me he knew."

"How did you find out?"

"I got one of those accidental texts. From Shawn." He leaned closer to me. Jace's grip tightened again, on alert. "Not a text someone would want to send to the wrong person, if you know what I mean."

I gasped. "No. Not a picture of—"

"Not that." He shuddered. "Thank God, not that. But a text with a lot of words that I wouldn't repeat to anyone. Ever. I couldn't delete it fast enough."

"But you didn't tell Lex about it?" Jace asked.

Gavin looked at him. "No. I was trying to think of a way to tell him. After your mom broke his heart all those years ago, I wasn't sure how to say it. I knew he'd want to know, need to know. I just . . . How do you tell someone that?"

My poor dad, I thought. He'd been as unsuccessful in the relationship department as I had been, although I wasn't sure the fault had been his all the time. Unlucky, maybe. But to be cheated on again. And Quinn. I still wasn't sure what to think of the possibility that he might be my brother. Fury swept through me. If she put some bullshit into Quinn's head about my dad being his dad to extort money from him, and was now moving on for more money, I'd have words with her that I'd not likely regret. There was a reason I closed myself off, and it was people like her looking to make a buck off of people like my dad.

Trembling swept through me. "I need to go to the bathroom."

I pushed out of our circle, but Jace held my hand tightly and turned with me. "Cass. Are you okay? Tell me the truth."

"I just need a minute. I'll only be a minute."

Reluctantly, he let go, and I fled into the house. I found the bathroom around the corner near the back of the stairway—luckily vacant—and shut the door behind me. I set my wine down and ran my hands under cold water to press against my cheeks.

That feeling in the pit of my stomach wouldn't go away. Shawn and Skyler seemed oblivious to anything going on when I'd talked to them separately. Did they have anything to do with him planning to get on that plane in the first place? Or being in trouble, having to run?

I stared at my reflection in the mirror, thinking the worst and not knowing what to think anymore.

"I need Jace," I told my reflection. "He's the only one who can help. I need to trust him. With everything."

Whirling around, I abandoned my wine and rushed out of the bathroom, only to run right into Watts. His arms came around me, capturing and cornering me in a dark part of the hallway.

"Cass," he breathed, leaning closer. "You look . . . wow."

He didn't smell like he'd been drinking, and he wasn't being pushy as he caged me against the wall. Even as lanky as he was, I knew he wouldn't be forceful. Watts wasn't that kind of guy. But he made no move to kiss me.

Tousled hair, smoking hazel eyes. Watts looked dangerously good. For someone else, I thought. Compared to Jace, he didn't hold a candle. Not anymore. It just wasn't there for me. Friends were about as close as Watts and I could get now.

"Things haven't been right between us since Chicago." He reached down, toying with the diamond necklace that rose and fell with each breath I took. "You can't say you haven't thought about it. About us. I have. A million times. Every time I close my eyes."

"Are you sure you aren't confusing me with the girl you had your mouth on in Chicago?"

He laughed, leaning closer. "I miss your wit, Cassie. I was nineteen and stupid."

"And I was sixteen, underage, and naïve."

His eyes shined. "Are you going to keep hanging that over my head? It was a stupid thing to do, and I regret it every day. I should have pushed that girl away. I did push her away, but you'd already seen what you did."

"Are you blaming me?"

When his hand slid up to cradle my jaw, I froze. The familiarity of his touch, even when he leaned closer, shocked me into stillness. Memories rushed through my mind, nine years sweeping right back as though it were yesterday. How much I thought I'd loved him.

I blinked, reaching up to pull his hand away from my face.

"Watts, no matter what happened all those years ago, it's done," I whispered. "I'm not rekindling this with you. I'd hate to jeopardize our friendship."

"Why?"

"Because she's with me."

My breath caught at the sound of Jace's deep voice behind us. Watts grudgingly turned, allowing me to escape the circle of his arms. Immediately, Jace swooped in, sliding his arm greedily around my waist and pulling me against him.

Watts' jaw flexed. "You said you weren't in town for that, yet here you are."

"Watts," I said. "This isn't what it looks like. Please, understand."

He threw up his hands and walked away from us without a backward glance. What could he possibly be thinking, trying to rekindle something from nine years ago? I didn't know what love was back then, and I still didn't know what it was now!

My dad hadn't been oblivious to Watts and me being a thing on that tour. He turned a blind eye, and I had a feeling he and Shawn figured that we'd end up together. That somehow my life would always have a connection to the band. It did, and it would. Just not in the way they probably thought it would. I held wonderful memories from that tour, regardless of Watts and me going our separate ways afterward. I heaved a deep breath.

"Tell me you're okay." Jace's voice washed over me.

I shook my head. "Yes."

I felt the rumble of his laugh. "There you go again. Shaking your head is telling me something different."

Lowering my cheek to his biceps, the roughness of his suit jacket oddly comforting, I hid my smile from him. I couldn't help it. "This is hard to deal with."

"Want to tell me about it?"

"What, my ex-boyfriend who wants to get back together with me after over nine years? I was sixteen and stupid. I'm not the same girl."

Jace smoothed his hand up my bare arm. "Can't say I blame him, but that's not the way to go about it."

Still curled against his rock-solid body, I looked up at him. "I need your help, Jace."

"Really? I didn't sense that."

I smacked him in the stomach, only to meet rippling hard abs. Dear God, how many crunches did he do to get those? He chuckled and pulled me out of the darkened corner and back into the crowd.

When he found out I'd left my wine behind, he offered to get me another glass, but by that time, I didn't want even another sip though I'd barely had a quarter of the glass I'd had.

Jace and I talked with Dave and Wes for a while, and before long, it was inching toward morning. I hated leaving Quinn alone at home, even knowing I had locked the door and activated the security system.

As we were leaving, I noticed Shawn coming down the stairs with Skyler right behind him, their hands interlocked. Her eyes widened when she saw me, and her face turned a shade of pink at being caught with someone she shouldn't be with. It was strange that I hadn't seen either of them all night, yet here they were, coming from the upper level where the bedrooms were located. The band had been partying here, along with members of other bands. It didn't take a rocket scientist to assume this was Shawn's house.

"Cassie," Shawn said, releasing her hand.

Ignoring him, I stared hard at Skyler, shaking my head slowly in disgust. Disgusted for them both since my dad had ditched town for a reason, but neither of them seemed to care. But I had to think about Quinn. She could take him and flee, and even after a week, it would break my heart. When I found my dad, it would break his heart, too. If Quinn turned out to be his, that was a different story. Without a doubt, I knew he had probably formed an attachment to Quinn.

Tread lightly, I told myself.

"Cassie, wait," Shawn tried again. "It's not what it looks like."

I watched Skyler stop on the staircase, waiting for Shawn to approach me. Did she think he would convince me that my eyes were deceiving me? That I didn't see two people close to my dad stab him in the back with their lies?

"He trusts you," I said through clenched teeth. "Does he know?"

He shook his head, eyes remorseful. "We didn't intend for this to happen. We didn't know he would take off out of town." My

eyes flashed. "You know why he left? Where he went?"

"I told you I don't. We don't know anything. Skyler was going to tell him, but then he left and we haven't heard from him since."

My stomach felt hollow while I stared at her. This time she didn't battle back with biting words. "I suppose you're incredibly disappointed that he wasn't on that plane after all. Would have made it so easy for her to move on."

Shawn gasped. "Cassie, it's not like that. Of course, we don't want him dead! We want to know what happened, just as you do. We didn't mean for any of this to happen. It just . . . did."

Casting a glance at Jace, I couldn't tell what he might be thinking. I didn't know what to think. Here were two people deeply involved in my dad's life that had been lying to him for months, or more, still carrying on even though he was gone. Maybe not dead, as he'd been presumed at first, but still missing. This was the reason I didn't trust anyone.

Jace waited for me to make my move, and I did—right the hell out of that house.

Chapter Twenty Two

When I woke up the next morning, my eyes felt like sandpaper, despite only having had technically one glass of wine and early in the evening. The ping of my phone stirred me from sleep. I glanced at the clock and groaned. It was way too early to be awake. I had forgotten what a fast-paced life I had flung myself into.

I almost ignored the message but then remembered the tidbits of information from the party. Tidbits, I scoffed. My dad's girlfriend was having an affair with one of his friends—his *band manager*. Stupid, ignorant me. Was that what she was doing when she wasn't here for Quinn? Peeling my eyes open more fully, I grabbed my phone and read the message.

Already snuggled deep within the thick white comforter and whisper-soft sheets, warmth spread throughout my body as if I had just taken a huge gulp of hot chocolate.

"Thinking about u," I read from the text message I received from Jace. "Thought about u all nite. I'l bring u tea. Say the word." I buried my head into the fluffy pillow and groaned, knowing I was done for and wondering whether he knew it or if this was simply his nature. I wanted to call Riley, but I didn't want to give Ty even a hint of this. Texting her was off-limits, too. I couldn't risk it getting back to Jace.

Phone still clutched in my hand, I looked back at the text. He had seen that I'd read it. I had to respond. Damn.

"I'd take tea, but I feel . . . " Frowning, I deleted the text. "I'd take tea, but I have some."

Ugh, I groaned and deleted that one, too. I didn't know what to say in response. Torn between asking him to come over with the tea and trying to come up with a witty reply, I settled on: "Glad u were with me last nite. May need tea later."

When he responded with a heart emoji, I flopped my head back down and tried to squeeze in a few more hours of sleep, wearing a dreamy smile. As if I could, with my mind racing with thoughts of only him. How could he be awake already? Ordinarily, I would be, but the days had been stressful lately, leading to insomnia.

I tossed around in bed for another hour before dragging myself out and downstairs to make my own herbal tea. Quinn had his eyes glued to a video on his phone, scooping heaps of cereal into his mouth with no regard for the milk dribbling onto the countertop.

"Morning," I said, reaching for a coffee cup.

I would need to invest in a teapot if I stayed longer than planned. The thought of booking a hotel room and escaping any confrontations with Skyler seemed viable but not with Quinn. He was alone entirely too much as it was. I wasn't about to do that to him, not with my dad still gone. At least when he returned from tour, he would be home in the evenings after studio sessions.

"Uh-huh," he replied, but it came out garbled.

I wanted to ask him if he'd seen his mom, but I didn't truly want to know. "What are you doing today, shortie?"

He shrugged.

"Want to go to the beach later?"

"The beach? What for?"

I laughed. "Walk around, maybe grab some lunch. If you don't want to . . . "

"Sure."

"I've got more calls to make today, and I'll probably be poking around in my dad's studio for a bit, but we'll go later on." I leaned against the counter, waiting for my water to heat. "Do you have a girlfriend?"

He pulled a face.

"I'm serious! At your age, you must think about girls. Talk to your friends about them. How they're so annoying but cute at the same time. And their little—"

I watched as his chewing slowed. "Cassie, stop." He slowly shook his head, eyes wide, which only made me laugh at how easily I could tease him. "No."

"Not a single girl you might have a tiny crush on?"

"Like Jace does on you?"

That threw me off. "What do you know about that?"

He grinned as if he'd caught me. The brat. "I saw him looking at you when he picked you up last night." His eyebrows waggled. "He likes you."

"You think?" I asked, then sighed. "Don't answer that. I don't want to know if he likes me or not. I'm not eleven."

"Almost twelve."

I chuckled. "When my dad is home, do you hang out with him?"

He stared at me. "Yeah. We play video games, and he takes me to the skate park. Sometimes he takes me to the studio to see the guys, but it's been a while. Mom just won't let me tour with him."

"Good. I'm glad he spends time with you."

Saved by the microwave beep, I took my tea and went back to my room to get ready for the day, hurrying away from the little twerp's laughter. He totally turned my questions about him liking girls around on me. And I loved it. My mind warred between thoughts of Jace, worries about my dad, and figuring out this home life thing with Quinn and Skyler. I knew I wouldn't avoid a confrontation with her; it would depend on when she stayed here, if she ever did.

With her being gone so much, it seemed she'd already ended her relationship with my dad. She would never admit it to me, even if I asked. I would have a big decision to make if my dad never came back. I cringed. Reporters were still camped outside, trying to get a statement from me about where my dad was. I still had no comment. As time passed, they'd eventually leave.

I was getting ahead of myself, but even when I stepped into the shower, I couldn't turn my brain off. Too many things were running through it. I settled for thinking about Jace. Once I started, I couldn't stop.

By the time I got out of the shower, I was no better off. I finished getting ready, grabbed another cup of tea, and headed down to the basement studio. As I shuffled through his papers, I found a bunch of handwritten music that made me wonder if the band had seen them. After that, I didn't think I'd get to anything of importance. Might as well organize his desk, I thought.

Hours had passed before the door opened and Skyler breezed in. I stopped, setting the papers down carefully as she closed it behind her. Oh, this would be fun. Her chin tilted up as she approached me.

"Do you really think you should snoop?"

I tilted my head, curious. "Afraid I'll find something I shouldn't?"

"No," came her snap. "That's your dad's business, not yours. He's still alive, you know. Just not here."

I leaned back in the office chair. "Are you sure about that? Because I sure the hell am not. No one knows where he is, and if someone does, they aren't saying. What the hell is going on, Skyler? Cheating on my dad? Really?"

Her eyes narrowed. "You heard Shawn last night. We didn't mean for it to happen. Just think of it as two friends walking down a stairway."

"Really? Is that what it is? Or are you just afraid he'll find out you're fucking the band's manager, who is also his friend? And what about Quinn? You've only been with my dad for three years, and you told him that Lex is his dad? What is wrong with you?"

"Lex *is* Quinn's dad!" she shot back. "You don't know anything. You don't live here to understand what happens."

"I'm not fucking stupid. I went to school, and three years does not equate to an eleven-year-old kid."

I should be ashamed of my language, but anger took hold and wouldn't let me go. I wanted to hold on to it. I wanted to lash out. Damn her.

It felt as if trying to erase vulgar words from my vocabulary had only built them up, making it impossible to stop the flow now. That was all it seemed I'd been doing lately. God, my entire life was flashing before my eyes, reverting back to my stupid adolescent years. I just couldn't stop myself anymore. I wanted to put my hands around her neck and shake her for what she was doing to my dad and Quinn.

She lifted her chin. "I'm not a liar."

"No, but you are hiding something. What is it?"

"I'm not hiding anything, Cassidy. You go on ahead and look through his papers, but I doubt you'll find anything in that mess."

"What did you do to my dad? Did you and Shawn do something to him that made him have to leave?"

Bitterness laced her laugh. "You watch too many movies. Like Quinn."

"That's all he has to do!" I leapt to my feet, ignoring the papers that flew off the desk from my sudden movement. "You aren't home for him. What else can the poor kid do other than watch TV and movies?"

She took a step toward me. Put your hands on me, I thought silently. I dare you. Do it. I tilted my chin up, seething silently behind my glare.

"You don't know a damn thing," she said between clenched teeth.

"You know what I *do* know? I grew up the same. Exact. Way. No one here for me. My mom wasn't there. And it was a lonely, miserable life. I learned to rely on myself. And here I am, twenty-five years old and still relying on myself." I nearly choked at my realization. "I'm the only person I can rely on," I finished softly, tears springing to my eyes.

Her eyes held a split second of understanding before she whirled away and slammed out of the room. I looked down at my hands, clenched into fists at my sides. When had I ever been so mad? I wasn't the type of person to get this irate.

Thank God the room was soundproof and Quinn couldn't hear anything that had come out of my mouth. Would he hate me for what I said to his mom? Feelings for Skyler aside, she was his mom. My mom was just as neglectful, though I understood part of it was because of her demanding career. It didn't stop me from loving her. It hadn't always been bad with her.

Sinking to the floor, hot tears trailed down my face and splashed heedlessly onto my hands. I couldn't remember the last time I'd cried. I held everything inside. I did yoga, I ran, I worked. Everything was like clockwork in my life. I took care of everything, and I did so well that I'd lost sight of it all. It took me a few minutes of just crying before I finally picked myself up.

Returning to the chair, I took a few deep breaths to calm down before I continued weeding through the papers. There was so much; it would take all day to get through it all. After a while, I checked my watch and decided it was time to get out of the house.

I'd get back to it later. My dad had to have something around here that would give me a clue about where he might be. Travel plans, receipts, anything. Based on the timeline I pieced together, the person he took a call from at the studio that day caused him to skip town. And he had wasted no time. There might be nothing here to find.

Desperation was setting in. I knew who I had to talk to: Ricky. When I last spoke with him, he made it clear he would not talk to me.

Quinn and I grabbed ice cream cones from a food truck near the pier and sat down in the sand to watch the surfers. This state, this beach, was the best for people-watching. The waves weren't huge, but the surfers were doing a pretty good job of catching them.

"Thought I'd find you down here."

I looked up as Mac joined us, plopping down in the sand and stretching out her long, suntanned legs as she tipped her freckled face up to the sun. I was happy to see she looked well, despite the threatening flowers I'd received yesterday. I hadn't forgotten about the dinner I had no choice but to go to tomorrow. It gave me the creeps, and I understood why Vissar would threaten me over it. He likely knew I wouldn't willingly go, not after our last conversation and my adamant refusal to become involved with him. I'd never mentioned it to Jace, and that had been on purpose.

"Looking for me?" I asked, popping the last of my cone into my mouth.

"I went to the house, but no one was home. Figured you were down here." She looked at Quinn. "Heya, Quinn."

"Hey," he said without removing his tongue from his ice cream.

I ruffled his hair. He quickly pulled away from me, clearly getting annoyed with my antics. I laughed, frowning when Mac caught my gaze. She didn't look happy about something.

"What's going on?"

"Cass, someone roughed up Dani. Bad."

My back straightened. "What?"

I couldn't have heard her right.

"Yeah," she breathed. "She's got some scrapes and bruises. Nothing broken or major. But someone wanted to scare her." Her eyes darted to Quinn, who was still working on his ice cream and ignoring us.

We stood up and walked a short distance away from him to ensure he couldn't hear us. I didn't think he'd know what we were talking about, but I also didn't want him to worry. He might be young, but I knew he was a bright kid.

"They still think she's me," I whispered. "She shouldn't have used my name at the party, Mac. What was she even thinking?"

"I don't know, but you heard her say they didn't believe her when she told them she wasn't you. And if they did, they'd be after you! Roughing you up. This could be unrelated."

Mac's deep brown eyes filled with fear. I didn't blame her. Vissar threatened to hurt Mac if I didn't meet him for dinner. Why would he send someone to scare Dani more unless he was afraid I wouldn't show up? I needed to talk to Jace.

"Shh," I said, glancing over at Quinn.

He was watching us but continued licking his cone. I didn't think he was paying attention to our conversation. If he was, he probably didn't know *what* we were talking about.

"Vissar knows who I am and that she's not me. Why would he send someone to do that?" I shook my head. "I'll sort this out. Jace won't like it."

"Jace?" Mac asked quickly.

"Since Kya told Jace where I like to go think, he's been helping me. He doesn't want me anywhere near Vissar, but I won't have Dani get hurt because of this. It's not her fight."

"The cops are investigating it. She's scared and not leaving her apartment."

"What a mess."

I quietly told her what I'd found out at Shawn's party last night about Skyler and waited for her reaction. She didn't know, which meant Shawn and Skyler had kept their affair under tight secrecy. Gavin wouldn't probably know if it hadn't been for that accidental text message.

"I might be here longer than I thought." Even as I said it, I knew I was kidding myself. I would be here longer than I thought—there was no doubt about that.

"What are you going to do?"

"I have some virtual client appointments scheduled for this week. I'll make sure they don't add any new appointments. If something happens after that, they can contact my clients and let them know I have openings." I didn't mention the dinner, not wanting to worry her.

"Do you have enough money to get by?"

I looked at her wryly.

"Right. Trust fund baby."

I nudged her with my shoulder. True, I'd inherited my mom's trust and kept most of what I hadn't used during college. Guilt kept me from using it frivolously. Jenna Nichols would still be alive if it hadn't been for me.

"You have famous parents, too, punk."

She linked her arm with mine as we walked back to Quinn and sat down. "So, what's up with this guy? Did you change your mind about dating?"

"No," I blurted, too quickly. "I'm not dating."

"You went out with Jace." Quinn shoved the rest of the cone into his mouth.

That little booger, I thought, selling me out to one of my friends. Mac turned her wide eyes on me in disbelief.

"Liar!" she accused. "Yeah, I know about the movie premiere. I just wanted to see if you'd fess up that you went with Jace. It's all over the buzz. You can't hide things from me."

"Kissed her, too."

"Quinn, stop talking," I ordered, but all he did was laugh, even with his mouth full. I stuck my tongue out at him. "I had to go out with him. It was to get information."

Mac crossed her arms. "Why'd he kiss you, then?"

I could never lie to Mac. She always had a way of seeing right through me. Looking at me like she had me right where she wanted didn't help matters. Words fled. They ran right away from me. I couldn't form a single word to answer her, even though he'd only kissed me on the cheek. From Quinn's view, he must have thought it looked much different.

"You are so busted, Casanova."

Quinn grabbed his belly, laughing until he fell back into the sand. "Casanova! That's a good one!"

I covered my face with my hands and groaned. "Shut up, shortie."

"You like him," Mac accused. "Here you are, giving me a hard time about trying to fix you up with him, and you like him!"

"Maybe."

My eyes narrowed into a stink eye at Quinn, who sat back up, still grinning like he'd never let me live down my nickname. God, Jace knew it, and now Quinn did. All's fair in love and war, I guess. I'd called him Shortie enough times now; he had to have some ammunition somehow.

"You should! He's hot," Mac said with a grin.

I glared at her. "He's more than that, but he only kissed me on the cheek. For now, he's helping me, and that's what matters. I can't let my emotions get in the way of this. We went out to get information, and that was that. I couldn't face the cameras alone."

But Mac hadn't finished with me. Not by a long shot. "You won't be able to stop your emotions from getting involved. And you know? That's okay. Live, Casanova! Live up to your damn nickname!"

I laughed when she raised her hands in the air as if summoning a storm or a goddess. Either way, I couldn't help but laugh right along with her, Quinn joining in too. Was she right?

Should I let Jace in more? If I did, I'd need to figure out how to navigate it carefully while trying to gather information about my dad.

Chapter Twenty Three

Cassie

I tried to hold back my disappointment when Jace wasn't waiting for us when Quinn and I returned to the house. I left Mac with a promise to update her on our plan, and we parted ways. Jace texted me back that he'd be over, but I didn't know why I had expected him to come right away. As much as it irked me, I understood that he might be caught up in something. He had a life here. His mom and brother were here, and he had his job working for Vissar.

Quinn settled at the breakfast bar for a snack, even after devouring a giant ice cream cone less than half an hour ago. I checked my phone again. No message from Jace. The message to my dad was still unread. I eyed Quinn as he devoured a plate of cheese and crackers, hesitant to ask him about food for later.

"What do you want for dinner?"

He looked up from his phone. "You're not leaving?"

"Not tonight. Jace is coming over."

Surprise lit his eyes. Without bothering to hide the grin stretching from ear to ear, he returned to his phone.

"He's not coming over to kiss me *on the cheek* again. He's helping me find answers." That seemed to brighten his mood, although he didn't take his eyes away from his video. "So? Dinner?"

"Pizza."

"Don't you ever get tired of pizza? It's such a stereotype."

He looked up at me. "What's with you girls and all your healthy stuff?"

"Touché."

I could compromise by ordering a salad with the pizzas, or I could just eat the pizza outright. It wouldn't kill me to relent occasionally. While Quinn snacked, I focused on making a list of all my dad's financials that I needed to review.

While Quinn went to his room to finish his homework, I headed up to the top level to take a few uninterrupted laps in the pool. I knew I should spend the time going through the desk drawers, but after the whirlwind of the last few days, I needed relaxation. It had been so busy that I hadn't taken time for any exercise, and I could feel it. I really wanted to go surfing, but that would have to wait for a better day.

The top level offered a spectacular view of the beach and ocean, with glass walls surrounding the three open sides of the deck. A sitting area with a comfy couch encircled the propane table fireplace, positioned nearest to the beach. A rectangular pool shimmered in the sunlight on the farthest side, simple and inviting. It wasn't huge, being a rooftop pool, but it was big enough for laps.

I dropped my knit cover-up on one of the nearby chairs and slid into the cool water, easing into a calm backstroke to start. My mind eventually cleared of everything that plagued me as I continued swimming laps until I spotted a figure at the end of the pool.

Slowly, I stopped and stood up in the waist-deep water. The afternoon had given way to evening, and the sun was getting lower. I must have lost track of time. Jace stood at the end of the pool, his smoldering eyes fixed on me.

"Quinn said I could find you up here." I noticed he had a plush white towel in his hand, but he wasn't offering it to me.

I stepped out of the pool, fully aware of his gaze consuming me. He could look all he wanted; that didn't mean he would ever touch me, even if I secretly fantasized about it. For the last ten years of my life, I had played strictly by the rules—rigidly so. And for what? It hadn't gotten me anywhere.

Dressed casually, he wore a loose-fitting cream-colored shirt paired with blue jeans and white athletic shoes. It didn't matter what he wore; he always looked good. He smelled even better, as the subtle scent of his cologne assaulted my senses.

When I stopped in front of him, staring at his sculpted chest through the thin fabric of his shirt, I realized that if this continued between us, I might lose control of myself. Would I eventually push him away, too?

"Are you going to give me the towel or continue enjoying the scenery?"

He laughed, impossibly low. "You already know the answer to that."

Snapping the towel open, he draped it around my shoulders. When he pulled me toward him, I contemplated letting him kiss me this time. I had barely lifted my eyes when he pressed a kiss to my cheek and moved away. Only then did I finally draw in a full breath. This man, I thought. I can hardly think around him.

"What time is it?" I asked, wandering over to the chair while I toweled off as much as I could before slipping on my cover-up. I rubbed the towel over the wet strands of my hair, leading the way back inside.

"Almost six."

"Shoot. I have to get dinner for Quinn. He's probably starving."

"Skyler's not here?"

I tilted my head while he followed me back into the house, stepping beside me. He knew the answer. Although I'd been here for two weeks, she had made only an occasional appearance. Quinn, however, had stayed most weekends when he wasn't at his friend Ray's house, as if he felt more comfortable here than at his own home. Maybe he did.

"Did you see her at all today?"

I recounted the events of the morning in my dad's soundproof studio as we walked to my bedroom, leaving out the explicit details of our argument, just in case Quinn could hear us.

Jace looked around my bedroom curiously while I went into the bathroom to change back into my clothes. When I returned, he was lounging on my bed with his head cradled in the palm of his hand. My breath hitched.

Ugh, he looked so good lying there. I couldn't help but imagine myself in bed with him. I closed my eyes, shaking away the images. "Quinn wants pizza," I said, opening them to see him sitting up.

When he reached for my hand, I tentatively let him take it, but he yanked me forward, and I fell against him. Scrambling to find my balance, I ended up with a knee tucked on each side of his hips. If I thought my breath had caught in my lungs before, straddling him was entirely different. Hyperaware of my uneven breathing, pounding heart, and trembling limbs, I tried to concentrate on something else—anything else. His fingers slid through the damp strands of my hair, curving against the back of my neck as his lips claimed my jaw, my chin, and finally, my mouth.

His kiss made me weak all over, and I knew it wouldn't end well if he continued, but holy smokes, I wanted him to keep going. Even if he'd done this thousands of times before, I didn't care. I hadn't gone out with that many men, but with Jace, the sensations flowing through me took on a whole new meaning. My heart raced as he sucked the breath right from my mouth until we breathed as one. Our tongues tangled, our mouths grew more urgent as I slipped my arms around his neck while he dropped his hands to wrap firmly around me, pressing me closer.

"Jace," I breathed.

A strangled groan slipped from his throat as if my saying his name only urged him on until I felt his hands on my bare skin along my ribs, caging me between them. My head fell back when he stopped kissing me for a second, giving him access to press his mouth against the hollow at the base of my throat.

"Not with Quinn downstairs," I whispered.

His eyes flashed as he pulled away from me, his lips swollen from our brief play. I couldn't help myself as I smoothed the pad of my thumb over his lower lip. Playfully, he nipped at it. Replacing my thumb with my mouth, I kissed him quickly before sliding off his lap.

Before I could get away, he grabbed my hand, stopping me from stepping too far. Our eyes met and held while his thumb traced a lazy path across my skin, igniting a shiver up my spine.

"This isn't over," he murmured. "Not by a long shot."

"Jace . . . I can't let my heart get broken. I might not recover."

What possessed me to say such a thing? I couldn't explain it. He didn't care about my feelings, especially my heart. I'd always kept everyone at a distance. Each breakup had made its impact on me, except for my split with Evan, which had been a blessing in disguise, though it still hurt how he'd ended it and discovering afterward that he hadn't waited long, if at all, to replace me. I'd never allowed myself to feel that way.

He stood, keeping my hand in his and lifting it to press a kiss to my palm. "Let's go feed the little monster downstairs. Maybe give him some company besides himself for once."

My heart stammered for a moment as he guided me out of the room, and within minutes, we were downstairs ordering pizza. Watching Jace sit and talk to Quinn about skateboarding while I placed the order, I felt a pinch in my chest. Pathetic, I told myself. I couldn't remember feeling this deeply for any man, and it had only been just over three weeks since I'd met him. What made Jace so different?

Hours later, after watching two action-packed movies with Quinn and devouring two huge pizzas, I sternly sent him off to bed. Jace and I stayed on the couch, staring at each other as though we were in a battle to see who would move first.

"Now that the little monster has gone to bed, what did you want to tell me?" he asked, looking so casual on the couch as though he belonged there.

"Someone roughed up Dani again. I'm pretty sure Vissar sent someone to do it, although I can't imagine why. But I can't have her getting followed and threatened in my place." I pulled my knee up and rested my chin on it as I looked at him.

His eyes flashed. "I can't have that happen to you."

"It shouldn't be happening to anyone, but it definitely shouldn't be her. She's not me, Jace. It's not right."

"Did she call the cops?"

"Of course, she did. You know as well as I do that if Vissar sent his men, it won't lead back to him. You forget that I know Reno Moretti. Men like them don't slip up."

I knew he wouldn't agree with me confronting Vissar, not when it would put me in danger. He was chivalrous. But I couldn't live with myself if Dani continued to get hassled and possibly hurt because Vissar thought she was me and that I had any information about where my dad.

"What do you think should happen?" his words came out slowly.

"We should start spreading the story of what happened that night. Like, 'Hahaha, do you know what we did?' I can't think of another way." I stretched out my leg, letting it dangle halfway off the couch.

He shook his head. "With Vissar, you have to be careful. I'm still not sure what he wants with you, other than the obvious."

"The man sent me flowers and wants to wine and dine me." I didn't bother hiding my shudder of repulsion. "But if he thinks I know something, I need to play along, if nothing else, so I can find out what my dad might have done that made him run."

The look in his eyes scared me. "I don't want you near him asking questions that could put you in danger. I'll find out what he wants with you. Not you."

I shook my head. "You're already in the middle. You aren't doing anything other than body guarding him, are you?"

His jaw flexed. "Not right now. If this is him sending his thugs after you, mentioning me will only get you into more trouble with him. Trust me. Please."

All I could do was nod, even though I doubted wholeheartedly that Vissar would send threatening messages knowing Dani wasn't me. Maybe eventually I would find out. And maybe it didn't even matter. "None of this makes any sense, and not finding any information is driving me crazy. And who is Natalia to you?"

"Natalia?" he asked quickly. "Why?"

They seemed more familiar than his employment should have allowed, and I couldn't help but feel a stab of jealousy. I had to be sure I could trust him first. After all, Jace was working for the man.

I searched his eyes, worry setting in. He knew something he wasn't telling me. "Who is she to you?"

"Vissar's daughter." He moved closer, his hand closing over my knee. "And nothing more, Cassie. But never underestimate her, either."

This was getting nowhere fast.

"Look, Natalia is staying at her dad's house. He won't let her leave. She did something that angered him."

Interesting, I thought.

"I can't believe I'm going to say this, but could my dad be involved with her? He wouldn't cheat on Skyler like she did him, though."

"No. She's friends with people in bands because she likes that kind of music, but I'm not sure she'd be dating anyone that much older than her."

That made sense if Natalia had made friends with Ricky and my dad. I frowned. It actually put a few more pieces together. I didn't need to have dinner with Vissar; I needed to have dinner with his daughter, but apparently, she was under house arrest by her own father. Oh yeah, she was involved in whatever had gone down.

I caught Jace looking at me. "You have to go, don't you?"

He nodded. "You want me to stay?"

Despite myself, I laughed lightly at his mixed message and thinking I must be rubbing off on him. "There you go, nodding your head and telling me something different."

His hand molded against my jaw as he drew my mouth to his. I melted against him, and his mouth moved slowly against mine. No hurry, at his leisure, as if he had me right where he needed me and I had no chance to escape.

"Not with shortie here," I whispered as soon as he allowed me a breath.

His groan was adorable. "Is this the equivalent of having kids?"

Good call, I thought. This must be exactly how it felt to have kids. I knew girls in high school who babysat for money and always had their boyfriends over to make out and have sex after they put the kids to bed. I'd never had the desire to babysit, but I felt a fierce urge to protect Quinn.

A smile curved my lips. "Guess so."

"I don't like leaving you alone here."

"Charming, but we have a security system. We'll be fine."

"You're sure you don't want me to stay the night? If I promise to keep my hands to myself?"

Oh, he was smooth. Resuming where we'd left off in my bedroom painted an intriguing picture in my mind. "We both know that won't happen, Jace."

When I walked him to the door, I should have known he wouldn't let it go. He leaned over to kiss me, his kiss sweet and lingering. There were many sides to this man, and I couldn't find one I didn't like yet, which concerned me.

"I meant what I told that guy last night," he murmured, his mouth hovering near mine. "You're with me."

The laugh that slipped out was shaky, almost nervous. "Last night was a deal we made to find out information. Just because we've hung out a few times doesn't mean—"

His mouth came down on mine, pushing me against the wall at the same time. I felt as if he couldn't hold himself back anymore, and I'd be lying if I said it didn't send a thrill directly through me. Yes, he had many sides. Had anyone ever pursued me with such rough abandon?

After making his point, he let me up for air but kept me pinned against the wall with his hips. "I'm not sure what you're doing to me, but I haven't been able to stop thinking about you," he whispered against my jaw, his hands firmly locked at my waist as if he didn't trust himself to put them anywhere else.

I must have been crazy to consider letting him into my life this way, but in the last few hours, he'd kissed me more times than I'd allowed anyone before a second date. Technically, we'd only been out once, and that was a fake date. It had to be his sinful looks and deadly charm. I couldn't be sure, but it seemed he was being honest with me. How else could I explain letting my lifestyle rules slide?

When he pulled away, his eyes searched mine. "Call me if you need me. I'm not so far away that I can't come back."

"Where are you staying?" I finally found my voice as he opened the front door.

"With Ezra and his friend Milo. Just north of the pier. We rent a small house." He must have seen the questions forming on my lips. "My mom doesn't have the room, and Ezra needed a place. Milo kind of comes with Ezra."

"I'm not sure I could live with my mom if she were still alive."

Tucking my bottom lip between my teeth, I thought about how I hadn't visited her gravesite. I knew I should. After going to school for it, receiving extensive training, and treating countless patients, I should take my own therapeutic advice. But I can't. I can't bring myself to visit her because I'm afraid—afraid to face my failures. Not just my failure to save her but also being the reason she died. If I had just said no that night, she wouldn't have overdosed.

I raised my eyes to his, afraid tears might appear. If he noticed, he didn't show it. Instead, he tucked my hair behind my ear.

Leaning against the open door, I watched him turn slowly, giving me one last impish smile over his shoulder before walking away. I didn't move until he got into his car and drove off, then closed and locked the door tight before activating the security system.

Chapter Twenty Four

I hated leaving her alone. After graduating from the police academy and joining the force, I had faced off against some of the toughest gangs. Against people who had hit their breaking point and no longer cared about their own lives or anyone else's. I had looked into the eyes of countless victims, and now I was working for a mastermind.

If it ever got out why I was really working for Vissar, my reputation as a ladies' man would quickly transform into that of a questionable character. I would lose any chance of getting a private investigation case if anyone thought I was doing illegal things for him. While I hadn't technically done anything illegal, I knew what Vissar was up to, and no one would trust me. Cassie would never trust me.

Out of the people I had met in my life, that woman . . . I sighed, rubbing my hand over my face as I thought about her in my arms. Tucked safely against me on the couch, at the front door, in her bedroom—it felt so right to have her there, the way she had all but melted into me. True, I had been with enough women who were pliant, but they were different. They knew what they were getting into. At least, I thought they did. I had never broken a single rule for anyone. Until Cassie.

Cassie knew what she was getting into too, yet she was holding back. She was pure of heart. She had told me she might not recover if her heart got broken, and I had to question myself. As much as I could tell myself this might be different, could I truly trust myself not to break her heart? Knowing what I was doing for Vissar and not telling her about it would devastate her, even if I was doing the best I could with what I had. She would hate me.

Yet I couldn't stop myself around her. It was as if I needed to touch her with anything I could—my hands, my mouth. I needed to claim her. The fact that Vissar had sent her roses, trying to get close to her while already having a damn wife, irritated me beyond reason. When that guy had her cornered, I saw red, and it took every ounce of strength I had not to rip him away from her and make him bleed.

My phone rang, interrupting my thoughts. When I saw who was calling, my mood soured instantly. It had been such a good evening, spending time with Cassie and Quinn. I genuinely liked the little guy. Listening to him talk about his interests made it clear he had no one else to listen to him. At least he had Cassie now, and her generous heart would do her best for him.

"Vissar," I answered. "What can I do for you this evening?"

"I have a job for you."

Closing my eyes, I tried to hide my deep sigh. I already had a job to do for him, and tonight I'd been doing it my way. He didn't know that I was purposely feeding him only what I thought would best protect her.

"Now, now, Jace, we agreed on an upfront payment for your services." His voice, clipped with an accent, sounded entitled. "Are you willing to listen, or must I find someone better suited for this job?"

I felt like beating my fists against the steering wheel. I owed Vissar for getting Ezra out of trouble with the people to whom he owed drug money. No one but Ezra knew about it, and he would keep his mouth shut.

"You paid me to do a job. I intend to see it through," I said through gritted teeth.

"Very good. You'll be picking up two young girls from a club downtown and meeting two men at a warehouse in Mid City. I'll text you the coordinates. Don't fuck this up, Jace."

"I told you I won't do those types of jobs, Vissar."

"Need I remind you what's at stake if you don't?"

"This wasn't part of our deal, Vissar, and you know it. If I do this, it won't end well. I won't let two kidnapped girls be sold into a prostitution ring. I can't."

"Who said anything about kidnapped?"

"I doubt these two girls are willingly being traded off to someone in a shady warehouse lot." My hatred for him grew every time I had to deal with him.

"If it doesn't end well, Jace, there is more at stake than just your brother."

I bristled at the unspoken implication, my stomach aching at the thought of Cassie getting involved with Vissar, or worse, getting hurt by him. He sometimes had me followed, but I always managed to lose them. If he was having Cassie followed by someone else too, it could mean trouble for both of us.

My jaw clenched so tightly I thought my teeth would crack. Lashing back at Vissar would only push her further into danger. If he knew I had any feelings for Cassie, there would be no stopping him from using it against me. And if Cassie had any feelings for me and Vissar caught wind of it, he would use it against her without hesitation.

"I won't hesitate to use anything to my advantage. You'll do this or suffer the consequences."

"What time?" I snapped.

"Two. Don't be late."

I checked the time. Good thing I never got used to sleeping much. "I never am."

"I'm losing patience with your lack of information on Cassie."

"No one knows where Lex went. It's like he dropped off the face of the earth. Cassie doesn't know anything at all. She's about as far removed from her dad's dealings as a person can get."

"Why is she here, then?"

Inwardly, I growled. He wouldn't give up unless I gave him something. He already knew about her friends; that was obvious since they'd been at his house. I just needed to provide him with the information about their work locations. I doubted he would harm them as long as we cooperated.

"The house has a robust security system," I sighed, praying he didn't intend to send his thugs to break in when Cassie and Quinn were there. "If you wanted me to get close to her, why aren't you asking me to break into her house?"

"I dislike being questioned," he snapped. "See that you don't fail this job tonight, Jace."

Vissar hung up without another word. Asshole. I didn't dare say it aloud, fearing the line remained connected. I had enough time to stop home briefly to change my clothes and wait for the coordinates before having to leave. Thankfully, I hadn't stayed with Cassie and had to make an excuse to leave. In other words, lie. It tore me apart not being completely honest with her. I was certain she would never get involved with guys who pretended to be the good guy but were committing crimes. What Vissar was telling me to do was not legal. In the name of putting people I cared about in danger, I had no choice but to proceed. But I had a plan. Cassie knowing anything about it would only put her in even more danger.

After stopping briefly at home, I went out again. But not before I sent a message on my burner phone to my buddies at the police department about what was going down tonight. They knew there were other people in danger and that if something interfered with what happened tonight, someone would die. I was only supposed to be an informant, not a transporter. The police would be on standby to follow these poor girls once I made the hand-off.

When I pulled into the dark alley behind the club, I dialed the number Vissar had Tito send me. Minutes later a door opened and two girls were thrown into my backseat. The massive guy reached out and smacked one of them in the head, as though she'd done something to warrant it. I didn't give a shit. No one did that to a woman around me.

"Hey!" I barked. "Knock that off."

He grunted and slammed the door.

I looked back at them, painfully aware of how scantily dressed and terrified they were. Adam and the team were hopefully near the location already.

"Listen to me," I said, keeping my voice low. "You will not say a word while I'm driving, and don't even think about attacking me. Both of you will be fine. Just stay there and keep quiet."

Silence responded.

As I pulled away, my eyes caught them huddled together in the rearview mirror, as though if they didn't, they would lose one another. Despair sat sourly in my gut. This was by far the worst thing I had been ordered to do for Vissar, and yet, it was the best since there was a chance they'd be saved. Spying on Cassie had been pretty bad, too, but seeing these two girls only deepened my hatred for Vissar. I was beginning to think he was purposely trying to make my life a living hell.

The warehouse area was poorly lit when I pulled in, turning off my headlights as I drove in and scanned the area for another vehicle and any signs of anything out of place. If Vissar had sent anyone to spy on me and suspected I'd double-crossed him, he would show no remorse in getting rid of me.

I thought about these girls, and the countless others around the world who had yet to be saved. They shouldn't have to endure whatever horrors they faced. I could only hold on to hope that the police would be able to tail the car after this exchange and make an arrest. Eventually, I wanted nothing more than to take down

Vissar once and for all.

Not long after I parked, a black minivan pulled in and drove toward us. I held my breath while I waited for them to make the first move. Of all the things I'd done as an undercover detective, of all the illegal actions I'd taken in the name of busting a criminal, this was by far the worst. Even my last case with Ty, when we handled so many drugs, wasn't this immoral.

As soon as a door opened and a man clambered out, I moved. Slowly, I opened my back door and motioned for the girls to get out. I took one of them lightly by the arm, noting how thin she was, assuming the other girl wouldn't take off running if I had one of them in my grasp.

My stomach churned at the fear in their eyes, propelling me forward toward the two burly men from the van. If anyone had followed the thugs here, other than my team of police on the lookout, Vissar would undoubtedly blame me for it. My heart pounded as I approached the van.

I couldn't tell the girls that everything would be fine. I couldn't make that promise when I didn't know when it would be. All I could do was commit as much to memory as possible.

One of the two men stepped forward to grab the girls, so I released the one I held. She bolted, and damn if she wasn't the fastest runner. I couldn't remember the last time I'd had to run full out. I sprinted after her and caught her around the waist.

"It's going to be fine," I whispered in her ear. "Just calm down."

It made me sick to my stomach. She trembled so violently that I thought she'd shake right out of my hold. "You just hang on."

As I brought her back, I kept my grip tight enough while trying not to hurt her while the two men eyed me with caution. They didn't trust me, and they had every reason not to.

"Who're you?" one of them asked.

"Who I am is no concern. I was asked to bring the girls and make sure nothing goes wrong," I replied smoothly, jerking my chin toward the fragile girl in my grip. "Like this."

He nodded once.

The girl wiggled in my grasp, but I reluctantly handed her over to the men. I thought I would be sick on the pavement as I did, but I held it together, my face a mask of granite for as long as I could. As calmly as I could, I waited for the men to take the two young girls to the van and pull away. I committed their license plate number to memory before turning back to my car.

Adam told me his team would tail them for a while before making the arrest to be ensure I wouldn't be implicated, but nothing made me feel better about this transaction. Until I knew for certain that these two little girls were safely in police custody, I wouldn't be able to sleep.

Alone in the vacant warehouse parking lot, I walked to the back of my car and threw up.

Chapter Twenty Five

Cassie

Across the table, candlelight flickered as Vissar made no move to hide his desire for me. I tilted my chin up a notch. I needed to keep my wits front and center, my pride be damned. In front of me, I had a glass of water. There would be no chance in hell I had wine tonight. Not around this man.

"Thank you for accepting my invitation to dine tonight." Vissar leaned back, swirling his bourbon in his glass, making the ice clink against the expensive crystal.

"Was this an invitation?" I feigned surprise. "Funny, I didn't read your message that way. It seemed more like a threat that you would harm my friend if I didn't come. In fact, that's exactly what it said. Kind of like how your men are hassling my friend Dani."

A slow, sinful smile curved his thin lips.

"I admit, and she does too, it was stupid of her to play such a trick at your gate last week. But to set them after her again, knowing she isn't me?" I tsked.

"Cassie, you are a beautiful woman. You're intelligent. I know we can help each other in this situation."

"Situation?"

"You get your father back; I get what he has of mine back."

"Ah, yes. Are you sure your wife didn't take whatever it is you're missing?"

"Veronica? No, she would never. She's visiting family in Greece."

I delicately raised my brow. "Is she from there?"

"I am. You might have noticed my accent. I hail from Mytilene, which is on the Greek island of Lesbos. Have you heard of it?" I shook my head. "Well, it's not as well-known as other cities in Greece. I haven't been back there for many years, but Victoria is attempting to mend fences."

I truly didn't want to know about his family. "Is Veronica your first wife?"

His jaw hardened as if I'd struck a nerve. "My second. My first wife met with an untimely demise when she tangled with one of my many enemies. I could not protect her."

"She was Natalia's mother?"

"Natalia's mother and my son, Giles. I remarried a few years ago."

I reached for my water, sipping it slowly. Did he really think I believed his tale of woe? Not for one second did I believe Vissar ever had a compassionate part in his body. He was the type of man who took without asking. I needed to stay wary.

"Vissar, if I could get whatever was taken from you back, I would have it to you in the time it takes to make a phone call. But I don't." I chose my words carefully, drawing them out slowly. There could be no confusion here. I needed to be clear. "I can't offer you more than that, but I can promise you that if I hear anything or find anything, you will be the first to know."

Well, I thought, Jace would be the first to know.

His mouth quirked. "You are the only bargaining chip I have, and I will keep you."

"That may be true," I said, anger simmering. "But in this case, I don't know where my dad, or whatever you're missing, are."

"I'll be hosting a charity event next weekend downtown." He motioned for the server to take our order. "I'd like you to attend."

My eyes narrowed at him briefly before I looked up at the server. "I'd just like a light salad, vinaigrette on the side."

"You heard the lady. I'll have my usual, Monte."

The server moved swiftly away, as though he wasn't comfortable around Vissar, and I didn't blame him. That he wanted me to attend an event with him was out of the question. If I'd known when I'd attended the art gallery, I would have steered clear. Whatever my dad had involved himself in, it clearly included more risk than I should be facing. And yet, I couldn't let it go. I needed to get him back.

"And if I refuse?"

The slight tilt at the corner his mouth sent chills through me. "You won't."

"I'll attend, Vissar." I lifted my chin. "But you'll tell me what it is you think my dad took from you, why you think he would do such a thing, and how in the hell you think I would know where he might be."

His eyes narrowed slightly. "I don't *think* he took something from me, my dear. I know he did. It's on camera. As to what it is, it's security footage and if released will have dire consequences to everyone involved, you included."

Damn it, Dad. "You have to know that I have nothing to do with this. And my dad isn't a thief. However he's involved, he was set up."

"On the contrary, I told him to return it or face the consequences and he thought the best thing would be to disappear. Unfortunately, that puts me in a terrible position since he's still in possession of it. And make no mistake, I will get it back."

In other words, it didn't matter if I knew where my dad was hiding or not. Vissar would use me as leverage to get that video back, even if it meant threatening me. My dad could bring it back and Vissar kill us all. I could head back to Seattle and still be in danger.

Vissar had me at his beck and call, and there wasn't a thing I could do about it.

A short time later, we had both dined in light, albeit strained, conversation, avoiding any more talk about the missing security footage or my dad. When a young busboy came to clear our dishes, his hands shook so badly that he knocked my water into my lap. I gasped, jumping from my chair and grabbing a napkin to wipe the wetness from my dress.

Vissar grabbed the boy by the front of his shirt, murder in his eyes. The fear in the poor kid's eyes made my heart freeze. The fire in Vissar's gaze was something to be deathly afraid of.

"Stop!" I said, grabbing Vissar's arm. "Stop! It's water. No harm done."

Holy smokes, I thought, as Vissar slowly loosened his hold and eventually released the boy. It took only a second before the kid scrambled away from us, and our server returned with a string of apologies. I grabbed another napkin and wiped the water from my skirt, waving my other hand.

"It's fine, just fine. Only water," I said. "It happens."

Vissar was furious, and nothing I could say would ease his anger. I tamped down my better judgment and touched his hand, looking into his eyes, hoping he would ease up.

"Vissar," I mumbled. "I'm fine. He didn't set me on fire."

Finally, the corner of his mouth quirked up. "People ought to be more careful. What if it had been red wine?"

"But it wasn't. And if it had been, the restaurant would have received a dry cleaning bill. No harm done. Truly."

He sighed heavily and nodded. Finally, I thought, and threw the napkin down on the table. I hoped this would conclude our dinner. I would need the week to prepare myself for his charity event. Who knew what else he would force me into doing. My thoughts strayed to Jace.

Vissar walked me to the front of the restaurant where his car waited for him. With a chaste kiss on the cheek, he left me and I went to my own car. Instead of getting in, I leaned against it and dialed Mac to find out where the girls were tonight. An hour later and I was at the club with Mac and Kya, sipping on a glass of water and enjoying the blare of the music, but soon the stress of my situation with Vissar caught up with me and I needed the solitude of home.

"I'm bailing," I said, leaning over the high top table to tell Mac and Kya. "I need to chill at home for a while. Figure out what I'm doing."

Mac's eyebrows drew together. "You're okay?"

"Babe?" Kya asked, laying her hand on my arm. "You're making us worry about you. You haven't been yourself tonight. Usually you have a glass of wine. All you've had is water."

I shook my head. "Everything is fine."

Mac barked out a laugh. "That's our girl. Make it home safe, okay?"

After hugging them both, I wound my way through the crowd and headed for the exit. With a nod to the bouncers at the door, I walked.

"Cassie."

I heard Jace's deep voice behind me, frowning when I stopped and turned around. "What are you doing here? Are you following me or something?"

"I was worried about you."

I noticed he didn't answer my question about following me. His fingers slid up my bare arm, pulling me abruptly to his side. I felt encircled by a sense of safety. His closeness chased away whatever chill was in the air.

Jace curled his arm around my waist, his fingers draped along my hip, curving intimately as though they belonged there, while he pulled me along the sidewalk toward the parking lot.

"You shouldn't be walking alone," he chastised. "You know that."

"I'm a big girl. I can handle myself, Jace."

"You couldn't have asked me to meet you here?" he asked, his hand pressing against my back. "And you shouldn't have to handle yourself. You could easily be grabbed into a dark alley. I'm in law enforcement, remember? Anything can happen on these streets, even in the best neighborhoods."

Probably how he'd tracked me down, I thought. Either that or Kya ratted me out again. She made no secret with her matchmaking skills.

Jace pulled me over to a vacant bench along the sidewalk, sitting me down. "I heard you went to dinner with Vissar tonight."

Our eyes met and held. I drew in a deep breath, knowing he'd be upset I hadn't told him about Vissar's threats. "He didn't give me a choice. There was a message with those flowers he sent."

His eyebrows shot up. "What did the message say?" he asked slowly.

"That I would meet him for dinner or there might be an accident on the set of the movie Mac's working on."

I heard him swear under his breath, smiling that he cared. I couldn't recall having heard him curse before.

"You can't let him get you alone."

I knew what Jace was saying had merit, but that didn't mean I needed to hear him voice it.

"I'm not . . ." Jace exhaled sharply. "He is more dangerous than you know, Cassie."

I laughed. "Do you think I'm really that innocent? I promise you, Jace, I have no desire to spend any time with him. But you don't have to sound so possessive. It's not like we're actually dating."

"Maybe we are."

I would have stood up if he hadn't locked his hands around my wrists in anticipation of my move. Stupid, I told myself. He probably knew every move in the book.

"Jace, I've been on my own for a very long time. I can handle myself without the cover of a fake relationship. Now, if you want an actual relationship—" He seized my lips as soon as I turned my head.

His mouth slanted against mine, not giving me a second to draw a full breath. Firm hands slid around my waist, pulling me toward him until I was almost sitting in his lap. His hand tangled in the hair at my neck, curling until he had me captive. Every sigh that escaped, he caught.

Slowly, he withdrew and looked into my eyes. "And what if I do?"

"What if you do what?"

It was the oddest thing to have all thoughts plucked from my head when he kissed me. I couldn't recall a time when I'd tuned out like that, melting into the moment. Only Jace could do that to me.

He gave me that wicked smile of his, pulling me against him but refraining from kissing me again. "Let's get out of here. I'll bring you home."

"I drove myself here."

"Then I'll follow you home to make sure you're safe."

When he walked me back to my car, I didn't flinch when he pulled me toward him and held me for a moment. I couldn't help but feel safe. Slipping a glance at him, I sensed myself entering unfamiliar emotional territory with him.

After helping me into the car, he kissed me and went to his own car to follow me back to the house. Oddly, I wished he'd been in the car with me for someone to talk to, but I needed to clear my head.

It seemed like we reached my house in no time at all, with Jace parking in the driveway after I pulled into the garage. After I climbed out and closed the garage door behind me, he took my hand and brought it to his lips, much like he'd done when we first met. Charming.

"Want me to come in?"

His voice, that low drawl, floated over me like a beckoning. My eyes fluttered, nearly closing at the feelings swirling within me. I knew what would happen if I told him yes, with Quinn not being home. I struggled to breathe.

"Not tonight," I said, disappointing myself as soon as the words left my mouth.

Oddly, he didn't look disappointed at my rejection. He kissed my knuckles again. "I respect that, Cassie." My brow shot up. "I respect you."

"You . . . do?"

"You know what you want. You know where I'll be when you figure it out."

With that, he pulled me into his arms and turned us, pressing my back against his car and nipping at my lips. I should have known it wouldn't be easy to escape. When I sighed, he caught the invitation and molded himself to me. I could feel every ripple of his muscles through our clothing. And I hated myself more for rejecting his offer. But I knew what I wanted, and it scared the living hell out of me.

Leaving me with another quick kiss, he led me toward the door before turning away. I understood why he had to leave me there. He didn't trust himself any more than I trusted myself.

"Damn it," I said, not realizing I had spoken aloud until he glanced back with a grin.

Standing on the doorstep, I watched him get back into the car and drive away. I cursed again, a little more colorfully this time, before turning around and leaning my forehead against the outer door, wondering what the hell I had just done.

Tonight, I'd be spending in my bed, alone. Alone in this house, and I would think of no one else but him. The way he felt. The way he tasted. I groaned. The way he smelled. What the hell was wrong with me?

I unlocked the front door, darting inside and leaning against the inner door for a moment. At this rate, I'd never get it together. As tempting as it was to whip out my cell phone and call him back, I knew I had to be strong. There would be plenty of time for that later. Right?

Instead, I stayed there for a few more minutes and wondered about all the what-ifs. What if I didn't get another chance and someone else came along and snatched him away from me? What if my dad suddenly came home, and there was no longer a need for me to stay? I would drive myself crazy if I continued to think of all the possibilities that could happen. As a therapist, I knew it wasn't good to dwell.

Chapter Twenty Six

Cassie

Shame filled me as I got into the car Vissar sent to pick me up for my trip to downtown LA, the exclusive event at a hotel looming. Dread and disgust washed over me during the drive. Thoughts of Jace's plans for tonight plagued my mind, and I hoped like hell he wouldn't be there. I may not have a choice about attending the event or having to go to dinner with him, but I knew I would eventually need to draw the line. I wouldn't be anything to him more than an unwilling companion. The thought of anything remotely more made me sick.

The car pulled up to the hotel, and I waited for the driver to open the door. I paused for a moment before stepping out, looking at the front doors as though I marched to my doom. My unease grew when one of his bodyguards met me in the lobby and led me to the grand ballroom, where dimly overhead lights illuminated white-covered round tables.

It felt almost like being on the red carpet again—except worse—when several eyes turned my way. Ice sculptures adorned the room, and tables were set with the finest silver and sparkling crystal. I scanned the crowd for Vissar amidst a sea of men in tuxedos and women dripping with diamonds, wearing the most expensive dresses, both short and long. I glanced down at the dress I'd worn to Vissar's house the first night, hoping I was dressed appropriately. This was as formal as he'd get.

Vissar spotted me, meeting us halfway and taking my arm from the bodyguard. With a familiarity that still surprised me, he kissed my cheek, even though I'd only seen him on a few occasions.

"You look lovely," he whispered. "Please, come in."

My eyes darted to the bodyguards standing at attention throughout the expansive room, searching for Jace and hoping he wouldn't be called to this event tonight. My heart sank when I spotted him near the raised platform at the far side of the room in the center. His eyes met mine, and my mouth turned downward.

"I was thinking you might not come," Vissar continued. "That would have displeased me a great deal."

"You sent a car for me," I replied, lifting my chin. "It would have been rude to ignore it. Not to mention you've threatened my friends."

He chuckled and drew me closer just as two impeccably dressed men approached. One was tall with bright green eyes and a full head of gray hair, while the other was only slightly taller than I was, with sandy brown hair.

"My dear, I'd like you to meet two of my business associates. This is Benedict Silva," Vissar introduced as the tall one took my hand and kissed my knuckles. "And Carl Fowler."

I turned to the other man, allowing him to do the same as Vissar smiled. "Gentlemen, Ms. Cassie Nichols."

"I do hope you will honor me with a dance later, Ms. Nichols," Carl said.

I smiled. "Of course."

As Vissar guided me toward a table at the front, closer to Jace, he waved over a server to bring me champagne. I sat down, feeling Jace's intense gaze devour me, making me uncomfortable. This was an event Vissar should have taken his wife to, not a woman he barely knew.

I tilted my head. "Why did you ask me to come to this, Vissar?"

His smile seemed cold. "I want you to enjoy yourself. We'll have plenty of time to talk later."

The server brought me champagne. It wasn't my usual choice, but I sipped it anyway. It wasn't long before our table was full and dinner was served. Vissar engaged in conversation with those around us, but it resolved entirely around business-topics I had no knowledge of. The women sneered at me, all older by at least fifteen years, while the men eyed me.

This night could not end fast enough, and I regretted coming with every passing minute. I could feel Jace's eyes on me, and for once, I hated it. I didn't want him to have to watch this, just as much as I didn't want to be here. When dinner concluded and the place settings were cleared away, I could finally get up and move around. I desperately wanted to go talk to Jace.

Vissar took me for a spin on the dance floor, thankfully keeping his hands in a modest place as he twirled me around.

"You've been avoiding me," he said.

"I've been doing no such thing. You answered my questions, and I told you I would come. Here I am."

He laughed. "I've booked the suite here tonight, Cassie. Perhaps you'd consider joining me."

I wanted to throw up. "No," I said tightly.

As he spun me around, I thought I should ease up on the champagne or risk getting into trouble tonight. The pitcher of water at the table hadn't lasted long and another glass of champagne had been poured for me. I needed to be careful. I didn't drink champagne. The last thing I wanted was to find myself in his room against my will.

"Are you unwell, Cassie?"

I sighed. "I'm fine. Just thirsty," I lied.

Vissar promptly brought me back to the table, waiting until I sat down and took a sip of my champagne before he sat down beside me. One more glass to take the edge off, but not enough to dull my senses, I told myself. When he crossed his legs and leaned back with his whiskey, he stared at me.

"You can't blame me for wanting you for myself," he said. "You are a desirable woman."

I snorted. "I'm leaving for Seattle soon."

"Oh, I don't think you are." He looked smug.

My eyes snapped to his. Did he know something I didn't? He had a look in his eyes that suggested he was up to something. I didn't like this. I wanted to fight him with everything I had, but he had all the power.

A tall man with liberally gray hair strode over to us. "Vissar, why don't you introduce me to your lady?"

Vissar flicked his gaze up. "Michel, this is Cassie. Cassie, this is another business partner, Michel Sawyer."

The man took my hand and kissed my knuckles. "My, you are lovely." I snatched my hand back, earning a deep chuckle. "And feisty. I love a challenge." He looked at Vissar. "You wouldn't mind if I took the lady for a dance?"

I watched Vissar, my breath held. He wouldn't dare let this man dance with me without asking first. At least others had shown the courtesy to ask. He barely acknowledged Michel, focusing on me instead.

"Take her."

I gasped.

"But mind where you put your hands, Michel. Cassie is mine."

As he gently pulled me from my chair, I tugged back, anger flashing in my eyes. Vissar merely looked amused, a smile teasing the corner of his lips. My heart threatened to beat right out of my chest; I was so angry.

"Absolutely not! You may ask me, but I might decline. It's rude to avoid asking someone directly for their permission."

Vissar's eyes glowed dangerously as he watched our exchange. The man inclined his head.

"My apologies, Ms. Nichols. Would you please honor me with a dance?"

As much as I didn't want to dance with him, he had apologized and asked nicely. When we reached the dance floor, he pulled me close, and I nearly cried in frustration as he made sure his hands were firmly on me. He had to be over twice my age, just as Vissar was, and I didn't know him at all. Disgusted, I realized I didn't truly know Vissar either. I had gotten myself into this mess, and I would need to get myself out of it.

As we danced, my eyes scanned the room for Jace, and rising panic hit me when I couldn't see him. Had Vissar released him from his duties tonight, and he left? My heart pounded, and my lungs struggled to take in enough air.

Michel tipped my chin up with his knuckle. "You're distracted."

"I'm . . . tired."

"A man like Vissar can only keep you entertained for so long."

My eyes narrowed at him. "Don't think for a single minute that I am with Vissar. I came here at his request, but we are not together. He is married."

He chuckled but said nothing else.

I steeled myself, prepared to finish the dance until the man's hand slipped down to cup my ass. My eyes shot to his as I gasped. He smiled deviously, but his grin vanished quickly when a hand on his arm pulled him away from me. Vissar took my arm and led me away without a word.

Once we were back at the table, I had to regain my composure. I needed to get out of this situation—and fast. Downing another glass of champagne, my head swam.

"I've tried to be patient," Vissar said. "I find I can no longer do that."

"He grabbed me," I reminded him.

His eyes flashed. "That wasn't what I was referring to. I will deal with Michel later. I'm talking about this situation between us, Cassie."

My eyes widened.

"Your father stole an extremely valuable piece of property from my home. I want it back." I opened my mouth to reply, but he held up his hand. "If I do not get it back, there will be repercussions."

"You blew up that airplane," I whispered.

"He wasn't on it," he replied tightly.

"How do you know the stolen security footage wasn't on it?"

His jaw tensed. "Because someone tipped him off, and he didn't get on the airplane when he should have. Someone saw him on the East Coast the day after that plane went down. Shall I continue?"

"I don't know where it is, Vissar. I don't know where *he* is. You are wasting your time if you think you can threaten me."

When he leaned toward me with that menacing look in his eyes, I shrank away and reached for my champagne to take a gulp. Oh, this was fire. This man wasn't about to back down.

"Forgive me if I don't believe you or your thieving father." "He doesn't steal, and he would never take something from you. He must have been helping someone." My eyebrows drew together. "Do you really think he's going to come running just because you're wining and dining me?"

He didn't answer me, but the way he looked at me didn't make me feel any better. Vissar had something planned, and I had a sinking feeling I was about to find out what it was.

He smiled, reaching into his inside pocket and withdrawing some papers. Not papers. Pictures. He tossed them onto the table in front of me.

"I want you to look carefully at these pictures. You have until the end of the year to either produce that security footage or your father. Because if you don't, anyone in your life could be profoundly affected by the outcome."

My eyes widened at the pictures on the table. Kya, Mac . . . Dani. I picked up the photo of me with Skyler. She'd come with me to the market just last week to pick up groceries, insisting she needed to pick up a few things. It was the only time I had gone anywhere with here. It was then I found out cleaning my dad's house was not her only job. There were other houses she cleaned to make ends meet, which explained her absence most of the time. I looked back at him, feeling the blood drain from my face.

"You've got to be kidding me."

"Your father thought he could evade me by disappearing. The next time you talk with him, make it clear that more than your life is at stake here."

I grabbed my clutch, stood up, and stumbled away from the table, heading for the door. Unsure of where to go, I made my way straight to the hotel lobby and then outside. I needed air. I hadn't spoken to my dad since the night his plane had gone down. How in the hell would I warn him?

The champagne swirled in my stomach, threatening to come up as I burst into the night air. The bellboy looked alarmed, probably because I looked pale. I'd just had the hell scared out of me. No one could get hurt because of this. Not if I could figure out how to prevent it.

"I need a ride home," I whispered.

He nodded, waving a car over. Once I climbed into the backseat, my head spun out of control as I gave the driver instructions. I had consumed more champagne than I realized and was determined not to vomit in this poor guy's car. I wasn't used to drinking champagne, unable to remember just how much of it I'd had. I groaned. Of all the nights I should have been keeping myself together, I'd been too focused on handling the stress of the evening. The further he drove, the more my stomach revolted. I managed to calm myself down enough.

"Drop me off at the beach by the pier," I said.

Not long after that, he dropped me off, and I walked unsteadily. Just for a few minutes into my walk, I realized it might have been unwise for him to drop me off at the vacant beach, but it was too late to call him back. I started down the path toward home, struggling to balance on my heels. My skin prickled with fear.

Even when I stopped to look around, nothing seemed out of the ordinary. I knew better than to walk alone, especially dressed as I was. Under the light of a streetlamp, I pulled off my heels and held them in my hand while I struggled to get my phone out of my clutch. My fingers trembled as I dialed Jace's number.

The only person who would know what to do now was Jace. I wasn't sure what had happened to him since the last time I'd seen him. Had he gone home? Was he still at the event, working?

I took the chance and dialed his number.

"Cassie?" he answered quickly. "Where are you?"

"Jace," I replied, taking a deep breath. A sense of security washed over me at the sound of his voice. "I need help."

Chapter Twenty Seven

"Where are you?" I asked again.

She smothered a hiccup. "I got dropped off at the pier."

"The pier?" I blurted. "What in the hell were you thinking?"

I would never admit to her that I'd been waiting for her to leave the event, hoping she would call. Watching Vissar show Cassie off to his business cohorts all evening, allowing them to dance with her and put their hands on her, had tested my limits. I hated her being with him. I hated him. Damn, but I wanted to see her. Be *with* her.

"Can you at least tell me where by the pier you are?"

"No," she whispered. "I don't know. It's kinda foggy."

Oh God, she didn't know where she was. The beach stretched for miles. "Do you see the pier?"

"Um. Kind of?"

"Go toward the street." I made a turn, glimpsing the moon through the foggy clouds, hoping she could get to the street where I'd be able to see her. "I promise you, I'll be there. Try to stay where there's light."

My heart thundered in my ears as I sped toward the pier. I wasn't far, knowing she would head toward her house. When I lost her ride in freeway traffic, I figured I'd go to her house and wait for her there.

"Cassie?"

"Yes?" she answered, sounding surprised, as if she'd forgotten I was on the phone.

"Are you walking?"

Laughter bubbled from her throat, a delightful sound that lingered in my ears even when she grew quiet. Drunk or not, she had a beautiful laugh. "I think you can call it that."

The speedometer pushed the limits of the streets, and I hoped I wouldn't get pulled over. A speeding ticket I could handle. What I couldn't bear was not getting to Cassie and having something happen to her while I was detained. I eased my foot back a bit, navigating slowly as I got closer to the beach.

"I'm almost at the beach. Can you see the street?"

"Can't tell in this fog. I'm walking on grass." She laughed again.

"You should be almost to the street. I'm near the pier. I'll get out and find you if I have to," I said. "What could you possibly be laughing at?"

"It tickles," she whispered. "The grass on my feet. Gaaaaahhh!"

Unexpectedly, I saw a figure stumble onto the street, and my heart jumped into my throat. I slammed on the brakes. Any closer and I would have hit her, even going slow. I jumped out and ran toward her.

I didn't care that she'd dropped her phone or skinned her knee. When I grabbed her off the ground and pressed my lips to her temple, a feeling washed over me. Relief, but something more. The feel of her hands sliding beneath the short sleeves of my t-shirt against my bare skin, gripping me as though I were the one thing that would keep her safe, made me feel more than I was.

"My phone," she murmured.

Using my headlights while keeping my hand on her, I found her phone on the ground. Thankfully, it didn't appear broken from the fall she'd taken. "Let's get you home."

Untangling her shoes, still wrapped around her fingers, I took them, along with her clutch and phone, and helped her back to my car. After tucking her into the passenger seat, I wondered how much she'd had to drink since I'd left. I knew she limited how much she drank when she was out, but I'd never seen her like this.

"I'm sorry," she said when I handed her things back to her.

"Don't be. I just want to get you home, which will be in about a minute."

I watched her lean her head back against the headrest, trying to ignore my heavily beating heart at the sight of her. She wore the same dress as the night I'd seen her at Vissar's house. I needed to regain my composure, I reminded myself. Tonight would not be the night for that.

I'd already broken almost every single one of my rules for women. I made the first move when I kissed her in her bedroom, even though she'd been straddling me. I'd pulled her into that position in the first place. I called her that day; though in my defense, it was to help her. And I was about to break another rule because there was no way I was leaving her alone tonight in her condition. I glanced at her and her bright eyes stared back at me. She might try to get me to leave, but the look in her eyes said something different. But we weren't going down that road tonight.

Silence in the house greeted us, and she leaned heavily against the wall, watching with wide eyes as I set the security system. I couldn't help but give her my most sinful smile as I took her arm to guide her toward the stairs.

"Do you need me to carry you?"

Her brows raised, and while I knew she rarely let people fully into her life, it made me wonder if anyone had ever carried her to bed before. Damn, but I was just a rule-breaker.

Before she could respond, I swept her up into my arms. My answer came when she laughed, throwing her arms around my neck.

Instead of laying her down on the bed as she probably expected, I brought her straight to the bathroom and sat her on the counter. Even after having had that many drinks, she looked perfect, though she tried to twist around to look in the mirror.

I caught her chin with my fingers and kissed her, tasting the champagne on her tongue. Damn if it didn't make me want a drink myself. I'd settle for her. "You look gorgeous," I said.

I gathered band-aids and antiseptic to tend to her scraped knee. She didn't bother to hide her gasps of pain when I brushed out some sand and dirt, but I tried to be gentle. I knew she was tough, and she probably wouldn't have uttered a word if she'd been sober.

Securing the band-aid over her knee, I glanced back up at her. "I'm going to check the house and make sure everything is secure. Get into your pajamas."

With my hands on her waist, I pulled her down from the bathroom counter and set her on her feet, although she swayed precariously. "What if I don't want to wear pajamas?"

"I'll put them on you myself, if I have to."

"You set the security system already," she pointed out. "There's no need to check again. And shortie isn't here."

"After what happened with your friend, I'm not leaving anything to chance. Not when Vissar is sending you threatening messages. Promise me you're okay to change and won't fall over?" I teased.

She nodded.

I left her by the bed, quickly checking the house and returning just in time to see her shimmy into a pair of sleep shorts. If she noticed me admiring her shapely legs and small waist, she said nothing. She had left her hair loose, and I wanted nothing more than to wrap my hand in the heavy mass, tilt her head back, and taste her slender neck.

Cassie stood next to the bed, blinking at me. Fine, I thought. I'd bite, but I'd be gentle. Two giant steps brought me to her, and I didn't give her a chance to stop me before I slid my hand under her hair and brought her lips to mine. The sudden pliancy of her entire body made my other arm slide around her waist for support.

"Are you going to ravage me now?" she murmured against my

mouth.

"No." But damn, I wanted to. "I don't take advantage of drunk women."

Her head fell back. "What are you going to do, then?"

Reaching around her while keeping a steady arm on her, I pulled back the blankets. "I'm going to put you to bed. Where you belong."

Even after she clucked a few times, she crawled in and stretched out like a cat after having cream. Inwardly, I groaned. Tonight would be a travesty. I'd be able to sleep next to this woman who had been under my skin for weeks, but I couldn't touch her.

"Jace," she whispered, looking at me with heavy eyes.

I took off my shirt and tossed it aside before sitting down to remove my boots. When I stood up to take my pants off, she stared. God, women had blatantly stared at me before, but the way she looked at me made my blood liquefy.

As soon as I stretched out beside her, she molded herself against me. Soft curves wrapped around me, making my heart thump steadily in my chest while my mind raced with the most indecent thoughts. I slid my hand beneath her, helping her get comfortable against me. I'd never cuddled with a woman, but something about her made me want to keep her safe. Here, with me, I knew she would be. Safe from me? I didn't know, but I wanted to try. And that spoke volumes.

"Cassie?"

"Mm-hm?" she murmured, and I knew she was almost asleep.

"You're safe with me."

Chapter Twenty Eight

When I woke up the next morning, I immediately regretted the amount of champagne I had consumed, although I would have been far worse off had I been drinking something stronger. Then I realized I had company. Recollections of last night flooded back as my limbs grew accustomed to the man sleeping beside me. Not just sleeping next to me. Jace's limbs twisted around me like a pretzel, the heat of his body causing mine to rise.

Carefully, I swiveled to look at him, half-expecting him to be staring back at me. My heart beat a steady rhythm under the arm he had curled around me, as if he meant to keep me in place with no chance of escape. He lay on his side, his other arm tucked under the pillow. Long legs tangled with mine; his knee was bent snugly between my legs while the other rested against the curve of my ass. All I felt was his heated skin against mine.

"You're staring," he said, his sleep-roughened voice muffled against the pillow, only making me want to turn and hide my smile.

"How do you know?"

"I can feel it."

When he flexed his arm and pulled me closer, cutting off my laugh, I asked, "What are you doing?"

"Getting more comfortable."

I would have protested, but I understood what he meant. This position was indeed more comfortable, pulling me right into him and holding me in a state of bliss. I sank deeper into his arms, burying myself closer to him until a chuckle rumbled through him.

"Thank you for coming to my rescue last night," I whispered against his bare chest. "I'm sorry you had to."

"I'm glad you called me." His fingertips skated up my hip. "What were you thinking, getting dropped off at the beach?"

"I told you I wasn't a big drinker. If it wasn't for Vissar . . . "

Jace stiffened instantly. "What did he do?"

"He threatened me. Again."

When his gaze snapped to mine and the line of his jaw hardened, I ran my hand along it, but he snatched it away. "What do you mean?"

"Vissar said my dad took his security footage. He wants it back, or my dad. He wants me to get one of them back."

Jace growled. "Or what?"

"He'll take out the people close to me—Kya, Mac," I whispered. "Quinn?"

I shook my head. Of the pictures he'd thrown onto the table, there hadn't been a picture of Quinn, thank God. Jace said nothing, but I could tell his mind was working on a solution.

"I need to get to Ricky. He has to tell me where my dad is so I can find this security footage and return it to him."

Jace relaxed a little. "We'll talk to Ricky. We'll make him talk. I have ways. Did he give you a timeline?"

"The end of the year."

"Good, that means he won't do anything in a rush."

He resumed tracing his fingers along my hip, eliciting a shiver. There were other things I would rather think about while Jace touched me like that, and we were both fully clothed. Well, almost.

"I wouldn't trust that's all he wants, Cass. Not by a long shot."

"It's all he'll get." I shifted, meeting his gaze. "He'll never have me."

Relinquishing my hip, his fingers danced up to my chin, tipping it to keep my eyes on his. The whisper-soft touch of his mouth against mine turned into a more urgent, pulsing sensation when he tilted his hips. I gasped.

"Let me take care of you."

"What does that mean?" I murmured against his mouth, my arms winding around his neck as he pulled me closer.

"You don't deserve any of this. You are a beautiful person, Cassie. Inside and out." I would have looked away, but his fingers found my chin again. It wasn't an answer, but it made me mush inside. "The kind of person who would do anything to make sure her friend isn't bullied or that a kid isn't alone."

Again, I tried to look away, only to find his fingers guiding my head to meet his gaze. The emotions swirling behind his electric blue eyes were nothing short of serious. They stole my breath. How wrong I'd been about this man. How in danger I was of falling head over heels in love with him!

"The kind of person who would do anything, even put herself in danger, to get her dad back."

I smiled, sliding my hand up to his wrist and gently pulling his hold on my chin loose. "That is nothing short of what any sane person would do. Would you do it? For your mom? Your brother?"

Saying that struck a nerve, igniting a spark in his eyes.

"Absolutely, I would. But I'm trained to do it."

"Then train me."

"What?"

"Teach me what I should and shouldn't do. Let me help you find things out."

He shook his head. "Training in what you're asking takes a long time and a lot of skill."

"I'm serious, Jace. Will he hurt me? If he forces me to go to another event or to his house for a party?"

"I've never known him to force any woman, but he is extremely persuasive. I wouldn't put it past him to persuade you to do something you don't want to do."

I gasped and tried to pull away from him, but he held me tighter. "I'm not about to let him touch me." A shudder of revulsion rippled through me. "I'd sooner die than let him touch me like that."

Sliding his fingers through mine, he brought the back of my hand to his lips. "I want your promise, Cassie." His eyes, deadly serious, met mine. "I can't stand the thought of him touching you."

"You have it. I swear to you."

"And if you're ever in a situation leading to that, you'll get out." I nodded. "He'll do whatever he can to try."

"How long have you known him?"

"What?"

"You said that for as long as you've known Vissar, he's never forced a woman. How long have you known him?"

He kissed me then. "Too long."

With a playful growl, he pushed me over, giving me no opportunity to ask more questions. Sighing, I slid my hands over his smooth shoulders while he molded his body to mine, proving how perfectly he fit against me. My fingers tangled in his short hair as his hand hitched up my leg.

"Oh," I said, feeling his reaction to me.

He answered with a wicked grin until I heard the beep of the alarm system going off, then abruptly stop. My eyes widened, wondering if Skyler had come home suddenly. Glancing at the clock, I saw was still a little early for anyone to be around.

"Cassie?"

I shoved Jace off me at the sound of Quinn's voice at the bottom of the stairs, Jace's deep growl against the pillow making me smile. Even though we weren't naked, I thought being in bed with Jace was embarrassing enough if Quinn caught us like this.

But the little stinker was fast, standing in the doorway of my bedroom a moment later with a silly grin on his face.

"Oh, hey, Jace," he said.

"Hey, kid."

Jace recovered from my shoving him off, though it wasn't as far as I'd thought. He slid off me and onto his side of the bed. My face warmed at the thought of him having a side in my bed.

"You're back early," I said, sitting up.

"Yeah, Ray had to go to church. They dropped me off. Are you making breakfast?"

I would have groaned, wondering how the kid wasn't still tired, if it didn't warm my heart to hear him asking me to make him breakfast. Didn't tweener boys stay up all night like adults did?

"I am," Jace said. "Give us a minute and we'll be down."

I sat up, looking over at Jace. He wasn't the only one that needed a minute to get bodily functions under control. All he had to do was touch me and I dissolved. Luckily, Quinn had gone to his room to put his things away and gave us a few minutes of catching our breath, letting our body temperatures come down.

"Guess I better start breakfast."

"You don't have to."

"I'm going to."

My mouth dropped open as he threw back the blankets and eased out of bed. I watched him stretch, awed by his finely honed body. He could claim to have only beer and pizza in his refrigerator, but this body belonged to a man who worked out. I'd seen him plenty of times without a shirt, but this time my gaze leisurely traced each crevice, ripple, and slope defining his torso. I wasn't afraid of anyone noticing.

Jace looked at me, and my face flushed with embarrassment. I fell over, burying my face in the pillows with a groan just before I felt a sharp slap on my ass, followed by Jace's deep chuckle as he left the room. Sitting up, I couldn't help but stare after him. In all my life, even in high school, no guy had ever slapped me on the ass. A smile pulled at my lips until I couldn't help myself, grinning and falling back into the pillow.

A half hour later, after giving myself a pep talk in the bathroom mirror and making myself halfway presentable, I found Jace whipping up French toast while an animated Quinn chatted his ear off instead of being buried in his cell phone. It took me a moment at the edge of the kitchen to appreciate the scene, my heart warming. Next to Quinn, a cup of steaming tea awaited me. Oh, my beating heart, I was in big trouble.

Never in my life had a man ever had a cup of tea waiting for me in the morning. Never. I don't think any of the men I'd been with even remembered that I preferred tea over coffee. Nearly stumbling into the kitchen, I slid onto the chair next to Quinn to watch Jace deftly lay another piece of bread in the skillet.

"The best syrup I could find is that store-bought stuff, loaded with sugar," Jace said without turning away from his task. "Not pure maple, unfortunately."

I shrugged, ruffling Quinn's hair, who surprisingly let me. He must be in a good mood, I thought. "I think we'll live."

After a few minutes of watching Jace, he plated a few slices and set them in front of Quinn. I couldn't believe how quickly the kid buttered and drowned his French toast in syrup, shoving forkfuls into his mouth as though he were starving.

"Did you eat at Ray's house at all?" I teased.

Jace turned. "How many would my lady like?"

Quinn leaned back, laughing, with his mouth full.

Oh. My. God. "Uh, two would be plenty."

I sipped my tea in wonder, my eyes never straying from the man in the kitchen. The kitchen wasn't completely unknown to me, though I hadn't delved into cooking enough to prepare an extraordinary meal, as I had told Quinn when we first started getting to know each other. Still, I knew enough. Having a man cook for me rendered me speechless, and watching Jace cook for me and Quinn melted my icy heart.

An hour later, after we devoured an entire loaf of bread, I insisted on cleaning up the mess while Jace and Quinn retired to the living room to play video games. I listened with half an ear to them as their chatter about the game, laughing and roasting each other while I loaded the dishwasher and cleaned up the stovetop and counters. I had to admit, the French toast Jace made from ordinary bread, eggs, and milk had tasted amazing.

The doorbell rang, dragging me out of my deep thoughts just as I was about to join them in the living room. Jace frowned at me, but I shrugged. I didn't know who would ring the doorbell mid-morning on a Sunday.

Lo and behold, the door opened to reveal another delivery guy holding a bouquet of red roses. I sighed, hoping they weren't from who I thought they were. The pit in my stomach from last night returned, threatening to erupt.

I caught Jace and Quinn staring at me when I brought the flowers into the kitchen, unable to hide the enormous bouquet as I pulled out the card. Sure enough, Vissar wanted to dine tonight. He claimed on the card that he wanted to apologize for last night. No threats this time, although I knew they were there. Just not spoken.

"Vissar?" Jace asked, turning back to the video game.

I tossed the card into the trash, sidling over to them and easing down onto the couch next to Jace. "He wants to have dinner tonight. To apologize."

The clicking of the gaming controls continued. "Who's that?" Quinn asked.

I bit my tongue to suppress the derogatory remark I wanted to make. "Someone who might know why my dad took off. I'm trying to find out what he knows, but he wants to take me to dinner."

"And I told you he wants more than that," Jace growled.

"And I told you that won't happen."

I pulled out my phone to text Vissar.

"What are you doing?" The clench in Jace's jaw betrayed his feelings.

"Texting him to say yes. I'd rather get it over with. You know what's at stake. I can't risk it."

He shook his head, though he knew I was right. "He'll never let you go."

"Jace," I whispered. "Tell me you'll help me."

He paused the game, earning a whining "Heeeyy!" from Quinn. When he turned to me, my heart sank. This had to be the worst position to be in. I hated it.

"I'll help you. But only because I'd rather die than see you with a man like him."

What he failed to say was that he would rather I be with him than Vissar, but I'd take it anyway. I glanced sidelong at him. Did he? Would he? I shivered. Everything he'd shown me suggested he would. But could I? And would it last?

Chapter Twenty Nine

How easily I'd slipped back into the old days of hanging out with my friends when I had nothing else to do-no school, no work. Other than taking care of Quinn on the days he was at my house and spending time with Jace when he wasn't working, my life had become completely open. Jace had obtained his license for private investigation and was juggling his work for Vissar while building up his clientele.

Suddenly, I had to take a long, hard look at my life and where I wanted it to go. Where did I belong? I wanted to continue to help people, but being a therapist in an office all week long for the rest of my life suddenly felt like a weight around my ankle. I enjoyed helping others and it was what I'd gone to school for along with countless hours of internships. But did I have to do it this way?

Watching Mac and Kya work the club crowd with their dazzling personalities, I hung back on the sidelines with my water. I'd heard that Ricky's band was playing at this club and jumped at the opportunity to corner him if he showed up. As easy as Jace thought we would be able to get Ricky to talk, we couldn't get him to talk if we couldn't find him. To my delight, he was there and performing. I leapt at the chance. I only needed to wait for the break. The girls were more than willing to indulge in a night out. Jace would meet me here as soon as he could.

Thankfully, Vissar had been busy with business and had left me alone, only sending flowers over the last couple of weeks. I seriously hoped he had forgotten about me, but each time a delivery arrived, my heart sank.

I hadn't had wine or anything else since the night Jace had to pick me up from the pier, even limiting how many parties I was going out to. I only agreed to come out tonight because it would be a chance to see Ricky in person and force him to answer my questions. I sipped my water, lowering it when I caught sight of a man making his way through the crowd. The length of his dirty blond hair was hard to miss, even though it had been a few years since I had last seen him. Oh, this was going to be good.

I set my water down on the low table next to me, waved to Kya that I was moving, and wasted no time pushing through the crowd to reach Ricky. No sooner had I gotten close than he noticed me. His mouth was set in a severe line, and his face hardened.

"Goddamn it, Cassidy," he said, grabbing my arm and steering me toward the dark side of the room. "I told you not to come down here, and here you are prancing around."

"Ricky, stop." I dug in my heels, forcing him to halt. "I know he isn't dead. You know he isn't either. Everyone knows that. Where the fuck is that security footage he supposedly took, and why was he involved in the first place? Where is he?"

He didn't give me a chance to respond. "You won't find him. He doesn't want to be found right now. And you are putting yourself in danger by being here. Stop messing around. You're going to get yourself hurt."

"Why, Ricky? Why?" I pulled my arm away from him, nearly spinning in a circle from the force. "Tell me why, and I'll stop."

It was only half the truth. I wouldn't stop, no matter what he told me. Especially now that he said my dad didn't want to be found. That only made me want to find him even more. Something was going on, and he had all but confirmed it.

His brown eyes met mine, hard. He looked like shit with his unshaven face and long hair tied back but in need of a good brushing. It appeared he hadn't slept and definitely hadn't been taking care of himself. He needed to be honest with me, and now was the time. I knew.

"What happened?" I crossed my arms, fully aware of why I was in danger. But I wouldn't tell him. Not yet. "Just tell me that much."

"Go home. If he can't find your dad, you could be leverage."

"You're damn right. So start talking. I've been here for over a month. Save me the trouble and just tell me."

He growled, looking up at the ceiling. "We didn't mean to get him into this, but we've been working on getting him out. In the meantime, you need to split. And I mean it. Natalia tells me you've already got his attention, so GO HOME."

I took a step back, my eyes wide. In all the years I'd known Ricky, I'd never seen him this angry. Normally, he was a laid-back kind of guy, likely because of all the weed he smoked. But this side of him scared me. Whatever was going on had terrified him.

"Tell me what went down," I whispered. "I can help."

He took a step toward me, and I felt the wall at my back. His eyes blazed with anger, teeth clenched together. "I'm telling you one more time: go home. Go back to Seattle and don't come back here."

I didn't realize until he walked away that he had made me shake from the vehemence of his words. One thing was absolutely certain: this was not the Ricky Monroe I'd known all my life. It left me even more puzzled than ever. Did Naomi know what he was up to?

I stayed where I was for a few minutes, with my back pressed against the wall. Now, I knew without a doubt that Vissar's daughter and Ricky were both involved. It didn't matter if I went back to Seattle; it was too late for that.

Jace found me against the wall when he arrived at the club, immediately alarmed when he saw me. Of all I'd been through in the last month, I think seeing Ricky like that scared me the most. What was wrong with him?

"What's wrong?"

"I just ran into Ricky. All he said was for me to go home. He was insistent, actually. I've never seen him like that."

Jace ran his hands up my arms, pulling me toward him and away from the wall. "Are you okay? And don't say yes and shake your head."

I laughed. "I will be."

"Do you want me to take you home?"

I pressed my face against his chest. "No. I'm not letting him chase me away from here. Not now or in the future." I looked up into his eyes. "He's never going to tell me what happened. But I know he was involved. And Natalia."

When his hands cupped my face, his fingers lightly drumming against my jaw, I could have melted right then and there. "I thought as much since Vissar hasn't let her leave his house, but I swear I saw her when I came in."

"Whatever happened, those three are involved. I wonder what was on that security footage he wants back so badly."

"Something incriminating, otherwise he wouldn't be so eager for it to be returned. You've been doing good at evading him lately. Keep it up, got it?" he grumbled, nipping at my mouth.

I nodded submissively, even though Vissar being busy was why I was easily avoiding him. His flowers reminded me of his presence and the ticking of the clock. Jace released me, slipping his hand around mine to pull me away from the wall and back to the table. Kya's grin broadened at the sight of Jace with me.

"Funny seeing you here," Kya said to Jace, tilting her head to the side. "And what a delightful surprise, too."

"Are you flirting with him?" My statement might have sounded accusatory, but my smile was anything but.

"I would never do that, babe."

Kya wouldn't. Even though I laughed, Jace didn't look amused by our banter. My eyes caught sight of Natalia drifting through the crowd toward us. Jace had been right. She was here. Vissar had let her out of the house.

"Lex's daughter, or should I say my father's new plaything," she smirked, stopping in front of us.

"Natalia, that isn't necessary," Jace said smoothly.

She ignored him, keeping her steely blue eyes fixed on me. "I assure you, it was. What did you say to Ricky to upset him?"

"Me? What did I say to upset him? Look, I don't know who you think you are to Ricky, but I've known him my entire life. He's like an uncle to me. Ricky never gets this pissed off. My question is what did *you* do to piss him off?"

"What did he tell you?"

"Other than to go home to Seattle, nothing."

I watched as she swirled the ice in her half-full glass, then took a drink. "You should. No good will come from you being here snooping around." She cocked her head to the side. "Unless you can find that security footage."

When she turned to walk away, I caught her arm sharply, despite Jace's presence. He lifted an eyebrow, amused.

She turned back, looking down at my fingers curled around her biceps and then back up at me. "Ow."

"Do you know something about it?"

Jace crossed his arms, waiting for her response. "If you know anything, it would be great if you'd let us know, especially since your dad is threatening Cassie about it when she knows nothing."

Natalia slowly drew her arm out of my grip. "I'm not discussing it here. And you," she leveled her eyes at me again, "should take Ricky's advice. Go home."

"Oh my God," I whispered as something my dad had said popped into my head. "You're Ricky's girlfriend. He told me Ricky's girlfriend was about my age. It's you."

She marched away without saying another word. As irritated as she made me, I now had a solid answer: My dad *did* have it. But why would he still have it, and where the hell was he? What did he intend to do with it if it was so incriminating?

I turned to Jace. "I'm not going home, by the way."

He responded with a grin, sliding his arm around my waist.

"You probably should, but I don't think that would deter Vissar. You could stay. What's keeping you in Seattle, anyway?"

I took a sip of my water, giving my throat some much-needed moisture. "Actually, I've been thinking about that lately. I enjoy helping people. It's what I went to school for, and I felt obligated to go into the field after I graduation, but . . . "

He raised his dark eyebrows, making my heart flip. "But?"

"Now that I'm not working in an office all week long, I'm finding it a lot less . . . suffocating. How can I still help people, but not in a stuffy office?"

"Do you ever think about opening your own practice? Or maybe doing therapy with kids? I see how good you are with Quinn, even though it's not therapy."

I thought about him, that little booger, realizing that I missed him when he spent nights at Skyler's place. It made me wonder what it would be like to have him around all the time, leading me to think about having kids. Being single more often than in a relationship, motherhood had never occurred to me. Now, suddenly, it could be a possibility.

Looking at Jace, I saw my future flash before my eyes and felt all the blood drain from my face. When I swayed, Jace put a steadying hand on my arm.

"Cassie? You okay?"

"No," I whispered. "I need air."

He wasted no time bringing me outside. As soon as the cool air hit me, feelings I had no business considering enveloped me. A life with Jace churned inside me like excitement for an upcoming event. The man I knew didn't seem the type to shy away from a relationship, yet despite how close we'd been to actually having sex, there had been no pressure. He was leaving it up to me, making it my absolute decision to move forward with him or not. He'd said we were together, as in a relationship.

But would he stay with me once I'd found my dad? He'd told me to stay, even after, but did he mean it? Ugh, confusion and uncertainty swept through me, making me feel nauseated.

"What happened?"

I blinked, unsure of what to say. How could I tell him I'd fallen hopelessly in love with him over the past weeks? I ticked off the number of weeks since Riley's wedding in my head. Six weeks since we'd met. Choking on air, I could only shake my head.

"I don't know, Jace."

"Come here."

When his arms slid around me, warming and comforting me, it made perfect sense to want him as I did. It didn't make it any less terrifying. What Evan had done hurt, and my feelings for him didn't seem nearly as deep as they were what I was feeling for Jace.

"I didn't mean to make you think so hard."

"Quinn isn't my kid. He lives with Skyler most of the time. I have a life in Seattle. A job," I said, as suffocating as saying it felt. "What the hell would I do here?"

He shrugged. "You'd figure it out."

I would. I had enough money. I just needed time to think. No decisions needed to be made until we found my dad, but I felt we were getting closer. The pieces were fitting together, at least. I knew one thing for certain: I wouldn't be going home. Not to Seattle, anyway.

We went back inside, but only long enough to say our goodbyes to Mac and Kya. Jace offered to bring me home, which Mac announced she had known he would. After saying goodbye to the girls, we left the club.

When Jace parked and walked me to the door nearly an hour later, my heart raced so fast I thought it might burst out of my chest. With Quinn not home, it would have been perfect. Except my head was swimming with confusion. Did I want to start something when I felt such overwhelming emotions? He'd always been respectful.

"Want me to come in?"

God, when he used that tone, I turned to mush. This had happened before, and I had turned him down, regretting it at first but then convincing myself that it was for the best. As I raised my eyes to his, I wondered if I would regret it if I didn't invite him in. I was terrified of what would happen if I did, yet I desperately wanted to invite him inside. My heart would win over my head, and I was afraid of hating myself in the morning.

"Cassie," he murmured, kissing the back of my hand. "If you aren't ready for this, just tell me. I told you before that I respect you. I would never pressure you."

"I . . ."

He pulled me into his arms, pressing me against the closed door and thoroughly plundering my mouth, leaving me breathing heavily and making it clear what I would be missing. I knew I needed to stop pushing people away. Stop pushing him away.

After leaving me with another quick kiss, he waited for me to unlock the door before turning away. I understood why he had to leave me there. He didn't trust himself any more than I trusted myself.

I hurried inside, quickly disarming the alarm, and smiled as I leaned against the door. I knew what I wanted. I wanted Jace. But I needed the courage to take what I wanted.

I turned on the lights, feeling deliriously happy, except for having let him go without being honest and having him stay. I caught sight of the kitchen, my eyes sweeping over to the living room.

And I screamed loud enough to wake the dead.

Chapter Thirty

The living room and kitchen were in complete disarray, clearly having been searched for something. I didn't need to go upstairs to know it was probably the same. The door at my back opened to Jace trying to come in after hearing my scream, and I scrambled out of the way. I let out a strangled cry and covered my mouth. Someone had been searching for something, and I knew exactly what it was they were looking for.

"Go out to my car and stay there," Jace said, handing me the keys.

I shook my head. "I'm not leaving you in here alone."

"Cassie, go!" he shouted, his eyes blazing. "Go outside and wait there. Stay out of the house. Do you hear me?"

Nodding, I hurried toward the front door.

I didn't care that the door was left open behind me; getting to the driveway was all I could think of. If the person who had ransacked the house was still inside, it terrified me to think they would hurt Jace. I had to remind myself that he was a cop and an undercover detective, experienced in countless dangerous situations, but I didn't think he had a gun on him.

I enclosed myself in his car, trying to focus on my breathing until he finally emerged minutes later. He opened the passenger side door, squatting down beside me.

"I called the cops. They'll be here any minute to do a sweep inside. I wouldn't be able to tell if anything is missing, so you might need to go back inside."

I swallowed the lump in my throat but nodded. He reached in, taking my hand and caressing my knuckles. We remained that way until the squad car pulled up minutes later. When Jace pulled me out, I recognized the officer I'd spoken to about my dad when I'd first arrived approaching with another officer.

"Ms. Nichols," he said, striding toward us and nodding at Jace.

"You can call me Cassie," I whispered.

"We'll need a statement and for you to take a quick look and let us know if anything is missing. If you can do that?" I nodded, comforted by Jace's hand on my back as we walked to the door.

With the entire house illuminated, I took in the full extent of the mess. Kitchen cupboards hanging open as though something had been hidden among the dishes and food, couch cushions upended, and plants knocked over. One hand tucked in Jace's, I covered my mouth with my other hand but didn't make a sound.

All of the artwork my dad loved still hung on the walls. If this had been a robbery, it would have been gone. No, this had been a targeted break in. We went upstairs, and I could have cried at the mess they'd made in Quinn's room. But nothing seemed missing. My room was the same, the bed crooked and dresser drawers pulled open, the closet door open with clothes scattered everywhere.

"Jesus," Jace murmured. "Made a point, didn't they?"

"Does anything look like it's missing?" Officer Davison asked, pen poised over his small notepad. "It doesn't look like there's any damage, just that they were searching for something."

I moved slowly into my bedroom, taking a peek at my jewelry. Nothing I owed had a steep price worth stealing, but everything appeared to be there. "It doesn't look like anything has been taken."

"Was the alarm system set while you were out?"

"I always set it."

Jace scoffed. "That's easily disarmed, Adam. You know that. These systems are too easy to bypass with a signal interference."

I raised my brow. That didn't make me feel safe at all. "Might have to get myself a dog," I murmured. "A big one."

After I gave Officer Davison my statement, Jace set the security system even as I laughed at it. From what I gathered, the security system wouldn't help against intruders. Not if they knew what they were doing.

"Call me if you find anything missing," Adam said before he and the other officer walked back to the squad car.

As I blew out a heavy breath, I leaned against Jace's car. He caged me in but didn't touch me. "Don't you dare shake your head and say you're fine." I gave him a half-hearted smile before he opened the door.

I slid into the passenger seat, dropping my head against the headrest as I waited for him to get in. How boring my life had truly been before coming here, I thought.

When he slid into the driver's seat, he reached over to take my hand. "I'm bringing you to my place." There was no question about it. "Shortie's at a friend's house?"

The corner of my mouth lifted slightly. "Yes. For the weekend."

Releasing my hand, he brushed his knuckles over my cheekbone. "We'll talk about this when we get to my place."

"They're looking for that security footage, knowing damn well it's not here. He's trying to scare me," I whispered.

Jace started the car, gripping the steering wheel so tightly that the whites of his knuckles briefly appeared. "I'm sure he is, but it's still a shitty thing to do. Your dad probably has it with him."

I stared at him. "I wish I could talk to him."

"Me too," he said wryly. "Whatever he's done or is doing, it's affecting you. And Quinn."

And that isn't something he would do, I thought. Lex Edwards would help anyone in need, but he wouldn't put anyone in jeopardy to do it, especially his daughter, even if I might not really be his daughter.

"You're fine with coming to my place?" he finally asked.

I looked at him. "Where am I going to go, Jace? They destroyed my bedroom."

He gave me a half-hearted smile. "Good. I'm not about to let you go back there. Not until I can inspect it more."

Jace hadn't been kidding when he said he didn't live far. He parked the car in the garage and ushered me through a door that led into a laundry room barely big enough for one person, then into a small kitchen. I wandered in as he closed the door behind us, glancing around the tiny house. There were doors on the left, presumably leading to bedrooms, and another door to the right.

"Your brother won't mind?" I asked.

When he turned on the kitchen light to a low setting, it illuminated a clean house. Three grown men sharing this cramped space, I mused.

I didn't realize I had stopped just outside the kitchen until Jace tossed his keys onto the counter beside me and pulled me into the kitchen. Still in my high heels, I teetered cautiously inside, even as he smiled.

"You're safe here, Cass."

I nodded, swallowing the lump in my throat. "I know."

"Ezra is probably out with Milo. They won't be back for a while, if at all." He went into the kitchen and opened the refrigerator. "All we have is beer."

"A beer is fine."

I leaned against the counter as he took out two bottles and popped them open. As soon as mine hit my hand, I tipped it back and chugged. The last time I'd had a beer was in college. His eyebrows raised.

"It's been a hell of a night," I said, cradling the bottle between my palms after pulling it away.

He stepped toward me, placing his hands on the counter to cage me in. "No one would think any less of you if you chugged that entire bottle, baby," he whispered.

All I could think about was how close he stood in front of me. We'd been this close before, but it felt different now. Quinn wouldn't be coming through the door, nor was he down the hall sleeping. My eyes met Jace's as he reached up to tuck my hair behind my ear, and my eyes fluttered closed. A second later, I felt his lips against mine. Blindly, I set my bottle on the counter behind me as he pressed himself against me.

Apparently, he had abandoned his own bottle because I could feel his hand sliding from my hips up my ribs, palming my breasts through the thin fabric of my dress as his tongue swept against mine. My head fell back as I gasped for air, his mouth, tongue, and teeth blazing a trail along the sensitive skin of my neck.

"Beautiful," he whispered, his fingers tentatively brushing against the hem of my dress.

Is that what he thought of me? My mouth opened just enough for him to accept the invitation with no mercy. His lips against mine sent sensations whirling through me. My mind raced, soaking him in while I burned beneath his touch. I felt his fingertips brush the skin of my thigh just beneath the curves of my ass.

"Jace."

He stilled for a moment, shuddering once before straightening and picking me up to set me on the counter. Instinctively, my legs wrapped around his waist. His eyes searched mine. "I don't know if I've ever heard anyone say my name that way before. You . . ." He reached up, tracing the line of my jaw with his finger. "You wreck me, Cassie."

My heart pounded. My desire for him to kiss me again prevented me from reaching for my beer. "I don't want to wreck you, Jace. I just don't want to be some girl."

The laugh he let out was low, nearly a growl. "You aren't just some girl. You aren't just *any* girl." His eyes sparkled dangerously. "You're *mine*, and I haven't said that to anyone for . . . " He hung his head for a moment before looking back up at me, his eyes still intense. "I haven't said that to anyone."

My heart skittered and thumped wildly. Fairly certain I would let him do anything he wanted after that, I slid my hands along his smoothly shaved jaw and leaned forward to kiss him. He didn't let me get even halfway before his mouth was on mine, his lips forcing mine open and his tongue sweeping against mine.

I groaned. Or he groaned. Either way, he pulled me off the counter, our beers forgotten, while he carried me out of the kitchen with my legs tight around his waist. He walked with me wrapped around him with such ease, as though I weighed nothing at all.

Although I didn't know how he managed to open the door to his room while holding me, it swung wide. I clung to him, my arms around his neck while he continued pressing his lips wherever he could reach.

He kicked the door shut behind us, and I paid no attention to my surroundings as he walked into a small bedroom, trying to divest him of his shirt while alternately kissing him everywhere. When I felt my knees hit the bed on either side of him, I lifted my head.

"I haven't been able to get you straddling me out of my mind since that day." The way he slowly eased out each word sent my heart racing.

His hands roamed beneath my dress, fingertips grazing the sensitive skin as his lips claimed the tender area beneath my ear. I managed to undo his shirt enough to pull it off.

When he lifted his head, his eyes bright with whatever was running through his mind, I could only stare at him. If he was looking for words, he'd need to wait. I didn't think I could talk right now. How had this man stumbled into my life?

"I think I broke your underwear," he whispered.

I let out a soft laugh and shrugged. A second later, I heard a quiet snap as he broke the other side, letting it flutter to the floor.

The feel of his palms sliding up each thigh, past my hips and ribs, pulling my dress up slowly, heated my blood to near boiling until he lifted it clear of me and flung it aside.

Stripped of everything, he had free access to whatever he wanted to touch. And touch he did. His hands slid, his mouth branded, and his teeth grazed until my head fell back in sweet agony.

"I want to touch you," I uttered.

"No," he groaned. "Let me touch you this time. Please."

He moved just enough to remove the rest of his clothes, resuming his exploration of my body as my temperature soared to impossible heights. I would be in danger of bursting soon if he didn't hurry, but I'd been right to think he'd take his time, just as he did with speaking. Jace was in no rush.

"I need to get protection."

He paused to look at me, hands on my hips and eyes hooded with arousal. I wouldn't budge, fully content to stay where I was for a moment, with my heart pounding ferociously in my chest.

I shook my head. "I promise you I'm clean, and I'm on the pill."

When he simply stared into my eyes with his molten gaze, I thought I might have shocked him. He expected a good girl. I might have shocked myself. That's what he did to me.

"Are you sure? I always wear one."

Instead of answering, I nodded, unable to say anything. I trusted him. Completely. He didn't need any further encouragement, reaching between us until I felt his hand on me, his fingers sliding against me, inside me. A gasp tore from deep in my throat.

"Cassie," he breathed, his mouth just beneath my ear. "Tell me again that this is what you want. Please."

"Does it feel like I don't want you, Jace?" I touched his face, gazing deeply into his eyes. "I want you, Jace. There's no doubt in my—"

He hooked his arm around my back, his hand on my shoulder, and abruptly pulled me down. I gasped, trembling at the feel of him against me, inside me. It hadn't been long since I'd been with a man, but I was positive he wouldn't fit all the way. Yet I didn't want him to stop, the sensations making me tremble. Dear God, I hadn't realized how much I wanted him until he pulled me down further, still not entirely in.

My mouth opened in a silent moan, his mouth covering mine as he used his other hand to pull me down the rest of the way, and I cried out in sweet torture, arching my back.

"How long has it been since you've done this?" he asked.

Of course, he had to ask me that. "Not as long as you think. You?"

He could crush me with just a few words, but the look in his eyes told me otherwise. "Longer than you think."

I gasped as his hands slipped away from my shoulders, smoothing around to my back and down to my hips, beginning to move slowly while keeping his eyes locked on mine. To be watched so intently while feeling him beneath me, inside me, around me—was unlike anything I'd ever experienced.

"I don't want to go too fast," he murmured, burying his face against my neck.

"It's too late for that, Jace."

"You're right, but I want this to last. Fuck, I want this to last."

Every touch of his mouth and hands branded me. He didn't know that if he broke my heart, I would forever remember this.

In the next moment, I was airborne as he lifted me and spun us around. I felt the bed against my back a second later, followed by him, as though he wouldn't let me go for even an instant. My fingertips brushed the ends of his hair, my legs cradling him as if we fit together perfectly. My lips swelled from the demands of his mouth, and I couldn't stop as he drove me to heights I'd never reached in my life.

"God, Cassie," he groaned. "I've never felt anything so perfect as how you feel clenched around me right now."

"Don't stop," I whispered, sliding my hands up the planes of his chest.

His body shuddered, and I couldn't tell if it was from my touch or what I'd said. I didn't care. Holy smokes, he had the smoothest skin beneath my palms.

He eased back, allowing me to adjust, but I reached for him. Leaning into me, he kissed along my jawline and then my lips, moving in sync with his hips until mine followed suit.

"Tell me if I'm going too fast," he whispered, then added, "No, don't."

I couldn't utter a single word as my legs clung to him, a symphony of sparks lighting through my body, bursting through every fiber of my being. Good God, how long had it really been? He made my body sing with the way he handled me. Wave after wave of pleasure hit me until I was gasping for air.

Gripping my waist, he ground against me and whispered my name as I moved my hips in time with his rhythm. Running my hands along his ribs, I let out a deep sigh and gasped his name as another orgasm rocked me.

"Come with me, Cass. Give it all you've got because I can't hold back any longer," he said, his voice low and husky.

Pulling me up against him, almost straddling him again, he used my shoulders as leverage to ensure he hit every single nerve I had. Fireworks exploded behind my eyes when I shouted out that final cresting wave, with his shuddering groan echoing right behind me.

When he dropped his forehead against mine, I wasn't sure I would recover from this. Together, we sank into bliss, his arms tightening around me. I couldn't remember ever being held so securely. He didn't need to say anything. He couldn't. I couldn't. We stayed where we were, breathing hard in the silence of his bedroom for several minutes while our heartbeats slowed.

"Did I hurt you?"

It was sweet of him to ask, but it wouldn't have mattered if he did. My heart still raced, my body still aching for him, though he hadn't withdrawn yet. I kept his gaze, smoothing my hand along his jaw.

"No. It was perfect."

Slowly, he moved away but didn't go far. He pulled back the blankets, and we crawled in, letting them swallow us up before he pulled me back to him, cradling me in his arms and kissing my temple. "Okay?" he whispered.

I nodded, pretty sure I wasn't able to speak with his body molded against mine this way. It made me want him more. He did that to me.

"Yes," I finally whispered.

Kissing the tip of my nose, he chuckled. "I think that's the first time you've ever actually been straightforward with me." He squeezed me tighter. "Best birthday ever."

I huffed and looked at him. "Jace! Why didn't you tell me?"

"Never had a birthday worth a shit, so don't make a big deal about it." He tucked my head under his chin, dancing his fingertips up my arm. "Sorry about your underwear."

I smiled, knowing that if he thought I would sleep soon, it wouldn't happen. And I was right; neither of us slept much that night. We laughed when we heard his brother and roommate come home and mutter about the beers we must have spilled in the kitchen in our haste. When I finally fell asleep, I rested deeply in his arms, feeling safe. It felt good not to be alone.

Chapter Thirty One

Morning came too early, but I needed water and to check my phone to see if Quinn had called or texted. I slipped out from Jace's arms, picked up his shirt from the night before, and put it on, making sure it covered all the right places before heading into the kitchen. Unfortunately, I had left the house in such a hurry that I hadn't been able to bring anything decent to wear. And now, no underwear, I thought with a smile.

Water would have to suffice for a toothbrush. As I reached up to assess how bad my hair was, I walked out of his bedroom and stopped at the sight of a guy in the kitchen with dark hair like Jace's, though even shorter. Dark eyes rimmed with red met mine. His eyes widened, then he shook his head.

"Should have known he had a woman here," he muttered as I padded slowly over. "I'm Ezra."

"Cassie," I said, staying out of the kitchen, feeling indecently dressed. "Sorry about the beers."

He shrugged, studying me with his reddened eyes. "Jace doesn't bring women here. Never lets them get close enough."

My eyebrows lifted. "You don't say."

"My brother may have a reputation, but it follows him around and never lets him go. He isn't the same as he once was." I opened my mouth, but he cut me off. "Women throw themselves at him all the time. It gets old."

Ezra opened the refrigerator and took out a jug of orange juice, lifting it in an offer to me. I nodded, not seeing a coffee maker, and I was certain they wouldn't have herbal tea for me. He poured us two glasses with a shaky hand.

"I can see that happening," I said, taking a few gulps to quench my thirst.

"So, what's your story?"

"That's a loaded question," I replied. "I met him at a friend's wedding in September. I live in Seattle."

"Ah. *That* Cassie."

"Excuse me?"

He pressed his lips together as if he shouldn't have said anything. "Just so you know, women don't walk away from my brother. First, they're attracted to him for obvious reasons, but once he talks in that smooth voice of his, it takes a miracle to pull them away. *You* walked away."

"I think that's enough, Ez."

We both turned at the voice in the hallway. Jace appeared, wearing only a pair of thin sweatpants slung low around his waist. I took another big gulp of my orange juice as he walked over, slipping his arm around me. When Ezra narrowed his eyes at us, I tried not to react as Jace's fingertips traced the edge of my shirt, just barely skimming the back of my thighs.

He dropped his chin to my shoulder. "You make a helluva sight in my shirt," he whispered. "Might have to go back to bed."

Ezra rolled his eyes dramatically. "Think I'll take my juice and go brood in my room until I have to go to work. Nice to meet you, Cass."

I winked at him as he brushed past us, while Jace worked his fingers around to the front of my shirt and slipped it down. A gasp tore from my throat. "Jace, your brother."

His teeth caught my earlobe. "Then you'd better get your sweet ass into my bedroom. Now."

Ezra's bedroom door had just closed before Jace scooped me up. We barely made it back into the bedroom, falling onto the bed in a tangle of limbs.

"Stay with me today," he said.

I tried to ignore his questing hands, intent on sidetracking me. "I have to put the house back in order. See what they might have destroyed." My breath caught when he found an especially sensitive spot, working it until my entire body tightened and exploded into a million stars.

"They're throwing a small party for me at my mom's. She's not able to travel well these days."

"Is she okay?" I whispered, my eyes closed as he undid the buttons of my shirt and covered the exposed skin with his mouth.

"She'll be okay. She was in an accident and messed up her back. Ezra and I are going over there later. I want you to come, and it's my party."

I smiled. Was he sure he wanted me to meet his mom? I didn't want to know. Instead, I plunged my hands into his hair and pulled his mouth to mine. "I'll say yes, but you need to do me one thing first."

I whispered in his ear, letting him easily overpower me while I laughed. Ezra shouted at us through the wall, but we only laughed harder until my gasps and his murmurs echoed throughout the room.

Cw

We went by the house to clean up what we could before heading to the birthday party. Silence and a giant mess greeted us when we stepped through the front door a short time later. Desperately in need of a shower, Jace urged me to get to it while he started putting things back in order.

After spending the night with him, I was fairly certain he knew every sensitive spot on my body. As though he hadn't already known several of them before, he knew them intimately now. It took us longer than it should have to get out of the house.

He would have joined me in the shower, but we wouldn't get anything done if we continued. Instead, I showered as quickly as I could and rejoined him just as Skyler came back.

"What the hell happened here?" she asked, throwing her bag onto the chair.

My spine straightened, thinking we'd gotten past this. "Someone broke in and ransacked the place, looking for whatever my dad has." I wanted to say something far different from that, but I held back.

Jace came up behind me with the garbage. Her eyes met mine. "How bad is it?"

"Every single room in this house, but we haven't gotten to them all yet. We'll get to what we can. It's not safe for Quinn here until this-whatever this is-blows over. Not even after school."

"He isn't going to like it, but I understand."

I watched her sashay across the room and up the stairs. Did she actually agree with me? I sputtered and looked at Jace, who merely raised an eyebrow. A minute later, she was shouting from inside her bedroom about the mess and reappeared at the top of the stairs.

"You have got to be kidding."

I shook my head as she stepped down the stairs. "Are you sure you don't know anything at all about what happened or where my dad went?"

"I already told you I don't."

Time to test the waters. I looked her in the eyes. "We're all in danger." She didn't show any sign of fear. "He has something that someone is looking for."

"Something that someone wants back badly," Jace added.

"Who?"

"Do you know who Vissar Loukas is?" I asked, watching her carefully for any sign of recognition.

"I've heard that name somewhere, but I don't think it's someone your dad hung out with. Did he do this?"

I nodded. "I'm pretty sure he had his thugs do it, looking for it."

"Your dad isn't into stealing. You know your dad." "But he helps people," I replied.

I looked at Jace, unsure how much I should divulge to her. Since we didn't have a strong relationship, I didn't know if I could trust her. He gave a slight shake of his head.

"Whatever they were looking for, I'm sure they didn't find it," she continued. "But they made a wreck of my bedroom. I don't appreciate that."

"Yeah, well, they made a mess of mine and Quinn's."

She scoffed. "His room's always a mess."

I turned away, reassembling the couch cushions to avoid saying something I would regret. At only eleven, he didn't deserve someone going through his personal space. As it was, I felt violated having anyone go through my things.

Skyler left us again, huffing about having to clean up her bedroom and not having time to do it. While Jace and I worked in the kitchen and living room, she stayed in her room and only retreated when she decided it was time to leave again.

"Interesting woman," Jace commented as we headed downstairs to see the damage done to my dad's studio.

This was the part I dreaded. Of all the rooms in the house, this was my dad's favorite. I didn't want to see what they might have done to it. The door was partially open when we reached the bottom of the stairs. Jace saw the worry etched on my face and curled his hand around mine, making sure he went in first.

Sure enough, drawers were stuck halfway out of the desk, with papers scattered everywhere on the floor. Pieces of his drum set lay strewn about the room. I clamped a hand over my mouth to smother whatever might have escaped while Jace squeezed my other hand.

Shaking him loose, I went over to the drums and sank down to my knees as tears spilled freely. Someone had broken his drumsticks in half and thrown them on the floor. My trembling fingers picked up what remained of one. The holes in the drums themselves only aggravated me further. Jace stared at me for a moment before lowering himself down and pulling me into his arms.

"Cassie," he whispered against my shoulder.

"Why would they do this?" My voice cracked. "Looking for something is one thing, but destroying his things?"

He didn't answer. I didn't expect him to. What kind of monster breaks into someone's house and destroys their belongings? I could have another drum set in here before the week was over, but it wouldn't be the same. He'd had this set for years. It was well-used and sentimental.

"He doesn't have a mean bone in his body and definitely never gets into trouble."

I lifted my head, searching his eyes as though he had the answers. He slid his palm against my jaw, cradling my face and wiping away tears with the pad of his thumb. My eyes closed when he pressed his lips to the tears.

"We'll get this put back in order before your dad comes home," he murmured.

When I opened my eyes, the seriousness behind his blue gaze stunned me. I threw my arms around his neck, releasing a deep sigh when his arms tightened around me, holding me against his chest and cradling me in his lap amidst the mess. I fell more in love with him at that moment. Had anyone ever held me this tightly?

We sat there for several minutes, as though he couldn't or wouldn't let me go. When the phone vibrated in my back pocket, I reluctantly pulled away from Jace to take it out. It was the same unknown number that had been calling.

With a sigh, I answered irritably. The only way to get this person to stop calling was to respond. "Hello?"

Pushing to my feet, Jace kept his hand cupped around my elbow.

"Hello?"

"Hey, baby girl?"

"Dad!!" I shouted, running for the stairs to maintain a good connection, with Jace right behind me. "Dad, can you hear me?"

"I've heard you've been sticking your nose into places it doesn't belong, putting yourself in danger. I told you to stay the bloody hell out of it."

"Where are you? Please tell me you're at least okay."

"Go home, baby girl. You're not safe."

"I'm not safe there, either, am I?"

"He'll kill you. Even if I told you, he'll kill you."

"Tell me where the security footage is and who else is involved. I'm not leaving."

"Cassidy Jenna Nichols, I'm telling you to go home right now. You're safer there than you think. Stop asking questions and go back to Seattle before you get hurt. Please."

"No," I said stubbornly. "But you can't come home. He'll kill *you*. I don't think he'll hurt me. He just wants it back, but he'll kill you if you come back. Can't you just send it back?"

"I can't do that. Not until we figure out how to bring him down."

"Who, Dad?"

"Bloody hell, baby girl."

The line went dead as soon as I reached the foyer. I wanted to crumple the phone in my hand, frustrated that I couldn't talk to him more. He was acting just like Ricky and Natalia. All three of them knew something but wouldn't let me in on it. Whatever it was, I could fix it. I turned to look at Jace, who had a surprised expression on his face.

"Anything?" he asked, coming up behind me.

I shook my head. "He won't tell me anything. He said something about figuring out how to bring him down. Whatever is on that security footage will, I bet. I don't know what that means. God, I hope he doesn't come home."

"He doesn't want to be found."

"Yes." I blew out a breath. "I'm in danger. But I'm not leaving. After that, I'm not sure how much more I can do today." I looked at him. "What time is the party?"

He reached out, sliding his hand up my arm. "An hour. Let's tackle your room and Quinn's. Then we can leave."

We tackled Quinn's room first at my insistence. Even though I told Skyler to keep him away from here, I couldn't live with myself if he came home from Ray's to find his room like that. It was Jace's brilliant idea to leave it a little messy, but I put his bed back together and fixed his dresser drawers. I left him a note, just in case he came home and wondered who had been poking around in his room.

By that time, I didn't care about my room. But Jace put the bed back together while I cleaned up the bathroom mess. Thankfully, I only had a few things for them to search. After the phone call from my dad, I knew they hadn't found what they were looking for, and they probably knew they wouldn't find it here.

Chapter Thirty Two

As soon as we walked into Valerie Taylor's home, she pulled me into her embrace. I'd barely made it through the door when she appeared, as if she had heard us pull up. Like Kya, she possessed a striking beauty with dark eyes and an olive complexion. This could not possibly be Jace's mother—she looked young enough to be his sister. The only hint that she might be years older were the telltale signs of tiny wrinkles at the corners of her eyes. I could see Jace in her hair and complexion but not in the lightness of his eyes. He must get them from his dad.

When I turned to look at him, he shrugged and gave me the wicked smile that turned my insides to mush.

"Cassie," she said, pulling away slightly, her eyes sparkling with unshed tears as she held my hands, "I'm so happy to meet you. Jace has never brought anyone to meet me."

"Mom."

The warning in his deep voice amused me as much as it sent a thrill through me. Hearing this, along with what Ezra had shared with me that morning, made it sound like I was growing on him. What I didn't tell him was that I couldn't wait to introduce him to my dad.

She released my hands and moved with deliberate slowness to let us in. I didn't wait for Jace, following her past the cozy living room with its small couch and television into a corner kitchen.

I understood why Jace didn't stay here. Although the house gave me a sense of comfort, it was small. I noticed a bedroom when we passed through the living room, and now that we were in the kitchen, I could see another short hallway leading to a bathroom and another room.

Jace pulled out one of the two stools and motioned for me to sit down while his mom withdrew two platters of appetizers from the refrigerator.

The kitchen barely fit more than two people. When he moved, she moved. I wouldn't be able to fit into the kitchen with them, but I couldn't just sit and watch, not with knowing that she'd been in an accident and hurt her back.

A smile teased the corners of my lips, even as I hurried to assist her by taking one of the platters to place on the counter. The counter space was tidy, with only a coffeemaker, a knife block, and a cookie jar shaped like a chicken in the corner—very minimal.

"Don't strain yourself," Jace said to her.

"I'm fine," she replied.

"You haven't been pushing it?" he asked.

"Like you're pushing me?" She winked. "No, I haven't been."

He leaned over to kiss her cheek, reaching around to grab some bottles of water to set on the counter.

"Make yourself at home," Valerie told me, gesturing to the stools at the counter.

The glance from Jace warmed me as I watched him continue to arrange the snacks and drinks. He might have a reputation for being a womanizer, but he knew his way around the kitchen.

"I should help," I said.

"Nonsense. You're a guest in my home, and you can rest easy knowing Jace has it under control. He always helped me with parties when he was younger."

"Mom," Jace grumbled, as if she had divulged his deepest secret. "Ezra will be here soon."

Looking at the display in front of me, I wondered who else might be coming. It seemed like enough food for a small party, even though the house was tiny. Of course, Jace and his brother could probably eat most of it.

"Are you sure there isn't something I can do, Valerie?"

She laughed. "It's Val, and no."

"Mom, sit down." Jace continued working his way around, putting out plates and silverware.

Val pursed her lips as she came out of the kitchen and settled on a stool next to me. "Booted from my own kitchen," she grumbled. "Can't say I'm fond of this."

"I don't want to pry, but is everything okay?"

I tried to keep it light, hoping she wouldn't take offense at my intrusion into her health. That was the therapist in me, I thought wryly.

"Someone bumped me with their car at the grocery store a couple of weeks ago." I gasped, but she laid her hand over mine. "Did a number on my back, but I'm on the mend."

"Oh no, did the person stop? What was their excuse for hitting you?"

"Unfortunately, the person didn't stop."

Instantly, I thought of everything that had been happening lately. Surely, Vissar wouldn't target Jace's mother, would he? "Did you file a police report?"

"You're starting to sound like Jace," she teased. "Of course, I did. And Jace has truly been a hero, coming over every few days to help me."

His eyes clashed with mine, warming me instantly before darting over to his mom with a warning glower. She met it with a laugh.

"You don't need to spill all my secrets, mom.," he murmured.

"Oh, shush. You brought her, Jace. Expect we'll get to know each other. And if she finds out that you were barely speaking at four years old and had to take speech therapy, so be it."

Jace snorted. Now I understood why he took his time speaking. He either did it on purpose or because he was used to it from growing up. Either way, I loved the way he talked, making me feel tingly inside.

"I'll be back to work in no time," she declared.

"Not before your doctor allows it, and you still have another few weeks before your check-up."

I tried not to admire his lean body while he stood against the opposite counter, taking a break from his preparations. Jace Taylor was an attractive man. It was no wonder women fell at his feet.

"What do you do, Val?" I asked.

"Event planning, although it's been slow for the last few years. It's been picking up lately. And you? Jace tells me you're a therapist. How did you get into that?"

Sharing this with her would give Jace another glimpse into my dark past. He was watching me, even though he didn't think I noticed. I didn't feel the need to go too far into detail yet.

"How much did he tell you about my family? About my parents?"

She shrugged. "Enough to know you lost your mom young and that your dad is nowhere to be found right now."

"He was on tour when she died. Since it was the middle of the school year, he called his best friend's mom, and she came to live with me, along with her two granddaughters. The oldest was going through a rough time, and I . . . helped her."

"But you were going through a rough time, too, weren't you?"

I nodded, feeling a tightness in my throat as I remembered how much I'd struggled even before my mom died. "I . . . " Glancing up at Jace, I took a breath. "I found my mom the morning after she'd overdosed. But when Naomi came with Riley and Hannah, Riley needed me more than I needed her. When listening to her, I found my passion." I frowned. "I think I'm good at it."

Jace smiled—one meant only for me. When Val looked at him, he turned and continued to putter around the kitchen until the back door banged shut, startling all of us.

"Ez!" Val shouted. "I told you not to slam the door!"

"Sorry! Geez!"

Ezra strode in, stopping to kiss her cheek before dumping wrapped gifts onto the table behind us. The door slammed again, and Val grimaced. Another man with shocking blond hair, nearly white, and a scruffy face joined us.

"Milo," she said. "Nice to see you."

Ezra straightened, grinning at me. "Well, hello, Sassie. You didn't meet Milo last night or this morning since you were so busy with my brother."

"Hi, Ezra," I said, trying to hide my blush.

Jace dropped a pair of tongs onto the platter with a loud clank. "Her name is Cassie. Use it, or don't say her name at all."

"Oh, I know. But the sounds coming from your bedroom all night long—"

Jace strolled out of the kitchen, and a scream tore from my throat as Ezra lunged at him, grabbing Jace by the throat. Val stayed seated but yelled at him to drop his brother while Milo tried to pry them apart. What a way to start a party.

I stood up. "Stop. Please."

Jace glanced at me, slowly lowering his hand from Ezra. I admired him for wanting to protect me, but why would Ezra grab him like that? Then, out of nowhere, Ezra grabbed him again, making him stumble back against the refrigerator as they wrestled each other standing up.

"Stop!" I cried, watching Milo rush past me to pull Ezra off Jace again.

"Ezra!" Val admonished.

If she had a room to banish him to, I imagined those would have been her next words. She didn't have to say anything. I rushed over to Jace, trying to see if he was hurt, but he turned and went to the sink to spit. I whipped around to stare at Ezra, who merely held up his hands.

"It's nothing. I bit my lip," Jace grumbled.

"What a party," Val said. "Nothing beats a party with two boys fighting, I guess. Cassie deserves an apology, Ez. And so does your brother. It's his birthday party. You didn't need to start it off this way, especially after everything he's done for you."

"Sorry, Cassie," he mumbled without meeting my eyes. "Sorry, bro."

I grabbed a paper towel, ran it under water, and handed it to Jace, who blotted the tiny bit of blood from his lip and rinsed the sink.

"Let me see," I whispered, nudging Jace over.

He was stubborn, not wanting to move until he finally sighed and allowed me to inspect his lip. I gently touched his lip, trying to hide my smile at his hiss.

"You'll be fine, you big baby."

His arm slid around my waist, yanking me closer until I pressed against him. Was it just me, or did the room suddenly go silent when his lips hovered over mine? "Course I will. I have the very best doctor."

"I'm not a doctor. Just a therapist."

Someone cleared their throat, but Jace didn't release me. He glanced over my shoulder, yet the muscles in his arm flexed, pressing me closer. I laughed. Everyone was watching us.

"Get a room, dude," Milo bellowed from the dining room.

Val swatted at him, instantly wincing at the pull on her back. Ezra smacked Milo upside the head for making his mom hurt herself. Milo merely shrugged and threw open the patio door to the small deck.

Within half an hour, more guests arrived, filling the small house and the deck area just off the dining room. Mostly friends and a few neighbors, but I felt oddly out of place. Once people discovered I was a licensed therapist, several sought conversations with me while Jace chatted with those he hadn't seen since his return.

I relaxed, realizing I was among friends and had nothing to worry about. Yet my mind wandered to the house, wondering if the break in had been Vissar's thugs and if he would do it again. My eyes found Jace across the room, and he looked up from his conversation, as if sensing my gaze. The slight tip of the corner of his mouth sent my heart into a tizzy.

"He likes you a lot." I looked up to see Ezra sliding over to the corner of the room, where I stood with my margarita. "I really am sorry about earlier. I was only teasing."

I looked at him, frowning. "It's fine."

He shrugged. "He's done a lot for me. I shouldn't have grabbed him like that."

"Look, I didn't grow up with siblings. I'd imagine your entire lives have been like that, no matter what you've done for each other."

"You really are something," he whispered. "He's broken his rule about having a woman over. And now you've met our mom."

My heart skipped a beat. I'd made him break two of his rules?

He smiled, looking boyish even with his eyes rimmed in red. Jace had told me that Ezra and I were the same age; he'd turn twenty-five next month. "He's not about to let you get away."

That panicked feeling returned and I couldn't tell if it was because of what Ezra said or if it scared me. Especially after last night, I realized I'd fallen deeper than before. There wouldn't be a way out of this without a broken heart. No other man had affected me like this—ever. Not even Watts when I was sixteen.

I sighed. "People don't get close enough to me for this type of conversation, to be honest. I'm private about my life."

"Closed off."

"Cautious."

"You're so worried about him breaking your heart?" He poured a cup of margarita, his hand shaking as he watched me instead of taking a drink. "What about you breaking his?"

I hadn't considered that. It took a moment for his words to sink in. I hadn't realized I had the power to do something like that. It wouldn't be on purpose. But now that I thought about it, reflecting on my past relationships, had that been what I'd done in some of them? After Watts broke my heart, betraying my trust, I started closing out anyone I dated. Was it to the point where walking away was the only option?

"You help people," he whispered.

"Yes. I help people with their problems."

The seriousness in his gaze made me think there was more to his statement than he was letting on. I could tell by the shaking in his hands and the redness in his eyes. The way he had attacked Jace earlier about something he had started made perfect sense.

"Like drugs?" he asked.

I needed to tread lightly, shifting into a more relaxed position as I watched him. I'd seen the signs before, having lived through them. It might have been many years ago, long before I became a professional, but I recognized them.

"I can help people with addictions."

His eyes were bloodshot, worry etched deep in the hollows beneath them. Paranoia, I thought.

I took a deep breath. "My mom died of a drug overdose when I was fifteen," I whispered, hoping it would draw him out. I never talked to patients about my personal life, especially not about my mom. "I was with her that night when she was getting high. I'm the one who found her the next morning. I'm the one who had to call my dad and tell him."

He hung his head, and as much as I wanted to reach out and comfort him, it would only spook him.

"I'm sorry again for what I said earlier. And for grabbing Jace."

A moment later, he stood up and left me. I sighed, my heart heavy, hoping he would accept my help now that he knew I could. His words about breaking Jace's heart spooked me, though. I still had not decided what I was going to do with my future.

It alarmed me enough to step out of the house before anyone could see me. Jace drove. I couldn't go very far, but I slipped out the front door and sat down on the steps to collect my thoughts and enjoy a few moments of quiet.

It took about half an hour before Jace found me. As usual, he said nothing as he stepped down to sit on the step above me. With his arms casually braced on his knees, he watched the street for a while before he spoke.

"Someone upset you?" he finally asked, his voice low.

He meant his brother but didn't say it. I shook my head. Ezra didn't upset me. He'd spoken the truth, making me realize it. All the while, I'd been hurting people by protecting myself.

"No."

"I heard what you said to Ezra," he said. "About your mom."

I stared at him. "It's public knowledge what happened to her."

"Not the part where you were with her. You told him you found her. It comforted him, knowing you have a history with it. With her."

My breath caught. I'd trusted him with so much already. Could I trust him with this? Should I trust him with the most intimate part of me? "No one knows I caused it."

His dark brows drew together. "Cassie, you can't think you're responsible for her drug addiction."

I shook my head. "I gave her the cocaine that night."

As my hands trembled, he grabbed hold of them and held on. "What do you mean? How could you have gotten cocaine for her? Weren't you fifteen?"

I couldn't believe I was about to admit this. He would think the worst of me once he heard it. "She was yelling at me to get her drugs out of her drawer. She'd been partying all day, and I don't think she had the strength to get them herself." I pressed my hands against my head. "She was screaming at me. I couldn't stand it anymore. I went to her drawer and gave them to her."

It was impossible to tell if I'd shocked him into silence or if he was digesting what I'd told him. What kind of kid gives their parents drugs they knew are bad? All that stuff they drill into our heads in school about saying no to drugs, and here I was, handing them over to her.

"The next morning, I found her next to her bed." I broke down, tears spilling over as I buried my face in my hands. Jace pulled me against him. "It broke my dad's heart when I called to tell him. God, he loved her so much." My tear-filled eyes met his. "I should have helped her, Jace. I should have flushed all of it down the toilet!"

"You can't blame yourself for that. You did what she was yelling at you to do." He squeezed me for reassurance. "Have you been carrying this around on your shoulders since then?"

I nodded.

"You need to let it go." He pushed my hair back from my wet cheeks. "Are you going to be okay?"

"Just a little tired, I guess."

He didn't bother to hide his smile. "I won't apologize. I was wondering if you wanted to spend the night tonight?"

My eyes lit up. "Are you sure you'd want that?"

He slid closer to me, took my arm, and urged me to stand up. Before I could question what he was doing, he pulled me down until I sat across his lap on that first step. I laughed, sliding my arm across his broad shoulders to keep myself from falling off, but his arm snaked around me, holding me securely.

He nuzzled my neck just below my ear. "There isn't anything I'd like more."

Shivers drifted up my back despite the warmth of the evening. Feelings aside, it felt good to be wanted. My fingers slid through the short hair at the nape of his neck, and a gasp escaped from deep in my throat when his teeth caught my earlobe.

"My place this time?"

"God, yes. I can't take any more grumbling from Ez." I smiled. "We'll be leaving soon. Ezra and Milo said they'd help clean up since we set up."

"You set up. I watched."

"And you can repay me later for that." His fingers splayed against the outer ridge of my thigh, gripping it as I wiggled closer. "For now, let's say our goodbyes before I shock my mom's neighbors with what I want to do to you."

Another surge of heat swept through me before I swung my legs off his lap and stood up. His arm looped around me as he stood, guiding us back into the party. How wrong I'd been when I first met Jace Taylor, I thought. He was nothing like I had imagined.

Chapter Thirty Three

"Adam, it's Jace."

"What's going on? We haven't heard from you in a few days. Assuming everything is going smooth and nothing to report," Adam replied.

Unfortunately, he was right. The wire I'd planted in Tito's car had yielded nothing useful, and I hadn't been able to plant a wire anywhere else that might incriminate Vissar in his illegal activities, most notably his trafficking. Until now.

"I've been summoned to meet with Vissar today."

After the incident with my mom being hit, I could bet Vissar wanted to meet with me for a more serious discussion regarding Cassie. His threat echoed in my mind. The next time he needed me for a job, it would be worse. I had to be smarter.

Time was ticking, and nothing had been produced to his liking, other than the little I had provided him. Knowing Vissar as I did, it wasn't nearly enough. I hoped to circumvent whatever threats he had coming my way. Protecting my mom and Ezra was one thing; protecting Cassie was a whole different matter. She was in direct line of danger.

"What do you need, buddy?"

"Another wire. If he lets me into his office, I can maybe plant it somewhere. His office would be the best place to catch him saying anything incriminating." I drew in a deep breath. "I want to take him down, Adam. I need to take him down."

Adam laughed. "I get it, Jace. We're getting there. You know as well as I do that we need something rock-solid to put him away. These guys always find a way out of doing any time. Someone else will always take the fall."

How right he was. Planting a wire in his office would give us something, but it could easily be contested in court with the right lawyer. I had to give it a try, at the very least. Too many lives depended on it.

"And the girls?" I asked.

"Safe and getting the help they need. They weren't able to provide us any information on other girls that might be transported, but we got them to safety. We couldn't have done it without your help."

Although it was a relief to have saved those poor girls, it had come at a steep price. "I'm glad to hear it, Adam. I hated to do what he told me that night, but saving those two girls makes me feel like I did the right thing."

"I'm sorry your mom took the brunt of his anger, Jace." Adam had been the first at the scene and took her report. "I still can't believe he would do that. What a bastard."

"Yeah, well, to Vissar, this is business and not personal." "Stop by, and I'll hook you up with a wire. If you can get it close to where he might take a phone call or talk with someone in person, especially if he blatantly admits something, that would be the best."

"I'm on my way."

After I ended the call, I looked out my car window at the skate park. Following Cassie had become risky, especially since she'd recognize my car, but I wasn't spying on her for Vissar this time. I was making sure she was okay. After he sent his thugs to break into the house, I'd never been so relieved that neither she nor Quinn had been there. The fact that I gave him the information about the security system crushed me.

With one last glance, I drove away from the park. Quinn had stayed every night at Skyler's house, whether she stayed home or not, and I hadn't left Cassie alone for a single night, and that had its own benefits. I wouldn't let her spend a night alone until she got another security system installed. We'd been researching the best options for something that couldn't be tampered with. Until then, I wouldn't leave her alone at night, even if she begged me to.

Two hours later, I parked near the delivery entrance of Vissar's mansion on the hill, the tiny button wire tucked neatly in my pocket. All I had to do was stick it somewhere around his desk. If he caught me, I'd be dead. But I was a professional. I had this handled.

My footfalls echoed in the vacant hallway as I walked in, carefully scanning for his guards. Given his level of security, there wouldn't be many today, but I needed to make sure. As I passed the first staircase, Natalia appeared.

"Well, look who the cat dragged in," she said, bounding down to me. "Haven't seen you for a while."

I stopped. "I've been busy."

"With your little girlfriend?" she smirked.

Natalia could smirk all she wanted. I wouldn't let her get to me. If Cassie ever found out what I had done, even if my actions were meant to protect her, she might never speak to me again. I'd take any time I had with Cassie I could get, and not take it for granted. Something I had never said of any other woman before.

"You know, it would be in your best interest to tell her what happened that night," I said. "At least put her mind at ease about why she can't see or speak to her dad."

Whatever good mood she might have had vanished. "Why would it even matter? Nothing is going to change, Jace."

I tilted my head. "I was surprised to see you and Ricky at that club. Thought your dad wouldn't let you out of the house?"

She shrugged. "He made one exception."

I would have smiled, but I knew she'd paid dearly for that exception. Related or not, Vissar made no exceptions unless he received something in return. And that something would be a hard thing to give up. He made sure of it.

"What did you promise him?"

She turned away. "He's waiting for you in his office."

Always elusive, I thought. Natalia wasn't all that different from her dad. She never answered when she didn't need to. But deep down, she had a heart, even if she rarely showed it. Vissar had none at all. He never did. I sighed, still wondering what she had given him in return for a night of freedom.

As soon as I turned the corner into Vissar's dimly lit office, he glanced up from his desk at the far end of the room near the window. Books lined shelves on the wall farthest from his desk, but otherwise, the walls were bare, except for one picture of a Grecian hillside.

Never having been in his office before, it gave me a sense of how dominating Vissar believed he was. It would give me great pleasure to take him down a few pegs. I strolled in, hands tucked in my pockets. His hulking bodyguard, Tito, stood in the far corner, ready for any action, his eyes blank.

"Jace," Vissar drawled, remaining seated. "Have a seat."

When I reached his desk, I braced my hands on it and leaned forward while inconspicuously pushing the wire just under the ridge. I took a deep breath, staring at him and waiting to see if Tito would rush me. Having stuck the small wire between my fingers, I hoped it was slight enough to go unnoticed. The small square device was bigger than I wanted it to be. Apparently, it worked.

"What do you want, Vissar? I have things to do today."

His jaw tightened. "Sit down. If I have to tell you again, I'll have Tito put you there."

I eased into the chair, leaning back and draping my arms over the armrests, eyeing him as he did me. Whatever this meeting was about, it wasn't good. Vissar rarely looked happy, but today he definitely wasn't.

"Why have you called me here instead of on the phone? It's not like you to invite me here," I asked.

"I do not answer to you."

"And I don't give a shit," I snapped. "You tried to run my mother down at the grocery store. Does a human life mean so little to you?"

When the corner of his mouth lifted in amusement, I nearly launched out of my chair. Everything had to be a game for him; he had to be better than everyone. He always had. This entire situation had grown tiresome. It needed to end.

"Consider that a warning, Jace. I told you when you were given instructions to transport those two girls that if anything went wrong, there would be dire consequences. The fact that my associates were arrested shortly after and charged with kidnapping only tells me that you had something to do with it."

"And I told you that I had nothing to do with it, and I didn't."

His eyes flashed. "Forgive me if I don't trust law enforcement."

"You should trust *me*."

As he leaned back, steepling his fingers, I knew he would get to the point soon. Certain he didn't want me in his office any longer than necessary, I didn't want to be sitting here as though I was in the hot seat. He shouldn't trust me any more than I trusted him, but that didn't mean I didn't bristle at the thought of him hurting anyone else I loved.

"While I appreciate the information you provided me about the security system at the house where Cassie is staying, you failed to mention that a little boy lived there."

My heart plummeted. It didn't matter what I did; it would never turn out for the best. I couldn't protect Cassie and Quinn without putting Ezra and my mom in harm's way. I ground my teeth.

"That boy has nothing to do with this, Vissar."

"Regardless, that information would have been best shared with me. You don't seem to understand the predicament our friend is in, and what she needs to get for me. I need anything, and I mean anything, I can use to bring her to heel."

I clenched my teeth. "She's not a dog, Vissar."

He leaned forward. "I need you to remember something, Jace. Everything you do, everything you say, as well as everything you don't do, and don't say, has consequences."

Chills skittered down my spine. It wouldn't matter if I demanded to know what he meant by that. We were all in danger. He wouldn't target me specifically. He'd go after every single person that mattered to me first.

Chapter Thirty Four

It was only the middle of the afternoon in early November when I looked at the latest bank statements. No activity. Jace could obtain phone records showing that my dad had taken and made calls to both Natalia and Ricky in the days leading up to when that airplane went down and he disappeared. Natalia was involved, but we already knew that she and Ricky had something to do with this. I just didn't know how. The thought that my dad might show up scared me to death. Vissar would get wind of it and kill him.

My phone buzzed on the counter. Seeing Shawn's name made me frown. I had heard little from the band since they hired a new drummer. Call it hurt, but I couldn't bear to think of the band moving on without my dad. After almost three months without him, they had no choice but to move forward.

"Hi, Shawn," I answered.

"Cassie," he said, his voice laced with despair. "There's been an accident."

My heart thudded, creeping into my throat. All I could think of was Quinn, even though he was at school. I couldn't bear the thought of anyone else being ripped from my life.

"It's Skyler," he said. "She's been hit by a car."

I stood up. Though there had never been any lost love between us, I never wanted her out of my life that badly. I thought we were fixing it. "How . . . what happened . . ?"

"Just outside of Venice. She was crossing the street when a car came out of nowhere and plowed right into her. It . . . it doesn't look good." His voice broke.

Without wasting another second, I grabbed my keys and purse and slammed out of the house. Racing toward the hospital, I didn't think about what I would do. I would do anything to help her. She was Quinn's mom. He didn't deserve to lose her or go through everything I had.

I didn't realize I'd hung up on Shawn until I was already down the road. I quickly dialed Jace, but he didn't answer, so I left a voicemail telling him what happened. When Quinn got home from school, I wanted him to hear it from me, not anyone else. No doubt if she was run down, she was badly hurt. Not like getting bumped in the grocery store parking lot, I thought, though that could have been much worse.

By the time I arrived at the hospital, I hadn't heard from Jace, but the emergency room was a flurry of activity. It was a busy day for them, and this latest accident had brought in at least one more patient. I checked in at the front desk, but since I wasn't a relative, I couldn't see her. I texted Shawn to let him know I was there, and he came out.

"What the hell happened?"

"All I know is that a car came out of nowhere and hit her. Cassie, even if she pulls through this, her head injury . . . "

I bowed my head. This could be my fault. It could be an accident, or it could be Vissar's doing. Things he'd been doing were stacking up fast. I had no way of knowing.

He placed his hands on my arms. "We have to brace ourselves for the possibility that she might not make it."

I pushed his hands away. "No, I won't accept that. I can't tell Quinn that when I get home!"

I turned to pace, my aggravation growing as I wondered how he could be so calm about this. First, my dad was gone, now his girlfriend, the woman Shawn had been involved with for months, if not longer.

When I looked up at him, he seemed like a shadow of himself. So much had happened. "Did you love her?" I asked softly.

It might not have been my place to ask, but I needed to know that she had someone here with her who loved her. Regardless of what happened, I needed to break this to Quinn. I needed to know that when I left here, she had someone decent here with her. I'd known Shawn my entire life, but I had no way of knowing how deep his feelings were for her.

I didn't expect him to ignore my question.

"Cassie, you should just go home. There isn't anything you can do here. I'll call you and let you know what happens, but unfortunately, you're going to have to be the one to tell Quinn. But there's something you should know before you go."

I paused at the seriousness in his voice. "Tell me."

"Skyler told me that Quinn is . . . " I raised my eyebrows. "Lex is Quinn's father."

"She told me that." I scoffed. "Quinn told me she told him that. I didn't believe it. How is that even possible? She didn't start cleaning his house until, what, three years ago?"

"They hooked up many years ago, once I believe, when she was on a break from her boyfriend. They never told anyone about it, and she didn't tell Lex that Quinn was his for a long time."

I spun around, unable to believe what I was hearing. It took a moment for it to sink in before I turned back to him. "Does my dad know?"

Shawn rubbed his eyes. "Yes. He's listed as the father on the birth certificate."

"What does this mean, Shawn?"

"It means that if something happens, you're going to have a decision to make. A big decision."

Thankfully, there was a chair nearby, and I felt around behind me until I could sit down with a thud. This was all happening too fast. "What decision do I have to make, Shawn?"

"You're his closest relative. You're his only relative."

The world began to tilt, and I leaned back in the chair. If that was true, it changed everything.

"Go home. I'll call you with updates. Try not to think about it, Cassie. Everything will be fine."

But as I drove home, I didn't believe it would be fine. It didn't matter what happened; nothing would be the same. I had a little brother. My dad had a son he never told me about, and I wanted to know why. By the time I reached the driveway, Shawn was calling again. I was terrified to answer.

"Hello?" I said, my voice sounding foreign to me.

When he was silent at first, I knew. I just knew. "She's gone, Cassie."

"God dammit!" I shouted.

My heart ached. It ached for Quinn, for my dad, and most of all, for Skyler. We hadn't gotten along, but I would never have wished this upon her. Over the last few weeks, I felt we had come to know what to expect from each other. But in the end, I wouldn't have wished her ill. Tears slid down my cheeks, which I quickly wiped away.

"Let me know if you need anything," he said quietly before hanging up.

I hadn't moved for a few minutes when my phone rang again. Expecting it to be Jace, I was shocked at the voice on the other end.

"My condolences for your loss," Vissar said smoothly.

My eyes widened. How the hell would he know anything about this? Unless . . .

"What did you say?" I asked slowly.

"It's such a pity for the young boy to have to grow up without his mother."

Apprehension snaked up my spine. "You son of a bitch."

"I'll leave you with one parting sentiment, my dear. I will take out every single person you care about if I don't get what I want. That I'll make certain of."

Tears of fury mixed with sadness welled in my eyes, spilling out when he ended the call without another word. The bastard had taken Quinn's parents from his life in the blink of an eye, leaving me the only person to protect him. The only thing I could do was pack him up and bring him to Seattle, but what would stop Vissar from following us there and taking his anger out on Naomi and Hannah? I sat in the car for a long time, ignoring Jace's call, struggling to control the torrent of emotions rolling through me.

I called Mac and Kya to make sure they were safe before composing myself enough to go inside and tell Quinn about his mom. Years of training hadn't prepared me for this.

Chapter Thirty Five

Cassie

In the years I had been a therapist, sitting down to tell Quinn that his mom was gone was the hardest thing I had ever done. Jace had been helping his mom all day but would come over as soon as he was finished. This was something I knew I had to face on my own.

So, I planned a funeral after all. I took on the expense since Skyler's assets were being held for the time being. Any assets she had would go to Quinn, who was underage. I refused to take any of that money for funeral expenses, anyway. That money belonged to Quinn.

When I told Quinn about his mom, he went stone cold, and nothing I could say would bring out the emotions I knew were brewing inside him. Instead, he stood up and went to his room. He needed to grieve alone. I understood that as much as it pierced my heart. When he did that, I had a good cry, too, which is how Jace found me. He comforted me like I wanted to comfort Quinn.

The cemetery was huge, with sweeping lawns and long pathways. It would provide much-needed privacy for the small ceremony. Since Skyler had no living family other than Quinn, it was up to Shawn and me to make all the decisions, and he was hardly any help. Jace accompanied Quinn and me, staying for the brief service. The band also came to the service out of respect, but there were few words spoken.

I pulled Jace aside as soon as the service concluded. "Can you keep Quinn occupied for a few minutes? I have something I need to do."

He reached out and touched my wrist softly. "You okay?"

"I just need to visit someone while I'm here."

Awkwardly, I twisted my bare legs together as the breeze kicked up and threatened to lift my skirt. He dropped his hand, but not before flashing an impish grin.

"Go on."

After a quick glance at Quinn, looking much older than his eleven years in his navy blue suit as he talked somberly to Wes, I started down the path toward my mom's gravesite. It took several minutes just to find it since it had been ten years since I'd been here, but once I located it, I stood and stared.

I sat down in the grass beneath the shady oak tree, folding my legs to the side. It was funny that now, being here, I didn't know what to say to her. Instead, emotions flooded me. It shouldn't have turned out this way.

"You were the best part of my world," I whispered. "You and Dad. The thing is, you were human. You made mistakes. God knows I have. When you hurt him, it hurt me. But we got through it. Telling me I wasn't his daughter . . . " I sucked in a shaky breath. "You didn't need to do that. It didn't matter. I'm still his daughter in every way but blood. And I'll be damned if I'm going to lose him."

A tear burned a path down my cheek, falling with a silent splash onto the back of my hand. I didn't bother wiping it away. Another tear followed, and I felt the burn at the back of my throat, more tears threatening to spill. Finally, I gave in and let them loose.

"I miss you every day. I should have helped you. Damn it, I should have." My voice cracked, and I sucked in a deep breath. "If I could do it all again, I would. I would save you. I would fight for you. Like I'm fighting for Dad. I might end up right there next to you, but I won't go down without a fight."

It felt good to let it out, as if a weight had suddenly been lifted from me. A trembling laugh escaped as I pressed the back of my hand against the tears dripping from the tip of my nose. "This is what I preach to others, but I could never take my own advice. I promise, next time I won't stay away for so long. I'm sorry it took me so long to come. You deserved so much better from me. I love you."

When I closed my eyes, I could hear her whimsical voice in my head, telling me she loved me back. I could hear her urging me to take the risks I needed to take and live life to its fullest, just like she did. Laughing, I thought it would be too extreme to live as fully as she did. While I loved her, we were two different people. Still, I needed to take a hard look at my life and stop pushing people away. People would hurt me, and I had to stop being afraid that someone would hurt me like Watts had hurt me. Like Evan had hurt me, though I'd been in such denial over that one. That was life. I needed to get over it.

"Cass?"

I looked up as Jace strolled toward me, hands stuffed in the pockets of his suit, looking entirely too sinful for his own good. The breeze ruffled his hair, which was getting longer and in need of a trim. I wondered if he intended to grow it long again.

When he reached his hand out, I accepted it and allowed him to pull me up. The security of his arm slipping around my waist and the swipe of his thumb brushing away the tears on my face only confirmed my feelings for him. If he walked away tomorrow, it would devastate me. I loved him so much it hurt. I tipped my face up to him, wanting so badly to confess my feelings.

"Is Quinn okay?" I asked instead.

He laughed, pulling me into step alongside him as we walked back. "He's fine."

Cʍ

Later, I lay on my bed in the silence of the house. I couldn't bring myself to go through whatever things Skyler had in my dad's room. It had been nine weeks, and I hadn't been able to sort through his belongings, as determined as I was that he would be back. Would he? Every day that passed, I lost more faith that I'd be able to get him home. I'd mentioned to Jace about taking Quinn back to Seattle, and he agreed that he'd like to get us as far away from Vissar as possible, but that Vissar would just send one of his thugs after us. I hadn't talked to Quinn about Lex being his dad since I'd arrived in September. Never asked him if he believed that Lex was his dad.

Jace had dropped me off hours ago while the band had offered to take Quinn out for ice cream and to the studio for a jam session. The look of joy in his eyes gave me hope that he would be okay after this. His birthday would be in a few weeks, and it was going to be a hard one.

Exhaustion claimed me, and I couldn't do anything but lie down, my thoughts swirling about everything that had happened over the last few months. Too much had occurred, and it was overwhelming, but I needed to get it together.

I heard the door open; quick footfalls were a telltale sign that Quinn was home. He didn't call out for me like he usually did when he came in if he didn't see me in the kitchen. Surprised, he came around the bed to the spot where Jace would sleep when we stayed here and crawled in next to me. I wanted to cry again.

"Did you have fun with the guys?" I asked.

"Yeah," he admitted. "They're so cool."

"They are. The coolest."

He lay on his back, staring up at the ceiling with his hands locked behind his head. He'd ditched the suit jacket and wore only the button-up shirt, making him look older. Such a handsome bugger, I thought. I needed to get my dad back. Soon. Quinn would need him now.

"Quinn?"

"Yeah?"

"Are you okay?"

He withdrew his hands from behind his head and rolled to his side until he was staring back at me. "I'm okay, Cassie."

"I have to tell you something I found out the day your mom died. Please don't be mad that I didn't tell you then; I didn't want to overwhelm you. It's about your dad." His eyes widened in alarm. "It's not bad."

"Mom told me Lex is my dad. Did she lie? If she did, and you're going to tell me who my real dad is and you're sending me away, I'm going to run."

The corners of my mouth lifted. What a little rebel, just like I was at his age. "There's no reason to send you away. Do you think it's true, even though you only came here about three years ago?"

He shrugged. "I think I just want it to be true since I don't really know."

"It's true. Lex is your dad, Quinn." He looked utterly confused. "Which means I'm your sister."

"But he's gone, too," he whispered. "So, I'm an orphan?" "Well, no. I'm your sister."

"You're staying?"

"Do you want me to?"

"Sure. Where else would we go?"

"We can go anywhere we want to, shortie. For now, we'll stay here. I'm still trying to figure stuff out, too. I'm just as surprised as you are right now. The last few days have been overwhelming."

I sat up and climbed out of bed, aware that he was watching my every move. I hoped this surprise would cheer him up. It had just arrived last week. I opened the closet and withdrew a long box.

Quinn sat up. "What's that?"

"I was going to give this to you as part of your birthday present." I sat down next to him and handed him the box.

When he took off the lid and opened it, I held my breath. Slowly, he pulled out the drumsticks nestled in the black velvet. "A pair of drumsticks?" he asked.

"Not just any drumsticks," I whispered. "Dad gave these to me when I was little—probably about your age. These were the drumsticks from his very first concert as the main act. It was a sold-out show."

His eyes grew wide like saucers, and he handled them with such care that my heart thumped wildly. I couldn't be certain, but I thought he might like them. It was a piece of Lex that he didn't have.

"I figured that since you don't know how to play, I'd give these to you and teach you—oof!" He launched himself at me, throwing his arms around my neck so quickly that I was lucky he didn't stick me with the drumsticks. I laughed, holding on to him. "Does this mean you like them?"

"I love them," he mumbled against my neck.

When he pulled away, there were tears in his eyes that he quickly swiped away. I had tears in my own eyes, never having had a little kid steal my heart so quickly. I was just a kid myself when Hannah came into my life, though I loved her now. Brother or not, Quinn was my responsibility now.

Chapter Thirty Six

Cassie

Quinn and I quickly settled into an easy routine that was not very different from before. I made him breakfast and got him off to school every day instead of only occasionally. I ensured he had snacks when he got home and made sure his homework was done whenever he had it, which seemed to be more often than not.

Since he could no longer be anywhere else but with me, I had a new state-of-the-art, super expensive security system installed at the house, complete with motion sensors, cameras, panic buttons, smart speakers, and a full internet backup. I wouldn't take any chances now that Vissar had upped the game.

On weekends, he wanted to stay at Ray's, and at his age, I couldn't blame him. At first, I hesitated to let him out of my sight, but after speaking with Ray's mom and hearing that they had a similar security system, I felt better.

Hanging out with friends was much cooler than spending time with a sister who had taken on the temporary role of parent. Neither of us knew how temporary it was. The only difference was that he didn't realize it at all. Only I knew otherwise.

Not hearing from Vissar worried me. Jace and I were on edge as we moved deeper into November. Too many incidents had happened and from what Jace had told me, he was still being sent to do his bidding, but less frequently. All it did was make us more concerned. In the meantime, Jace had been working surveillance for the clientele he'd been building for his private investigation practice, leaving me with far too much time on my hands.

My running shoes pounded the pavement on the path winding along the beach across the street from the house and I swiped my arm across my forehead to wipe away the sweat. Quinn had gone to school, Jace was off to do some work for a client, and I had been slacking on my daily runs. I couldn't complain though, having kept up with my yoga. It still felt good to release my pent-up energy.

Mornings were the perfect time for a run, but getting Quinn off to school sometimes took longer than I expected. Unanticipated motherhood to an almost twelve-year-old boy brought new challenges every day, like the homework that didn't get done over the weekend, which we had to scramble to finish this morning. That meant I had to drive him to school.

I smiled at the irritated memory. It just meant I had to be more vigilant about making sure his homework was done. Cutting right, I slowed my run into a jog to cross the street. Today would turn out to be a beautiful day, I thought as I neared the house and nearly stopped at the white van in my driveway.

"Highly suspicious," I murmured, walking cautiously closer.

A man wearing a plain black baseball hat and a uniform with a name badge opened the driver's side door and slid out as I approached the driveway. He carried a clipboard, which seemed legitimate, as though he were here to check on something.

"Ma'am," he said. "I'm with the security company, here to make sure everything has been set up correctly. Would you mind if I looked at it?"

I stopped, making sure I wasn't within arm's reach of him. Not only something in his eyes made me suspect that his reason for being here wasn't true, but the new system had been installed for over a week, and they'd already called to confirm everything was working properly.

"What company did you say you were from?"

As soon as I asked, the side door of the van swung open, and a man lunged for me. I opened my mouth to scream, turning to run back the way I'd just come, when a massive hand clamped over my face and an arm latched around my torso, lifting me clear off the ground. No matter how hard I struggled, this man held onto me as though I weighed nothing.

Pulled into the van, the door slammed shut. It didn't stop me from struggling against my assailant until I felt a pinch in my neck, and everything slowly faded to black.

⌒〜

Aches in my arms and legs greeted me when I first came to, peeling open my gritty eyelids a moment later. All I could see was darkness, but wherever my assailants had brought me offered no comfort. I felt like I was lying on a bed of rocks. Oddly, my hands and feet were not bound. I pushed myself up.

"She's awake," I heard a gravelly voice say.

"Where the fuck am I?" I snapped.

"Calm down," someone said. "Someone wants to talk to you. Just lay back down like a good girl until we get there."

Like hell, I thought. Presuming we were still in the van they threw me in, it lurched into motion and I pitched to the side. There had to be a safer way to transport me. I braced my hands wherever I could find stability and waited it out while I tried to clear my head. Every once in a while, I would see a flash of lights. No one spoke.

The chilling thought entered my mind that Vissar had me kidnapped so he could put me into one of his trafficking rings, making my stomach roll. I couldn't imagine what it would be like, but I knew it wouldn't be good. My thoughts raced with scenarios on how to get out of this. They hadn't tied me up, which was good, but I didn't know where we were, and whatever they'd injected into me still made me feel lethargic.

Wait. It seemed the only thing I could do.

It turned out, I didn't need to wait much longer before the van lurched to a stop. The side door slid open, and meaty hands plucked me out, setting me on my feet. I swayed, hardly able to feel my legs.

"Stand up," the man snapped.

"I can't feel my legs!" I bit back. "Give me a damn minute."

I recognized where we were. I should have known that Vissar would try something. He'd had his men pick me up instead of sending me flowers with a threatening note as he usually did. The guard holding me up looked familiar, but the driver didn't. If I'd recognized him, I would have run in the opposite direction as soon as I'd seen the van.

As it was, the situation I found myself in now couldn't be reversed, and I'd need to face it. Face Vissar, the bastard. The rolling of my stomach hadn't stopped, especially as I thought about anyone attempting to rescue me. It was fully dark now, and though I had no idea what time it was, Quinn had likely called Jace when he noticed I wasn't home. I pulled my phone out of the sheath on my arm.

"No," the guard said, yanking it out of my hands.

Crap.

"Can you walk now? Mr. Loukas doesn't like to be kept waiting."

I shifted from leg to leg. "Yes," I answered tightly.

We moved toward the door, the guard keeping one hand on my arm and my phone in his other hand. I just needed to text Jace and tell him not to get any fancy ideas about storming in here to rescue me. I would handle this. It could be that Vissar just wanted to see me and nothing more, although drugging me was a new low, even for him. Regardless, I wouldn't hold back my fury this time. He hadn't seen anything yet.

Chapter Thirty Seven

Cassie

I found Vissar in his office behind a massive desk, reading documents. From that vantage point, he looked extremely important, but I didn't care. This man had no right to pluck me from my driveway.

"What the hell—"

He held up his hand, signaling me to stop talking, without taking his eyes off what he was reading. Not a good way to cool my anger. I walked toward the desk, head held high, regardless of whether he could see it and slid into the chair in front of him and crossed my legs.

For a full five minutes, I surveyed the dimly lit room, which exuded a dark wood and masculine feel. The soft glow of lights illuminating the sections of the bookcases lining one wall created a warm ambiance, while the lamp on the desk provided additional light. When I looked back, Vissar's hard gaze was fixed on me.

"How dare you?" I asked.

"How dare I?" His laugh fueled my anger. "I have given you ample opportunity for weeks. Weeks, Cassie. How dare I?"

My chin lifted defiantly. "You gave me until the end of the year! I have nothing to give you. You had no right to send your bodyguards to come for me."

"Let's not mince words here, Cassie. I'm tired of waiting." He slouched back in his leather chair, exhaling heavily.

I rose.

"Sit. Down."

I sat.

"From this moment forward, you are a guest in my home." When I opened my mouth to protest, he held up his hand again. "If I want you to accompany me somewhere, you will. If I want you to stay here to entertain, you will. If I can't get what I need back, you will remain here."

Timeline be damned! He'd gone back on his word. Not that it mattered. I had no idea what my dad's plan was with this security footage. Ricky and Natalia hadn't told me a damn thing, either, which meant they had no idea what to do. The only alternative I had was to take a deep breath as irritation flared to life.

"And you think your stupid footage will just show up because I'm here?"

"I might settle for you instead."

A quick laugh burst out of me. "You bastard."

"Much to my regret, what I've tried to do thus far hasn't worked. You've never been in any real danger." His eyes darkened. "Although my intentions toward you have been honest, if not dark."

A low growl of frustration escaped him when I stood up. "I would tell you what you can do with your intentions, but I think you can figure that out on your own. I'm not staying here, Vissar."

As soon as I turned, he snapped his fingers, and two bodyguards blocked the doorway. A red haze shaded my vision when I faced him again. He meant to keep me here to draw my dad out of hiding.

"Oh, and I'll take your phone. We won't need you to contact Jace."

My eyes widened as the guard stepped forward and handed him my phone. "You have no right," I bit out. "I have every right."

I marched up to his desk. "You keep me here, Vissar. Let's see how that works out for you."

He stood, hoping to intimidate me. I didn't care. I crossed my arms as my blood pumped through my veins. This man could easily have me killed.

"What are you going to do, Vissar? Keep me here indefinitely because you're jealous that Jace is twice the man you are?"

His hand shot out and slapped me, snapping my head back and leaving my face burning where he had struck me. I covered my heated cheek and turned my glare on him, saying nothing. No one had ever hit me before.

"I think you'll find that isn't the case. In the meantime, you'll be provided a room of your own." His eyebrows rose. "Unless you'd prefer to share mine."

In response, I snickered. "I'll take my own."

When Vissar motioned to the two men at the doorway, they approached, and I had a feeling we were far from finished. One of them took my arm and led me away.

"We'll see," he called after me. "Tito, make sure Natalia knows that we will be having a guest for a while. And make sure she tells her friend Ricky. He'll want to know about our guest, so it hastens the return of my property."

I dug in my heels. "Are you keeping my room guarded?"

"No. You are free to use whatever you need in the house, but please do not leave the grounds. It's for your protection. I can't have you getting hurt out there. I'll have what you need brought to you."

How kind, I thought bitterly, as I was led out of the room and toward the back stairway. Seething with anger, I yanked my arm away from the guard and walked up the stairs unaided. One of them swung open the door to a bedroom that overlooked the front of the house, providing a magnificent view of the ocean, although I could hardly see it in the dark.

Just as I was about to step in, another door opened, and Natalia emerged from her room. Her eyes widened for a moment before she let out a laugh and walked to me, shooing away the guards.

"Your dad wants to make sure you know that Ms. Nichols will be a guest here, and you should make sure your friends are made aware of this," Tito said before he turned and left the room.

I didn't need a confrontation with her right now.

"What are you doing here?" she asked, following me into the spacious room.

"What do you think?" I snapped, dropping my empty phone sheath onto the bed in the center of the far wall between two open balconies. "Like you, he's keeping me prisoner here. And you know why."

Natalia clucked, closing the door behind her and shutting us in together. "He hit you." Her eyes narrowed, studying my face and the mark he'd caused. "Didn't I tell you to leave it alone? You should have gone home and stayed far away from here."

I turned, folding my arms in front of me. "Look, I know you don't have the same relationship with your dad as I do with mine, but I intend to bring him home. Eventually. You can't tell Ricky I'm here."

Her eyes grew wide. "Get comfortable then, because my dad isn't about to let you go anywhere until he gets it back. And Jace can't get you out of this. Not without pissing my dad off enough to commit murder."

That was the last thing I wanted to happen.

"Can you do me a favor?" I asked, sitting down on the edge of the bed and glancing at her.

"Favors are costly around here." "Call Jace. Tell him to not come here."

She sucked in a breath, and I looked at her sharply. What did she know that she wasn't telling me? Instead of answering, she walked to the door, pulling it open harder than necessary. She looked back at me, meeting my gaze. "I can do that."

Before I could ask any more questions, the door slammed behind her. I flopped back on the bed, my head pounding. As much as I needed Jace right now, he had to stay away. As a cop, I knew he would want to leap into action and save the day. I hope he knew better than to storm this fortress. He'd get himself killed. The thought hurt my heart worse than my face hurt.

I had nothing with me—not even my phone—in a house where I didn't trust the man who would sleep just a few doors down. Checking the door, I saw it had a lock, which I snapped into place immediately. Not that it would keep him out if he really wanted in. I shuddered as I walked into the private bathroom.

I found a toothbrush and toothpaste in the drawer, as if he had known he would have a guest here. He probably did. A man like Vissar was cunning enough to always be one step ahead of everyone else. He didn't get to where he was today by being foolish.

After brushing my teeth, I slid into bed, fully dressed out of fear of sleeping in anything less. It didn't matter if I locked the door; I didn't feel secure, and I wouldn't feel safe until I was putting this house in my rearview mirror, hopefully never to return. After this, I would never involve myself with Vissar again.

Chapter Thirty Eight

"You look like you're enjoying your little vacation."

I looked up from my book as Natalia walked into the pool area, sashaying in her black one-piece swimsuit beneath a sheer cover-up. She sat down beside me, easing back in the lounger chair by the pool. Unfortunately, the weather wasn't warm enough to use the outdoor pool, so we had to settle for the indoor one.

It had been two days since I'd become a prisoner here, and I had never felt so depressed. I had avoided Vissar as much as possible, even when he sent almost a full wardrobe and every necessity I might need. When his servants brought everything up, I had the alarming thought that he intended for me to live here, given how much he had bought.

Slamming the book shut, I set it down carefully before glancing at her. "This is not my idea of a vacation. I need to get out of here."

She scoffed. "That isn't going to happen."

"Funny you say that. Why is he keeping you here?"

"Because I pissed him off, just like you."

I found that hard to believe. Vissar was a hard man, but she was his daughter. Why keep her here? She must have had something to do with that security footage, and that was likely why he was furious enough to keep her here. Why else did he tell his guard to make sure she told Ricky? Still, keeping her here wouldn't do him any good.

"I call BS," I said. "You know exactly why he's making you stay.

You can come and go, though. I saw you at the club when Ricky's band was playing. He must be easing up."

"You don't know shit," she shot back. "My dad doesn't do anything without something bigger and better in return. I had to . . . to-"

"Had to what?"

Stubbornly, she wouldn't look at me. Whatever she'd promised her dad had cost her something she didn't want to admit. I hoped it had nothing to do with my dad's whereabouts.

"Tell me you didn't give him my dad's location, at least."

She shook her head. "I don't know where your dad is."

"We can help each other if we work together."

"You don't understand." Her eyes met mine, filled with terror. "He'll kill me if he thinks I'm working against him. He could have killed me for my part in that security footage. He let me out that night because I sabotaged one of Gavriel De Luca's drug deals. A big one. I got there first."

I sucked in a breath. It had nothing to do with me and my situation, but it would infuriate Gavriel and Reno. I would hate to be around either of them when they found out. No wonder Vissar had so many guards. Two powerful families against one. That couldn't be good for business.

I swung my legs over the chair to face her. "I think you need to tell me exactly what you know, don't you? There are more lives at stake than just mine."

"Are you talking about Jace? He can handle himself."

"Not if he comes storming after me and your dad kills him."

At least she had the decency to look guilty. "Jace knows better than to do that. Besides, he would have done it right away if he was going to play the hero. And I called him like you asked me to."

That softened me up, even though she aggravated me to no end. "Natalia, start spilling what you know. About my dad, about this damn footage. Everything. I need to know."

"I swear, if you say a word of this to my dad, I might kill you myself." She swung her legs onto the chair and leaned back. "It can't look like we're doing anything other than girl talk here. He has eyes and ears everywhere."

I picked up my book and lay back in my chair, pretending to read. Our chairs faced the pool, but that didn't mean there weren't cameras everywhere in here. If I were a mastermind needing this much security, I would.

"That security footage has him in a big trafficking deal. There shouldn't have been footage in the first place, but he was blackmailed. He paid dearly to get it. Almost ruined him."

"So, now my dad has it and he's afraid he'll release it?"

"If your dad releases it, my dad will kill me. That's why he hasn't done it. But if your dad brings it back, my dad will kill him anyway. That's why Ricky and I haven't been able to figure a way out of this mess. We don't know what to do."

"Why did my dad get involved in the first place?" I asked, not looking at her, knowing she held onto some bitterness about this.

"Your dad offered to take it, so Ricky gave it to him at that party I invited them to. I thought I interrupted the frequency of the cameras, but it caught just the tail end of the trade-off. Your dad said he'd take the blame, thinking my dad wouldn't take out a hit on a famous musician. But we were wrong. After he saw the footage of his own house, he threatened to kill your dad and anyone he loves if he didn't bring it back."

"He disappeared with it to save everyone involved."

She didn't need to respond. I knew it had been his only way out of the mess without putting anyone in harm's way. "I tipped your dad off about the hit, but we never thought my dad would take down a plane. Especially risking that the security footage survived the crash and be discovered."

"Where's my dad?" I asked, my heart racing at the thought of finally knowing where he'd gone.

"I don't know where he is. I told you that already."

My heart sank. "And he still has the security footage?"

She laughed. "Honestly, you don't have a clue about these types of games, do you?"

"I'm a therapist, not a criminal."

This time, she threw her head back in laughter. "God, I really do like you."

I hadn't expected her to say that. Throughout our conversations, Natalia had seemed aloof, as if she disliked me immensely. I hated to admit that she was exactly as I thought she would be. She was just as cunning as her dad, but in a way, a little more amiable. We could be friends. Not close friends, but maybe more like acquaintances.

"Can I ask you something else?"

"Maybe."

"Jace . . . is there, or was there, something going on between you?"

She turned to me and pushed her sunglasses down to stare at me. "You're serious? There never was, and there never will be, anything between me and Jace. Absolutely *never*. I promise you that. He's all yours."

"What makes you say that?"

"I see how he looks at you. All the years I've known him, he's never looked at any woman that way."

There it is again. "Years? How long have you known him?"

She looked away. "Long enough."

There was more to her story than she was letting on. Jace had mostly grown up here. I knew Vissar was from Greece, but I didn't know when he'd come here. Something very disturbing about how quickly she shut down that conversation settled deep within me.

"If I find a way out of here, how mad will he be?"

"You should know. You've been flirting with him for months."

"That is not what I've been doing," I said, maintaining my dignity. "But you're wrong. I don't know your dad well enough to know how mad he'll be when I'm not here."

She shrugged. "Then do you really care?"

"What about you?"

"What about me?"

"His wrath won't come down on you, will it?"

"Aw, are you starting to like me a little?"

The glare I gave her was anything but friendly, but she only laughed as if this were a game to her. It was all a game, I thought bitterly.

"If I help you escape, yes. But it's not anything I can't handle. After all, I managed to get evidence that could put him away for a long, long time out of here, and he didn't kill me for that." She glanced my way again. "How are you planning on escaping?"

I tilted my head. "How would you?"

Chapter Thirty Nine

Cassie

For almost two weeks, I avoided Vissar as much as possible. We went out twice during that time; he showed me off to his business associates, accompanied by a warning that if I said anything to anyone about being forced to live at his house, not only would no one believe me, but I would deeply regret it. After everything he'd done, I had no doubt he was telling the truth.

He hosted one party at the house, but I stayed in the shadows as much as I could. Not once did I see Jace, and Natalia avoided me, too. If Vissar caught wind of our conversation by the pool and had taken it out on her, I wouldn't blame her for wanting to steer clear of me.

While I did my best to avoid Vissar, he hadn't attempted to come into my bedroom, although he had mentioned sharing his bed any chance he could. I needed to get out of this house. I missed Quinn. I not only missed Jace, I craved him. The outside world was vast compared to this small slice of confinement, and I needed to escape or be stuck here.

I memorized when Vissar left and he returned home. I noted every delivery that arrived at the house and the times they came.

From my balcony, I watched Vissar leave the house. As I did every day, I dressed for a run. Running without my phone to listen to had taken some getting used to, but Vissar refused to give it back to me. Bastard, I thought wryly as I stepped down the winding back stairway. Typically, I went out the back doors and down the path Jace had first taken me when I first arrived at this house, but as soon as I reached the bottom, I noticed Natalia at the far end of the hallway in the foyer near the other two staircases. What the hell was she doing? It looked like she was trying to get my attention. My suspicion rose, but since she was the only one in this house I could trust, I walked toward her. I supposed I'd need to start my run from the other side of the house today.

It took a minute to reach her, given the length of the hallway and the number of rooms in between, and she appeared impatient when I arrived. She blew out a breath.

"You've been avoiding me," she accused.

I straightened my back. "It's not you I've been avoiding, Natalia."

Her smirk was answer enough. "As much as you probably dislike me, I'm the only ally you have right now. And you know it. Give me your hand."

"What? Why?"

"Just hold it out."

She glanced down toward both ends of the hallway while I reluctantly extended my hand. As much as I hated to admit it, she was my only option at the moment. I had no choice but to trust her. She slapped my hand, and when I looked down, I saw my phone.

"Put it in your pocket," she whispered urgently. "It's dead, but you have it now."

"How did you get it?"

"Let's just say I stole it back for you." She turned to head back upstairs. "Have a nice run today, Cassie."

While she walked up the curving stairway, I slipped it into the tight pocket of my capri running pants and continued down the hallway to the side door at the end. The door was for deliveries, but today wasn't a delivery day based on the information I'd tucked away in my memory.

As soon as I stepped outside into the bright sunshine, I started toward the path just as a white van drove up the long driveway.

Weird, I thought. It's not a delivery day. Maybe it was a special order. I went to the edge of the path to stretch when the van parked, watching a man with a clipboard get out from the driver's side and look at me.

"Ma'am? Are you able to sign for a delivery?"

I sauntered cautiously back toward him. "What are you delivering? I'm not sure I can sign for something. I don't live here."

"We're delivering some red roses, a lot of them, but I need someone to sign for them before I can get them out of the van." He took another step toward me.

"There are no scheduled deliveries today," a guard said, stepping out from the side door of the house and coming over to me. He snatched the clipboard from the man's hand.

I gasped when the man shoved me aside, throwing himself at the guard. When I hit the pavement painfully, I rolled away from the two men grappling on the sidewalk. I heard gunshots and covered my ears until someone grabbed me under my arms and hauled me up.

What was going on? I heard the screech of the van door open, and a pair of hands pulled me roughly inside before the door slammed shut. It was dark in the van, and I could hardly breathe, suddenly rolling sideways when the van's engine roared and careened backward out of the driveway. I heard more gunshots and screamed, squeezing my eyes shut.

I fell back against someone as we swerved hard to the left, recognizing the powerful arms banded around me even before I lifted my gaze to the brilliant blue eyes. He clung to me, probably even more since I wasn't securely seatbelted in like he was, but his arms held me as if they would never let go. I couldn't stop the tears from flowing as I buried my face in his chest.

Once the van had made it far enough away without further threat, Jace released me just enough to let me settle into my seat and secure my seatbelt, but he pulled me right back against him, kissing my head.

"I swear, I won't let you out of my sight again."

"How in the hell did you get me out of there?"

He grinned. "Friends."

"I never thought I would get out of there. He . . . "

Jace set me back. "He didn't touch you? Hurt . . . you?"

"He hit me once, but otherwise, no."

I looked into his eyes, drowning in their depths just before he pulled me roughly against him and seized my mouth with his. There was nothing gentle about it. He kissed me with his entire body and refused to let go. I accepted it because my heart couldn't stand the thought of being apart from him again.

Chapter Forty

"I don't think I've ever had anyone touch my tattoos quite like that before."

I continued to trace the wide black swirl over the outer curve of his shoulder with the tip of my finger, eliciting a drawn-out shiver from him. If I could lie here in his arms and touch his tattoos all day, I would. We'd made it back from his daring rescue, with Jace taking me directly home. With the new security system in place, we felt secure enough, even though Vissar would be furious when he found out I'd escaped. Jace had made sure his mom, Ezra and Milo were put up in a hotel, not trusting Vissar to come after them.

Quinn was spending the night at Ray's again, and I spoke with his parents to let them know of the potential danger he might be in. They assured me that the security system couldn't be hacked and that he'd be fine. As much as I wanted to see him to make sure no one had hurt him, I needed this time with Jace. The night wasn't enough for me, especially as I looked at his smooth skin the next morning.

"Like how?"

"I'm not sure. Like you aren't expecting something from me." He turned to look at me so quickly that my hand fell away, only to be swept up by him and trapped between us when he leaned over me. "Like you're expecting me to ravish you."

"Ravish?" A seductive smile curved my lips as I lifted my unhindered hand to slide against the curve of his jaw. "I'm not expecting anything. I'm waiting for it."

His growl rumbled through his chest as his mouth came down on mine, capturing my lips into submission while his leg slid between my thighs. His fingers traced the sensitive skin of my inner thigh, producing a gasp from me, and he took every opportunity I allowed him.

Flames ignited at the touch of his fingers; my head falling back from the overwhelming riptides of heady pleasure that his easy actions wrought. While his lips traced a path from the column of my neck downward, my fingers drifted through his soft hair.

"You have no idea how many times I've imagined this over the last few weeks," he murmured, his warm breath against my already heated skin, intensifying the temperature of my inner core. "God, you feel amazing in my hands."

"Jace," I whispered as I saw stars, a tidal wave rippling through me as though we hadn't just been at it all night.

"When you say my name like that," he said against my breast, gently biting the inner swell and teasing me with everything he had, "it only makes me want to take you higher."

"I'm not sure you could—" My eyes shot wide open when he shifted and flexed his hips, my body still getting used to the size of him stretching me.

He kissed his way up, drawing my hand to the headboard and curling my fingers around the rung. "Hang on for me, baby."

My fingers curled tight. As soon as he started moving, shoving my knee up to my chest until I could feel him everywhere, I was grateful that no one was around. I was certain the neighbors could hear me moaning because he hadn't lied.

He took me to heights I'd never felt before. I flung my other hand up and hung on for dear life while he made sure I knew I was his. My legs were weak by the time he gently disengaged my hands and pulled me back down, kissing a path up my torso. He lay half-sprawled on top of me while I continued to draw lines over his tattoos.

"Are you trying to do that again?" he said, his voice muffled against my stomach. "If so, you're going to have to give me a few minutes."

"Jace," I whispered, wanting so badly to share my feelings for him.

"Hmmm?"

"Nothing."

He laid his head back down. "My mom has a doctor's appointment today. She's hoping to get cleared to go back to work."

"Is she still having issues?"

"No, but I don't trust her not to tell me what her doctor says." I laughed. "I'm serious. She's always trying to hide stuff like that."

"You act like she's eighty, Jace! She's not even fifty yet."

"Well, I'd like her to make it to eighty."

When he shifted and rolled away from me, I immediately felt the loss of his warmth.

"Let me take her," I said, rolling onto my side as he stood up.

I watched him walk to the bathroom, admiring his naked body as he moved. Holy smokes, we'd never make it out of this bedroom if I couldn't keep my eyes off him. He turned halfway, grinning at me when he caught me staring.

"Really?"

"Yes." I sat up, keeping the sheets pulled around me. "I like your mom. I need to get out after being trapped for so long. It will help me."

"Stay alert. I don't trust Vissar not to follow you and attempt to grab you again. He's got to be furious."

"I intend to."

The way he stared at me made it hard to tell what he was thinking until he abandoned whatever he was going to do and strode back to me. Kneeling on the bed, he scooped me into his arms and sealed my mouth with his. The sweep of his tongue and the caress of his hand sliding up my ribs to curve around my breast sent shivers through me.

"If you're sure," he murmured, moving his mouth to just under my ear while his other hand slipped down and around the curve of my ass, pulling me against him.

"We won't get anywhere if we can't keep our hands off each other, Jace," I grinned, keeping my hands on him.

He sighed. "I know. I'm getting into the shower. Her appointment is at ten."

I glanced at the clock. "Did you . . . uh, need help in there?"

Jace stood up, sweeping me off the bed and into his arms, carrying me into the bathroom while I laughed the entire way.

An hour later, I pulled up to Val's house and parked in her single-car driveway behind her convertible Mustang. Since the clinic was near her house, she told me to pick her up there instead of the hotel. The day boasted stunningly bright sunshine and warm temperatures—just right for putting the top down on the Miata. I wasn't sure if she would prefer to take my car or hers, but I felt more comfortable driving, especially if she was still experiencing back discomfort.

When I knocked on the screen door, I could hear her talking to someone, and a moment later, I saw her poke her head out of the kitchen and wave me in. Glancing at my watch, I hoped she knew we'd need to get going soon, or she'd be late for her appointment.

Before I left, Jace made sure I had the address for the clinic, a list of questions he wanted me to ask, and the time of the appointment—again. The man was anything if not thorough. I suppose, as a former undercover detective, he had to be.

The screen door let out a tiny screech as I opened it, and I slowly walked into her spotless house. Whoever she was speaking with on the phone wasn't my business, and I didn't want to appear to be eavesdropping.

"I don't want you to keep getting mixed up with him," she said urgently as I entered the kitchen and set my clutch on the counter, sliding onto the stool. "That's all I'm going to say about it. Cassie's here, and I have to get going."

Trained to listen for things left unsaid, I tried my hardest not to dwell on who she might be talking to. Apparently, it was someone who knew me, as she hadn't explained who I was to the caller.

She smiled and gave me a hug. "Ready to go?"

"I should ask you that. How are you feeling?"

I followed her to the door, noticing she walked with a straighter posture. "I'm feeling much better. Much stronger."

While she locked the door, I jogged down the steps to the car. "That's good to hear. Jace will be happy to know that. He gave me a list of questions to ask the doctor, assuming you'll allow me to listen in."

Her irritable groan told me all I needed to know when we got into the Miata. "He means well," she explained. "I really hope you can forgive his pushiness."

I grinned, remembering months ago when Jace tried to get me to leave town, to leave Vissar's party. She wasn't wrong. He was pushy, and he meant well. Jace only did it to protect me, and for good reason. I hadn't heard from Vissar today, but he had to know what happened yesterday and that he no longer had me contained.

"I have my own way of handling it, I suppose," I said, starting the car and backing out of the driveway. "You're right. He does mean well."

She glanced at me. "I hope you know he isn't anything like his uncle."

While I drove, I tried not to look confused, even though I didn't have a clue what she was talking about. I'd never met his uncle, so I had no way of knowing whether he was like him. Had he been at Jace's birthday party, and I just didn't remember?

"His uncle?"

"Vissar."

I felt my breath catch in shock. All the blood seemed to drain from my face, settling in my stomach, where it curdled like sour milk. Blinking, I concentrated on the road, grateful I hadn't pulled onto the main road yet.

"Vissar?"

"My brother. Well, stepbrother. My mother remarried when I was five. Vissar has always been vicious, and I've tried to keep the boys away from him. He's got his claws sunk into Jace, though. I hope you don't think poorly of him. He did it for Ezra."

It would have been helpful if he'd told me that Vissar was his uncle months ago. Not that it would have mattered. We'd still be in the same position. But it made a lot of things clearer now. I felt a little queasy, having thought he'd been sleeping with Natalia. They were cousins, even if not blood-related.

"Cassie, are you okay?" she asked. "Did I say something to upset you?"

I shook my head. "I . . . I didn't know. What do you mean he did it for Ezra? Is that why he's doing jobs for Vissar?"

She tucked her hair behind her ear. "If he didn't tell you, he's going to be pissed at me. Please, Cassie, don't blame him for not telling you. I'm sure he had his reasons."

"I'm sure he did, but things might have been different if he'd told me right away. I always wondered why he was working for Vissar."

"He should be the one to tell you, but since I've opened my big mouth, I should probably just explain it. Ezra, as you know, has a drug problem. Back in August, he got into trouble with some men he owed money to—more money than Jace and me have. They were going to kill him unless he came up with it. Jace made a deal with Vissar to help Ezra and pay off these men."

"How long?" I needed to know for my sanity how long he'd be working for him. "How long will he be doing these jobs?"

"Until Ezra's debt is paid."

"So, whenever Vissar says."

"Jace and Ezra are his nephews. He won't make him do it forever."

"Is he doing illegal things for Vissar?"

"Jace doesn't tell me about the jobs. I hope not, though. He worked very hard as a police officer and then as an undercover detective. Jace takes that line of work seriously. If Vissar asked him to do something illegal, Jace would put up a fight about it."

That I could understand, knowing Jace. He might not have the same moral code I did, but he was in that line of work for a reason. Jace had to help people; it was ingrained in him. If Vissar asked him to do something illegal, especially if it would hurt someone, it would pain Jace to comply.

"And if Jace refuses to do any more jobs for him?"

When Val met my eyes, saying nothing, I knew.

"Which one of them would Vissar hurt if Jace refused to do anything else for him?" I asked.

"Ezra," she whispered. "He needs Jace for his connections."

"He'd kill his own nephew?"

She glanced away. "And now you know why I never wanted my boys to get mixed up with him. That's why Fred and I used to fight all the time. He didn't want me to have any kind of relationship with my brother. He's my brother."

"I thought you said stepbrother."

"He's still family."

"He's the one who hurt you, isn't he?" I asked. "Jace did something to make him angry, and he had someone try to hit you when you were at the grocery store."

She nodded. "Can't prove it, but he asked Jace to do something illegal, and, well, you know Jace couldn't do it. We were lucky it wasn't worse."

I wrestled with my emotions during the short drive to the clinic, even while Val chatted happily with me. The situation grew riskier by the minute, and I had just made it worse by leaving. But Jace was a good person, and memories from that morning surfaced, making me blush.

Val allowed me to speak with the doctor and ask the questions that Jace needed answers to, but I didn't stay for her actual physical exam. While I waited in the lobby, I itched to call Jace and ask him, but I decided to wait until I saw him before bringing it up. It wasn't worth starting a potential argument. Being related meant nothing. It just meant that what Vissar was doing to this family needed to end. Soon.

Chapter Forty One

Cassie

I dropped Val off an hour later with a clean bill of health and a release to return fully to work. Her mood soared after that, even though I thought she seemed fine before the appointment. We had lunch, which I insisted on paying for since she wasn't fully back to work, and then I dropped her off.

I had just pulled onto the highway when Jace called.

"Everything is fine," I said before he had a chance to pepper me with questions about what the doctor said.

"Where are you?" he asked, his voice demanding.

"I just dropped your mom off at her house. Why?"

He let out a deep breath. "I'm at the hospital. Ezra . . . he's in bad shape."

My heart thudded uncontrollably. "What happened? Did he overdose?"

"He got the shit beat out of him. I'm lucky I got him here in time, but . . . it's . . bad." My hands gripped the steering wheel as I tried to keep my focus on the road when all I could think about was Jace and Ezra. Poor Ezra. "Cassie, I was afraid he'd gotten to you, too."

"Vissar. Because you came for me." That bastard, I thought. "Did you call your mom?"

"Yes. I told her to get back to the hotel and not come here yet. Not until we get things figured out. Milo should still be there under strict orders not to leave. Where is Quinn?"

"He's still at Ray's house," I said. "I'm coming to the hospital.

I'll be there soon."

For the second time within a month, I found myself at the hospital, but this time not in the emergency room. A nurse led me into a hospital room, where I found Jace sitting next to Ezra. He hadn't been lying. Ezra's face was more bruises and cuts than skin. He had bandages on his head, one eye swollen shut, a busted lip, and stitches on his cheek.

I covered my mouth as tears started to fall. Jace stood up as I walked into his arms. "This is my fault," I said against his chest. "I should have stayed there."

"No." He pulled me away, keeping his hands on my arms and looking into my eyes. "No. Absolutely not. This is Vissar's sick and twisted way of controlling people, Cassie. This is not your fault. Stop taking that on yourself. I thought the hotel would be safe enough, but Ez has a problem. He slipped out to buy some drugs while Milo was sleeping. I don't know how Vissar's thugs found him."

When he pulled me over to the chair to sit, I shook my head. I needed to stand. After dropping off his mom, the information she gave me still tumbled around in my head. I imagined how he must have felt seeing me with Vissar. It made me sick to my stomach.

"Sit down," I whispered. "I need to tell you something."

Worry creased his brow. "What is it?"

"Sit down. Please."

Jace sat down but slyly changed the course of the conversation. "How'd it go with my mom?"

Funny you should ask, I wanted to say. Instead, I replied, "One hundred percent back to normal. Her doctor gave her the go-ahead to fully return to work. She was so delighted; she almost skipped back to the car, but I stopped her."

The side of his mouth quirked up. "Figures. When it happened, she wasn't used to being laid up. She can't stand to be inactive. This really did a number on her."

He reached for my hand, sliding his fingers along mine and

running the pad of his thumb over that sensitive spot on the back of my hand. Whenever he did that, it made me stop thinking altogether. I lost all argument with myself.

I straightened. "She said you came back to help Ezra out of a mess, but you came back to help her too, didn't you? He's truly evil, isn't he?"

Molten blue eyes stared into mine, holding my gaze with a seriousness that stole my breath away. He would do anything for his mom. Anything for his brother. It made me wonder if he'd do anything for a woman, having never been in a serious relationship in his life. That was what worried me.

"Yes." He tilted his head. "What else did she say?"

I drew in a deep breath. "That you aren't anything like your uncle."

The movement of his thumb immediately stopped, his eyes remaining on mine. "I suppose she told you that Vissar is my uncle?"

"Why didn't you tell me?" I whispered.

"I don't know."

"Come on, Jace." I pulled my hand away and paced around the room. "That's not a valid answer, and you know it."

"Shame? Shame that I'm related to him? About what he does."

I stopped pacing and faced him. "That has nothing to do with you."

When he stood up, I thought he would walk toward me, but he stayed where he was. "I'm working for him, Cassie. He does horrible things. He's threatened people in my life if I don't do things for him. You have beliefs that are completely against everything I'm doing."

"Your mom already confessed that her accident at the grocery store may have been because you didn't do something he told you to do. Something illegal." He just stared at me. "I once told you I had no right to judge others for their lifestyle unless I wanted them to judge mine. I don't do that unless it's hurting me. Jace, I know what he does. You know I do. I don't agree with it. Are you helping him with this trade?"

He shook his head. "I can't tell you. It only puts you more at risk if I do."

I walked to him, sliding my arms around his waist and looking up at him. "I wish you would have told me. I'm disgusted even being in his company."

"Think of how I felt," he whispered, lowering his mouth to mine without touching.

"I do because I couldn't bear the thought of you in the company of another woman."

"You never have to."

"You swear he didn't touch you?" I shook my head, even though he'd already asked me that a few times. "Good, because I'd have killed him."

When his lips finally pressed to mine, tentatively at first, my body relaxed against him. He pulled me roughly against him and deepened the kiss. His fingers cradled my neck, holding me prisoner to his mouth until my knees weakened. But he wasn't done yet. Not by a long shot. His arm banded around my waist, and he picked me up with that one arm, sitting down in the chair with me on his lap.

"Jace," I cried out. "I'm mad at you."

He grinned, though his mouth was still on mine. "Doesn't seem that way."

"Tell me what happened with Ezra. And why did you need to bail him out? Couldn't Ezra have gone to Vissar himself for the money he owed?"

Jace sighed, keeping me locked in place. "When we were kids, I was a little shit and stole some candy from a store once. I got caught, but Ezra took the blame for me. I'll never know why he did that, but it changed the course of his life forever. I tried to tell my dad that it was me, but since Ez already confessed, he didn't believe him. Ezra was always in trouble. He has a learning disability, and he's just slower than me. I told you my dad is a real asshole, right?"

I nodded.

"He was always picking on him. The older we got, the worse it became, and he eventually started hitting him. Sometimes I couldn't stand it, so I took it for him. Mom could tell something was going on and confronted him once, but it just got worse, even though we never told her what was happening up in Seattle. Eventually, Ez started getting into drugs. He got kicked out of school and came right down here. Never went back. But the drug use has just gotten worse and worse. I got into law enforcement because I felt guilt over stealing that candy and to protect people like Ezra."

A red haze came over me, filling me with anger at what Ezra had to go through and for what Jace had to endure just to protect him. Vissar was taking advantage and now taking it out on both of them. I stood up and turned away from Jace, but he caught my wrist.

"Don't even think about what you're thinking."

My eyes flashed. "I won't let him get away with this."

"For now, you are."

Jace stood up, cupping my face in his hands and kissing me. He dropped his forehead to mine.

"Cass," came a croak from the bed.

Jace and I spun around to look at Ezra. He couldn't open his eyes, but he must have heard us. We ran to his side, but I didn't want to touch him anywhere.

"We're here, Ez," Jace said. "Just rest. You'll be out of here in no time."

"He'll pay for this," I whispered.

"So sorry," he croaked. "Sorry, sorry, sorry."

"It's not your fault, Ezra." I looked at Jace, wondering what Ezra was apologizing about. Why did he keep saying he was sorry?

"It is. Vissar. Knows. Everything."

My breath caught.

"Everything?"

"Lex's kid."

I covered my gasp with my hand and ran to my clutch to dig out my phone. With shaking fingers, I dialed Quinn's number. When the call connected, I took a deep breath.

"I'm displeased with this turn of events," Vissar answered.

Chapter Forty Two

Cassie

"Quinn has nothing to do with this, Vissar. Please. I swear I will get you the security footage back."

I winced at his sinister laugh. None of us were safe. "I don't believe for a moment that you would hand it over to me. Not after you've been speaking with Natalia. I know she told you what's on it."

"Natalia has told me nothing."

"Don't," he snapped, and I jumped as if he were right beside me. "Don't lie to me, Cassie. Not now. Not after everything we've been through."

Jace's hand wrapped around my arm, steadying me as my hands trembled. I had to be stronger than this. Vissar wasn't going anywhere, and while I didn't know Natalia well, she had helped me when I was there. That counted for something.

"Here is what's going to happen," he continued. "I now have another bargaining chip. You have three days to bring me the footage. Contact your father, or do whatever you need to do to get it back. I don't care. I expect you by nine o'clock on Wednesday evening."

I didn't want to ask, was afraid to ask. "Keeping me in your house won't make it appear. It's pointless."

"I only need the footage back, or someone is going to die. And since you aren't here, and your brother is, that's good enough for me."

I gasped, covering my mouth. My eyes widened in fear as I met

Jace's gaze.

The phone tumbled from my grasp, landing on the bed as I covered my mouth with my hands, hot tears spilling from my eyes. I turned into Jace and buried my face in his chest. His arms came around me, protecting me, shielding me. But who would protect Quinn? I sobbed harder, thinking of him wrapped up in this. Sweet, innocent Quinn.

"I have to go," I whispered, horrified to tell Jace the truth just yet. He'd storm over there and try to kill Vissar himself. "He has Quinn. I thought he was at Ray's. He must have gotten him somehow. I told Ray's parents not to let him out of their sight."

"Cass, stop." Jace put his hands on my arms and pulled me away, looking into my watery eyes. "Breathe. What did he say?"

"I have three days to bring back the security footage." Jace raised his eyebrows. "I have to go. I'm not losing anyone else because of him."

He gave me a shake. "And I'm not about to lose you."

My eyes widened.

"You heard me, Cassie. I won't lose you. I'm going to call Ty. We've battled the worst criminals together. We'll come up with a plan."

I nodded, feeling numb as Jace grabbed his phone to call Ty. My phone rang again, and I hesitated to look, fearing it might be Vissar. But I had to check, just in case it was Vissar calling to let me speak with Quinn. It was Natalia.

"Hello?" I answered, my voice cracking.

"Cassie," she said in a hushed tone. "I only have a minute. I'm watching the kid. Don't worry about him. My dad won't do anything to him."

"Do you promise?"

"I promise."

The line went dead before I could say anything else. I looked at Jace as he paced, talking with Ty. I sank down onto the chair. There was still one person I could call. I wasn't sure he could even help me with this.

I had to.

"Cassie," Reno's deep voice rumbled through the phone. "I trust you're recovered from your ordeal?"

"How did you know?"

"I couldn't leave you, not with your boyfriend speaking on your behalf as he did. It was rather admirable of him to put himself in front of me like that."

"He's not my . . . " Hold on. What the—? "What are you talking about?"

"He must not have told you he contacted me just after you disappeared. Actually, he contacted Riley, and she put him in touch with me. I understand the predicament he would be in, having worked in law enforcement like Ty. It's always refreshing to know I have someone on my side should I ever need it."

I sucked in a breath, glancing at Jace, who was still deep in conversation with Ty. He made a deal with Reno on my behalf? He had all kinds of tricks up his sleeve.

"In that case, I need your help again."

He sighed. "Sweetheart, what did I tell you before?"

"You said that you were there if I ever needed your help."

"Right, and now you're in a position where you need another favor. Jace was kind enough to pay it for you."

"I never said I needed a favor. I need your help, Reno."

"What is it you need my help with?"

"Vissar has kidnapped my brother. He's only twelve. I need your help, your guidance, on how to kill him. How to kill Vissar." My voice rose, and so did my heart rate.

"This is likely something that Gavriel will want to involve himself in, since Vissar has been such a thorn in our sides. It just so happens that I'm down for a visit. Why don't you come by tomorrow?"

"I'll be there."

"And do bring your boyfriend."

"He's not my . . . " I glanced at Jace, catching his gaze. "I'll see you tomorrow, Reno. We appreciate the help you've given, and I won't forget it."

Chapter Forty Three

Cassie

The eight-foot-tall black iron gates of the De Luca family home opened automatically as we pulled up. My mouth fell open at the size of the house. Riley hadn't been kidding when she described her first impressions of it during Regan and Cameron's wedding in March. Vissar's house was massive, but this pristine two-story home, with its perfectly manicured lawn, was something else entirely.

Thick, shady trees loomed overhead as Jace drove up the long driveway that wound around to the front of the house. I clambered out without waiting, staring up at the imposing structure. Reno and Gavriel were waiting inside while my anxiety gnawed at my stomach.

I snapped out of it when Jace's hand touched my back. "Okay?" he whispered.

I shook my head. "Mm-hmm."

He only laughed, sliding his hand from my back to my hand, threading his fingers through mine before pulling me up the steps to the large oak double doors. We didn't even knock before one of them opened, revealing Regan, her pale golden hair piled on top of her head.

She pulled me into a hug, surprisingly strong for such a petite woman—even after having just given birth three months ago. "I'm so sorry to hear about your troubles," she whispered in my ear before pulling away and staring into my eyes. "Pops is in his office with Reno."

I stepped into the enormous foyer, still gripping Jace's hand, where Cameron stood cradling Nicco in his arms. At almost three months old, he had grown considerably, his fists waving around as he tried to grab at anything within reach. I understood why Regan had her hair up; if not, he might have yanked on it.

"Wow, look at him!" I said, smiling at Cameron. "What a cutie!"

"He's about to go down for a nap," Regan said, closing the door behind us. "Do you want to hold him before Cameron takes him upstairs?"

I hadn't held him since he was only a week old at Riley and Ty's wedding in September, when he hadn't been nearly as active. However, something deep inside me urged me to accept. I held out my arms. As soon as I had him snug in my arms, his hands stopped waving, and he stared up at me with huge blue eyes. We locked gazes, and my life flashed before my eyes.

I had never thought about being a mother until Quinn, and he was twelve now. As I drew my finger down the softness of his chubby cheek, his pouty lips curved into a gurgling smile. My gaze darted up to Regan, who had slipped her arm around Cameron, leaning into him and smiling knowingly at me.

"Motherhood changes *everything*," she murmured, gazing up at Cameron.

I felt like an intruder in their moment and looked back down at baby Nicco, who was still staring up at me in wonder. Leaning down, I kissed his little forehead and inhaled that fresh baby scent. Dear God, I thought, then quickly moved over to Regan and handed the baby to Cameron. What was happening to me? She just kept grinning at me, as if she knew a deep secret. I looked back at Jace, who raised his dark eyebrow.

"Don't let her rattle you," Cameron said with a chuckle, turning to go up the huge winding staircase behind him, with Nicco cradled in his arms. He called back, "I'll meet you in the office."

Regan tilted her head to the side and took a deep breath.

"Come on. Let's see what they have to provide you for advice."

To the right was another set of double doors like those leading into the house. These weren't heavy oak but a lighter wood, still effective in closing against intruders. Regan gave me one last look, as if to question whether I really wanted to do this, before she swept the doors open.

Facing the circular driveway, with a vast window behind him, Gavriel De Luca sat behind a large desk, while Reno sat in a chair to the right. As Reno stood up, Gavriel remained seated. Both men exuded an air of dominance. I couldn't imagine Vissar in this same room. It would be lethal. As we walked through, I stared at the left wall, covered from floor to ceiling with bookshelves. Directly across from the library wall was a small living area furnished with a dark brown couch and chairs.

"Breathe," I reminded myself as my feet moved toward the intimidating man behind the desk. He wore reading glasses, which he removed as we approached. Reno put his hands on my arms, just below my shoulders, and kissed my cheek.

"You're looking well, sweetheart," he said, then looked at Jace. "Mr. Taylor, good to see you."

Jace nodded, extending his hand. "It's Jace. I appreciate your help, Mr. Moretti."

Reno released me and stepped back. "Cassie is . . . special." I'd heard that before and disagreed. I wasn't any different from the next woman. "She's not quite like anyone I've ever met before. Mysterious, with a hidden strength. Wouldn't you agree, Jace?"

"I would."

Gavriel cleared his throat. "If we could get on with business, I have other matters to address today."

Regan snapped her gaze to her dad. "Pops, they've driven all the way across town, which is no small endeavor. You can at least give them a minute to breathe before jumping right into it."

"It sounds like you're having an issue with one of our biggest threats, Ms. Nichols," Gavriel said.

I met Gavriel's gaze. "I do."

Desperation drove me to this point, despite my morals. I would kill Vissar, even if it meant going to prison. I hadn't even told Jace what I planned to do. I just wanted Quinn back, unscathed.

Cameron joined us quietly, standing behind Regan and placing his hands on her shoulders.

Gavriel reclined in his chair, the massive mahogany desk separating us, his fingers steepled as he regarded me with hard eyes. I didn't know him like I knew Reno, and even with Reno, our acquaintance had its limits. However, as fathers of two women I deeply respected, I didn't need to know them well. Reno stood close to him, arms crossed and tapping his chin as if lost in thought. They were intimidating, but not as threatening as Vissar.

"Very well, Ms. Nichols. What is it you need from us?" Gavriel asked.

"I need to kill Vissar, and I need your to help to do it. Or at least tell me how. I'll be facing him, so please tell me what I need to do."

"No!" Jace exploded, stepping in front of me as if to shield me. Cameron, at least, anticipated his movement and grabbed his biceps to restrain him. A person didn't just lunge around men like Gavriel and Reno. Jace shrugged off Cameron's grip, refusing to back down. "I'll do it, Cassie. Don't you dare tell me you're going to charge in there to save Quinn."

Gavriel raised his brows. "It makes no difference to me who does it, Mr. Taylor. But she has more at stake in this game than you."

I tried to move Jace out of the way, but he wouldn't budge. It was like trying to move a slab of granite.

"Cassie, you don't know anything about killing someone," Regan said.

Gavriel's eyes intensified. He braced his hands on the desk and rose slowly, moving with the grace of a predator. He pulled open a drawer and handed me a gun. "I need someone to take out

Vissarion Loukas, and Ms. Nichols is in the perfect position to do so. I say let her do it."

I took it, surprised at how awkward it felt in my hand.

"I'll do it," Jace insisted again, swiftly taking the gun from me as though he didn't trust me with a firearm.

"No." I finally got around him, allowing him to keep his arms circled around me while I looked into his eyes. They silently pleaded with me not to do this. "I've already put enough people in harm's way. I can't live with myself if something happens to you, Jace."

His gaze found mine as his knuckles brushed against my cheek. "He'll take you out before you even have a chance to. And even if you did, his guards will kill you for it. Cass, I've killed people before in my line of work. It isn't something you want on your conscience. I don't want that for you."

"Argue all you want, but I like the idea of having him out of the way." Gavriel retrieved his cigar and took a puff.

I held Jace's gaze without turning toward Gavriel and replied, "Yes, I'll do it. However, there is one problem."

Gavriel raised an eyebrow at me, waiting for an explanation.

"I've never shot a gun before."

Jace's jaw hardened so much I thought it would break, his eyes taking on a glossy sheen. I gripped his arm, shaking my head. He needed to get any thought of going after Vissar himself out of his head.

"Don't," I said. "He'll kill you the second you step into his house."

"Isn't there a way we can get in there and take him out so she doesn't have to, Gavriel?" Reno asked.

Gavriel shrugged. "She'll be in the perfect position since he's ordered her there."

I looked at Reno and nodded. It would be fine. I'd figure it out or die trying. I wouldn't let Quinn stay there and die. But I would need help to do it. I'd never handled a firearm before.

"Thank you," I told Gavriel before I turned to leave the office.

Reno caught my arm. "Are you certain you can do this, Cassie? Killing a man isn't as easy as you think, especially a man as well-guarded as Vissar. You know what will happen if you fail."

"I'm certain. There is no other way." I looked back at Gavriel, who was watching us cautiously. "I just need someone to tell me the best way to do it."

With that, I stalked out of the office, Jace right on my tail, regardless of who followed me. In the foyer, I trembled violently. I was terrified about what I was about to do, but as I'd told Reno, there was no other way. That was the truth.

Jace reached for me, sliding his fingers around my arm. I could tell he was angry that I hadn't told him about Vissar's plan for me. I met his gaze just before he crushed me into his arms.

I heard the click of the office door behind me, though I didn't turn. Regan and Cameron joined us, everyone talking at once. My ears rang, and my vision swam. I blinked several times.

"Cassie," Regan said. "Are you sure about this?"

"She came here for advice," Cameron said. "If she does this, she'll earn the utmost respect from our families."

Regan's eyes flashed. "But this, Cam? It's not reasonable to send her in there. God, it would be better for me to go than her."

I had never seen Cameron look so angry. "Fuck no, that will *never* happen. We are not getting involved in this any more than we already are."

Jace released me as I faced them.

"Stop," I whispered. "I'm doing this. If I don't, he'll kill Quinn, and that's not a risk I'm willing to take."

I had to remember the horrible things Vissar had done, especially to the young girls with promising futures whom he sold into prostitution for profit. My resolve hardened. I might be next unless I did something about it.

"I need a plan. Please, someone help me with a plan. I can't just go in and shoot him. His bodyguards will take me out."

Chapter Forty Four

Cassie

The guards at the gate recognized me immediately when I pulled up, and the tall iron gates opened a second later. The thundering of my heart only increased as I approached the front of the house and the side garage. I purposely parked close to the door to make a quick getaway if needed, but I realized when I stepped out that it was pointless. I'd need the guards to open the gates for me to leave.

Spotlights hidden in the perfectly manicured shrubs bathed the house in soft light, with the interior lights only adding to the glow. Vibrantly hued flowers sprouted from the shrubs around the perimeter. My heels clicked on the pavement, bringing me closer to the front door. As I walked in, I could hear his favorite classical music softly playing in the study, filtering through the high vaulted ceiling and into the hallways passing from the foyer through the living room. The house took time to navigate, given its massive size.

Vissar sat in his chair, a glass of vintage Irish whiskey in his hand. Dressed in a white shirt open at the collar and a pair of dress pants, he looked deadly. His eyes drifted to me as I walked through the door into the spacious room, decorated in dark walnut and muted lighting.

The gun in my oversized handbag at my side, the Glock G19 Gavriel had given to me, made me nervous enough. I didn't know when I'd be able to reach in and grab it without being seen, especially with Vissar's guard stationed in the room. But I had it.

Cameron showed me how to use it and let me fire it to get accustomed to handling it. As if I'd ever adapt to handling a firearm.

"I was wondering if you were going to come." Vissar set his glass aside and rose to meet me at the center of the large imported rug that covered the length of the floor.

Before I could utter a word, he slid his hand around to the base of my neck and gripped it hard. I gasped as he crushed his mouth against mine. This was not what I signed up for when I thought I would be coming here to kill him.

When Vissar pulled away, his eyes met mine, shining dangerously. That look, one I had become familiar with, confirmed that something had irritated him, and I had a feeling it had nothing to do with my timing. I sucked in a breath, his hand still banded around my neck.

"You've gotten close to my nephew, Cassie. I'm interested in knowing just how close you've become." His tone and accent were more pronounced than I ever remembered.

"I don't know what you mean. Jace and I aren't that close," I lied.

He gave me a hard shake by my neck, his jaw taut. "Do not lie to me."

Something had gone wrong. I was the bargaining chip, and I was here. Why would he care how close I'd gotten to Jace? This was not how I had planned this evening to go. If it derailed, I didn't know if I'd be able to recover.

He withdrew his hand from my neck and cupped my face with both hands. I tried everything to calm my breathing while he stroked his thumbs over my bottom lip, but I couldn't stop my lips from quivering at his unwelcome touch.

"You're scared," he whispered. "You should be."

"I need to see my brother before I give you anything," I choked out.

"You should know that from the start, I had Jace watching you.

Those pictures that I showed you at my charity event? How do you think I was able to start harassing your friends, beginning with the one who looks like you? And your dad's girlfriend? She was easy to get rid of. Jace provided me information, and when I asked for pictures so I could get you right where I wanted you, he provided them, too."

My stomach plummeted. No. Jace knew I had trust issues. He wouldn't have done all that and put the people who mattered to me at risk.

He continued, "Information about your security system so I could have my guards break into your father's house, search it, and scare you? Jace gave me all that so I could pass the information on to my guards on how to get in undetected. I knew your dad wasn't stupid enough to have my security footage there."

My mouth dropped open, but I quickly recovered. "You're lying."

Scrambling to remember when I first ran into Jace here, I recalled he'd offered his help, but he'd tried like hell to get me out of this house. If he was spying on me for Vissar, why would he push me to leave that night? The beach the next morning. I felt sick. He had offered his help.

"And my little trafficking ring with girls? Jace helps me with that too. I've made a lot of money with his help."

At that moment, I thought I would throw up. Jace wouldn't do something so vile as to help Vissar with his trafficking ring. He was in law enforcement, sworn to protect people. I swayed. Had he truly been forced to help Vissar instead of saving those young girls?

Damn him, I thought. I had trusted him—the first person I'd trusted in ten years—and he had shattered that trust with lies. Not telling me about his relation to Vissar was one thing, and I could get over that. That was minor. But this? This hurt. My heart faltered, but this wasn't over yet. I raised my eyes to Vissar.

"I want my security footage. That information ties the trafficking to me, and I need it back. Did you bring it?"

I opened my mouth to tell him that I didn't have it, but he interrupted me.

"Bring in the rest of the players in this game," he told the guard at the door.

My eyes widened when two guards dragged Quinn in first, looking terrified but unharmed, followed by Jace. He didn't look beaten up, but the two burly guards had a hold on him that he wouldn't be getting out of, though it looked like he was still trying. My stomach dropped, seeing him in a different light now that Vissar had told me everything I didn't know about Jace.

I whipped around to Vissar. "I don't know what you want from me! I don't have your security footage, and I can't get it for you! I don't know where my dad went."

Vissar shook his head, walking around to his desk and withdrawing a gun from his desk drawer, much like Gavriel had done, except this gun wasn't handed over to me. Instantly, I stiffened, ready to reach into my bag for mine. The way he was looking at me sent a chill up my spine.

"I don't believe you. For that, I have no choice but to get rid of you. It's such a pity to have to kill you, my dear. I truly liked you. Once your dad gets word that I killed his precious daughter, he'll no doubt come for his son."

My eyes widened.

Jace pushed against the two guards holding him just as one grabbed my arm to pull me out of the room. "Vissar, stop this!" he growled. "She doesn't have it, and you know it. This has been dragged on long enough."

Vissar jerked his head at the guards restraining Jace. "He's of no use to me now. You can kill him."

No matter what Jace had done, I didn't want him to die!

"No!" I cried out, lunging after them, only to be held back by iron muscles clamped around me.

Quinn, having heard that they were going to kill Jace, shouted and struggled like I did, but was easily held in place. We were screwed. There was nothing we could do to stop this as we helplessly watched them take Jace away.

"What's going on in here?" I heard Natalia's voice behind us.

"Not your concern, Natalia," Vissar bit out. "I thought I told you to stay out of my business-and out of my office."

When she came into my view, I saw her vicious smile and thought about how well she would get along with Regan. Or not. They'd either become friends or bitter enemies. She walked like a predator stalking her prey, seemingly unconcerned about the guards in the room.

"You've had the audacity to keep me here for months, Dad. Save it. Your days are finished because I'm going to release that footage and you will burn for it." She stopped next to me. "Cassie? You're going to kill her? Jace, too? Are you out of your damn mind?"

Vissar's jaw clenched, and a glossy sheen of malice filled his eyes. If I wasn't mistaken, there was no love lost between him and his daughter. Something strange was unfolding, I thought, while holding my breath. I had to wonder what she was doing.

"What do you know about my business?"

She tossed her head back and laughed. "I know everything on that footage. After all, I am your daughter—your own flesh and blood. Learn from the best, or don't learn at all. You don't think Giles will get all the credit, do you? Just because I'm a woman, I can't take over an empire like this? Except I won't be using it to sell young women. Don't think for a minute that what's on that security footage won't hold up against you in court, because not only have I seen it, I've made copies."

I looked at Vissar, who looked ready to commit murder. Except he didn't have the gun pointed at anyone. Yet.

"How much did you get for your last sale, daddy dearest? Ten, fifteen grand?" She turned back to Vissar. "And how old was she?

Sixteen, seventeen?"

"Again—"

"Tell me! I deserve to know that, at least. I suppose I can question the guards, and they'll tell me. Especially Tito. He certainly does like money—"

"Enough," Vissar snapped. "She was seventeen, and I received twenty grand for her. Now, tell me exactly where every single copy of that footage is, or I will put a bullet in every one of you."

If he thought Natalia would give up, he was mistaken. She had come in here for a reason. If it was her attempt to help or rescue us, now was her time. But she held up her hands.

"I can't tell you that. That would erase months of trying to take you down. Months," she spat. "Imagine my delight when I came across that delightful footage, showing you examining these young girls for sale. My, my, but they are going to love you in prison. Not only that, but the footage shows you accepting the cash. Talk about damaging evidence."

"You bitch," Vissar growled. "Just like your mother. She was easy enough to get rid of. All it took was an overdose, her body easily disposed of in a barrel at the bottom of a swamp where no one would ever look."

I was going to be sick. I doubled over, clutching my stomach and vomiting on his expensive rug. The guard immediately released me with a retching sound, as though he might vomit right along with me. Guess some of Vissar's guards had weak stomachs. After being so nervous about coming here, not much came out, but it was enough to buy me time to pull the gun out of my bag.

I slowly reached into my bag. Just as soon as my hand slipped inside, a guard grabbed my biceps from behind. But that wasn't all. In the distance, I heard gunshots. Small pops that were getting louder.

"I don't think so, asshole." I heard Natalia say, followed by two quick gunshots before I was suddenly released from the guard's grasp. Quinn, free from the guard who'd been holding him, stood paralyzed in fear.

My ears were ringing, but I looked over to see Natalia returning with a gun aimed directly at Vissar. I should have known she wouldn't walk away without a fight. Scrambling, I withdrew the gun from my bag. This was far different from when Cameron had shown me how to use one, and my hands shook uncontrollably. I wouldn't be able to shoot straight if I pulled the trigger, I thought wildly.

The gunshots were getting closer. Whoever was shooting outside these four walls was drawing nearer, and my heart rate quickened.

Vissar laughed as he raised his gun. I glanced at Natalia. Why wasn't she shooting him? He was going to shoot one of us or Quinn! Do something! My hands trembled so badly that if I pulled the trigger, I'd likely hit the wall. But I couldn't allow him to shoot his first. I had to stop him.

The gunfire was so close I could hear it echoing in the hallway. Slamming my eyes halfway shut, I squeezed the trigger. The shot forced me to take a step back, but I missed Vissar entirely, just as I knew I would. All I did was give him enough time to raise his gun, and he wasn't aiming it at Natalia or Quinn. He had it centered on me.

"No!" she shouted, shoving me aside as two gunshots rang out simultaneously.

We hit the ground together, my head colliding with something solid, and all I could see were blurs. I blinked a few times. There was no way his bullet hadn't hit one of us. Was it me? I could hardly move; my eyelids felt so heavy.

"That was for my mother, you bastard," I heard Natalia murmur nearby.

I felt hands on me, pulling me up and patting me down. They ran along my legs and arms, hauling me into a sitting position even as my head fell back. Strong, insistent hands touched my torso and turned me over.

"Cassie!" I heard Quinn, felt his smaller hand slide into mine.

"Where are you hit, baby?" I heard Jace's deep voice on the other side of me.

I blinked, trying to clear my vision enough to see him. I extended my hand, feeling his bulletproof vest beneath my fingertips, but I couldn't see him.

Was I dreaming? Did I get hit and hallucinate this? I could still hear gunshots, but my ears were ringing so badly.

"Natalia," I whispered. "That bitch pushed me."

Jace crushed me against him, kissing my temple, my cheek, my nose, and my mouth. I felt his hands on my chin, trying to keep my eyes open as he whispered to me.

"That was entirely too close," he said, sliding his hands to cup my face. "I love you, Cassie. I hope by now that you know I do."

I must be hallucinating if Jace Taylor just told me he loved me.

Chapter Forty Five

Jace

I'd barely made it to the room when Vissar's gun went off. All I saw were Natalia and Cassie hitting the floor. Cassie's head struck the massive floor vase with a sickening thud. I couldn't get to her fast enough, motioning to my law enforcement buddy to see to Natalia. I let Quinn hold Cassie's hand while I checked on her, knowing everything that had happened had traumatized him.

After frantically searching Cassie for a bullet wound and finding her safe, other than probably suffering a concussion from the blow to her head, I couldn't stop the words from spilling out. I needed her to know. I didn't want to go another damn day without her.

"Keep your eyes open, Cass," I said. "An ambulance is coming."

Her head fell listlessly to the side. "Did I get shot?" she whispered. "Did he kill me?"

Pushing her hair away from her face, I smiled. "No, he did not. Natalia got hit, but it looks pretty minor. I'm not sure which of you shot, Vissar, but he's dead."

"I did," Natalia said from behind me. "And I would do it again, the bastard. He was going to kill her. It was self-defense."

After everything she did to help me and the police department take down Vissar, I had no doubt it would be determined to be self-defense. She'd been preparing for this for a long time, helping me by being my inside eyes and ears.

"Take Quinn to get checked out," I told one of the officers.

"No! I want to stay with Cassie," Quinn cried, struggling when the officer reached down to pull him away.

"Shortie, she'll be fine," I insisted. "We'll be right behind you. I swear."

Tears streaked down his face as he reluctantly released her hand, allowing the officer to pull him away and out of the room.

I held Cassie, looking down at her as her eyes met mine. The relief that Vissar hadn't shot her hit me like a freight train. I couldn't lose her. Not now. Not after everything we'd been through and after everything we would probably still go through.

"Did you tell me you love me?" she asked.

"I did. And I do."

"How could you possibly love me when you lied to me?" Her whisper was so deadly that I wondered if she was about to pass out. "You lied to me, Jace."

"Everything I did, I did to protect you. Yes, he ordered me to watch you. And it's a good thing, too."

She tried to sit up, but I held her firm.

"A good thing?" she spat, wincing. "Tell me how taking pictures of me out with my friends was a good thing! Or how giving him information about my security system helped. Tell me how having to bury my little brother's mom is a good thing. Tell me about how helping Vissar trade young girls for sex trafficking is a *good thing*."

"You don't understand," I responded slowly, my heart aching with the hope that she would forgive me for everything I did. "If he hadn't had me do it, he would have had someone else do it. At least I had control over who I was taking pictures of."

She snorted.

"He already knew about Kya, Mac, and Dani. I had to give him something else. He was getting suspicious, and there was no way in hell I was going to give him a picture of Quinn."

She looked away. "You could have told me, Jace. I trusted you."

More officers poured into the room, followed by paramedics to assist Natalia. I helped Cassie stand up slowly, but she didn't say another word until she glanced over at Natalia, who smirked at her.

"Thank you," Cassie said.

"It was my pleasure."

"I bet it was."

Cassie let me lead her out of the room, slowly heading down the hallway toward the door. Quinn watched us come out of the house from his perch on the hood of a squad car, relief in his eyes.

An ambulance waited at the side door, and I sat her down on the back ledge, allowing the paramedic to shine a flashlight in her eyes and assess whether she was well enough not to go to the hospital.

Though Natalia had a gunshot wound, she complained the entire way. The bullet had grazed her enough to warrant a hospital visit, but she refused to go in an ambulance.

"Listen to me," I said, taking Cassie's hands. "I won't let you go. I don't care if you think I lied to you. I did it to protect you. Had someone else spied on you, it would have been much worse."

She shook my hands loose, looking away from me. Damn it, she was going to be stubborn about this and not listen to reason. I refused to lose her because of this. Cassie was an intelligent woman with trust issues, but she needed to understand my position and everything I'd done.

"How could you have helped him exchange young girls, Jace?" she whispered. "That you had any part of that at all makes me sick to my stomach. I can't even look at you right now. I could have gotten past you telling him everything I've been doing, but that."

She turned her blue eyes on me, taking the punch of her hatred straight to the chest. It wouldn't matter what I told her or how I explained what I did to help those young girls. Would it? She wouldn't believe me. Whatever trust she had for me had been shattered as soon as Vissar told her I'd helped him with that. It was inexcusable, regardless that I'd saved those girls. Every single one of them.

"I'm going to have to drive you and Quinn home," I said, standing up straight but looking down at her. "I'll drive your dad's car and-"

"No. Someone else can drive us home. Not you."

Fuck . . . that might have hurt worse than the look in her eyes. I leaned back down, taking her chin and forcing her to look at me. Her eyes flashed with fury, but I didn't care. She was going to listen to me.

"I want you to know that I meant everything I've ever said to you these last months. Every. Single. Word."

She pushed my hand away, tearing her gaze from mine at the same time. I blew out a breath. This was going to be an uphill battle. One I had never faced before. After receiving the go-ahead from the paramedic, I motioned Adam over and explained to him that she and Quinn needed to be driven home. Her car, too.

Watching her drive away with anyone but me damn near snapped my heart in two, especially the fact that she wouldn't look at me. Despite how hard I'd tried to straddle that fine line, it hadn't been good enough. It would never be good enough. Cassie's trust, once broken, would never be earned back. Ever.

Cᴡ

"Heard about your heroic rescue," Ty said after he picked up my call. "Again. Are you trying to make me look bad with all these rescues?"

I scoffed at his tease. "Natalia's the hero, not me. She knocked Cassie out of the way and took the bullet for her. Cassie escaped with a bump on the head and a massive headache."

"What's going on, Jace? You don't sound like yourself. Can't hide it from me."

If he only knew half of what was ravaging every part of my head and heart right now. Half afraid he would run straight to Riley, I hesitated to call him. But Ty was my best friend for a reason. We'd been through more shit together than anyone else. He knew me better than my brother did.

"Come on, spill it."

I took a deep breath. "I love her. Shit, I tried so hard not to. And when I saw her fall, when I thought he'd shot her . . . hurt her . . . " My voice broke, like it had when I was going through puberty.

"Dude," Ty whispered. "Does she know?"

"That I love her? Yes. But she won't talk to me. She knows I had to spy on her, take pictures, knows I had to help him herd young girls for his trafficking, though I had the cops collect them before it went any further than that, and now she doesn't trust me." He gave a low whistle. "She won't listen, Ty. I broke her trust. And I broke it bad."

"I told you from the start she had trust issues. But I'll tell you, when I was in that position and Riley got hit by a bullet, I'd never been so scared in my life. I thought my heart would beat right out of my chest when I saw her go down. And when she refused to see me afterward, it ripped my heart right out."

"But you figured it out."

"If she hadn't come to me when she did, I would have gone to her. Jace, fight for her. This is a woman who made you break all your rules. If you don't fight for her, there's a chance you might never find another like her." He laughed. "The infallible Jace Taylor, in love. I never thought I would see the day."

"Well, save it because I haven't gotten her back."

"You will. You're a pushy son of a bitch."

Ty's laughter gave me a flicker of hope. A bit of hope, but it had to be enough. I needed to go to the house and pray that Cassie would listen to me. Not having a clue what I would say to her, I had to make her listen. If she didn't, it would break my heart to walk away from her. I couldn't do that. I wouldn't.

"If you breathe a word of this to Riley, I'll come up there and beat your ass. Impending fatherhood or not, I don't give a shit," I warned. "This absolutely stays between us, Ty."

"I don't keep things from my wife."

"You're going to keep this from her. At least until I can talk some sense into Cassie. *If* I can talk some sense into her."

"Good luck, Jace. Knowing Cassie, you're going to need all of it."

After I hung up, my nerves were so jumpy I almost felt like a teenager again. She couldn't have gone far with Quinn, and I knew she wasn't about to uproot him to Seattle without warning. I only hoped that she'd be home. I'd never had to rely on charm so much, but I would do it if necessary. Our future depended on it.

Chapter Forty Six

Here I was again, but under different circumstances this time. This time it was for me. The waves of the ocean washed against the sandy beach, retreating with a gentle pull. Regan was right when she told me that winter on the West Coast was far different from winter here on the East Coast. It wasn't as warm as it had been before. I wore a pair of shorts, but added a hoodie. I sat on the beach instead of dipping my feet into the water like I had months ago.

After talking with the school, I pulled Quinn out for a few days and called Regan to ask if I could use her beach house in Cape Haven. Quinn and I needed this time to recover. I needed it to get away and think. I needed time for myself. Over the last few months, things had spiraled out of control, disrupting my straight-laced life. I had been so focused on getting my dad cleared and staying away from danger that falling in love with Jace hadn't been part of the plan.

We had just arrived here last night. I slept alone in the master bedroom suite while Quinn slept in the bedroom I had slept in when I was here for Riley's wedding. He was inside playing on his portable video games while I decided to come out to the beach today in bare feet to sit and reflect. Sitting on the beach in Cape Haven felt no different from doing it in LA, except it was cooler outside.

As soon as we arrived, I felt a deep longing inside. I missed Jace. I missed him so much it hurt. Looking back over the last few months, I realized he had made me a better person, despite having lied to me. I understood what he had said about being the best one to control it. I replayed in my mind what would have happened if someone else had been spying on me, taking pictures of Quinn and me at the beach or at the skate park. This could have turned out differently if it hadn't been for him. Would I have visited my mom's gravesite if he hadn't been there? Would I have faced Vissar like that if not for him?

I had run from him like a damn fool when he finally told me he loved me. I pulled my knees up to my chest and rested my chin on them, watching the waves roll in. As hard as I tried to hide my true self, I had been genuine around him. I had shared things with him I hadn't told anyone else. Things I wouldn't have considered revealing to any of my other boyfriends. Not even my friends knew some of what I shared with him.

When I arrived, I called Riley. After she let me have it for not calling her and talking to her during the entire time I had been in danger, she finally calmed down enough for me to tell her I was in love.

"You're what?" she shouted. "With who?"

"Jace," I admitted.

I think she was stunned because she said nothing for a minute. "I can't believe it. And here I thought you wouldn't trust anyone, especially him."

"I'm still working through my trust issues, Riley. He took my trust and shattered it, despite knowing all of my struggles. He did things for Vissar. Unforgivable things."

"Yeah, about that. Did you listen to his side of what he was doing?"

I started to tell her I didn't need to hear his side. His involvement was bad enough, but something made me stop. I hadn't allowed him to explain. Not a single word.

"You know he was working with the police department the entire time, right? Every time Vissar sent him out to pick up the girls and bring them to the drop site, he alerted his friends at the police department, and they would pick them up. He saved every single one of those girls that Vissar sent him to transport."

"Wait-"

"Let me finish," she snapped. "Don't you want to know how the police got to you so fast? Jace risked everything to plant a wire in Vissar's office. When you and Natalia confronted him and got him talking, he confessed all kinds of things. The cops were close enough. Jace would be dead right now if they hadn't been."

My heart jumped into my throat. Why didn't he tell me any of this himself? He hadn't even tried. "How . . . how do you know all of this?" I shook my head. "Ty. I should have known."

"Jace is the one person you should trust, Cass. Ty tells me everything, and he wouldn't lie to me. Not unless he had a damn good reason to. Some of the things I've told you about Jace weren't true. I didn't know that, though. That's because I thought they were true when Jace and Ty were undercover. Jace isn't really like that. He doesn't go around chasing women, and—"

"Riles, stop," I finally said. "I know. I've spent enough time with him to see that he doesn't chase women. In fact, I know about his rules—well, some of them. If anything, he tried to keep me away, just like I tried to keep him away."

I laughed. We were both in such denial.

"Rules? Like, what rules?"

"I don't know all of them. Ty probably does. You'll have to ask him. But I'm in Cape Haven, trying to figure out what I'm going to do. I've always been there for you, but I've never wanted to admit that you've been there for me, too. I owe you so much."

She snorted. "You don't owe me anything. And I'm warning you, if I'm crying when Ty comes back in here from exercising the dogs, I'm blaming you."

I laughed, wiping away a tear as the center of my chest ached. "What if I've lost him, Riley? I pushed him away, just like I've pushed everyone else away. It hurts to think I might have lost what we had."

"Oh my God," she whispered. "You really are in love with him. Look, I thought I'd lost Ty, too. Fight for him, Cassie. Unless you talk to him, you won't know. Take the time to relax after everything you've been through, then go back and fight for him."

"I miss you so much."

"I miss you, too, but I hear Ty coming back with the boys."

"Don't you say a word to him, Riles."

"I won't. Yet."

She hung up before I could say another word, making my heart thump. If she told Ty, he'd call Jace and could ruin everything. I didn't want Jace to hear anything from Ty that I couldn't say to Jace first. There was so much I had yet to figure out. Sleep refused to come after talking to her, and I lay awake listening to the gentle waves washing against the shore. It was a good thing, too, because Quinn had nightmares now, and I'd been awake to comfort him back to sleep. Morning came too soon, and here I was, sitting on the beach, still lost in thought.

What I needed to figure out was whether I wanted to leave my life in Seattle behind and live in California again with Quinn. I closed my eyes, wondering if Jace would even forgive me for running out on him. I had behaved so foolishly after he confessed his feelings. I'd broke my own damn heart this time.

Jace didn't do relationships, yet he had bent his rules to be with me. The one time he opened up, I made him feel like a fool. He had to hate me by now. I was certain that if I tried to contact him, he might not respond. As much as it hurt to think that, I knew it was well-deserved.

I looked down the vacant beach, contemplating my life in Seattle. Naomi and Hannah didn't need me, and a change might be good for me. Maybe moving back to Santa Monica would be refreshing. I'd be closer to Quinn and my dad, if he ever returned.

Standing up, I brushed the sand off my palms onto my shorts and looked back out at the wide expanse of the ocean. It was time to truly start living my life, regardless of whether Jace would be in it. As much as it hurt to think he wouldn't be.

As soon as I turned to go back to the house, I saw Jace approaching me. My breath caught at the sight of his dark hair ruffling in the breeze and my heart felt like it lept into my throat. He wore blue jeans, no shoes or socks, and one of his thin button-up shirts rolled to his elbows. His gaze locked onto mine, sparkling with intensity.

"Jace, I—"

He reached me in two seconds, one hand curling around my neck to pull my mouth to his while his other arm hooked around my waist, hauling me against him. My head spun, thoughts skittering away as he took possession of every part of me. God, I loved this man. Like no other before him, he held my entire heart in the palm of his hands, and I knew I would do anything to keep him.

With wild abandon, he kissed me, one hand holding my head as if to say I couldn't move until he had enough. The other arm banded around me, keeping me close. I felt possessed. I felt loved.

When he finally tore his mouth from mine, his eyes still shining dangerously, he kept his hands where they were, staring into my eyes. I'd never forget the moment I first saw him on this beach. It ignited a fire within me I hadn't known existed.

"When I thought Vissar shot you, that you might die, I didn't know if I could go on living without you. I felt what Ty must have felt when Riley got shot," he whispered, his voice rough and unhinged. "From the moment three months ago when you walked away from me at the wedding, I knew I had to have you. I just never knew it would be like this.

"I love you, Cassidy Nichols. I broke every single one of my rules for you, and I'm about to break one I never knew existed."

He reached into his pocket and pulled out a ring. I stared down at it, mesmerized by its sparkle. A simple diamond ring, nothing big or flashy. Elegant, the perfect size for me. My eyes darted back up to his, my lips parted.

"I will marry you," he continued. "Whether you like it or not. Today, tomorrow, I don't care when. If you want to live in Seattle, we'll live there. If you want to move to LA, we'll move there. Where you go, I go, because I won't go another day without you. I won't sleep another night without you by my side."

I gasped, and he kissed me again, not giving me a chance to respond. Did he think I would run away again? Not this time. I threaded my fingers through his hair, meeting the slant of his mouth against mine until he groaned.

"Jace," I said, swallowing my fears. "Can I say something?"

"If it's telling me yes and that you love me back, then yes. Otherwise, no."

I laughed. "I love you back, and I will marry you."

He picked me up, and I shrieked, locking my legs around his waist. I cupped his face and kissed him again.

"I love you. God, I tried not to. You know I tried not to. But I do. I'll marry you. I'll have your kids. I'm so sorry for running away and doubting you, but I was scared."

He pushed my hair out of my face. "I know. You didn't just make me break my rules; you made me shatter them. But we'll be scared together. I promise you, we're in this together, Cass. I won't let you fall if you don't let me fall."

When he set me back down, keeping my hands locked in his, I tilted my face up. "You don't know how refreshing it is to hear someone say that. All my life, I've been on my own, relying on myself."

He shrugged and leaned down. "Me too, in a way. And you know what? When I saw you hold Nicco, I haven't been able to get the image of you holding our baby in your arms out of my mind. You will make such a beautiful mother, Cassie."

I grinned. "Someday." "Someday."

"I'm so sorry I didn't give you a chance to explain yourself. All those girls that you saved . . . you saved me. Us."

He brushed his knuckles against the curve of my jaw. "And I'd do it again. It was a very fine line I had to walk, but I would do it again. I might make smarter choices when it comes to the people in my life, but I would save every single one of those young girls again."

My heart soared, loving him all the more for saving those young, innocent girls from the horrors they might have faced. He truly was good, even if he was pushy.

As we turned to go back up to the house, our hands linked, I couldn't help but think about what he said regarding where to live: Seattle or LA. I had been contemplating that constantly since Quinn.

"So?" he asked, opening the gate to the house. "Get married now or later?"

"Later," I said. "If there's any chance I can get my dad back, I want him to walk me down the aisle or give me away, or whatever we decide."

He nodded. "You don't have to decide right now, but have you considered where you want to live?"

I grinned. "Honestly, I need a change in my life. I want to move back to Santa Monica. I would hate to take Quinn away from his friends, and I have a feeling Ezra is going to need my help."

He kissed my knuckles. "You are a wonderful woman, Cassie."

Chapter Forty Seven

We spent another day in Cape Haven before heading back to Santa Monica, and I had to admit that the warmer weather was a delightful change. We were lucky to be on the same flight. I drove my dad's convertible back while Quinn insisted on riding with Jace. By the time I pulled into the driveway, Jace's car was already parked.

"Shortie, I'm back!"

I dropped my bag on the floor just inside the door as Jace came down the stairs, looking like he'd just been in Quinn's room. He smiled at me, and I could tell he hadn't lied when he said he didn't want to spend another day without me. He insisted on coming here and let me know he would stay tonight instead of at his place.

Out of the corner of my eye, I saw someone coming up the stairs, and my eyes widened when my dad appeared. He'd cut his hair shorter than when I'd last seen him, and his face was scruffy. I shrieked and launched myself at him just as he reached the top. "Hey, hey, hey, baby girl," he said, catching me in a hug.

"It's all good now. I'm home because you refused to give up. Ricky says he's sorry, by the way."

I pulled back, my jaw set. "Yeah, he's on my shit list right now. He could have at least told me where you were. Where *were* you?"

He looked around my shoulder at Jace. "Who's this? Not the bloke who broke up with you in a text?"

"You must have been holed up in your studio and didn't hear anyone come home. Dad, this is Jace." I turned halfway around to look at Jace and smiled. "Jace is my fiancé."

"Whoa, whoa, whoa," he said, releasing me and straightening as he looked at Jace. "Says who?"

Jace extended his hand. "I'd have asked permission first if we knew where you were. It's nice to finally meet you. You have an amazing daughter."

My dad raised a tawny eyebrow. "Don't I know it? So, you're going to marry my baby girl, huh?" He scratched his chin. "No one else has ever been worthy of her."

"Okay, now answer my question. Where were you?" I demanded.

"I went overseas. Your aunt has a cottage in Surrey. Man, it's so good to be home," he said, walking into the kitchen. "Who were you calling for when you came in?"

"Quinn. Where is he?"

He reached into the refrigerator, pulled out a few beers, and offered one to each of us. "In his room, I presume," he said, opening the beers and handing them out. "I heard about Skyler. That's a damn shame. I really loved her. Thought it would stick."

"I'm sorry too," I said. "We didn't always see things the same way, but I think we were making progress."

"I'm going to miss her. I'll go visit her grave in the next day or two so I can pay respects. Quinn can come, too." He swiped at his cheek, looking inconspicuously like he was wiping away a stray tear.

Jace and I sat down on the stools while my dad leaned against the counter, sipping his beer. I was happy to have him back, but I needed answers. There were things he needed to know too.

"Did you talk to Gavin? Or Shawn?"

"They hired another drummer, but that makes no difference now that I'm back. It wasn't my fault."

"It was your fault, Dad!" I said. "You offered to take that footage for Natalia, and while I understand, people got hurt! Where is it, anyway?"

"I brought it with me, but there's no sense in releasing it now that he's gone. And you." My dad jerked his chin toward Jace. "Heard about you. You worked with your team in the police department and saved a lot of girls."

"You're amazing," I whispered, sneaking my hand into his.

"Bloody hell, knock it off," my dad muttered. "You remind me of when your mom and I were in love. We were inseparable. I loved her so bloody much."

It was now or never, I told myself. If I didn't ask him now, I wasn't sure I would ever have the courage to do so.

"Speaking of which, I need to tell you something."

He looked at me as though he'd never heard me be serious before. "What?"

"When Mom died, I'm the one who gave her the drugs." I swallowed the thick lump in my throat. "She was yelling at me to grab them out of her dresser, and she'd been partying. I was so mad at her. I did what she wanted and ran to my room."

The way he looked at me, the deep sorrow in his eyes, made me want to look away. Jace's hand on my back reassured me he was there. We were in this together, like he said.

"I found her the next morning, and I've carried that guilt with me forever. I was so angry with her. Angry with her because . . . she told me you weren't my dad."

He stared at me. Really stared at me. I wanted him to say something. Anything. Yell at me if he had to. Suddenly, he started laughing, throwing his head back.

"This is not funny," I said. "Why are you laughing?"

He calmed down enough to look at me. "She was trying to pull one over on you. Not sure why. We had some genetic testing done when you were a baby because we have a risk of sickle cell disease in my family, and your mom was worried that it might have passed to you."

I blinked. She lied to me? All these years, I'd believed that he wasn't really my dad, and I'd never know who my dad was because she was gone, and it was all a lie? Now I was really mad.

"I wish you would have asked me when she told you that! Geez, Cass. You've been carrying this around with you since you were . . . what, fifteen?"

"Yes," I bit out. "It wasn't long after that when she overdosed. I should have gotten her help. I ran into Dar months ago. She said you and Mom were trying to reconcile right before she died."

He hung his head. "Yeah, we were trying to give it a go. Our schedules were tough, though. With me being on tour and her being on set for movies, usually in different locations, I'm not sure it would have ever worked."

"What about Quinn?"

"What about him?"

"You know that he's yours, right?"

"Yeah. Did Skyler tell you that?"

"Quinn told me, but I didn't believe him. Skyler told me, and I didn't believe her either. Why the hell didn't *you* tell me?"

He smiled. "Bloody hell. That happened so many years ago, and I didn't know for a long time. Then she told me after I got her away from that dim fucker. I didn't want you to think I'd replaced you."

I looked at Jace. He smiled back at me, rubbing his hand along my back. Everything was going to be fine. It had to be.

"I want you to listen to me very carefully."

I watched his smile slowly disappear.

"I had a tough life growing up without either of you around. Quinn has been living the same way. No one home after school, making his own meals and snacks, watching TV alone. While you aren't on tour, you *will* make an effort to be here for him, and if I hear otherwise, I'm going to be pissed."

The smile on my dad's face returned full force. "I won't let you down, baby girl. We won't be going on tour again until next summer. I'll bring him with me."

I grinned. "And teach him how to play?"

He brightened. "He wants to learn?"

"You bet your ass he does. And I passed on the drumsticks you gave me when I was his age, so teach him, would you?" I smiled. "Oh, and I'm moving back here."

Jace slipped his arm around my waist.

"Naomi and Hannah can still live in the house, but I'm moving back here to be closer to you and Quinn. And Jace has family here too. That way, if you need me, I'll be here and for Quinn as well."

I looked up at Jace, and he leaned down to kiss me, whispering, "I love you, Casanova."

Chapter Forty Eight

I couldn't remember being this nervous. Trying to shake it out and roll my neck didn't help. Everything I'd been through didn't come close to this. Going through police training, busting up drug rings, saving young girls from prostitution, nearly watching my girlfriend get shot. None of it held a candle to this.

"Damn, Jace! Calm down," Ty growled.

We stood in the ballroom of the De Luca family home, waiting to head down to the altar set up at the edge of the perfectly manicured lawn, just past the shimmering pool. Regan convinced Gavriel to allow us to use his backyard for our wedding. The girls were upstairs in Regan's childhood room getting ready while I waited with Ty and Cameron.

These weren't just nerves. I couldn't wait any longer. I'd waited long enough to make her my wife. Wearing that engagement ring on her finger for the last two months wasn't nearly enough for me. I wanted more. I wanted it all.

Cameron and Ty glanced at each other, grinning. Assholes, I thought, just as Lex and Quinn came in from the hallway, Quinn looking grown-up in his tuxedo. The smile he wore said it all. Despite everything he'd been through, this kid was lucky. I wasn't sure if he was happy that Cassie and I were finally getting married or if he was excited about taking off on his first tour with Lex once school was out in a few months.

It hadn't taken long for the band to realize the drummer just wasn't working out, and they'd taken Lex back. Who could blame them? After getting to know him better, I saw he was a decent guy, and I'd heard some of the music he'd written. Impressed, I could see why Cassie wanted to learn to play the drums when she was younger. Discovering that she could play and watching her do it shot a pulsing thrill right through me. If Lex hadn't been home, I would have taken her right upstairs to her bedroom. As it was, I had to convince her to come live with me, Ezra, and Milo until we could find a bigger house.

Ezra had finally relented and gone to treatment, though it had taken a while for him to be released from the hospital. Today marked just under two months sober. He had a long way to go, but with Cassie now living with us and her skills as a therapist, he was thriving. She was even helping him get his General Education Degree so he could pursue secondary classes. I'd never known a more patient woman than her.

"You look funny," Quinn said.

I laughed, reaching down to ruffle his hair like Cassie always did, but he sidestepped me quickly. Lex's deep laughter filled the vacant room. This kid was quick. I'd give him that.

"It's about bloody time you put a proper ring on my daughter's finger," Lex said, stopping next to us. "She's not just for any bloke."

Ty's hand clamped down on my shoulder. "She's getting the very best with this one, Lex. He broke every single one of his rules for her. Every one."

"I'd like to hear about these rules," Regan said, joining us with Nicco on her hip. "Seems to be such a secret. Do tell."

I sighed. Only one other person knew my rules. Cassie didn't even know all of them. Lex shot me a knowing look. If I didn't spill, I knew he'd have something to say. "Look, I set these rules to protect any woman from getting involved in my life. Working undercover has its dangers for a guy who cares about anyone."

"Uh-huh," she said. "What are they?"

"Cassie already knows I broke one of them with her, but she doesn't know the rest. Never make the first move, which almost got shot to hell the minute I went to her house." I smiled, recalling that night fondly. "That was after I called her. In my defense, it was to see if she needed help."

Ty shook his head. "I'm calling bullshit on that. You called her because you wanted to call her. Seeing if she needed your help was just the excuse."

Damn best friends, I thought. "Think whatever you want." Regan cleared her throat. "The others?"

"Never spend the night with a woman. Don't take a woman to meet my mom." Regan rolled her eyes. "And don't bring her to my place."

"Sounds like a lot of poppycock," Lex said. "Maybe you shouldn't tell my baby girl your rules. It makes you sound like a prick."

I laughed. "Pretty sure she thought that when we first met, and she was right. But it worked out. I'll be marrying her in less than half an hour, so that's the rule I never set."

"She owes me a thousand bucks, by the way," Regan said over her shoulder as she sashayed toward the open doors, looking back at me before stepping outside. "Easiest bet ever won."

My eyes darted to Cameron, who looked just as confused. He shrugged. "I hope you're ready to have your hands full. It's never a dull moment, and I wouldn't change it for the world."

Cameron went after Regan, leaving the rest of us. I took a deep breath, itching to get on with this. Ty checked his watch and nodded just as Naomi and Hannah joined us. Quinn looked at Hannah, his eyes bright.

"Let's go," Ty said, ushering us out into the bright sunshine. "Don't want to be standing here gawking when your bride comes down. Not a good way to start off your marriage."

My mom and brother, along with Milo, were already standing by the altar, next to the officiant we'd hired for the service. The same one Regan and Cameron had used when they got married, for the second time, a little less than a year ago. I didn't bother to invite my old man, who would have made an excuse not to attend anyway. Milo and Ezra were trading jabs while Mom tried to wrangle them in. I breathed in deeply, watching the guests gather in the rows of white chairs.

The wedding wouldn't be a huge affair, as neither of us had a large circle of friends, but we had enough to hold a proper ceremony. Cassie didn't want a big, flashy event, but she also didn't want to get married in the courthouse. We'd spent enough time there in the last few months due to Natalia's trial for killing Vissar. Natalia flashed me a grin when I walked down the aisle past her. She'd gotten off on self-defense.

Mac, Kya, and Dani had come along, as well as Cassie's friends from Seattle. Mac was a little put out that Cassie didn't ask her to stand up for her, but Cassie explained that she owed it to Riley. I had invited friends from the police department who just had to see this to believe it. I laughed as I stepped up next to the officiant.

"Are you ready?" he asked.

"I was ready months ago," I replied smoothly, taking my stance next to him while the guests found their seats.

Ty came to stand beside me. Riley would come down before Cassie, and I held my breath, waiting to see her because I knew Cassie would be right behind. I knew beyond any doubt that the sight of Cassie would steal my breath. She had that effect on me every time I looked at her, every time I remembered she was mine and that she'd said yes.

My heart pounded in anticipation when Riley appeared, wearing a purple gauzy dress that did nothing to hide her pregnant belly. She walked with ease, even though she was due in less than a month. I didn't know how Cassie had talked her into standing up for her at our wedding right before she was ready to give birth, but I suppose they had enough time to get home before she had the baby.

My breath caught in my lungs when I saw Lex's head above the hedges, sporting a pair of dark sunglasses, with Cassie on his arm. It took all my restraint to stay where I was and not rush over to her, sweep her into my arms, and kiss her senseless.

The wedding dress she'd chosen mirrored her personality perfectly; a simple, slim white sheath that fit her body beautifully. I knew without needing to look at the back that it was open.

Mac saw to that. No veil, her hair flowing down, and she clutched a small bouquet of daisies. Cassie caught my eyes, and I had to take a deep breath or risk passing out.

Time seemed to slow as Lex and Cassie walked toward me, slower than it should have been. I just wanted her to reach me so I could put my hands on her, even with an audience. By the time they reached me, my breathing had become erratic, and I had to take another deep breath while Lex kissed her cheek and handed her over to me.

"Take care of my baby girl," he said.

I managed a nod, taking Cassie's hand and pulling her closer. Wanting to pull her right up against me, I had to remind myself again of our audience and question why we'd invited these people. She smiled at me, the same smile she'd shown me on the beach all those months ago. Dear God, I think my heart was melting at the sight of her.

"Mine," I mouthed.

When color rose high on her cheeks, I knew she understood me. Never again would she be alone. She'd always have me, and I would never let her go. It had taken me too long to find this woman. Who in their right mind would let her go?

After we said our vows, the officiant had barely finished speaking before I pulled her against me and captured her mouth. The breathy sigh that escaped her only made me smile as I slid my hands down to her hips, just in case she didn't already know that I would never let her go.

Someone cleared their throat. I didn't care. I could stand here and kiss her all day if she'd let me. When Ty tapped me on the shoulder, I growled and pulled my mouth away, keeping my hands firmly where they were.

"Eventually, we want to get to the festivities," he said with a wink. "But I understand what you're going through. Maybe you two could hurry it along, so everyone can congratulate you at least?"

I looked back down at Cassie. "Are you ready?"

She nodded. "No."

Only she would do that. I shouted, swinging her up into my arms and carrying her down the aisle amid whistles. "I love you," I said. "More than life. Never doubt that."

When she looped her arms around my neck and pressed her face against my shoulder, she whispered, "I'll never doubt you again."

Acknowledgements

It's always difficult to make sure I thank everyone who has supported me. Most people who have already know exactly what they've done. So, as usual . . . to those who have supported me through this last year: family, friends, neighbors, acquaintances, friends of friends, community, everyone who stops by booths at craft shows or author events, or follows me. There are not enough words to express my gratitude to those who have helped me along. It's hard to fathom this is my fifth book!

Tonya, Emily and Jessica, my rock star beta readers for your unbiased, honest opinions. I appreciate you more than you will ever know.

And most of all, I want to thank my editor, Becky Wallace, for the massive amount of help you give me with my books and also for pointing out how far I've come! It's always nice to hear when your editor points out that a book is "compulsively readable"!

Find more books by

Jodie Leigh Murray

by scanning the QR code below

Books are also available through:

Amazon

barnesandnoble.com

Bookshop.org

Tertulia

Select Bookshops